Second Chances

DEBRA WHITE SMITH

HARVEST HOUSE PUBLISHERS

EUGENE, OREGON

Cover by Koechel Peterson & Associates, Minneapolis, Minnesota

SECOND CHANCES
Copyright © 2000 by Debra White Smith
Published by Harvest House Publishers, 2005
Eugene, Oregon 97402
www.harvesthousepublishers.com

Library of Congress Cataloging-in-Publication Data

Smith, Debra White
    Second chances / Debra White Smith
        p. cm. — (Sisters suspense series) (formerly Seven sisters series)
    ISBN-13: 978-0-7369-1668-4
    ISBN-10: 0-7369-1668-7
    1. Divorced women—fiction. 2. Clergy—fiction. I. Title.
PS3569.M5178 S44 2000
813'.54—dc21   99-048824

Printed in the United States of America

05 06 07 08 09 10 11 12 / BC / 10 9 8 7 6 5 4 3 2 1

To my friends
Theda Day and Melissa Grimes.

The Seven Sisters

Jacquelyn Lightfoot: An expert in martial arts, private detective Jac is "married" to her career and lives in Denver.

Kim Lan Lowery: Tall, lithe, and half Vietnamese/half American, Kim is a much-sought-after supermodel who lives in New York City.

Marilyn Douglas Thatcher: Once married to Gregory, Marilyn struggles to rebuild a life for herself and her daughter Brooke. The daughter of Fred and Natalie Douglas, Marilyn works as an office manager for a veterinarian.

Melissa Moore: A serious nature lover, Dr. Melissa Moore recently established a medical practice in Oklahoma City.

Sonsee LeBlanc: A passionate veterinarian known for her wit, Sonsee lives in Baton Rouge.

Sammie Jones: The star reporter for *Romantic Living* magazine, Sammie is an expert on Victorian houses, art, and finding the perfect romantic getaway. She and her husband live in Dallas.

Victoria Roberts: A charming, soft-spoken domestic "genius" who loves to cook, work on crafts, and sew, Victoria is married and lives in Destin, Florida.

Second Chances Cast

Brooke Thatcher: Marilyn Douglas Thatcher and Gregory Thatcher's four-year-old daughter.

Clark McClure: Known as "Leopard," Clark was recently released from prison. His driving desire is revenge.

Fred Douglas: Marilyn Thatcher's father and Natalie's husband, Fred is a strong Christian and an active church member.

Gregory Thatcher: Once a prominent minister, Greg divorced Marilyn Thatcher to marry Sheila. He is Brooke's father.

Joshua Langham: The minister of Victory Chapel Community Church, which Fred and Natalie Douglas attend, Josh lives across the street from Marilyn Thatcher. He's also known as "Panther."

Natalie Douglas: Married to Fred Douglas, Natalie is a devout Christian who loves and supports her daughter, Marilyn, and granddaughter, Brooke.

One

⌒

"Mom! Mom! There's a huge dog in our garden. Mom! He's tearing up the tomato plants and pepper plants!" Four-year-old Brooke's distressed voice preceded her entry into the cluttered bedroom.

"Oh, no," Marilyn Douglas Thatcher groaned. She dropped the denim skirt back into the box from which she had taken it. Last week she had put off unpacking everything so that she and Brooke might plant their first garden together. Marilyn so loved fresh vegetables and had long dreamed of sharing the fun of gardening with her daughter. Perhaps that dream would also end in disappointment.

With the blonde-haired Brooke pulling on her hand, Marilyn rushed through the quaint cottage and out the back door. In horror, she gasped and stopped. Like a frisky pony, a jubilant Saint Bernard frolicked among her tender plants.

"See, Mom, I told you." Brooke turned distressed brown eyes to her mother. "He's makin' a mess!"

"You can say that again," Marilyn growled. In one second, she relived the hard work they had put into that small garden. Her father had tilled it. Then Marilyn had meticulously removed the grass and mixed in the fertilizer. Carefully Marilyn and Brooke had placed each plant and seed into the soil. Because it was already early June and a bit late to plant, they had expended extra effort to ensure their garden a healthy start. Now this overgrown mutt from...from Mars was destroying their tomatoes and peppers and looked to be heading toward the row of freshly sprouted green beans.

With a surge of bravado, Marilyn charged the unsuspecting animal. "Get out of there!" she yelled. Bending over near the garden's edge she retrieved a clod of dried dirt. Unmercifully, she hurled the clod toward the dog's hindquarters. The dirt met its target and produced the desired effect. With a yelp, the overgrown puppy tucked his tail between his legs, flattened his ears, and raced from the garden. Incensed, Marilyn ran after him, waving her arms and hollering like a mad woman.

Only Brooke's startled wails stopped Marilyn from the one goal that burned through her mind—*strangle that dog!* But Brooke, unaccustomed to such raging, needed comforting. Marilyn let the terrorized Saint Bernard escape. Winded from her running, she trotted back to her distraught daughter.

"It's okay, honey." She knelt and gathered Brooke into her arms. "Mom's just fine. I got angry at the doggie, that's all."

"Pick me up," Brooke cried.

Marilyn gathered her daughter into her arms. Everyone agreed Brooke was a miniature clone of her mother—the same blonde ponytail, the same doe-brown eyes, the same fair complexion—except Brooke possessed her father's long straight nose; Marilyn's nose was the pug variety.

With Brooke sniffling against her neck, Marilyn stood and trudged across the tiny backyard dotted with dogwoods and oaks. Now she would be changing into work jeans and repairing a garden rather than finishing the unpacking.

Two years ago, Marilyn's parents had lovingly opened their Eureka Springs, Arkansas home to their divorced daughter. After a couple of years of working part-time at the local veterinary clinic, Marilyn had recently taken the full-time position of office manager. Her salary, plus her ex-husband's child support, gave Marilyn enough income to embrace independence. She had been ready. Last week, Marilyn and Brooke had moved from her parents' house and rented the little cottage. For the first time in her life, thirty-year-old Marilyn was living on her own—really on her own. Independence proved to be an adventure, to say the least. All week she had been dealing with leaky water faucets, mowing the yard, and having the oil changed in her car. Now a Saint Bernard on the rampage. What could be next?

"Er...excuse me," a male voice called as Marilyn reached for the sliding-glass door.

She turned to see a vaguely familiar, thirty-something man approaching from the side of the house. He was the type who might get lost in a crowd: average brown hair, average gray eyes, average height and weight, average black business suit and white shirt. He seemed unusually apprehensive. Nervous. Ashamed. With a sheepish smile, he cautiously met her gaze. "I believe my...um...dog just introduced himself?"

Immediately, Marilyn transferred her irritation from the Saint Bernard to its owner. This guy had a lot of nerve letting his dog run loose in the neighborhood!

"Yes, he has," she said acidly. "And he destroyed my garden!"

Brooke tightened her grip on her mom's hand.

"I'm sorry." With a kind smile, the man decreased the distance between them to mere feet. "I just let him out for a few minutes. When I went back into the house to answer the phone, I figured he would stay in my yard." The smile increased. There was *nothing* average about his smile—one of the most engaging smiles Marilyn had ever encountered. A smile that lit up the man's soft gray eyes. A smile that somehow soothed her irritation.

Marilyn felt herself returning that smile. "I guess it wasn't your fault." She glanced toward the violated garden. When she looked back, the Saint Bernard, his nose caked in dirt, skulked behind his owner. His tail produced a pathetic twitch. And Marilyn giggled. Perhaps the stress of the move, of being a single parent, of trying to perform her new job had left her delirious. The giggle increased to outright laughter.

With obvious relief, the man joined her.

Brooke even produced a muffled chuckle.

"I'm sorry," Marilyn said through tears. "It's just—this isn't funny—I'm sure..." More laughter. "Mom always said I had an offbeat sense of humor. I ought to be using that dog as a scarecrow, and here I am *laughing!*"

When all the chortles had scurried away, the man extended his hand. "By the way, I'm Joshua. Joshua Langham. I live across the street. All my friends just call me Josh."

"Nice to meet you, Josh." Once more, Marilyn wondered if she had met this man before. His name even seemed to strike a chord in her memory. Eureka Springs, population 1,900, was the kind of town where everyone knew everyone. Perhaps they had met in the grocery store or post office at one time or another.

"I'm Marilyn." She shook his hand. "Marilyn Thatcher," she added as an afterthought. Marilyn desperately wanted to shake her ex-husband's name, but Brooke couldn't. Even though the Reverend Gregory Thatcher, Ph.D., had destroyed their home, his last name still united Marilyn with her daughter.

With a hint of recognition playing on Joshua's face, she fully expected him to ask, "Have we met before?" Instead, he said, "If you don't mind, I'd like to repair the damage to your garden. Do you think your husband would mind?"

"Not in the least," she clipped bitterly. "He and his new wife don't give one flip about my garden."

"Oh," Josh said respectfully, but a faint trace of humor sparked in his eyes.

Marilyn produced another spontaneous grin. Discreetly, she looked for a wedding band, sure of finding one, only to discover Josh's ring finger void of gold. Warning bells began a cacophonous clanging in her mind. Marilyn was not in any way interested in starting a relationship with a man. She had told her own mother last week, "A relationship with a man couldn't be farther from my mind," and she had meant it. Despite Joshua's average looks, he possessed an endearing charm that had probably impressed more than one woman. In short, Marilyn sensed she could become attracted—seriously attracted—to Joshua Langham. The warning bells clanged louder. She still wasn't even sure she had sorted through all her leftover love for Gregory. Despite his affair and abandonment, Marilyn had found she couldn't just turn off her feelings. The last couple of years she had swung from disdaining her former husband to realizing her disdain sprouted from disillusioned love. Nonetheless, even if she had no feelings for Gregory whatsoever, Marilyn would *not ever* marry again. *Period.*

"Your doggie was not nice," Brooke accused. "You need to put him in time out."

With an indulgent smile, Josh extended his hand to Brooke. "I completely agree with you, delightful lady. And what's your name?"

"Brooke." Timidly she shook Josh's extended hand.

"You look exactly like your mother, ponytail and all. Do you know that?"

"Yes, I do," she said with pride.

"Would you like to help me fix the garden?"

"Can I?" Brooke's eager brown eyes implored her mother for permission. Apparently *little* girls weren't immune to Joshua Langham's winning ways, either. Brooke normally took longer than five minutes to accept the overtures of a new friend.

Marilyn hesitantly peered into Josh's inquiring eyes. She had yet to give him permission to repair the damage and wondered if she should. It would be so much easier to politely refuse and not get tangled in a new friendship.

"I would feel so much better," he said as if he could read her thoughts. "It's the least I can do." Another infectious smile.

And Marilyn couldn't remember why she had even hesitated. From a practical standpoint, she desperately needed the help. Furthermore, his repairing the dog's damage was certainly ethical.

"Okay," she heard herself saying. "Let me get my jeans on and we can work together."

"That's great. I'll go change into some jeans myself. Then I'll put 'Farmer Ben' in the house and be right back."

"You actually keep him in the house?" Marilyn queried.

"Yes. He's company."

"Rather large company, I'd say. What's his name, anyway?"

"Blue."

"Blue?"

A teasing light danced in his eyes. "Yeah, haven't you heard of it? That name's been around a long time."

"But for a *Saint Bernard?*"

"I had a mutt during childhood. His name was Blue. That dog and I went everywhere together. He died when I was twelve. I'm not sure I'm over that one yet. I named this dog Blue in memory of the other one, I guess." An embarrassed shrug. "That sounds kind of sappy for a grown man to be sentimental about a dog who died more than twenty years ago, but it's the truth."

It's not sappy. It's being sensitive, Marilyn wanted to counter. "That's touching," she said instead.

He averted his gaze, suggesting he was a bit disconcerted that he had revealed so much of himself to a new acquaintance. "It's touching, all right," he said with a smirk. "Especially when Blue is *touching* your garden."

Marilyn and Brooke shared a giggle.

"I'm going to change. Be back in a minute." He whistled to Blue and walked back around the house.

"I like Joss," Brooke said.

"So do I," Marilyn answered, despite her reservations.

When she had rented the cottage in the cozy neighborhood on Emporia Street, Marilyn had envisioned a quiet community of mostly retired people living in the white-frame houses dotting the lane. It looked like one of the neighbors didn't fit *that* description.

Once again bells of caution echoed through Marilyn's mind. A year ago she had thought herself attracted to an ex-schoolmate. Eventually, she had realized the attraction was based on her friend's subtle similarities to her ex-husband. Since then, Marilyn guarded herself against any romantic involvement. She wasn't going to ever get married again, so why waste her time on romance? She could live a long, long time without having her soul ripped out again. One day she had been a pastor's wife. The next, a divorcee. That experience left her turning her back on romance...and God.

Thoughts of God and church brought the usual uneasiness twisting through her chest, but the idea of stepping into a sanctuary also evoked other feelings. Nausea, for instance. Her life with Gregory had centered around church. Despite her dear mother's gentle coaxing, Marilyn hadn't dared attend one church service since Gregory's desertion. She had even sold the piano she expertly played because the instrument represented her years as the sanctuary pianist. Anything to do with church was simply too painful to tolerate. Yet something inside Marilyn insisted Brooke needed a place of worship. Perhaps she would compromise and allow her mother to start taking Brooke on Sundays.

Pushing aside all these troublesome musings, Marilyn turned for the house. Josh would be back any minute. The garden repair must be expedited because an enormous amount of unpacking still remained. She had taken a week off from work to move, and tomorrow was her last "vacation" day.

Within minutes, she rummaged through her unfolded laundry and found a pair of faded jeans for both her and Brooke. After changing, they exited the house to discover Josh, on his knees, hands in the dirt, whistling cheerfully.

"Joss!" Brooke squealed, bounding ahead of her mother.

Her eyes stinging, Marilyn bit her lip. She wondered how much of Brooke's spontaneous fancy for Josh reflected the child's hunger for a father. Marilyn's dad had graciously stepped into the role of Brooke's father, and Gregory did take her to his Little Rock home one weekend a month. But none of that was the same as having a daddy who lived at home. *Why has God allowed Brooke and me to experience so much pain?* The same question that had tormented Marilyn for two years troubled her once more. Some days she felt as if God had betrayed them. The double weight of Greg's breach of faith had left Marilyn weeping herself to sleep many nights. With a feigned smile, she approached Josh and the laughing Brooke.

"Joss is silly," Brooke exclaimed as he repositioned a tomato plant. "He called me Ladybug." Her high-pitched giggle seemed to dance from limb to limb on the surrounding trees heavy with lush foliage.

"Well, you are a little Ladybug," Marilyn said, smiling. With her gloved hand, she tousled her daughter's fine hair then exchanged an indulgent glance with an admiring Josh. At once she discerned that Brooke wasn't the only one who had riveted Josh's attention.

Marilyn, her mind reeling, forced herself to focus on the row of peppers. She bent and picked up a bedraggled plant to place back into the soil. Fifteen minutes. She had known Joshua Langham fifteen minutes, and already he affected her. Affected her deeply. What had become of the steel wall she had erected between her and the opposite sex? In the face of Josh's smile, that wall had melted like ice before a furnace. As Brooke continued to monopolize Josh, Marilyn mutely righted the rest of the bell pepper plants, discarding those beyond saving. While the smell of earth filled her senses, she desperately tried to reconstruct the wall, but it stubbornly refused to resurrect.

In a matter of minutes, they had salvaged what was left of the plants. Josh stood, bowed, and extended a chivalrous hand to Marilyn. She reluctantly placed her gloved hand in his and stood, all the while vowing to promptly remove herself from this man's presence.

Too many encounters like today would be more than dangerous. I'm simply not ready.

"Now I go to my office, mates," he said with a feigned Australian accent. "But may I beseech the presence of your company for a picnic tomorrow?"

His smiling eyes reminded Marilyn of a pleading Cocker Spaniel's. How could she refuse him? *Grit your teeth and say "no"—that's how,* a persistent voice in her head insisted.

"Oh, can we, Mom? Can we?" Brooke tugged on Marilyn's floppy T-shirt.

"Well...I—I just have so much unpacking to do, I don't think—"

"I'll be glad to help," Josh said eagerly. "I'm off all morning and most of the afternoon. We can unpack in the morning and picnic at noon." He shrugged and gave another arresting smile. "It's the least I can do. We're neighbors now, right?"

She groaned silently. *Mere minutes ago, I was trying to escape him. Now escape seems impossible.*

"Please, Mom," Brooke begged as Marilyn's silent deliberation continued.

"Look," Josh said, "it's not like I've got chicken pox or anything. One little picnic never hurt anybody. If it will make you feel any better, I can invite Mr. Wasson down the street. He's 120 years old and has a humdinger of a cane you can beat me with if I in any way make you feel uncomfortable." His eyes sparkled mischievously.

Marilyn chuckled. "Why do I feel as if Mr. Wasson doesn't exist?"

"Probably because he doesn't," Josh admitted, producing another carefree shrug that spoke of his guarded anticipation.

Once more, she considered the offer of his help from a practical standpoint. Simply put, Marilyn was beginning to feel as if she might never finish the unpacking. Joshua's help would certainly hasten the end of the task.

"Okay," she said at last, hoping she wouldn't regret the decision.

Two

⌒

As if he had been socked in the stomach, Reverend Joshua Langham collapsed onto his antique bed's hunter-green comforter and stared blankly at the wall's only décor—a landscape painting in muted blues and greens. When he had heard Marilyn's enraged screams and saw Blue running for his life, he had hoped to encounter a sweet-looking lady who probably made cookies for her grandkids. After all, most of the neighborhood residents seemed to be retirement age.

Wow! What a surprise!

When he had rounded the side of Marilyn's house, there she had stood, in blue jean cutoffs, hands on hips, blonde ponytail, no makeup, a smudge on her cheek. In short, Marilyn was the personification of the all-American woman.

"God bless America," he muttered. Shaking himself from his reverie, Josh stood and began changing from his dusty jeans back into his suit. He had observed someone moving in across the street during the last week, but up until yesterday he had been busy finishing his own unpacking at his church office. A month ago, he had taken the position as pastor of Victory Chapel Community Church. Just off Highway 62, the white country church with a green roof looked like an image from a postcard. He had spent so much time organizing his church office and home that he had missed any previous opportunities to introduce himself to his new neighbor.

Only after Marilyn's bitter comment about her ex-husband did Josh begin to remember one of his church members, Natalie Douglas, discreetly requesting prayer for her daughter. Natalie had never mentioned Marilyn's name, but she had sketched the details of the devastating divorce and mentioned that the daughter would be moving onto Emporia Street.

Josh recalled seeing Marilyn at McDonald's the week before. Humorously, he had told the Lord that he would take a clone of Marilyn as the wife he had been praying for.

That day in McDonald's Josh had assumed Marilyn was married because of Brooke's presence. Learning she was single left him thoughtfully musing about God's sense of humor. Could God be chuckling, even now, at Josh's amazement that the very woman he had jokingly prayed about now lived across the street?

Nonetheless, Josh would most definitely proceed cautiously from this moment forth. Even though he found Marilyn attractive, he would never become romantically involved with a woman who wasn't seriously committed to Christ. And Natalie seemed truly concerned for her daughter's spiritual well-being. Marilyn had once been a pastor's wife. Was her focus still on God?

Joshua's life was no longer as private as it had been before becoming a minister. A whole congregation now looked to him for moral guidance. He couldn't, he wouldn't, fail them or his Lord. Tomorrow's neighborly picnic would give him a chance to better acquaint himself with Marilyn and decide if he should develop his initial interest. He hoped this new acquaintance was the beginning of God's answer to his prayer for a godly wife.

As he removed his smudged blue T-shirt, Josh glimpsed the tattoo on his right shoulder—the ebony face of a feline.

"The Panther." That's what his friends had called him all those years ago. What would his congregation think if they learned his whole story? Trying to force his dark past from his mind, Joshua hastily crammed his arms into his starched white shirt and began fastening the buttons.

Within minutes, he had replaced his tie, given Blue's ears a scratch, and closed the door on the small white home he had purchased. Noticing the collection of mail in the black box attached to his house, Josh pulled out a fist full of letters and advertisements. Expecting the usual array of bills and miscellaneous correspondence, he paused momentarily to glance through and make sure nothing was urgent. But his casual glance turned to a wide-eyed stare of disbelief. The top letter so arrested his attention that he didn't even glance at the others. The typed address on the white, legal-sized envelope looked respectable enough, but instead of a return address, one word marred the upper left corner.

Leopard.

Nausea crept up Josh's throat. His lips trembled. His legs weakened. He collapsed against the door as he was hurled back in time....

They had been a fraternal pair through high school and early college. While Leopard fully embraced the life of criminal darkness, Joshua concentrated on breaking the laws of God. At the time, Josh had thought he was wiser than Leopard. A dangerous misconception. Joshua soon learned that those who associate with criminal activity are often as guilty as those who orchestrate it. At least that was the opinion of the FBI.

Fifteen years ago, Joshua had been forced to divulge incriminating information regarding Leopard to the authorities. Amazingly, Leopard had never retaliated. Furthermore, the plea bargaining had kept Joshua's criminal record clean.

Looking back, Josh knew God had miraculously protected him.

As Josh stared at the mysterious letter, he wondered if Leopard had finally caught up with him. The ebony feline on his shoulder seemed to warm with the intensity of his fear and regret. Would all those years of flirting with darkness, of rebelling against God, of running from a call to ministry ever end? Now that Josh had finally completed his Master of Divinity and dedicated his life to God's work, could his past still resurrect itself and taint his world today?

"Oh, Lord," he breathed as his fingers shook, "I don't even want to open it." Gritting his teeth, Josh folded the envelope and slipped it into his suit pocket. The rest of the mail he dropped back into the box. He would read the letter after he had mustered the strength to face the darkness.

That night Marilyn received a shock as she at last recalled the reason Joshua's name sounded so familiar.

"Mother, why didn't you tell me your new minister owned the house across the street from me?" she demanded into the cordless phone, feeling somehow betrayed. "I had no idea—"

"Why are you so upset?" Natalie Douglas asked in a perplexed voice.

With a long sigh, Marilyn collapsed onto the blue-and-cream striped sofa she and her mom had found at a "nearly new" shop. Wearily, she rubbed her eyes and propped her aching feet up on a half-empty box of books. While groping for words, she stared at the vanilla candle burning on the Queen Anne coffee table. Marilyn didn't want to explain to her mom. She didn't want to tell her she found Joshua Langham's boy-next-door smile incredibly attractive. He *was* the boy-next-door! He was also a *minister.* All the doubts Marilyn had experienced after agreeing to the blasted picnic doubled.

What is the matter with you, Marilyn Thatcher? You seem perpetually drawn to pastors. This is disgusting! It's worse than disgusting—it's sick! The very last thing she wanted or needed was another preacher in her life. And here she was living across the street from one. A single, charming one at that! Was God playing some kind of practical joke?

No, it's the calling, a soft voice urged. Clamping her jaws, Marilyn snuffed out that voice. She had once felt a calling to be a pastor's wife; she felt it as strongly as Gregory had felt the call to be a pastor. *Those days are over,* she thought bitterly. *Gregory chose to end our callings. And God let him.*

"Dear?" Natalie's hesitant voice broke into Marilyn's thoughts.

"Hmm?" she answered absently.

"Are you okay?"

"Fine. I'm fine. I'm sorry I snapped at you. I'm just exhausted." After repairing the garden, she had spent the whole day laboring over box after box. Amazingly, Brooke had cooperated beautifully. She had played in her new room, looked at her books, and watched a few kiddy videos. Thirty minutes ago, Marilyn had tucked Brooke into bed.

Now it looked as if she was going to have to say goodbye to her mother and make another phone call. First to information, then to Joshua Langham. Under no circumstances was she, Marilyn Douglas Thatcher, going to become involved with another minister—even as friends. Joshua could stay on his side of the street, and she would stay on hers. She didn't want him helping her unpack. She didn't want to share his picnic. She didn't even want to fall into any cozy habits like feeding that overgrown mutt when Joshua was out of town.

After another weighty pause, Natalie replied, "Well, okay. But it's just not like you to be so short. I hope you're taking care of yourself." Her voice dripped with concern, but Natalie seldom interfered. "I guess I'll see you Thursday morning when you bring Brooke over?"

"Yes. And thanks again, Mother, for watching her. That means so much to me."

"I'm the one who should be thanking you."

The moment of tension dissolved, and another call beeped over Marilyn's conversation. Within seconds, she had bid adieu to her mother and answered the new call. The chorus of hellos didn't surprise her in the least. At last! The voices of her six "sisters"—her dearest friends from the University of Texas—eased her distraught mind with their comforting tones. Model Kim Lan Lowery, the compassionate beauty. Sonsee LeBlanc, the witty veterinarian. Dr. Melissa Moore, nature lover. Sammie Jones, the intense reporter who pursued art. Victoria Roberts, domestic genius and the romantic among them. And private detective Jacquelyn "Jac" Lightfoot, the athlete and the one they had all decided would never get married. On landmark occasions they always arranged a conference call to support one another. Marilyn's starting a new life of independence was most definitely a major event.

"So, how are you settling in?" Kim Lan asked, her high-pitched voice reflecting her mother's Vietnamese heritage.

"Yeah, got any single men for neighbors?" Sonsee quipped.

With Melissa, Sammie, Victoria, and Jac chuckling in the background, Marilyn rolled her eyes and muttered, "Oh, brother."

"Hey, I'm a woman with my priorities straight," Sonsee declared, voicing her motto for life. Straight priorities had given Sonsee the strength to finish veterinarian school.

Kim Lan, New York supermodel, made an enormous job of clearing her throat. "Well, while you're busy keeping those priorities straight, maybe Marilyn would care to expound on her newfound independence."

"Actually…" Marilyn debated whether or not to tell her best friends about Josh. But the seven friends had never held anything from each other since college. Why start now? "Actually, there *is* a single man across the street."

All six of Marilyn's sisters howled with laughter.

"I love it!" Victoria Roberts declared.

"You would, you romance junkie!" Marilyn snorted, glancing out the window to note the lights glowing from Josh's windows.

"So what's his name?" Kim Lan asked at last.

"Yeah, and what does he do for a living?" Sonsee queried.

"His name is Joshua Langham," Marilyn supplied. Pausing, she bit her lips. "And…and he's…um…he's a minister," she added haltingly.

Silence—the kind that whispers a significant, *Oh*.

"Well, how's the unpacking coming?" Kim Lan asked, and Marilyn wanted to crawl through the phone to hug the neck of the woman who had become one of the most recognized models in the United States. Kim Lan had a gift for being in the right place at the right time and saying the right thing.

For the next fifteen minutes, the seven friends chattered as if they were still college women. But at last the call came to an end with Kim Lan suggesting their next sister reunion be in New York. Every six months the friends got together for a two-night slumber party, shopping spree, and general fun.

"New York sounds great!" everyone chimed.

"Great! And I'll pay everyone's travel expenses this time," Kim Lan suggested.

Marilyn smiled at the resulting lame protests. Kim Lan's modeling career had made her incredibly wealthy. All the sisters knew that.

"Yes, yes, I insist," Kim Lan continued.

"Well, if you think you can afford it," Marilyn said dryly.

With another round of snickers, the semiannual reunion was set for New York in five months, and everyone eventually agreed to Kim Lan's offer to foot the traveling expenses.

Hanging up the phone, Marilyn felt as if she had received a special hug from her dearest friends. They had been an inseparable unit in college and had been able to maintain their close bond for almost a decade. Kim Lan, Sonsee, Melissa, Sammie, Victoria, and Jac were the only siblings Marilyn had ever known. Those six had supported her through the divorce and given her the courage—and even the financial help—to face life on her own. The only way Marilyn could ever repay their loyalty was through her own steadfast love.

Eyeing the phone, Marilyn mused over the other conversation she must not neglect. After getting Josh's number from information, she pressed the buttons on her cordless phone. When his answering machine picked up, she breathed a sigh of relief.

In a politely cool voice, Marilyn informed Josh that she had reconsidered his offer of company the next day. "I hope this hasn't upset your schedule too badly," she ended, trying to appease her conscience.

Marilyn hated disappointing a man as kind and considerate as Joshua. But his alluring qualities, rather than being to his advantage, only raised a battery of reasons to avoid him. The fact that he was a pastor posed itself as his biggest fault. Marilyn would run from Joshua Langham—run and not look back.

When the phone began ringing, Joshua jumped. He had just removed his tie, collapsed on the burgundy leather sofa, and retrieved the mysterious letter from his suit pocket.

Should I answer the phone? Is the call, like the letter, a shadow of my past? Every muscle in his body tensed, as if he were anticipating an attack.

All day, the letter had tormented Josh. While he visited those in the hospital. While he enjoyed dinner with a church family. While he began his notes for next Sunday's sermons. And every ticking minute seemed to echo his fate. Ultimately, he would be forced to face the letter in his pocket. Yet he feared that the letter—a virtual Pandora's box—would release an aura of evilness that would plunge him into despair.

The telephone continued to ring. Breathlessly, Joshua waited while the answering machine picked up. The volume was turned down, so he only heard the typical clicking when the message began and ended. Woodenly, he reached out to turn up the volume and push the replay button. Marilyn's restrained voice filled the room. "Hello, Joshua. I'm sorry, but I don't think I'm going to be able to fit the picnic in after all. Also, thanks for your offer to help with the unpacking, but I can manage..." Her voice hesitated, and there was an awkward pause. "I hope this hasn't upset your schedule too badly."

A mixture of relief and disappointment washed over Josh. For the first time since the phone rang, he breathed deeply. *Marilyn. The call was from Marilyn—not from his past.*

"Oh, Lord," he pleaded, "this letter, whatever it says, has thrown me into a tailspin. I cannot start hyperventilating every time the phone rings. I've got to be stable. For You. For the church. Please, Lord, please, don't let this escalate into something ugly."

Once again, the panther tattoo burned his shoulder in shame. He gritted his teeth. He could no longer put off reading the letter. With short, jerking rips he opened the end and turned the envelope to shake out the contents. Nothing fell out. He pulled against the side and peered inside.

Empty. He blinked.

Why would Leopard send an empty envelope? Was it a prank? Had Josh jumped to conclusions? Desperate for other clues, he examined the postmark: Los Angeles, California.

Unleashed terror rushed upon him like a wild beast bent on ravaging its prey. As if he were trapped in the downward spiral of a deadly nightmare, Josh spontaneously ripped the envelope into myriad tiny pieces. When finished, he wadded the fragments and tossed them into the rock fireplace. Desperate to expunge the evidence, he rubbed his clammy palms against his pants to remove the clinging remnants. In seconds, Josh raced to the kitchen, retrieved a box of matches, and ran back to the fireplace. His fingers trembled. He struck the match. At last the flame appeared. Accompanied by the smell of sulfur, it devoured the scraps.

"Oh Lord," Joshua cried, resting his arm and forehead against the mantel, "I thought I had shaken my past. Is it going to ruin my ministry?"

At twenty years of age Josh had finally turned from sin and embraced his Lord. From that moment forth, he felt as if a shaft of light extended from heaven to him. And the call to ministry returned. The first time Josh felt the call in his teen years, he ran. Because his father was a minister and

had unmercifully crammed religion down Josh's throat,
Joshua had vowed never to become a pastor. If being a
pastor meant all the regulations that imprisoned his family,
then he had no desire to align himself with such a profession, with such a God. Only after years of running, had
Joshua comprehended how wrong, how pitifully wrong, his
father had been. An experience with God wasn't about rules.
It was about love—supernatural, unconditional love. And
that love might be the only thing that could keep Josh sane.
If the churning black clouds of his past wound into his present, Joshua Langham could easily be devoured by a ravenous tornado of shame and anguish.

Three

~

Marilyn awoke with a start. The voice of a monstrous train, growling, roaring, snarling, filled her cluttered bedroom. The lightning flickered across the walls like a million windblown torches. Her heart lurched then pounded in panic as one word assaulted her.

Tornado.

Her mind replayed the ten o'clock news and the meteorologist's report of approaching storms and a tornado warning for all of northwest Arkansas—a regular occurrence for much of Arkansas in late spring and early summer. Marilyn had anticipated the usual rain, lightning, and perhaps some heavy winds. Even though she had toyed with the idea of a tornado, she had dismissed the thought. Eureka Springs, surrounded by the Ozark mountains, *never* had tornadoes. According to her parents, the closest one had been ten miles east, in Berryville, and that was in the 1960s. But apparently nature was ignoring the past and producing the improbable. Like rubber, the trees outside her window bowed to the ground. Then the sound of splintering wood, and the strong, horizontal rain lashing her windows moved her to action.

Brooke.

She lurched from her bed to race across the narrow hall toward her daughter's room. Marilyn found Brooke on the floor, paralyzed by fear. The continual lightning revealed the child's face contorted in terror, but Marilyn couldn't hear her wails. The furious wind stamped out the possibility of any other noise getting through.

Without a word, Marilyn snatched up her daughter, stumbled toward the hallway, and entered the linen closet. She fumbled for the thick comforter she had placed on the shelf mere hours before. Marilyn clumsily shut the closet door, sat down, wrapped the comforter around them, and covered their heads.

Brooke, her body shaking with sobs, clung to her mom's neck. As the house shuddered against the furious clouds, Brooke and Marilyn cried. One question continually curved through her mind: Would their little cottage be sucked skyward, gnawed to bits, and spit out by the insatiable beast lurking overhead?

Oh Lord, save us. Even if You can't save me, save my baby. The sweet floral smell of Brooke's shampoo heightened Marilyn's panic. Then the old resentment returned. *Gregory Thatcher, where are you? We need you! Even if you couldn't do anything, we need your presence!* And the independence Marilyn had come to relish seemed to mock her. It was that independence that had forced her to do the work of three women in the last week. To say she was exhausted was an understatement. That exhaustion had caused her to sleep so soundly she hadn't awakened until the tornado hit the neighborhood.

She thought the roaring couldn't increase in volume, but it did. The tornado sounded as if it were just outside the closet door. But gradually the growling diminished to a distant echo of its fury. Marilyn's terrorized tears subsided, and she finally heard Brooke's choked sobs. Her ears aching, Marilyn clutched her daughter and muttered, "Everything's fine. Mom's here. The storm's almost over. We're going to be fine. We're safe."

"I want D-D-Daddy," Brooke wailed.

"I understand, Sweetie." Marilyn bit her lips against a new rush of tears and started to tell Brooke that she wanted Greg, too. But did she really?

———

Groaning, Joshua tried to move his legs but an unforgiving beam pinned him to the floor. He was flat on his stomach in his own bedroom, trapped under his collapsed roof. His left leg felt as if it had been severed below the knee. Laying his cheek against the floor, he tilted his head forward and strained to see if his leg had indeed been amputated. The diminishing lightning revealed the shadowed outline of his lower leg turned at an odd angle. It appeared to still be connected. *Probably have a nasty fracture,* he thought. As if to validate that supposition, his leg throbbed anew.

The storm, demanding, unrelenting, had blown up quickly and escalated at an alarming rate. Josh, burdened with a restless night, had awakened at its onset. Despite the whipping wind, he had groggily mused on his bizarre dream—a gigantic leopard chasing his attractive blonde neighbor. With the storm ripping through the trees, Josh had concluded that, given his receiving the mysterious envelope, Marilyn's canceling their picnic was for the best. Marilyn Thatcher didn't need a man in her life with the kinds of problems his past might birth.

Then the tornado had struck. The telltale roaring jolted Josh from his troubling thoughts. The tree had crashed onto the roof quicker than he could race for the hallway. The same tree now lay below a gaping hole in the wall and roof.

What now?

He could barely move.

No one can hear me.

No one to help.

The phone sat across the room.

Then a faint whine penetrated the damp darkness. "Blue?" he called into the damp darkness. "Where are you, boy?" The Saint Bernard usually slept on a mat outside Josh's room. Was Blue also injured?

The quick padding of paws and Blue's wet tongue on his cheek reassured Josh that the dog had escaped harm. With a whimper, Blue placed his clammy nose against Josh's neck and sniffed.

Another jolt of pain clamped Josh's leg in its iron teeth. He moaned. He must get medical attention—and soon.

"Blue," he croaked, "go find help, boy."

The dog barked once.

"Help. I need help."

Another bark, and the dog scratched at Josh's arm.

"Go find somebody," Josh growled impatiently.

The dog backed away, hesitated, then trotted up the hallway.

Closing his eyes, Josh drew a deep breath against the nausea knotting his gut. The smell of the decreasing rain seemed to taunt his very soul. It dripped from the shattered roof and onto the beige carpet on which he lay. The cool night air, coupled with the soggy carpet, kept him shivering.

Blue's pathetic barking, whining, and scratching at the front door only added frustration to Josh's growing list of emotions. Gritting his teeth, he pushed against the floor, arched his back, and tried to pull himself from the trap. The result was another breath-snatching stab of pain—this time in his leg *and* ribs. With an agonized cry he collapsed onto the floor. His upper lip and forehead beaded in cold sweat.

The dog, responding to his master's voice, raced back into the room. Another bark. Another whimper. Another lick on the face.

"Blue," Josh called, "crawl over...over the tree." He swallowed. "Can you crawl—crawl through the hole in...in the wall?" Concentrating on his own words was requiring more effort as the agony from his leg and ribs threatened to snatch his consciousness.

More barking. A howl. A whine.

"Josh?" a familiar voice called as a flashlight's beam caressed the floor around him.

"Marilyn," Josh croaked.

Yapping hysterically, Blue tried to climb over the tree toward the voice.

"Are you okay?" she asked. In the background Josh could hear more voices. A child's, a man's, and a woman's.

"Not exactly. The roof—the roof g-got me."

Then a muffled conversation Josh couldn't understand.

"How can I get in there?" Marilyn called. "The front door's still locked, believe it or not."

"There's a...a key to the front door under the rock—" He gasped against the agony. "—the rock in the flower bed."

Last week, Josh had locked his keys in the house. He had been forced to kick the door in, which resulted in replacing said door. At the time he was furious with his own bent to absentmindedness, so he had three extra keys made. One he left under the rock. The other two he placed in his office desk at church. Now, Josh was glad the whole incident had occurred. God had been looking out for him.

Within seconds Marilyn, with Blue close behind, picked her way through the demolished room's debris. Then she was bending over Josh. The flashlight illuminated her face, making her blonde tresses and concerned eyes seem the countenance of an angel. Soon she answered the questions flitting through his mind.

"After the storm, Mom and Dad called to check on me. Brooke and I were so shaken, I asked them to come over. When they got here we saw the tree on the side of your house. Dad went back to my house to call for an ambulance. He'll be back in a minute."

As she talked in dry, practical tones, Josh had the faint idea that she was trying to remain calm just for him.

She directed the light toward his leg. "It looks like you're pinned down." A pause. "How badly does your leg hurt?" And this time her voice quivered.

"Before I found Christ, I...I could have told you. But I—" Another groan. "I quit using such strong l-lang-language."

"I understand." A note of worried indulgence laced her words.

"Th-Thanks."

She sat down by him, and the faint smell of jasmine accompanied her. Gingerly Marilyn touched his arm. "Dad will be back soon. Maybe he and I can free you." She retrieved the bedspread and gently settled the dry end around his torso.

"You're an-an a-angel," Josh breathed. He only wished he could stress how much he meant it.

"If one of the qualifications for being an angel is being scared senseless, then I guess I'm angel material. I've lived in Eureka Springs most of my life, and this is my first tornado—here or anywhere."

"Your house?"

"I lost some windows and the two oaks out front. The rest of the neighborhood—let's just say we're all going to be planting trees. Right now, yours appears to be the only house with significant damage. But the streetlights are out, of course, so it's hard to tell. The tornado must have been off the ground enough to keep from demolishing the whole town."

"God," Josh rasped.

"Yes," she whispered, "It had to have been." Her flashlight once again trailed around the room. "It's amazing you're still alive," she said with a shiver.

"I agree."

Fleetingly, Josh wondered if he would meet his demise soon anyway. If Leopard had indeed found him, the possibilities of his survival could be slim.

The flashlight's beam flitted across Josh's left shoulder then settled inches from his face on the floor. Marilyn sat motionless, wordless. He glanced up at her curious eyes. Despite the intensity of his pain, Josh felt a stifled question poising itself between them. He sensed without even asking that she had spotted his panther tattoo. As usual, Josh had gone to bed dressed only in his pajama pants. In the summer, he didn't bother with the shirt.

Once again, the shame of his past raised its ugly head. Should he tell her how the panther came to be? Then he remembered his troubled dreams and the huge feline beast chasing a screaming Marilyn.

No, I won't tell her, he decided.

He had already decided to keep his distance from Marilyn, so the less she discovered, the better.

Josh locked his fingers together and placed his forehead on them as new shivers of shock and agony wracked his torso.

The arrival of Marilyn's father, Fred, preceded the paramedics by only minutes. Within half an hour, the crew had freed Joshua, braced his leg, and loaded him onto a gurney.

Marilyn gave his arm a last reassuring pat, and Josh produced a faint smile directed in her general direction. Once more, he recalled that humorous prayer he had voiced when he saw her in McDonald's. The sentiment had been nothing more than a masculine appreciation for her physical attractiveness.

There is so much more to a relationship than physical attraction, he thought.

The ambulance doors closed, and Joshua was prepared for the ride. Despite the effects of pain on his tired mind, he carried with him a new awareness that Marilyn could easily epitomize everything he desired in a woman. More important than any physical attributes, she possessed a profoundly caring spirit and a sweet disposition. Her ex-husband must have been crazy to let her go.

At noon the next day, Marilyn walked down the hallway of Carroll County Regional Medical Center and shied away from analyzing all her motives. Earlier that morning Josh had called and asked a favor. "Would you please bring my shaving gear and, if my dresser survived the storm, some clean clothes? You know where the key is." Marilyn had hesitated, but her genuine concern had prompted her agreement. The man needed assistance. After unpacking all morning, she had picked up his clothes and deposited Brooke with a friend. Still in her work jeans, she now approached Josh's door. She pondered the irony as she remembered her decision yesterday to evade him.

But avoiding an attractive, single minister when he was up and running was one thing. Avoiding a neighbor in need was cruel. So, for the moment, Joshua Langham was a neighbor in need. Nothing else. Once he recovered, Marilyn would withdraw into her world and encourage him to do the same.

She hesitated before knocking on his door, wondering what her six sisters would think of her. Kim Lan would most likely raise her perfectly arched brows and produce a teasing smile. Sonsee would undoubtedly lead Melissa, Sammie, Jac, and Victoria in a round of snickers. "Oh, give it a rest," Marilyn muttered as if her friends were present.

Deciding not to mention this visit to the gang, Marilyn tentatively knocked on Josh's door.

A smiling nurse met her.

"May I go in?" Marilyn asked.

"Sure. I was just removing his lunch tray. Are you his wife?"

"No," Marilyn said uncomfortably as she averted her gaze. The smells of a hospital lunch enveloped her.

"Oh," the nurse said with meaning.

That only increased Marilyn's chagrin.

"He's napping, but you're welcome to leave what you've brought." The nurse pointed toward the duffel bag Marilyn carried.

"Okay, thanks." Wondering at her own disappointment, Marilyn tiptoed into the room, deposited the bag on the bedside chair, and turned to leave. But a glimpse of Joshua halted her in mid-stride. His haggard face, relaxed in sleep, would be hard to pick out in a large crowd. Only his heavy brows gave him a distinct mark of character. Fleetingly, Marilyn reflected on the day before when his infectious smile had transformed his features, and his soft gray eyes had sparked with mirth.

Then she remembered the panther tattoo. With a touch of guilt, she strained for a glimpse of the ebony feline, but the hospital gown covered it. Joshua Langham must be a man with a past. There was no other explanation. The mystery only added to his appeal.

As if he had sensed her scrutiny, Joshua's eyes snapped open. His startled, haunted, gaze seemed to pierce Marilyn's soul. She jumped. An electrified pulse surged between them like a bolt of last night's lightning.

"Hi," he finally said, as if the intense moment had never existed.

"Hi."

He attempted to stifle a yawn. "You brought my things?"

"Yes."

"Thanks." Another one of those million-dollar grins flashed. Despite his day-old stubble and the dark circles under his eyes, Marilyn experienced the same response she had before. Her well-constructed wall crumbled around her feet. Once again she needed to run. Run—or she wouldn't be held accountable for her actions.

She had been wrong. Joshua Langham wasn't simply a neighbor in need. He was a man. A single man. An incredibly alluring man. A man with an intriguing past.

I should have never come to visit him, she acknowledged.

"Won't you s-sit down?" he said as he languidly motioned toward the chair where she had deposited the duffel bag.

"Sure," she answered. Wondering if she had completely lost her mind, Marilyn plopped the bag on the floor and sank into the chair. "How...how are you feeling?"

"Oh, I've had b-better days." With a painful wince, he glanced toward his left leg, elevated in its walking cast. "Seems I'm a bit beaten up or I'd let you have my chair."

"Right," she said dryly.

"At least they say it's a c-clean break. A compound fracture, b-but clean. And my ribs..." He gingerly touched his right side "...are having marital problems."

"Oh?"

"Yes, they...they've separated." His brows drew together as if the very mention of the ribs increased his discomfort.

She rolled her eyes. "Well, I always look forward to that—separated ribs and a compound fracture."

A drowsy chuckle. "Where's the Ladybug?"

"You mean Brooke?"

"Who else?"

"I left her with a friend who has a little girl the same age as Brooke." Marilyn wondered if they had been having these comfortable conversations for life or if it just seemed that way. Had she only met Joshua Langham yesterday?

A dry cough, a painful flinch, and he reached for his empty water glass, sitting on the bedside tray.

Marilyn stood, took the water pitcher, and supplied him with a fresh drink.

"Thanks," Josh acknowledged before sipping the water through a straw.

"Are they saying when you'll get to go home?"

"Tomorrow, I think."

Her mind raced ahead to his inability to tend domestic duties. Who would help him?

"Have you ever had a broken leg before?" she asked.

He eyed his walking cast. "Not when I was living by myself." A sheepish smile crossed his face. "You wouldn't happen to have the number of a good maid, would you?"

"Uh, no." She clenched her jaw to stop herself from offering any help. With a full-time job, a four-year-old, and her own housekeeping, Marilyn had precious little time to play the good Samaritan. An onslaught of guilt left her feeling like a selfish shrew.

"I can help with the meals," she blurted. "It won't be any trouble to make enough for one more."

Yes, I've lost my mind. I need to exit, and swiftly, before I volunteer to scrub his walls with a toothbrush or something else equally insane!

"I appreciate the offer, b-but I'm sure when the ladies at church hear about—about this, I'll be covered up with food." A drowsy slur laced his words.

"Maybe they'll help you with the dishes and laundry, too."

"Maybe." With another yawn, he set his glass back on the tray. His eyes drooped closed, his shallow breathing grew rhythmical.

Marilyn attributed his lethargic state to the pain medication. Taking her cue, she decided to slip out. But just as she reached for the door handle, Marilyn remembered she had tucked his mail into her oversized bag. She immediately scooped it out and gently placed it near his hand. That way he would see his mail when he awoke.

For the first time, she noticed the letter on top. A letter with a cryptic return address: Leopard. Her eyes widened. She swallowed. Then doubts, doubts, and more doubts. *Who is Leopard?*

An inky panther tattoo covered Joshua's shoulder. Was he called "Panther"? A lump of fear, the size of a tight fist, sprouted in her midsection. If Josh was a man with a dark past, did the darkness also taint his present?

Four

Leopard gripped the bulging manila envelope and dumped the contents onto an ancient roll-top desk that had once belonged to his grandmother. The yellowed newspaper clippings tumbled out into a disorganized heap. Fifteen years ago he had meticulously clipped and saved these articles because he suspected that, one day, they would be of utmost value to him. That day had arrived.

Settling into a torn, leather chair, Leopard picked up an article. He coldly studied the aging print then reached for another. Every article featured him, his alleged dealings with the military police, his admission of guilt, and ultimately his sentence. But several articles also mentioned Joshua Langham.

Joshua...the Panther...my supposed best friend. Spewing forth a caustic grunt, Leopard reached for the packet of pencil-thin cigars, which usually lay close. This time the cigars weren't there. With steel-like hands, he snatched a pack of nicotine gum and shoved two pieces into his mouth. He chewed like a brutal lion consuming his prey. As part of his plan, the cigars had had to go. When he faced Joshua, Leopard wanted no traces of recognition in his former friend's eyes. Any use of tobacco, especially the telltale cigars, might strike a chord of remembrance. As much as he enjoyed his smokes, Clark would gladly give them up in order to successfully complete his revenge. There was no room for risks in his perfectly orchestrated plan. Squinting, he continued to appraise the pile of yellowed clippings.

Due to his parents' assistance, Leopard had managed to settle into this small Los Angeles apartment. His father had hired him to load trucks for his shipping business, and Clark McClure was once again in the real world. With a wicked chuckle pulsating from the depths of his dark, dark soul, Clark glanced around the sparsely decorated apartment. Menacingly, he pondered what *Reverend* Joshua Langham's home must be like. During the last fifteen years, Joshua had probably married, sired a brawling brood, and was blissfully enjoying his freedom.

A freedom that had been stolen from Clark.

Abruptly, Leopard stood. Chomping furiously on the wad of gum, he stalked toward the bathroom. He was already late for work, but his father most likely would say nothing. The aging man so desperately wanted Clark to fully "recover," as Clark's mother put it, and be a good boy, that he was willing to overlook discrepancies. Even Clark's older brother, Sinclaire, had declared all was forgiven regarding the military secrets stolen from his office, and vowed to forget his younger brother's encroachment against him. Clark wondered if his family understood that he could never forget, could never "recover." Not until Joshua Langham paid for running his mouth to the FBI. What had started as a harmless, immature offense sixteen years before had turned extremely ugly.

Leopard peered into the full-length mirror and stared at his muscular form, clad only in faded jeans. The face, lean and tan, strongly resembled his "perfect" older brother's—a face at one time handsome enough to turn more than one woman's head. Only the barely discernible trail of a knife marred his cheek—a souvenir from his first weeks in prison. As far as he was concerned, that scar represented Panther's betrayal.

He glanced toward the leopard tattoo gracing his left shoulder. He and Panther had gotten their tattoos the week before high school graduation. The symbols that had started as a juvenile escapade soon marked them both as the dealers of darker deeds. Resembling their chosen feline counterparts, Leopard had been quick and agile and able to slip from the hands of the law at any given moment. Panther had seemed more attuned to stalking after nightfall, more likely to hide his accomplishments in ebony shadows. That trait had enabled Panther to tuck his guilt away safely in the darkness and convincingly point to Clark as the perpetrator. The ultimate deceit.

Clark's burning need for vengeance left his cold, amber-colored eyes void of anything but the sharp wariness of a wild cat. Indeed, Clark McClure felt nothing now but hatred and the need for retaliation. Something deep within wanted to taste the love from his mother and father, wanted to embrace his brother's forgiveness, wanted to truly enjoy his nieces and nephews, but he couldn't. Not until he dealt with Panther. He would feel again only when he destroyed Joshua Langham's reputation, only when he sank his claws into Josh's life and ripped holes into his every accomplishment, only when he devoured Panther's very soul.

Joshua jerked and opened his blurry eyes. Someone was hovering over him.

Leopard? Was it Leopard? Blindly he tried to strike out with his right arm, but the sharp pain in his ribs allowed him to produce nothing more than a gentle shove.

"Hey, it's just me," a soft voice protested. "Marilyn. Remember?"

Struggling to focus, Joshua relaxed against the bed and recalled the last several minutes. His attractive new neighbor had retrieved some things from his home. Had he dozed off while Marilyn was talking? As the initial fear vanished, Josh stifled a dry chuckle. Those painkillers must have been potent for him to have gone to sleep with such a fascinating guest in the room.

He produced an apologetic smile. "Sorry. I guess you just surprised me."

Marilyn's stiff grin seemed more a wary grimace than a friendly overture. "I was actually leaving and remembered I had your mail, so I placed it here—" She glanced at the mail atop the covers and guiltily looked back at him "—so you'd notice it."

Yesterday's image of Leopard's letter leapt into his mind. Had Leopard sent another reminder of the deceptive web of their pasts? Joshua fumbled for the collection of correspondence, bills, and flyers to discover yet another plain white envelope. His chest tightened. A fresh stab of pain tore at his ribs. As he suspected, the envelope bore a Los Angeles postmark with Leopard typed in the upper left corner. Urgently, he tore at the envelope. Once more it was empty.

His throat constricted. His stomach churned. His head spun with the implications.

Why is Clark contacting me? Isn't he afraid I'll go to the police? A surge of terror rushed upon him. *But with what? Mailing empty envelopes to people is not against the law!*

Josh also didn't want his congregation to discover just how close he came to doing time in prison. If he were to report these letters to the police in a town as small as Eureka Springs, the whole citizenry would discover the past now rising to haunt him. Thoughts of the past brought with them an onslaught of guilt—enough guilt to drown all of Arkansas. How could he have ever allowed himself to slip into the bondage of sin to the point of divulging national security secrets? People could have died. And he would have been to blame.

It had been one thing to harm his own body with the parties, to harm his own soul with the sin, to devastate his parents with his willful disobedience, but to have almost been responsible for murder...

Joshua shivered as if winter's icy fingers had wrapped around his very being. No, that was one thing he did not want his congregation to discover. He wouldn't divulge anything about the letters to the police. Not yet. Perhaps the whole thing was nothing more than a joke. Immediately, he dismissed this possibility. Numbly he reminded himself that Leopard usually played for keeps. He would never indulge in pranks.

"You're scared," Marilyn whispered.

Joshua started. He had been so focused on his own terror that he had forgotten Marilyn. But there she stood. The personification of a summer day. The all-American woman. He thought about Brooke, the living image of her mother. He remembered the dream from the night before...that horrible leopard chasing a screaming Marilyn. *What would happen if Leopard were serious...really serious...and discovered that Marilyn and Brooke were becoming a serious part of my life?* Josh wondered.

"Stay-stay away from me," Joshua blurted, at the cost of another burst of pain from his ribs. "J-just go home and pre-pretend I don't exist."

"You're in some kind of trouble, aren't you?" she accused, her brown eyes widened in alarm.

"I can't say."

"Who's Leopard?"

"You read my mail." The accusatory note sharpened his words.

"No. That—that letter was on top," she said defensively, pointing to the torn envelope. "I just glanced at it when I laid it near your hand, just like you'd glance at—at anything... I..." She trailed off lamely then took a decisive breath. "Are you the Panther?" she asked.

Silence, as cold as a tombstone settled in the room. Joshua stared up at her. "Why would you say that?"

"I saw your tattoo last night. I thought you knew I saw it."

At once, he remembered being trapped under his fallen roof and Marilyn's angelic form outlined by a flashlight's beam. He remembered the hushed moment when he felt her looking toward his shoulder. Once more, the panther tattoo condemned him to reliving the past. Joshua turned his head and stared toward the sink. A host of questions swirled between them like so much debris caught in last night's roaring tornado. If only the funnel had grabbed Josh and hurled him to another continent where no one had heard his name, where Leopard could never find him.

Awkwardly, Marilyn stood beside Josh's hospital bed and scrutinized him. The more she learned about Joshua...the more she knew she should avoid him...the more fascinating he became. Who was this Leopard, and how did he fit into Josh's past? What about him made Josh blanch at the very sight of that envelope?

An empty envelope. Why would anyone mail an empty envelope?

"I think I made a mistake in asking you to bring my belongings, Marilyn," Josh said in a voice as chilly as a cavern's frigid air. "Please accept my thanks," he continued, deliberately avoiding eye contact, "and do like I said—"

"In other words, you can stay on your side of the road, and I'll stay on mine? Is that it?" Marilyn snapped, suddenly aggravated by this whole ordeal. Within the last twenty-four hours, this man had managed to turn her nice, predictable life into one upheaval after another. First, his dog destroyed her garden. Then that offer for the picnic she was forced to weasel out of. As if that weren't enough, he had to go and get himself injured in the tornado. Now, when she should be finishing her unpacking she was standing beside his hospital bed, feeling as if she had been thrown into an Alfred Hitchcock movie. And furthermore, yesterday's decision to avoid him seemed nothing short of an insult when he demanded as much.

"*Pulleeeze* forgive me for intruding into your life," she said sarcastically, all the time wishing she could stop her caustic remark. What in the world was the matter with her? Joshua had just given her the exact thing she wanted— license to avoid him.

Josh stared fully at her. "I didn't mean that the way you took it," he snapped. "It's just…" The slur of sleep had vanished from his words. Josh picked up the empty envelope. "There's a lot I can't tell you, but this is the second one of these. The first one came yesterday. And—"

"And?"

"I have no idea what's going to happen."

Marilyn bit her lips until they ached. Then she blurted, "Are you involved in something illegal, Joshua, because if you are—"

"No!" he barked, then flinched in pain. "I'm a man of God, Marilyn. Good grief! I'm pastoring a church!"

"Yeah, I understand all the restrictions that's *supposed* to put on a man," Marilyn commented.

"And what is that supposed to mean?"

"It means, Reverend Langham," she said derisively, "that my former husband didn't let the fact that he was pastoring a church stop him from running off with his secretary two years ago."

"Yes, I know that," he snapped.

Marilyn's mouth fell open. "Exactly how..." Then she pieced together the source of his information. "Did my mother tell you?" she demanded.

Joshua wearily rubbed his forehead in defeat.

"Exactly what else did she tell you about me?" Marilyn commanded, her mind splattered with irritation. How could her mother have stooped to such betrayal?

"It was-wasn't like that. Your mom is just concerned for you sp-spiritually," he mumbled as if his discomfort once more manifested itself.

He paused to wince, and Marilyn experienced a tiny touch of pity for him. But in light of her current exasperation, the pity dwindled.

"Your mom just requested that I p-p-pray for you and briefed me on the d-d-details. All she told me is basically what you just said, and I figure that's probably public... public knowledge anyway." He drew his brows together and momentarily closed his eyes.

"So, did you learn all this before or after you asked me on that picnic?"

"Before."

Marilyn prepared to further express her vexation when Joshua opened his eyes and raised a hand to silence her.

"But I didn't put it all together until after I returned home from repairing the garden. Then I remembered Mrs. Douglas requesting prayer for you."

"Well, what all *did* she request prayer for? Did she also request that you pray about asking me on the picnic? It's hard for me to believe that you conveniently forgot who I was until *after* you extended your invitation!" Marilyn growled, removing the keys from her purse.

"I'm telling you the truth!"

More than ready to escape this tense conversation, Marilyn walked toward the end of his bed, and with a flourish she was far from feeling, turned to face him again. "Just for the record, you don't have to worry about my staying on my side of the road. I'll be happy to comply."

The struggle to find a comfortable position caused Joshua's baggy hospital gown to slip from his left shoulder. Marilyn instinctively glanced toward the ebony tattoo. Joshua labored to pull his gown back into place, then broodingly stared at her. Silently he worked his jaw muscles as if daring her to speak again. But the panther had been uncovered, and Marilyn imagined the dark beast crawling from Josh's shoulder to menacingly prowl between them. A chill danced up and down her spine, and Josh's words wove their way around her neck like a boa constrictor trying to squeeze out her very breath. She glanced at that torn, empty envelope that still lay atop the covers. His words from only moments before echoed through her mind: *There's a lot I can't tell you, but this is the second one of these. The first one came yesterday. And...I have no idea what's going to happen.*

Marilyn looked back at him. His pained expression had not changed. Still brooding, still irritated, still challenging. And despite herself, despite her exasperation, despite her better judgment, Marilyn couldn't ignore the fact that Joshua Langham was an incredibly alluring man. There he lay in a hospital bed—his left leg in a walking cast, his hair rumpled from sleep, frowning like an ogre—and the man still affected her.

All the more reason to stay on your side of the street, sister, she admonished herself. Without another word, Marilyn turned and began striding toward the door.

"Happy trails to you, too," he muttered bitterly.

Marilyn stopped, gritted her teeth, and entertained the notion of stomping the few feet back to his side and telling him to get off his high horse.

But the room's door slowly swung inward, and Marilyn stood staring at her mother.

"Hello, Marilyn!" Natalie Douglas said with a relaxed smile, a smile that held not one trace of surprise.

Marilyn watched in consternated silence as her mother waltzed into the room and deposited a lush ivy on the wide window sill. One of the reasons Marilyn had left Brooke with a friend was because she didn't want to tell her mother she was going to see Joshua. With all that had happened after the tornado and last night's phone conversation, Natalie Douglas clearly understood her attractive pastor and Marilyn were well acquainted. However, Marilyn did not want her mother to get any ideas about her relationship with Joshua being anything more than a distant neighbor-to-neighbor friendship. Nevertheless, Natalie's pleased expression confirmed every assumption Marilyn had desperately wanted to avoid. Frantically, she turned to Josh, hoping he would provide some explanation. But his attention was focused on his devious task. Surreptitiously, he slipped that telltale envelope under the covers.

Natalie turned from her mission with the ivy and approaching her pastor's side. "Now, how is the most charming young man in America doing today?"

Marilyn wanted to roll her eyes. The new pastor had undoubtedly smitten her petite blonde mother, and Marilyn figured the rest of the congregation probably shared Natalie's feelings.

Josh produced a suffering smile, and the change in his countenance shocked Marilyn. He looked so amazingly natural, no one would ever believe he had just been involved in a tense, heated conversation with a new acquaintance, or that someone named Leopard was sending him suspicious envelopes. As he and Natalie embarked upon a light conversation, the marked difference in Josh left Marilyn all the more flabbergasted.

When the two of them turned to her, as if they expected her to answer a question, Marilyn stared back at them in round-eyed uncertainty. "I'm sorry. I didn't catch what you were saying," she said, trying to hide the stiff undertones in her voice but failing miserably.

"We were just wondering about the rest of the neighbors, Marilyn," Natalie said, a curious gleam in her eyes. "Have you spoken with anyone this morning? Was anyone hurt during the tornado by debris or breaking windows or anything along those lines?"

"No, not that I've heard," Marilyn supplied absently. "I only talked to Mrs. Morgan, who seems to be the neighborhood..."

"Gossip?" Joshua supplied with a hint of humor.

"Oh, you..." Natalie teased playfully touching his arm.

Marilyn groaned inwardly. Joshua Langham had Natalie Douglas captivated beyond reason. If only her mother understood what lay under those covers.

"Anyway, Mrs. Morgan said everyone was okay," Marilyn said stiffly. She refused to give in to Joshua's feigned cheerfulness because something dark and sinister lay beneath his blithe expression.

She studied the spot where he had pushed the envelope under the sheet. *Are there other things he's pushing under the covers and hiding from his congregation...and me? He'd said the envelope didn't relate to anything in which he was presently involved, but is he lying? Does the letter reflect only past activities?*

She pondered Brooke—her trusting spirit, her gentleness, her vulnerability. If something illegal was occurring across the street, Brooke could clearly be in danger. The last thing Brooke needed was more despair on top of a daddy who had abandoned her. *Perhaps I should move again,* Marilyn considered.

The thought of another move assaulted her with an onslaught of anxiety. She had no vacation time left. Moving again would throw her and Brooke into another tailspin of turmoil. Marilyn was so ready for rest, for peace, for some semblance of a normal existence. But were rest, peace, and normality possible when living across the street from Joshua "The Panther" Langham?

With a foreboding shudder, Marilyn wanted to run from her own thoughts. Saying a quick goodbye, she rushed for the door. She needed to talk to someone—and soon. Marilyn prayed Kim Lan was home. Even though she loved all her sisters and considered them her best friends, Marilyn always called Kim Lan first when she needed support. The two had struggled through Biology 101 together, which the other sisters breezed through. The late nights of studying and pleading with God for divine grace during finals had created a bond between Marilyn and Kim Lan that remained strong to this day.

Five

⌒

Joshua watched Marilyn's hasty retreat and wished he could run after her and somehow assure her that things simply were not the way they seemed. The blasted envelope from Leopard did not reflect anything in his present. He had not been lying when he said he initially didn't realize Marilyn's relationship with Natalie Douglas. He had no choice but to shuffle that envelope from Leopard under the covers and behave in a natural and charming manner with Mrs. Douglas. Marilyn's expressive face hid little, and Joshua had easily interpreted exactly what she was thinking: *You're a fake!*

Couldn't Marilyn understand that he could not afford any member of his congregation gaining even the tiniest suspicion of his worries with Leopard? A tense tendril coiled around his stomach. What if Marilyn told her mother about the communication from Leopard? Even though he had planned to avoid Marilyn from this moment forth, he must remember to admonish her not to tell a living soul about the appearance of these mysterious envelopes.

He glanced up at Mrs. Douglas, who stared after her daughter with enough concern to fill the scenic valley in which lay Eureka Springs. Clearly this dear woman and the rest of his congregation had enough worries of their own without discovering Josh's grave past and the possibility of that past destroying his future.

"I think the more I pray for her, the further she is from me," Mrs. Douglas fretted, turning her full attention to Josh. "I was so hoping when I found out the two of you would be neighbors…"

What exactly was Mrs. Douglas hoping? That he and Marilyn would hit it off and marry? Josh suppressed a derisive chuckle. Even if the issues of those dreaded envelopes didn't separate them, Josh clearly saw that Marilyn was not fully recovered from the divorce that had obviously shattered her. And as a pastor, he had no business even thinking of Marilyn as anything more than a woman in need of prayer and divine healing.

"Keep praying for her," he said gently. "She's still got a tough journey ahead of her."

"Yes." Natalie sighed and turned kind, blue eyes to Joshua. "My husband has been nothing but faithful our whole marriage. I can't imagine… And what's even worse is that Marilyn admitted to Greg that she wasn't completely faultless, and she was willing to go to counseling, forgive him, and rebuild the marriage, and he…he just…and he was even a pastor!"

A tiny tear seeped from the corner of Natalie's eye. Marilyn wasn't the only one whose soul was plundered by Gregory Thatcher's sins. But that was the way sin always worked. The dark deeds impacted not only the life of the sinner, but also the lives of everyone that sin touched. Josh thought of his own parents, of their grief, their devastation during his years of rebellion. Without the constant reminder of his own past, he could easily want to hunt down Gregory Thatcher and lambaste him for his horrid choices. But Josh was forever reminded of the paths he had once chosen.

True, he had never deserted a wife and a child, but he, like Gregory, had made immoral choices. Even worse, Josh had almost been responsible for the deaths of Americans.

As Natalie Douglas flitted around the room and nervously chattered about the next church social, Joshua prayed: *Dear God, help Marilyn forgive her ex-husband and embrace Your forgiveness. And Gregory...Father, help Gregory Thatcher seek Your forgiveness. And, oh dear Lord, help me. Help me see that I could very well be in Leopard's shoes. Show me how to love him, oh God, because right now I can't. Direct my path, Father, direct my path in Your ways...*

Looking over her shoulder, Marilyn slipped through the front door of her quaint cottage and locked it behind her. She walked several steps toward the living room's large picture window, yanked on the drapery cord, and allowed the shadows to embrace her. She covertly inched the heavy floral curtain away from the window frame, just enough to secretly peer across the street toward Josh's house.

A strange man, dressed in dark clothing, walked down the lane and paused in front of Josh's yard. The hair on the back of Marilyn's neck rose. What was the man up to? Was he Leopard?

As he stepped behind a tree lying near the road, Marilyn strained to catch a last glimpse of him. Should she call Josh and alert him to the strange man's presence? But perhaps the man's appearance wouldn't surprise Josh. Perhaps this man was part of whatever that panther tattoo represented. Then she recalled Josh's stricken, pale face as he tore open the envelope from Leopard. He had clearly been alarmed, frightened, and concerned. When she had questioned him regarding whether or not he was involved in anything illegal now, he had been adamant, even aghast, that Marilyn would doubt his integrity. Perhaps her qualms about Josh were unfounded. And, if so, he should be alerted that a strange man was snooping around his house.

Abruptly she turned from the window and snatched her cordless phone from its cradle on the end table. In a matter of seconds, she flicked on a lamp, looked up the hospital's number, punched it into the phone, and asked the operator for Joshua's room. Sidling up to the window, Marilyn continued to stare across the street. Just as Joshua's voice came over the line, a large dump truck with "City of Eureka Springs" printed on the door slowed to a stop in front of Josh's house. Two other men, dressed exactly like the first man, hopped out of the truck and began examining the trees lying partially in the road.

Marilyn wilted with relief and collapsed onto her sofa.

"Hello? Hello?" Joshua repeated in a sleepy voice.

"Joshua?" she responded.

"Marilyn?" A slight pause. "Are you okay?"

"Yes, yes, I'm fine." A soft chuckle erupted from her.

"What's so funny? Don't tell me...you couldn't wait to talk to me again. After all, it has been fifteen whole minutes," he said drowsily.

"Don't flatter yourself," Marilyn growled, berating the impulse that made her call him in the first place.

The satisfied snicker on the other end made her want to ask him how one man could be so exasperating. He had seemed like nothing short of Prince Charming yesterday when she first met him. But now, somehow, the Reverend had turned into a guy...just a guy...a magnetizing guy... who...who...suddenly seemed thrilled at the prospect of engaging in verbal sparring, as long as Marilyn was his partner.

"I thought you were going to stay on your side of the street—"

"I am on my side of the street," she snapped. "I'm sitting in my living room." Marilyn stopped short and abruptly changed the subject. "I take it my mother is no longer there?"

"Why?"

"Because you're back to your *real* self!" Annoyed beyond words, Marilyn disconnected the call and plopped the receiver onto the table. With a huff, she jerked the drape cord once more and beckoned the late morning sun to fill the cluttered living room. She rubbed her forehead as she watched the trio of men begin to clear the sidewalks and roads of the fallen limbs that cluttered the neighborhood. How could she have been so paranoid? She had arranged for a babysitter in order to continue her unpacking, not to make trips to the hospital and spy on her neighbor's yard.

When the phone rang, she assumed the caller must be Joshua. Undoubtedly he was calling back to ask why she had called him in the first place. Up until the fourth ring, Marilyn toyed with the option of letting her answering machine take the call. Then she remembered she had yet to unpack her answering machine. At last she recognized that, even if the machine *did* answer the call, she would eventually be forced to explain the reason she had called him.

Gritting her teeth, she grabbed the phone, pushed the talk button, and began speaking before the caller had a chance to even say hello. "I called you because I saw some strange man in your yard," Marilyn said defensively. "As things have turned out, it's the city cleanup crew trying to do something about all the trees from the tornado. That's all I wanted, and I'm sorry I bothered you."

"Ummm, thanks for your concern," a soft feminine voice said, "but I live in New York, and there have been no tornadoes here."

"Oh no," Marilyn moaned, flopping back onto the couch. "Kim Lan! I thought you were somebody else!"

"As in the minister who lives across the street?"

"Oh, great. Can I never hide anything from you?"

"No. Nothing. I can see right through you! I was calling because I wanted the lowdown on him, but the main thing is—are you and Brooke okay? I heard on the national news this morning that Arkansas was hit hard with tornadoes last night."

"Yes, we're fine." Immediately, Marilyn suspected she would receive five more phone calls just like this one from her other friends. She warmed with the thought. This group of sisters was nothing less than a godsend.

A high-pitched tone interrupted the call. This time, Marilyn decided the caller *must* be Joshua, and she chose to ignore the beep.

"I hear an interruption in our connection," Kim Lan said. "Is that your call waiting, or are we having trouble with the line?"

"It's another call. I'm sure it's him, and I'm not going to answer it!"

"Yes ma'am," Kim Lan said mockingly. "He must be getting under your skin."

"You can say that again!"

"I believe it. You were weird last night on the phone, especially when Sonsee was laughing about a man living across the street. What did you say his name was, anyway? Casanova?"

"Ha, ha, ha. Very funny," Marilyn said dryly. "His name is Joshua Langham."

"That has a nice ring."

"Would you just please explain to me how I get myself into these situations?" Marilyn questioned, ignoring her friend's comment.

"Beats me! If I knew the situation, maybe I could help you figure it all out."

The phone beeped again.

"Oops!" Kim Lan said with a giggle. "Sounds like he's Mister Persistent."

"Well, he can just persist awhile," Marilyn snorted as her oversized tabby cat languidly jumped into her lap. While she scratched the cat's ears, Marilyn began pouring out her troubles. She shared all her emotions, all her reactions, and all her misgivings of the last twenty-four hours. Everything except the issues of Joshua once being "Panther" and those disturbing envelopes from the mysterious Leopard. Something inside her insisted that she keep all that information to herself.

At the end of Marilyn's story, Kim Lan posed a troubling question, "So if he asks you out—and I'm not talking about on a neighborly picnic—are you going to accept?"

"No way! After what Greg did, I've sworn off men—totally, completely, for *life!* You couldn't pay me to get involved with another man. And even if I haven't completely sworn off men, I've certainly sworn off ministers! I don't care *how* attractive he is! Forget it!"

"Is this something you've prayed about?"

The phone beeped again. "Let me get my other line," Marilyn said, ready to grasp any diversion from answering Kim Lan's direct question, even if it meant talking to Josh.

Marilyn pushed the appropriate button. "Hello," she said crisply.

"I've been trying to call you," Joshua said. The sleepy tones had vanished to be replaced by an influx of irritation.

"Sorry," she said without feeling, "but I've got a long-distance call on the other line."

"You hung up on me."

"Well, you aggravated me!"

"Would you please tell me why you called in the first place?"

"I called because there was a strange man in your yard. By the time you answered, I saw he was with the city clean-up crew."

"Oh, thanks!" he said sheepishly.

"You're welcome."

"Well, while I'm on the phone, I guess I sorta owe you an apology for...for earlier today as well as just now on the phone. But I—I've been on edge lately..." His voice trailed off, and Marilyn began to hear the voice of the Prince Charming who appeared in her backyard the day before. On the heels of that association came images of the panther on his shoulder and the intrigue it implied.

"It's okay," she said. "I guess I should apologize, too. You weren't the only one who was snappy."

He sighed wearily. "Marilyn, I hope you believe me when I tell you that I promise I am not involved in anything sinister. This...this letter is something totally related to my past. I promise—I pledge on the Word of God that I am trying to serve the Lord with my whole heart and that's where I've been for the last fifteen years."

"But before that?" The words popped out before she could stop them. Her mind raged with curiosity to discover exactly what Joshua's past had been. Names like Panther and Leopard sounded as if they were related to an evil gang of sorts.

"Before that... I'd rather not talk about it."

"I'm sorry. I shouldn't have asked." Marilyn wondered what had possessed her. "I've only known you a day. I have no business asking such—"

"It's okay. If I were in your shoes, I'd feel the same way," Josh interrupted. "But I don't want to talk about it all. There are some things I am deeply ashamed of."

"Okay," Marilyn said, her mind whirling all the more.

"And one of the reasons I persisted in calling you back is because I would appreciate your silence regarding the envelope you saw from Leopard." He paused meaningfully. "I've told no one about my past, except that it was dark and that I glorify God for delivering me from sin. I would appreciate the details being left unstated."

"For instance, you don't want the congregation to find out you have a panther tattoo on your shoulder?"

"Exactly. And Marilyn?" he added with a gentle nuance that seemed to weave its way through the phone and sedate her defenses.

"Yes?" she said. The caressing undertones in his voice left her unsuccessfully fighting the warmth that wrapped around her spirit. Marilyn had never understood what it meant to be a wife who was treasured and cherished. If only Greg had spoken to her as gently as this man just did. Marilyn bolted up from the couch and began pacing between the boxes cluttering her living room. She must get a firm grasp on her reactions to Joshua Langham and stay by her former resolve to avoid him at all costs.

"My asking you to stay away from me...that was for your own safety, not because of any aversion on my part."

The ache in Marilyn's soul escalated into full-blown panic, and her pulse pounded like an impatient drum.

"I understand," she whispered.

"And I also want you to understand that your mother may mean well, but I would never allow her wishes or...suggestions to influence my choices."

"Okay," Marilyn squeezed out, her knees wobbling. She had to get off the phone with him—and *fast!*

"It would be a lie for me to say I don't find you extremely attractive, but..."

Marilyn walked toward the window, leaned against the frame for support, and watched the cleanup crew working on their huge task.

"But...I don't think either one of us is ready for anything more than friendship right now, and a distant one at that."

"I never expected anything more from you," Marilyn said, frowning slightly. Did Joshua somehow think she had made a play for him? But how could he possibly feel that way after she had canceled their picnic? Furthermore, he was the one who asked her to deliver the toiletry items from home. She would have never gone to the hospital to visit him otherwise.

"Good," he said.

"Great," she replied, once more riding the emotional pendulum from attraction to irritation.

"Then I'll be praying for you," he began, sounding too professional for Marilyn's frame of mind. "And if you need anything—"

"I'll call," she snapped.

Silence. The kind that screams, "What should I say now?" But then another call beeped in over Marilyn's conversation.

"Oh, no! That's probably Kim Lan beeping back in! I totally forgot she was on hold!"

"You mean Kim Lan Lowery, of course," Josh said jokingly.

"Yes, as a matter of fact. We're the best of friends."

"As in the supermodel Kim Lan Lowery?"

"Yes, the supermodel. And don't be so surprised. Well, gotta go." Without waiting for Joshua's adieu, she pressed the appropriate button and jumped back into the conversation with Kim Lan.

Thankfully, Kim Lan never once mentioned Marilyn's seeking God about her decision to avoid Joshua. As they ended their conversation with Kim pledging prayer for her friend, Marilyn reflected over the irony of Gregory Thatcher's past comments regarding Kim's lack of spirituality. Up until the last few months, Marilyn had agreed with Greg, but recently Kim had seemed more interested in the things of God than ever. How ironic that while Marilyn was virtually running from anything that reminded her of God or the church, one of her dearest friends seemed to be growing closer to the Lord.

As she hung up from her phone call and busied herself with finishing the unpacking, Marilyn recalled those years of earnestly following God. She remembered counseling seekers at an altar of prayer. She mentally recounted the Tuesday morning ladies' prayer breakfasts that resulted in miraculous movements from the Lord. Marilyn had been a good pastor's wife...no—a great pastor's wife.

Why did Greg have to go and ruin it all? Why did God let him? The anger welled up within Marilyn's throat and intensified as she contemplated the pain Greg's leaving had inflicted on Brooke. As if her mind were bent on tormenting her, Marilyn recalled those first weeks after Greg had moved in with his girlfriend. The shocked church board had generously given Marilyn a month to relocate from the parsonage. And every night of that month, two-year-old Brooke had sobbed, "Daddy! Daddy!" until she cried herself to sleep.

These memories left Marilyn despising her ex-husband. The whole situation would have been much easier for Marilyn to forgive if Greg had left only *her*. But considering how he had devastated little Brooke...

Stubbornly dashing aside a hot tear, Marilyn tore into one of the final boxes. Ironically, the box contained family photos she hadn't seen since moving from the parsonage—the picture albums she had once put together with exceptional care. While arranging them, Marilyn had mused about her and Greg and Brooke leafing through them in twenty years. But any possibility of that happening was now nonexistent. How could such a small word—"divorce"—a mere seven letters, represent so much desolation?

Marilyn had spent the first year after the divorce feeling as if her insides had been ripped out, shredded, and left to rot in the sun. She had come to the conclusion that divorce was nothing short of an emotional abortion. Greg, however, had somehow convinced himself that divorce was an answer to their problems. Divorce had never been an option for Marilyn. Rather, it was a bigger problem. A bloody, brutal, soul-scarring trap.

With a resigned sigh, she stroked the leather-bound album lying atop the stack of others like it. And for the first time ever, she understood that most of her anger now stemmed more from the pain Gregory had caused Brooke than the pain he had caused her. She would be lying if she said she was completely rid of all bitterness from his disavowal. But somehow she seemed to be growing past the hatred she had once felt for him. Yes, hatred. She had truly hated her ex-husband for quite a few months.

But no longer. Now, today, sitting on the floor facing all those old family pictures for the first time since he left, Marilyn simply wanted to put the whole thing behind her and start life anew. There was no sense in continuing to hang onto the past or reflect over what might have been. The bottom line was that it wasn't going to be. Gregory had made his choice. Even in the light of Marilyn's admitting her own faults, begging him to go to marriage counseling, and promising she would forgive him, he had still chosen the other woman. Perhaps, as her mother had said, their family's breakup was more a direct result of Gregory's allowing Satan to influence him than a seeming lack of God's concern.

"Oh, Lord," she pleaded spontaneously, "please help me forgive Greg for what he did to me. I desperately need to let go of this anger. It's been two years. I need to move on." She blinked against the tears stinging her eyes. That was the first time she had prayed, truly prayed, since the divorce. As a result of that prayer, an old, recognizable warmth filled her soul. God had heard her. He was still there. He was still waiting to embrace her with His unconditional love. How could she have ever been so furious with Him?

With a choking sob, she covered her lips with her fingertips. *Oh, dear God, forgive me for...for all the anger toward You. And, Lord, I feel like I'm making progress toward forgiving Greg for the way he hurt me, but Brooke...oh, Father, I still want to just...just retaliate for his forsaking little Brooke.*

Marilyn recalled a few times during her years as a pastor's wife when women had expressed similar emotions to her. She had been so prepared with her pat answers and her ready replies, so judgmental in her thoughts about anyone who struggled with hatred, unforgiveness, fury, or even temptations of violence after someone had inflicted emotional injuries. Shaking her head, Marilyn chuckled at her own naïveté. If nothing else, this divorce had taught her that sometimes life got messy, and that sometimes the emotions were equally messy, and that sometimes it took time—

precious time —for the injured party to allow God to spiritually, emotionally, and mentally heal him or her.

The firm knock on the front door startled Marilyn from her teary musings. Without a thought, she stood and opened it to encounter the very subject of her heavenward pleas—Gregory Thatcher, Ph.D.

Six

Leopard entered The Party Shoppe amid the rows of stores in the Century City Shopping Center. He nonchalantly strolled between racks of party costumes and stacks of custom accessories. Dance music and the smells of scented candles enveloped him to create a festive atmosphere. Clark, still chewing the nicotine gum with vengeance, paused to allow his eyes to adjust from the bright June sunshine. Narrowing his eyes, he gazed around the store, searching for a wig section.

"May I help you?" a young lady, dressed as Peter Pan, asked as she appeared from between the costume racks.

Clark produced a lazy smile and noticed the pile of costumes she had been pricing. "Yes. Do you carry wigs?"

"Yes, we do. We carry anything you'd want for a costume party, as well as gifts and supplies for any other kind of party."

"Great." Clark hesitated and increased his smile to the bewitching variety while orchestrating his lie. "I've got a wealthy friend who is throwing a costume party. He doesn't have much else to do with his time or money than offer a reward for the one who is the least recognized. If I win, I could carry home a thousand bucks. Can you help me?"

"Of course." The young, petite blonde walked toward the back of the store. "We've got all sorts of stuff here—wigs, eyebrows, mustaches, even beards—all in a variety of colors, including gray."

"Great!" Clark scrutinized his watch to see that his few minutes late for work had now passed the hour mark. But that was okay. He would tell his father he had a flat or some other lame excuse. Within half an hour, Leopard had purchased a gray wig, a scraggly gray beard, a mustache, and eyebrows to match. To round off the whole disguise he had also bought some thin plastic "wrinkles" to place around his eyes. He deposited the bag in the seat of his classic 1970 Cutlass Supreme—the very car he had been driving when he sped away from Vanderberg Air Force Base sixteen years ago. His shirt had been stuffed with the computer printout from his brother's office. The printout proved more valuable than Loepard had ever dreamed.

As he gripped the steering wheel, enjoying the feel of the powerful V-8 engine, Clark reflected over his years at Leavenworth and all his planning for this day.

Easing into the west-bound traffic on Santa Monica Boulevard, Clark mused over the pending trip to Eureka Springs. The plan had its possible pitfalls, including his being able to slip away without his parole officer's knowledge. With the calculation of a bloodthirsty predator, Clark would deliberately think out his strategy and find solutions to each obstacle, one at a time, until he had woven a flawless tapestry of action and artifice. He had been contriving fifteen years to complete his vengeance. If need be, he would allow himself a few more weeks to perfect his scheme. In the meantime, Clark would continue his correspondence with Panther. By the time Leopard got to the Reverend Joshua Langham, the victim should be consumed by worry, fear, and doubt.

Marilyn stared into the face of her ex-husband, the man who had turned her head the first time she saw him. He was the epitome of tall, dark, and handsome. Standing just over six feet two, he created a dignified presence when he walked into a room or stood behind a pulpit. His keen eyes, the color of emeralds, spoke of sharp intelligence and quick wit. Five years ago, Marilyn would never have imagined he would think of deserting her. Even though he had been more a dictator and less the model husband, she had believed he possessed a greater sense of integrity than his choices implied.

"Hello," he said simply.

"Hello," Marilyn returned, amazed that she felt no dread, betrayal, or love. In the place of the whirlwind of emotions she had experienced over the last two years, peace now existed. Peace like a placid azure sea. A peace only God could convey.

Marilyn recalled the first time she had seen Greg after the divorce. She had forced herself not to fall prostrate at his feet and beg him to please, please reconsider his horrid decision. But today, she felt none of that. Only release. Today she had to stop herself from frolicking around the room in a delirious dance of unrestraint. What a thrill to have no desires whatsoever to beg for a second chance with a man not remotely interested in her. Even though she could not deny that what he did to Brooke still gave her reasons for struggle, Marilyn decided she would not take Gregory Thatcher back if he came wrapped with a twenty-four-carat gold bow.

"Well," Gregory said, eyeing her curiously, "today's the day I'm supposed to pick up Brooke. Remember?" He looked past Marilyn. "Is she all right? We were worried after the news of the tornado."

"Oh, no! I totally forgot about your coming!" Marilyn covered her mouth in consternation. "Yes, Brooke's fine. And I'm sorry about forgetting!"

Why am I apologizing? she thought, as a surge of the old bitterness rushed through her. *With no remorse, he destroyed our home. I don't owe him any apologies!*

As the caustic thoughts invaded the peace God had so newly imparted, Marilyn recognized the trap. She would easily fall back into her old patterns of despising Greg if she didn't purposefully choose to train her thoughts in the ways of the Lord.

"Come on in," she said. Opening the door wider, she breathed a prayer that she would have the strength not to undo the work the Lord had begun in her soul. "Excuse the mess. I just moved this week."

"I take it Brooke isn't here?"

"No, she's with a friend."

A perverse voice within Marilyn gleefully giggled because Brooke wasn't readily available. Gritting her teeth, Marilyn squelched the voice.

"Well, you seem to be doing okay," he said casually as he stepped into the quaint cottage and glanced around.

"Doing great!" she said cheerfully, refusing to give in to the temptation to doubt her peace. "Just give me a second to pack Brooke's bag and grab my keys and purse, and you can follow me to where she is. It's only a couple of streets over."

"I left Sheila out in the car..." His voice trailed off.

"Oh. Well, go ahead and go on back out to the car," she continued amiably. "I'll be right out."

Gregory persisted in eyeing her curiously. "You seem... different," he mused. "What's going on? Got a new boyfriend?"

Marilyn's thoughts jumped to Joshua Langham, and she immediately dashed aside all images of him. "No," she answered, "you couldn't give me another man right now."

A spark of something akin to ire flashed through Greg's eyes, and Marilyn wondered why her words had annoyed him. Silently he turned and walked from her living room.

Marilyn contemplated the other times she had encountered Greg. In the past, she had barely been able to keep a civil tone with the man. Their meetings had been strained with strong undercurrents of hostility. The equilibrium Marilyn felt during this meeting, although not struggle free, was nothing short of a miracle. A miracle that had begun only moments before beside that box of photos. For the first time, she had beseeched God to help her truly relinquish her pain to Him. For the first time, she felt His presence, supporting her desire to move away from the agony of the past. For the first time, she had begun the journey of forgiving Greg for what he had done to her.

With a sigh, she thought of last night during the tornado when Brooke had said she wanted her daddy. Marilyn still had miles to go in forgiving Greg on Brooke's behalf. But she was thankful, so thankful, and eternally relieved that she had at last begun the journey of healing.

As Gregory picked his way across the limb-strewn yard, Marilyn recalled Sheila Thatcher. The tall brunette had previously made her feel dowdy, despite the claims of her mother and the compliments people had given her. Sheila was much younger, and her beauty was more blatant. Sheila seemed more animated, more apt to draw a crowd around her. Marilyn had initially loved Sheila; apparently, so had Gregory. But today, Marilyn felt tinges of pity for Sheila. She briefly scrutinized Greg's profile before he got back into the new Cadillac and wondered just how committed he was to the young woman. Every time Marilyn had encountered Sheila during the divorce and afterward, the young brunette had exhibited an "I won!" attitude.

What exactly has Sheila won? Marilyn wondered. *Well, Sheila, one day you may wish you had never entered the race. If Greg would divorce one good woman who was willing to forgive and move on, he might just as easily divorce a second one.*

Within minutes, Marilyn had packed Brooke's bag, grabbed her keys, and headed out the door. But the telephone, seeming destined to ring every-other-minute, began another round of incessant peals. With an impatient groan, Marilyn answered it.

"Hey, this is Sonsee! What's going on with the man across the street?"

Marilyn stifled a chuckle. "Thanks for asking if I'm alive after the tornado!"

"Oh, I know you're alive. I've already talked to Kim. Besides, if you were dead, you wouldn't have answered the phone!"

"Great deductive reasoning, Watson," Marilyn said through outright laughter. Sonsee LeBlanc had always been able to make her laugh.

"You sound different," Sonsee said. "I told Kim I feel like something's wrong with you, or…anyway, we're all worried."

"No need to worry. I'm fine. But listen, Greg's out in the driveway with Sheila. I've got to go get Brooke for him. I forgot this was his weekend."

A meaningful pause. "Are you sure you're okay?"

"Yes, why?"

"Because this is not normal behavior for you. The last time Greg picked up Brooke, you were on the phone wailing with me, Kim, Melissa, Sammie, Victoria, *and* Jac."

"How did you find out I called all of them?" Marilyn asked, unable to deny the lump forming in her throat. Truthfully, she didn't relish the idea of Brooke going with Greg.

"That's beside the point. The point is, all this cheerfulness is just not normal for you. At least not during the last two years, anyway."

"No, it isn't normal. And, well..." Marilyn swallowed hard, "even though I'm doing much better, it's still a struggle. But, Sonsee, God is good. I'll call you later and explain everything."

"Even about Joshua Langham?"

"Yes, even about—hey! How did you find out his name?"

"You told us last night on the phone, remember? But well, Kim 'The Informer' Lowery told me," Sonsee said in a contrived, ominous voice.

"Goodbye, you!"

"Bye! We'll talk tonight," Sonsee said.

"Great! Call me!"

In a matter of minutes, Marilyn had sprinted across the front yard and plopped into the driver's seat. For the first time in two years, she did not feel inferior to the tall brunette who claimed the spot beside Gregory that once had been hers. She took a cleansing breath, gripped the steering wheel, and determined not to fall back into the old despair and anger.

Oh, Lord, just help me through this weekend without Brook, she pleaded. And with each word, she felt the presence of God draw nearer and nearer.

By Saturday afternoon, Joshua had arrived home with the assistance of Natalie and Fred Douglas and a couple of other church members. As he had anticipated, the dear ladies had filled his refrigerator with a variety of casseroles and salads. Several church members had also begun repairing the roof in his bedroom. So far they had cleared the room of all debris and erected new beams and a roof base of plywood and felt. All afternoon, people had been there working inside and out. Several ladies had even started replacing the wallpaper where possible.

At last Joshua sat alone. As the evening sun began its slow descent, he was ensconced in a recliner in the guest room. With his left leg awkwardly propped on the footrest, he listlessly watched television and tried to stay the growling of his stomach.

On his lap lay his latest mail, along with another envelope from Leopard. By this point, Josh was considering calling information to see if he might discover Clark McClure's phone number. Some primeval urge suggested Josh should verbally confront Leopard about the whole business, but a constraining force stopped him.

Grabbing the empty envelope from his lap, Josh violently crumpled it into a hard ball and slammed it into the nearby trash can. The envelope hit the bottom of the metal container with a rocklike thud. He methodically dealt with the other mail and put it aside. Restlessly, he reached for his crutches and lowered the recliner's footrest. He awkwardly pulled himself up and began the deliberate, difficult journey toward the kitchen. Thankfully, his sore ribs were on the right side, and his broken leg was on the left. Nonetheless, the crutches pushing against his armpit inevitably caused darts of pain to shoot out from his ribs. Despite Josh's discomfort, his stomach's incessant growling could no longer be denied. This would be the first meal since he broke his leg that he had prepared for himself. Thankfully, the refrigerator was full of precooked food. The gentle padding from behind reminded Josh of his ever-present canine companion.

"Well, Blue, it's just you and me, ol' boy. I have no idea how I'm going to fill my plate and keep my balance, but maybe I can manage. Too bad you don't have hands instead of paws."

Wagging his tail, Blue produced a sympathetic whine. The loyal dog, who had stayed with one of the church members during Josh's absence, had not left his master's side since Josh had arrived home. He seemed to understand his owner's precarious circumstances and was offering as much sympathy as a two-year-old Saint Bernard could.

Within minutes, Josh had maneuvered himself into the tiny kitchen and managed to retrieve a plate from the cabinet along with a Mexican casserole and a dish of green beans from the refrigerator. With feelings of grand accomplishment, he began dishing out his supper and eyeing the casserole's layers of cheese with the voracious appetite of a man who has seen one too many servings of hospital food.

"And into the oven," he said to Blue, waving his arm in a chefly manner before depositing his plate into the ancient microwave and turning the stiff knob. While a heavenly aroma filled the kitchen, Joshua remembered the salads and decided to round off his entrée with a nice helping of something that looked like it came from the portals of cherry heaven.

Carefully, he opened the refrigerator, leaned on his crutches, retrieved a glass bowl, and swiveled toward the nearby cabinet. But his former culinary victories decreased his caution and he lost his balance. Struggling to remain standing, he clutched the bowl of pink confection and teetered on the brink of disaster. When his crutches slipped from beneath his arms, Josh lost control of the bowl and ultimately his own destiny. The beautiful glass dish crashed to the floor, spewing the congealed salad across the pale linoleum. Like Goliath in the face of David's stone, Joshua tumbled to the floor. Barely missing Blue, he managed to brace his fall and keep his injured leg out from under him at the expense of breath-snatching pain erupting from his ribs. As the smells of cherry Jell-O and Cool Whip engulfed him, the microwave's bell dinged cheerfully.

Exasperated, Joshua looked at the mess, the shattered glass, and the dots of pink all over the kitchen cabinets. At once his refusal of his mother's offer to come stay for a couple of weeks mocked him. Blue consolingly licked Josh's cheek. A glance toward his canine companion proved the dog was likewise dotted in pink.

With a sad chuckle, Josh stroked Blue's ears and shook his head in defeat. "This is going to take some getting used to. Looks like I need more help than you can offer." Immediately, Josh's thoughts flew to Marilyn, standing beside his hospital bed offering to cook for him. He had assured her he would be well fed, but Josh wondered if her offer would extend to cleaning up this mess. He wasn't certain he should call her because a lot had happened since their first meeting. Josh hadn't heard a word from Marilyn since their bizarre phone conversations the day before. In his heart, Josh recognized they should avoid each other, but another part of him—a lonely, bereft side that would enjoy the companionship of a woman of integrity—urged him to call Marilyn. He did, after all, need help. And given all the work his devoted congregation had extended on his behalf, he hated to call on any of them again—besides Marilyn was close by.

With great difficulty, he managed to pull himself up from the floor and stand. His left leg throbbed in protest, and he remembered he hadn't taken his latest dose of painkiller.

Maybe Marilyn would retrieve that from the bathroom as well. Crutches in place, he hobbled to the cordless phone hanging on the wall that separated the kitchen from the living room. With anticipation and dread, he grabbed the phone, collapsed into a kitchen chair, and pressed in the number that had become part of his memory—Marilyn's number.

As the phone began ringing, Josh's own words mocked him. He had told Marilyn to stay away from him. He had suggested they maintain a distant acquaintance. He had declared he would be lying if he said he didn't find her attractive. That was an understatement.

And the side of him that was lonely urged Marilyn to pick up her phone. By the sixth ring, Josh was certain she wasn't home. But just as he pulled the receiver away from his ear, a breathless hello sounded over the line.

"Marilyn?" Josh said, his stomach twisting with the timbre of her voice despite his common sense.

"Josh? Is everything okay?" she rushed.

"Yes. Everything's fine, except..." He eyed the mess on the floor and noticed Blue was helping himself to a taste. "No, no, Blue!" Josh scolded, momentarily ignoring Marilyn. "That's got glass in it. It'll cut your tongue. Come here, boy."

Blue dubiously observed Josh as if he didn't want to trust his owner's judgment on this one.

"You're at home?" Marilyn asked.

"Yes. I thought maybe you saw my grand arrival this afternoon." After a bit more coaxing Blue sidled up to Josh's legs.

"No. I've been out back most of the afternoon, working in the garden and yard."

"Oh...well...that's great. The reason I called, Marilyn, is that I've got a huge mess over here. You would think a grown man would be able to heat up his own supper without a catastrophe, but it didn't happen that way. Anyway—"

"I'll be over in two seconds. Just let me wash my hands."

With a surprised blink, Josh stared at the phone and slowly pushed the off button. He had expected at least a token hesitation. Instead, he'd received nothing short of prompt willingness. She hadn't even given him the chance to properly pose his question. Self-consciously he looked down at his tattered gym shorts and shirt, then shrugged in defeat. He ran a hand over his rumpled hair, only to feel a streak of the pink stuff leave his hand and lodge in his hair. With a frustrated grunt, he noticed that the previously undetected residue on his hand had also graced the cordless phone with a dollop of pink as well. Josh had long since accepted the fact that he fell far short of being conventionally handsome, but a voice within urged him to take extra care with his grooming, especially in the face of encountering a beauty like Marilyn.

With a derisive chuckle, Josh looked toward the checkered dish towel hanging precariously over the side of the sink. If he could just reach it, he might be able to rid himself of the effects of pink Jell-O. But the ache in his leg and rib cage insisted he remain seated. So he did. Joshua placed his chin in his elbow, inhaled the torturous smells of Mexican casserole and green beans, and awaited Marilyn's arrival.

Seven

❧

As she crossed the street and stepped onto the front porch of Josh's blue-trimmed frame home, Marilyn lambasted herself for acting like an eager teenager impatiently awaiting Joshua's call. She hadn't even given the man a chance to ask her to come over. Obviously that had been his intent, but she should have at least allowed him the opportunity to voice his need and then casually agree to help.

Without knocking she turned the doorknob and discovered it was locked. Deftly, Marilyn retrieved the key from under the large rock in the flower bed overflowing with petunias. She gave a faint knock, unlocked the door, pushed it open, and called into the house, "It's me. May I come on in?"

"Yes! Welcome to bedlam," Josh said, a streak of humor in his words.

Marilyn, closing the door behind her, saw Josh sitting at the kitchen table, left leg extended clumsily before him. The small, airy home offered a ready view of both the living room and kitchen to anyone entering the front door. After a few steps toward the kitchen, Marilyn spotted the refrigerator, door ajar, and a pink, sloppy mixture all over the white linoleum.

"So, this is the broken glass you were afraid Blue was going to cut himself on?" she asked, whisking past Josh.

76

"Yes. The drawer to the right of the dishwasher should have all the towels you need. And there are clean bowls and spoons in the dishwasher if you want to try to scoop that stuff into something."

"Okay, thanks." While she methodically dealt with the mess, Marilyn avoided so much as a glance at Joshua. As much as she wanted to concentrate on the task at hand, their every encounter spun through her mind like a recurring dream bent on tormenting her. That first meeting when he had thoroughly charmed her. The night of the tornado when he was trapped under his fallen roof and she had noticed the panther tattoo. The comfortable chat they had enjoyed in the hospital that had turned to tense verbal sparring. His teasing chuckle when she called about the strange man across the street. Then this evening, when she had fallen all over herself to run to his assistance.

Her recent conversations with her six sisters seemed to mock her. One by one, she had told them, "You couldn't *pay* me get involved with another man—especially a minister!" Yet her hands now trembled with his nearness. The longer she worked on cleaning the floor, the closer Josh seemed to move toward her. But that was crazy. He was stuck in the kitchen chair.

"Where's the Ladybug?" Josh asked as Marilyn wiped the final traces of pink from the floor and cabinets.

"This was Greg's weekend to have her," Marilyn said in a matter-of-fact voice. "She'll be home Sunday night." She determined to keep her back to Josh and exit the premises soon. If the man weren't in such a pitiful state of disability, she would have told him to clean up his own mess. *Maybe...* Feeling as if she were in a hurricane of emotions, she suppressed a baffled sigh.

"Does that bother you?"

She dumped the shards of glass mixed with the dessert into a plastic-lined garbage can.

"Bother me?" she echoed, more in an attempt to stall for an answer than to prompt Josh's explaining the question. Brooke staying with Greg *did* bother her—a lot. She worried the whole time about how Sheila treated Brooke. She worried the whole time whether Greg was spoiling Brooke or being too harsh with her. But the courts said Greg got his weekend every month, and the whole month of July on top of that. There was nothing she could do about it. Furthermore, Brooke needed her father, despite his forsaking their family.

"Yeah, bother you," Josh repeated, as if he sensed she fully understood his question.

"Well, how would you feel?" She pivoted to face him and her worries over Brooke were swept away by an onslaught of giggles.

"What's the matter?" Josh's face lit up with that arresting grin of his.

"Oh, not much, you just look like you've been baptized in pink, that's all. It's dotted on your face and shirt, and there's a long streak in your hair." She retrieved a clean towel and tossed it to him.

"Thanks." But his attempts at ridding himself of the sticky confection only smeared it further.

On impulse, Marilyn dampened a handful of paper towels and walked toward him. "Here. Let me help. How did you get it into your hair?" she asked, dabbing at the long streak atop his head.

"From my hand."

Silently, Marilyn continued her vigil while gradually becoming aware of just how close she was standing to Joshua— to this man who had a way of demolishing the carefully structured walls she built around herself. This man whose spicy aftershave reminded her of just how void her home was of masculine influence. This man whose dark past only intensified Marilyn's fascination. This man who had told her he found her extremely attractive then had asked her to maintain a distant friendship.

Marilyn had gradually comprehended that the only way to maintain a distant friendship with Joshua Langham was by avoiding him altogether. Any contact with him brought with it a host of unsuitable reactions—clammy palms, increased pulse, trembling knees. As much as she wanted to, Marilyn couldn't ignore her attraction to Josh. She had meant it when she told her sisters and ex-husband that she wasn't interested in a relationship. As soon as she removed herself from Joshua Langham's presence, she would remember that, but being near him now threw her mind and pulse into a tailspin that removed every vestige of common sense from her grasp. With each encounter, the reaction became stronger, despite the fact that he had a way of thoroughly exasperating her.

"There. I think that's most of the pink stuff," she said, desperate to end this encounter. Even though a significant pink streak remained, she had removed most of the dessert. "You're going to have to really wash your hair, though."

"Thanks," he said, glancing up with an infectious smile. "The way things are shaping up, I'd say you're turning into my rescuer. First from the jaws of a tornado, now from the aftermath of culinary disaster."

Marilyn fully intended to reply with something flippant but the words caught in her throat. The retort was fully stopped by the admiring light in Joshua's silken gray eyes. She desperately wanted to distance herself from him, but she couldn't seem to muster the strength. And the faint light of admiration slowly glowed into the fire of attraction.

Somewhere, a clock ticked off the seconds, and Marilyn felt as if that clock were counting the minutes until she melted into a warm heap.

Why are you even over here? a persistent voice questioned.

Run! Run! Run! Run!

Now! Now! Now! Now!

Run now! Run now! Run now!

But Marilyn didn't run. She continued to stare at him, to be drawn into the web of his thoughts through the expressions of his eyes. He had the kind of eyes a woman felt as if she were drowning in. Velvety gray eyes that reflected undercurrents of secrets, tenderness, and passion. Eyes that were not easily forgotten.

But don't forget, you idiot, he's a pastor! You have been there and done that! Have you lost your mind?

As if Josh heard her very thoughts, he abruptly looked toward the kitchen window. Marilyn felt as if she had been suddenly released from an electromagnetic current. She stumbled backward. Breathlessly, she deliberated what to do. Escape or collapse on the spot? Escape seemed the most logical choice. Marilyn bolted toward the front door.

"Marilyn?"

Joshua's strained call stopped her in her tracks. She didn't answer him, but she didn't move either. Her back tingled as she felt his gaze upon her.

"Are you still in love with Gregory?"

The question crashed against her like an unexpected tidal wave.

"What?" she gasped, whirling to face him.

"Are you still in love with your ex-husband?" His bland expression in no way reflected the undercurrents of tension pulsating between them.

"Why do you want to know that?"

"It's something I need—I'd like to know."

Speechless, Marilyn marveled at the timeliness of Josh's question. Two months ago, she couldn't have supplied an appropriate answer. But that moment of prayer yesterday had begun the purging of her feelings for Gregory Thatcher and reawakened her interest for the things of God. Marilyn could at last deny any love for Gregory. But her feelings for her ex-husband were not the business of this man she had only just met. With every hour, Marilyn felt as if her path was being woven more tightly with the path of Joshua Langham. The more she shared of herself, the more risk she ran of becoming involved...attached...ensnared. Something Marilyn never wanted to happen again.

"I don't feel this is something the two of us should discuss," she parried.

"You don't love him anymore, do you?" Josh's narrowed eyes seemed to penetrate her very soul.

"Was there something else you needed before I go?" she asked pointedly.

Silence.

"Yes, as a matter of fact, there is," he said flatly. "I was wondering if you might retrieve my pain medicine from the bathroom counter and also get my plate out of the microwave. I'm terribly hungry, and my leg is killing me."

Silently Marilyn walked down the short hallway to discover the bathroom on the left. She grabbed the prescription bottle from the counter and glanced into the mirror to see a large smudge of soil along her cheek and dots of dirt on the front of her floppy gray T-shirt. At this point, she didn't even care.

Determinedly, she deposited the medicine bottle on the kitchen table near Josh's hand. Resolutely, she removed the warm plate from the microwave, grabbed some silverware, and set them next to him. Purposefully, she retrieved a soda from the refrigerator and placed the can by the plate. Her spine stiff, Marilyn turned to leave. As an afterthought, she walked back to the refrigerator, removed another container of congealed salad, found a bowl in the dishwasher, and served a generous portion of the orange dessert into the bowl. After replacing the salad, she plopped the full dessert bowl next to Joshua's plate.

"Thanks," he said bluntly.

"You're welcome," she said in an equally blunt tone. With that, Marilyn paced back toward the front door, planning to go home and unplug her phone until she could change her number.

Boring. Marilyn wanted her existence to be boring, planned, predictable. She had experienced enough upheaval for one lifetime and was ready for her days to plod along, for one hour to melt into the other in a comfortable routine. Joshua Langham threatened any possibility of a comfortable routine. She hadn't felt comfortable since she met him.

"How do you feel about starting back to church?" Joshua asked, as if he had just inquired the time of day.

Marilyn once more stopped short as his question ricocheted around the room. Again, she whirled to face him. "How did you find out I'm not going to church?" she blurted, then held up her hand. "Wait! You don't have to answer that. My mother told you. Right?"

"Yep," he said as if that admission was of no consequence to him. He filled his mouth with a forkful of casserole and chewed ravenously.

"What *hasn't* she told you?"

"Ummm...your shoe size," he said after another bite.

"This is not funny!" Marilyn said in the army sergeant voice she reserved for Brooke's most disobedient moments.

"I never intended it to be funny," he said to a forkful of green beans. "We need a pianist. We're willing to pay, and your mother told me—"

"That I play superbly," Marilyn said, waving her hand like an accomplished conductor.

"Exactly!" Josh smiled.

"No thanks!" she said firmly, so infuriated with her mother that she could have roared until the universe collapsed.

"Wow! You must do some quick praying," he said mockingly.

"What's that supposed to mean?"

"It means…" He turned to expose her to a piercing stare, "aren't you even going to pray about it?"

Marilyn recalled a similar question from Kim Lan, except she had asked if Marilyn had prayed about dating Josh. Why was everyone suddenly so bent on investigating her prayer life? The truth of the matter was, until yesterday she hadn't had much of a prayer life since the divorce. She was doing all she could to hang onto the forgiving spirit toward Gregory. Furthermore, she had spent her gardening time trying to talk herself into the fact that she needed to begin the journey in forgiving him for what he did to Brooke. How could Kim Lan expect her to juggle all that with praying about dating Josh? And how could Josh expect her to pray about getting back in church as the pianist? She wanted to scream, *Give me a break, will you?*

Instead, she placed her hands on her hips and said, "Do you have any idea what I've been going through the last few days?"

He shook his head.

"Well, let me tell you. I have, for the first time in the two years since my divorce, decided that I must forgive Greg—put the whole thing behind me, release any feelings for him, and move forward. I have made a new commitment to spending time with God. I have decided it's not right for me to be angry with Him any longer. And, furthermore, I have come to the conclusion that for my forgiveness to be complete, I must also forgive Greg for abandoning Brooke. If you had told me a month ago that I would have come to this point by now, I would have laughed in your face. And right now, Joshua Langham, the last thing I need is people putting more things on me to pray about," she said making imaginary quotation marks in the air with her index and middle fingers.

"Wow, Marilyn, I'm sorry," Josh said sheepishly. "I didn't mean to make you feel—"

"And while I'm baring all," Marilyn continued, "I might as well go ahead and tell you that no, I am not in love with Gregory anymore. But I'll tell you like I told Greg *and* Kim Lan—you couldn't pay me to get involved with another man."

"I guess I've been put in my place then," Josh replied, raising his brows to suggest a combination of flirtation and disappointment.

Marilyn desperately wanted to stomp her foot, firmly agree, and then make a grand exit. Instead, she silently stared at him. Once more that energizing current flashed between them. Kim Lan's words flooded her mind like a tortuous chant: *So, if he asks you out—and I'm not talking about on a neighborly picnic—are you going to accept?*

"Well, you're the one who said we should only be distant acquaintances," she finally said, sounding much weaker than she intended.

The phone's ring cut off Josh's reply. He picked up the phone near his elbow and answered the call.

Her knees trembling, Marilyn hurried toward the door, not certain she could get away fast enough.

"Leopard!" Josh yelled.

Her hand on the doorknob, Marilyn stilled. The image of Josh's panther tattoo invaded her mind. The concerns, fears, and worries of the last few days washed over her like angry waves bent on destruction. What kind of sinister darkness was Joshua Langham dragging from his past?

His embarrassed, "I'm so sorry," preempted the phone's short beep as he disconnected the call.

Marilyn spun to face him. "Is he calling you now?"

Josh pushed aside his plate, placed his elbows on the table, and rested his forehead against the heels of his trembling hands. "No. That was some old lady with the wrong number. When I answered, she paused and I could hear a Los Angeles news program on TV in the background. I was certain Leopard was... Never mind. It doesn't matter."

"Did you get another envelope today?"

"Yes."

As hard as she tried, Marilyn could conjure up nothing appropriate to say. "I'm sorry" seemed trite, and that was all she could think of. Instead, she silently exited, walked across the street to her new home, and stared in shock at the car pulling into her driveway.

∽

Leopard smiled with satisfaction as he replaced the receiver. He clicked the stop button on the tiny cassette recorder that he had held to the mouthpiece. He had recorded the opening words of the evening news in order to play the tape just when Josh answered. That way Josh would hear the call was from L.A. When Josh went ballistic, Leopard had feigned a high, shrill, elderly voice and hesitantly said he must have the wrong number. That short phone call left Leopard satisfied. After only a few empty envelopes, Joshua was becoming almost neurotic.

He placed the recorder beside the pile of newspaper clippings that still cluttered his desk. Several of the articles would damage Joshua's reputation once his congregation read them, but Leopard had narrowed his choice down to two. Squinting, he picked up the yellowed article that lay atop the pile as he slowly tormented a piece of nicotine gum between grinding teeth. The chosen article, titled "The One Who Got Away," featured a great shot of Joshua, leaving a brick building head bent as if he were being dogged by reporters. The journalist did a great job of making Joshua sound just like the weasel he was—a stinking scoundrel who had turned the tables on his friend and gotten off without so much as probation.

Abruptly Clark stood, grabbed the two articles, and strode toward the cluttered apartment's door. An office supply shop was just around the corner. Within an hour, he would have taken care of one more detail of his strategy. He wasn't certain of the size of Joshua's congregation, but a hundred copies of each of the articles should be sufficient for the mailing he was planning. Once he got into Panther's office and copied the church roll, he would have all he needed to proceed.

With a wicked chuckle he paused to examine his appearance in the mirrored surface of the clock hanging near the door. An old man stared back at him. A graying old man who wore shaded glasses. Clark reached for the gnarled cane resting against the door frame. He had purchased the cane at Goodwill, along with the ancient, musty suit and scarred shoes he wore. This trip to the office supply shop would be his first attempt at masquerading as a harmless elderly gentleman. But it would not be his last. In the coming weeks, Leopard would perfect his routine until no one, not even Panther, would recognize him.

Eight

~

Brooke tearfully tumbled from her father's red Cadillac and ran toward her mother. Marilyn dropped to her knees and wrapped her arms around the love of her life.

"Mommy, I missed you," Brooke whimpered.

"I missed you too, Honey, but I wasn't expecting you until *tomorrow* night." Marilyn cast an inquiring glance toward a troubled Gregory who trudged toward them like a man dragging a two-ton weight in his wake.

"I'm sorry." The dark, weary circles under Greg's eyes spoke of hours without sleep. He deposited Brooke's overnight bag at Marilyn's side and produced a grim smile. In the two years since their divorce, Gregory had never returned early with Brooke. If anything, he would call and request an extra night. While Marilyn did miss Brooke, she often agreed to Greg's request for more time because the child needed her father. Unlike Marilyn, Brooke trusted her dad with childlike simplicity and had yet to comprehend the depths of his betrayal.

"Sheila isn't feeling well," Greg said, shrugging his shoulders.

"She's got a baby in her tummy, and she's a grouch," Brooke sniffled.

"Sheila's pregnant?" Standing up, Marilyn picked up Brooke and held her close.

Greg gave a silent, sober nod.

"Well...congratulations," Marilyn said with moderate enthusiasm. Although Brooke always spoke fondly of Sheila, Marilyn wondered how Sheila's treatment of Brooke would change were she to have children of her own. This added one more piece to an increasingly complicated puzzle.

If only you had stayed with us, Gregory, Marilyn thought while placing her cheek against Brooke's soft hair. As in the past, a serpentine bitterness slithered into Marilyn's soul, but today she immediately squelched the tendency and shot a prayer heavenward. *Oh, Lord, deliver me from this vengeful spirit. I'm struggling...I need Your strength.*

She looked back at Gregory who eyed her curiously, just as he had when he picked Brooke up the day before. He reached into the pocket of his polo shirt and extended a sealed white envelope.

Marilyn silently took the child support check and mechanically thanked him.

"I added a little extra this month," Gregory said.

She blinked in surprise. Even though Greg maintained an impeccable record in his support payments, Marilyn never expected him to pay extra. "Oh?"

"I thought the extra might help you get settled in," he said, nodding toward the quaint cottage.

"Thanks. You must be doing quite well." She glanced toward the Cadillac and wished to put a quick end to this strained conversation. Taking child support money from a man who once promised to love, honor, and cherish proved awkward enough. But trying to deal with the implications of his overpaying only heaped tension on top of tension.

"I'm working for Sheila's father now. He owns a couple of real estate agencies there in Little Rock."

"Oh, I thought you were still with the bank," she murmured.

Shortly after Greg's ministerial credentials were removed by his church's national board, he had waltzed right into a high-power position at a local Little Rock bank. Up until today, the two of them had never discussed Sheila's family. Marilyn wondered why Sheila would have taken a job as a church secretary if her father was so undeniably successful. She recalled that Sheila had first attended as a visitor, and then gladly applied for the job as office secretary when it became available. Perhaps, even then, her motives had been less than pure.

For some reason, Marilyn thought of Joshua Langham. She scrutinized Greg, looking for any signs of anything that reminded her of Josh. Perhaps if the minister across the street in some way resembled Greg, that would answer the reason for her irrational attraction to Josh. If that were the case, she would be able to once and for all firmly renounce any feelings that might be growing for Joshua. She certainly didn't want to fall into the trap of being involved with a man just because he reminded her of her former husband. That would be nothing but confirmation that she was still in love with Greg.

As she continued to peer into Greg's face, desperately searching for anything that would remind her of Joshua, Marilyn began to panic. There was nothing—absolutely nothing—about Gregory Thatcher that reflected Joshua Langham. Their looks were poles apart. Josh's average height, brown hair, and gray eyes were nothing like Greg's athletic height, near black hair, and intense green eyes. Her mind raced to their personalities. Greg was forever the strong, choleric leader who could be a dictator if he chose. Josh clearly exhibited a more easy-going charm. Marilyn imagined he made everyone he encountered feel welcomed and loved.

And that was the problem! she mentally acknowledged, slightly irritated.

"Was there something else you wanted to say?" Greg asked, observing her with an odd expression.

"No...no...I just..." Marilyn sputtered to an awkward stop. "I...uh...just thanks for the extra money. It was very thoughtful. I wish you all the best in your new job." Still holding Brooke, she bent to retrieve the child's bag and rushed toward the house.

"Oh, Marilyn? One more thing—"

Marilyn halted and swiveled back to face him.

"Yes?"

"I...I know that I'm supposed to have Brooke most of July, but I don't think...this year, it doesn't seem to be going to work."

"Oh?" Inwardly, Marilyn shouted with joy. She detested the month Gregory had Brooke. Even though Brooke usually came back home two weekends in July, during the other weeks Marilyn felt like she was undergoing an emotional amputation.

"Yes. Sheila isn't doing well in her pregnancy. Nothing serious, but we just found out last week that she's pregnant, and she's terribly sick. I was wondering if we might be able to wait until later in the year for me to have my month with Brooke, once Sheila starts feeling better."

"Okay. I understand. I'm sure we can work something out. After all, despite the water under the bridge, we're still rational adults, right?"

"Yes."

Marilyn didn't even look at him again. She didn't want to. She just wanted to go into her cluttered home, sit on the couch with her sweet daughter, read a few picture books, and spend some time cuddling. Marilyn closed the front door behind her and glanced out the ancient door's window to see the red Cadillac cruising up Emporia Street. For the first time in two years, the ache of losing Greg no longer plagued her. She had no desire to run after him. No need for his hug. No feelings of missing him again. Instead, she thrilled in embracing her daughter and gloried in her independence.

"Praise the Lord," she breathed. "Praise the Lord!"

As she turned from the door, Marilyn caught a glimpse of a shadowed figure standing at the front window of the house across the street. Joshua Langham, leaning against his crutches. Marilyn felt as if he were peering straight into her eyes. Her hands trembling, she abruptly lowered the mini-blinds that usually covered the window. And Kim Lan's question haunted her once more.

Have you prayed about dating Joshua?

I'm afraid to pray about Joshua. The realization hit her hard. *What if God wants me to get involved in another relationship?* Another wave of panic crashed against her soul. *What if my calling to be a pastor's wife hasn't been swept away by Greg's renunciation?*

With great determination, she buried these troubling thoughts and settled on the couch with Brooke in the crook of her arm. Mischievously, Marilyn tickled Brooke's tummy and the little girl squealed with laughter. They playfully toppled over and spontaneously hugged each other.

"I missed you so much, Mommy," Brooke said.

"I missed you, too, Brooky."

"I don't like Sheila as much as I like you," Brooke said, her big brown eyes as candid as ever.

"That's great, Honey, because I like you better than anybody else in the whole wide world."

"We're best friends," Brooke said sweetly.

"Yes. Best friends." Marilyn's eyes stung. "Brooke, darlin'?" She stroked aside the stray wisps of blonde hair that sprang from Brooke's ponytail. "Was Sheila terribly mean to you?" A spiral of fear whirled through Marilyn, but she needed the answer.

Brooke's eyes filled with unshed tears. "She…she hurt my feelings and I…I couldn't hold it."

"What do you mean, Sugar?" Marilyn asked against a lump in her throat.

"Daddy went to the store, and while he was gone, Sheila yelled at me for breaking a little cup on the shelf. It was an accident, Mommy. It really was!"

"I believe you," Marilyn crooned.

"And…and…I started crying when she yelled at me. Sheila told me that if…if I didn't stop crying before Daddy came home that she'd spank my bottom. I couldn't stop, Mommy. I tried. But…but I couldn't hold it."

"And did she spank you?" Marilyn's pulse increased and her palms grew clammy as something akin to blind rage rushed through her. Carefully, she schooled her features into a loving expression.

"Yes. Right when Daddy walked in. And he…he told Sheila no, no!" Brooke shook her finger at Marilyn's nose and puckered sternly.

Brooke's recounting of Gregory's response spawned a certain relief which helped assuage Marilyn's fury.

"Did Sheila spank you hard?" Marilyn asked kindly.

"Yes. And it hurt, M-Mommy!" Brooke paused to pout. "And Daddy told her that the next time she does that, he's gonna spank *her* and let *her* see how it feels!" Once more, Brooke shook her finger at Marilyn's nose. "And Sheila ran into her room, and she didn't come out all night. But that was just fine 'cause Daddy slept on the floor with me in my room."

"Oh?" So that accounted for the dark circles under Greg's eyes. All apparently was not well in paradise. At one time, Marilyn would have chuckled in vengeful glee. Instead she experienced a heavy realization that Gregory was probably getting a dose of his own medicine. From her own painful experience, she would not wish that on even him.

Before opening one of Brooke's favorite picture books, Marilyn discreetly examined her daughter's bottom for any signs of bruising. How horrible to be in such a wretched situation! To be forever worrying if Sheila might spank Brooke too hard or unfairly. Marilyn began reading the book, which was about an adorable puppy, until the phone's peal cut through her animated recitation. During the first ring, Marilyn suspected the caller was Joshua. Marilyn decided to just let it ring. If the caller wasn't Joshua and the issue was important, the caller would leave a message or try again.

"I'll get it!" Brooke declared, lunging for the end table where the cordless phone sat.

Marilyn reached to restrain her eager little girl. "No... no..." she desperately urged, just as Brooke spoke a cheerful hello into the receiver.

"Joss! It's you!" Brooke squealed. "I told my Daddy we had a new neighbor who calls me 'Ladybug.'"

"Oh great," Marilyn muttered. *What must Greg think? But who cares what Greg thinks!*

"Yes, Mommy's here. Yes, you may speak to her, *please.*"

Marilyn put the phone up to her ear and gave a restrained greeting.

"I was calling because I noticed Greg bringing Brooke home, and you'd said she wasn't due home until tomorrow night. I'm just checking to make sure everything is okay. She isn't sick, is she?"

"No. Everything's fine. I guess you can chalk up her early return to a bad case of pregnant stepmom nerves."

"What?"

"Gregory's wife is expecting," Marilyn said bluntly. "And it would seem that she needed a break." She guiltily glanced toward Brooke who, thankfully, had been diverted by Tab, their cat.

"Oh," Joshua said, with the sound of a smile in his voice. "Looks like I'm starting to act like a nervous uncle here or something."

"Thanks," Marilyn said, warmed by the genuine concern in his voice. This was not an excuse phone call—a call to inquire about Brooke in order to talk with Marilyn. The man cared about her daughter. And despite his number-one fault—that he was a pastor—Marilyn found herself liking him. She finally let herself admit it. Yes, she especially liked Joshua Langham. Even without that ensnaring grin of his, she still would have liked him. He was the kind of man most anybody would like, and Marilyn saw a long, successful future in front of him. Joshua Langham was probably everybody's dream pastor.

But despite her admission, Marilyn firmly compressed her lips. Whether he was likable or not in no way changed her stance. She would not—and could not *ever again*—be a pastor's wife. Period.

I will not develop any sort of relationship with this man, she thought, *regardless of how nice he is.*

Joshua hung up the phone and hobbled toward the recliner in his bedroom. He had been heading toward the bedroom when he glanced out the window and noticed the tall, dark stranger standing in Marilyn's yard. When he saw Brooke in Marilyn's arms, he deduced that Marilyn's former husband must be delivering Brooke back a day early.

Once in the bedroom, Josh lowered himself into the worn blue recliner and switched on the television to blankly stare at the Saturday night movie. When he first noticed Marilyn's former husband, Josh wanted to tell Greg just how stupid he had been to throw away such an enchanting wife and daughter. During Josh's brief acquaintance with Marilyn and Brooke, he had somehow taken on the role as their neighborly protector. The very idea that Greg would have hurt them both so deeply left Joshua reeling with righteous indignation. How could a man do such a thing?

Then Joshua remembered. He remembered his own past. His own choices. His own sins. Even though God had forgiven him, he still wondered if he could ever forgive himself. Occasionally, the memories of living life on the wild side washed over him and produced a renewed surge of guilt, frustration, and thoughts of what might have been had he not lent himself to sin.

"Oh, God, help me," Joshua muttered, placing his elbow on the recliner's arm and wearily resting his forehead against his palm. "And help Gregory Thatcher. If the man ever wakes up and realizes his mistake, he's going to be miserable."

As he continued musing on Greg's leaving Marilyn and Brooke, Joshua's thoughts gradually wandered from Gregory to focus solely on Marilyn. At last he relived that moment when she had attempted to get rid of the gelatin in his hair. Joshua understood all too well the emotions that had flitted across her face like successive waves slapping against a beach. He understood the emotions because he had experienced every one of them himself. Admiration...attraction...confusion...fear. With a sigh, he wondered if Marilyn was indeed the answer to his prayer for a godly wife.

And given Natalie Douglas' continual comments, the middle-aged lady seemed to already be humming the wedding march. Joshua could see the matrimonial designs in Natalie's eyes every time she looked at him. But it just wasn't that simple. While he was indeed ready to get married, and while he wanted a wife to round out his life and ministry, he had no idea what Leopard was planning. And Marilyn had vehemently declared that she was done with romance. So despite the fact that Joshua had begun to dream of Marilyn at night, despite the fact that her earlier remarks about renewed prayer attested that she was indeed a woman serious about the Lord, he doubted that he and Marilyn could ever be more than neighbors.

Nine

○───

Two months later, Leopard ignored the terms of his parole and left Los Angeles without permission. He planned to be gone only one week. No one, not even his parole officer, would miss him. He asked his father if he might have a week off from work to take care of some personal matters. The elder McClure agreed, even though a host of questions plagued his eyes. Questions Clark never attempted to answer.

At the L.A. International Airport, he boarded the 7:20 A.M. flight to Dallas, where he would board a shuttle flight into Northwest Arkansas Regional Airport in Bentonville. From there, he would rent a nondescript car under the alias on his driver's license, John Magruder, and drive the remaining hour into Eureka Springs.

Deftly he handed the airline stewardess his ticket, accepted the returned boarding pass, and hobbled along the carpeted tunnel that led to the 757's smiling crew.

"Hello, sir," a young stewardess said respectfully. "May I see your boarding pass?"

"Yes," Clark said in a feeble voice. He extended the slip of stiff paper and, taking extra care to pitifully hunch his shoulders, leaned heavily on his gnarled cane.

The pretty oriental woman scrutinized his boarding pass, and Leopard wondered what she would think if she knew a young, attractive male was evaluating her beneath the disguise of a worn-out old gentleman. "You're in seat 23A." She gave him a sympathetic glance. "But that's a window seat. Would an aisle seat suit you better? I think we're going to have some vacancies this trip. I'd be glad to relocate you."

"Yes, thanks. That would be nice," Leopard said weakly and cooperated with great humor as the young woman extended extra effort in ensuring his comfort. She even offered a pillow and a soft drink.

Once he was secure in his seat, thoughts of his mission resurrected themselves, and the humor spawned by the stewardess died. Images of Joshua left Clark scowling. During the last two months, he had continued to occasionally send Joshua an empty envelope, gradually decreasing them until he stopped a couple of weeks ago. Hopefully, the whole thing produced the desired effect. He knew from his carefully placed phone call that Panther had been initially anxious. He hoped Joshua had stayed on edge until the last envelope arrived. By now, he should be feeling somewhat relieved that the envelopes had stopped showing up in his mailbox. That was exactly where Leopard wanted him—with his guard down.

As passengers continued to board the plane and clumsily store away their carry-on luggage, Leopard reflected over the last two months. Dressed as he was now, he had gone out into public day after day until he mastered his act. The final test had been posing as an old street person and approaching his own father for money. His father had taken him into a nearby restaurant, fed him, and offered to buy any other necessities of life. But Leopard had solemnly declined further help. That final test had assured him that no one, not even Panther, would recognize him. "John Magruder" was ready to exact his revenge.

At last the final passenger had settled into his seat, the "fasten seat belt" light came on, and the plane began taxiing toward its specified runway. Clark lightly stroked the gray beard, whose adhesive slightly irritated his skin. But any irritation was worth the opportunity to repay Panther.

Josh decided to wash his reliable, five-year-old Ford truck for the second time that week. The truck didn't need to be washed, but he was lonely this Friday evening and the Ladybug usually noticed when he was outside. During the last couple of months, she had become a regular at his house. At first, Brooke had chatted with Josh while he sat outside to enjoy the cheerful neighborhood and rest his injured leg. But once his cast was removed, the two friends weeded flowerbeds together, washed the truck, played hide and seek, and tossed a ball around. Despite his better judgment, Josh was becoming increasingly attached to the blonde cutie. In short, she had him right where she wanted him—ready to do her bidding. Marilyn, on the other hand, kept her distance.

Josh rummaged through a dresser drawer for a pair of gym shorts and a T-shirt. He quickly removed the confining business suit and donned the casual clothing. Thankfully, his bedroom had been completely repaired from the tornado damage and everything was back to normal. The envelopes from Leopard had even stopped arriving. Josh considered that nothing short of an answer to prayer. Perhaps Clark McClure's harassment was short-lived.

With great anticipation, Josh gathered the worn blue bucket from beneath the kitchen sink and filled it with the appropriate bottles of cleaning paraphernalia. Because Blue usually made washing the truck impossible, he was left inside to sit, ears pricked, staring outside as his owner closed the storm door. Humorously, Josh recalled Brooke's concern that they would wash off all his truck's green paint. The child had certainly provided Josh with more than a few chuckles. He stepped off the front porch and surreptitiously eyed the house across the street. Marilyn's cobalt-blue Chevrolet was there. So was the sporty white Toyota that had arrived yesterday. But neither Marilyn nor her daughter were to be seen. Walking toward the trusty truck, Joshua inhaled the smell of hamburgers on an open grill. Fleetingly, he wondered if the odor was coming from Marilyn's backyard. None of his elderly neighbors ever grilled that he was aware of. His mouth watered. His stomach growled. And Joshua shamelessly listened for Brooke's elated call of "Joss! Joss!"

Thirty minutes later, he was finishing up his unnecessary job and still straining to hear the enraptured cries of a four-year-old. He was still lonely, sweaty, and alone.

As always, Josh reflected over the possibility that he might remain a bachelor for life. He had often wondered what would have happened if, after high school graduation, he had gone to a Christian college, as his father had dreamed. Joshua would have been surrounded by Christian young women, one of whom might very well have become his wife. At thirty-five, Joshua could have been married a decade. He could be the father of a charming little girl like Brooke, who would have filled his life with laughter. But why continue to pine over what might have been? Marriage and a family wasn't what had happened. He had chosen another path. A path that still brought him great shame. Although he was extremely fulfilled as a pastor, and the church was already showing steady signs of growth, he felt as if a part of life were passing him by. Brooke helped to alleviate some of those regrets, but not this evening.

Stepping back, he examined the glistening paint. With one last, longing look toward Marilyn's cottage, Josh turned off the water, collected his various cleaning supplies, and trudged toward his glass front door. As he opened the door, Blue lunged from his post just inside and, growling in fury, rushed across the front lawn. Joshua's left leg produced the typical ache as he attempted to maintain his balance while trying to grab Blue. Looking across the yard, he noticed a familiar tabby cat scurrying up one of the few oaks the tornado hadn't annihilated. Brooke's cat.

With a calculated smile, Joshua set his bucket inside the front door. In a matter of minutes, he had locked Blue back inside the house and coaxed the gentle cat down from the tree. This was the perfect excuse to investigate that scrumptious smell and perhaps have a brief visit with Brooke. If Josh were lucky, maybe Marilyn would invite him to stay for dinner.

I'm shameless, he thought. *But I'm also lonely...and hungry.*

❧

"Marilyn? It's me, Greg."

"Yes?" Marilyn answered as she cradled the cordless phone between her ear and her shoulder while grabbing the paper plates from the pantry. Greg was due to pick up Brooke in the morning and keep her until early next week. They were going on a father-daughter excursion, and Greg had even rented a cabin in the Ozarks. The little girl was beyond excited about spending so many days with her daddy.

A long pause left Marilyn more than uncomfortable. She stopped near the kitchen counter, not wanting to go outside while talking with her ex-husband.

"I don't know how to say this," Greg said at last.

"You aren't coming for Brooke," Marilyn blurted.

"How did you know?"

"It just figures."

"What are you implying?"

"It means that Brooke has been looking forward to this for weeks. You weren't able to keep her the month of July because of Sheila. I figure Sheila's throwing a fit about this, too."

The old resentment welled up in Marilyn. She darted a desperate prayer heavenward. This business of trying to keep a forgiving spirit was a full-time job. Her wounds were well on the way to healing, but these wounds against Brooke that continued to be inflicted were almost impossible to deal with. Marilyn was learning that forgiving something in the distant past was much easier than forgiving an ongoing situation. Gregory's ending their marriage now rested in history. But his allowing his younger, pregnant wife to dictate his time with Brooke was quickly becoming a habit.

"This is not easy for me," Gregory said evenly. "I looked forward to the trip as much as Brooke did."

"Poor baby," Marilyn snapped back, slamming the paper plates against the kitchen counter.

"Marilyn, if you would just listen to me. Sheila is in the hospital, and she might be having a miscarriage."

With a defeated sigh, Marilyn rubbed her temples and wondered why she was so ready to strangle Gregory at the slightest mishap. She was supposed to have begun the journey of forgiveness. It looked like she needed to get back on the path.

"I'm sorry," she said at last. "It's just that..." Marilyn swallowed against her tightening throat. She hadn't cried over this miserable situation all summer. Why was she starting now? Now, of all times, when she was on the phone with the man who had destroyed her life. Gritting her teeth, Marilyn blinked against the threatening tears and exerted more willpower than she had ever dreamed she possessed.

"Don't worry about a thing. I'll tell Brooke and—"

"Would it be okay if I came and got her tomorrow morning and spent the day with her there in Eureka Springs?" Greg asked, his voice dripping with guilt. "Then, as soon as Sheila gets out of the hospital we can plan another excursion."

"Yes, yes, that would be great," Marilyn said quickly as a wave of relief washed over her. At least Brooke would still get to see Greg. "Every morning since you set the date, Brooke has asked, 'Is it today, Mom?' I just hate to have to disappoint her, that's all. It rips my heart out." The final words escaped her lips like a whisper being swept along the river of agony.

Gregory's weighty silence left Marilyn all the more uneasy.

"Well!" she said with feigned cheerfulness. "I've got to go. Kim Lan is here. We're cooking burgers."

"Okay," he answered in a tight voice, and another painful encounter ended.

Marilyn schooled her features into a pleasant mask, grabbed the paper plates, and headed out the door. She didn't want her true emotions to ruin their cookout. Tonight she would try to explain to Brooke about Greg, or perhaps she would simply let Greg do the explaining. Hopefully, the fact that Kim had surprised them with a visit would take some of the edge off of Greg's canceling their mini-vacation.

She systematically began putting paper plates in the appropriate places on the picnic table. Glancing over her shoulder, she smiled as Kim made a grand endeavor of flipping the hamburger patties on the grill. The oriental femme fatale wore an oversized chef's hat that she had found in one of Marilyn's kitchen drawers. Marilyn vaguely remembered unpacking the thing and wondering if it had belonged to Greg. Brooke stood in a sturdy lawn chair beside Kim, watching her every move in rapt admiration. As far as Brooke was concerned, Kim Lan epitomize everything feminine. Her father had been an American soldier whose beautiful Vietnamese wife entered America as a refugee. Kim Lan possessed the exotic features of the orient and the willowy height of her American father. The combination dazzled Brooke. For weeks after one of Kim Lan's visits, the child usually wanted to color her hair black and let it grow to her waist "like Kim Lan's."

As Marilyn distributed the napkins and drinks beside the paper plates, she wondered what her life would have been like had she chosen to sign with the modeling agency. She looked at her daughter. No amount of money or fame could ever compare to having Brooke. Even though her marriage had failed, God had used it to give her an adorable little girl. Marilyn would never regret her choice not to pursue a modeling career.

The sound of a man discreetly clearing his throat startled Marilyn. She turned to face Joshua Langham, holding Tab.

"Hi," he said, wearing the grin that would undoubtedly stop traffic in downtown New York.

"Hi," Marilyn replied. Other than the necessary neighborly hellos and distant waves, they hadn't spoken in two months. Marilyn finally decided that her irrational attraction to Josh had been nothing short of an overreaction due to stress. After all, she had just moved and was trying to juggle new independence while unpacking and keeping up with Brooke. Add an engaging, single man to that picture, and Marilyn had simply been too stressed to rationally deal with it all. That explanation had seemed sensible two weeks ago, but not this evening with said engaging man standing only feet from her, holding her cat, and wearing those worn-out shorts and T-shirt. At once Marilyn's theory about her initial reaction to him vanished. Her pulse jumped just as it had when she cleaned the pink gelatin from his hair.

With traces of Greg's disturbing phone call still troubling her soul, the last thing Marilyn needed was to be attracted to another man. She wanted to vehemently tell Joshua Langham he could take himself *and* his winning smile and go back from whence he came.

"I brought your cat back," he said, glancing toward Kim Lan like a man who could not believe his eyes.

"Thanks," Marilyn replied blankly.

"Blue had chased him up a tree, and I thought I'd rescue him before he was in need of emotional therapy." His face lit up with humor.

"Oh, well, thanks," Marilyn repeated, wondering if she sounded as breathless to him as she did to herself. *This is beyond ridiculous,* she thought.

"Hi!" Kim Lan stepped from close behind Marilyn and extended her hand to Josh. "I'm Kim Lan Lowery."

Marilyn wanted to groan. Undoubtedly Kim had left her duties at the grill to curiously scrutinize her sister's guest.

"Nice to meet you. I'm Joshua Langham."

"Yes, Marilyn has told me about you," Kim said smoothly, her public graces ever intact.

"Oh?" Josh looked at Marilyn as a hint of pleasant surprise flirted with the corners of his mouth.

She lowered her gaze to his worn running shoes and toyed with the idea of ripping that crazy chef's hat off of Kim Lan's perfectly shining hair and stuffing it into her mouth.

"Joss!" Brooke squealed before rushing into her friend's arms.

Marilyn had allowed the friendship to blossom over the summer, not certain what complications might ensue. Brooke needed the input of a man in her life—more than the one weekend out of the month Gregory had her. True, Marilyn's dad had taken seriously his role as Brooke's father figure, but his arthritis limited his physical activities. Josh, on the other hand, could play catch, and chase, and hide-and-seek until Brooke was all played out. Marilyn had watched them during the last few weeks, evening after evening, as they played in Josh's front yard. At first she was afraid Brooke was a nuisance to Josh. Now, she wasn't certain who enjoyed the activity more, Josh or Brooke. Of one thing she was sure: Whenever Joshua Langham *did* get around to marriage, he would be an exceptional father. That was one of the downfalls of this relationship with Brooke. If and when Josh did marry, Marilyn wondered if his new wife would smile on his friendship with Brooke. Of late, Greg's wife certainly didn't seem enamored with Brooke, and she was the child's stepmother.

Kim Lan turned toward Marilyn and raised her flawlessly arched eyebrows as if she were conspiring all sorts of matrimonial designs in that busy mind of hers.

"It's not what it looks like," Marilyn said through gritted teeth. She grabbed a paper plate, walked to the grill, and began scooping the hamburger patties onto the plate. Desperately, she tried to focus on the task at hand and tune out the animated conversation, but all she could hear was Kim politely asking Josh to stay for burgers.

Oh, great! Marilyn thought. *She invites him over to my house, and I get to have a nervous breakdown!*

By this point, Marilyn's hands, knees, and lips were trembling. All she could see in her mind's eye was that moment when she tried to remove the pink stuff from Joshua's hair. The man might as well have kissed her. She must have been momentarily comatose to have even remotely believed that her initial reaction to him had been a stress-related response. As Kim Lan's charming laugh floated along the warm evening breeze and mingled with the call of a distant whippoorwill, her question from two months ago began a tormenting chant in Marilyn's mind: *Have you prayed about dating him?*

Marilyn plopped the fragrant burgers on the picnic table and rushed into the house. The cool air enveloped her and chilled the perspiration that had beaded along her forehead and neck. Taking a cleansing breath, Marilyn gripped the edge of the sink and determined to control herself. She splashed her face with cool water, blotted her cheeks with a towel, retrieved a cola from the refrigerator, popped the tab, and greedily drank it.

"Are you okay?" Josh asked from close behind her.

Marilyn jumped reflexively, sloshing the cola all over her white walking shorts. "You scared me," she said, placing a hand on her chest.

"I'm sorry. I thought you heard me come in."

"I was thinking. I didn't hear you." Marilyn busied herself with cleaning up her mess. Anything to keep from looking into Josh's eyes.

"Kim Lan asked me to stay for burgers, but I didn't want to agree until I made sure it was okay with you," he said softly.

"Of course it's okay," Marilyn heard herself saying. But what else could she say. Anything else would be rude.

"When you told me you were good friends with Kim Lan Lowery, I never suspected I'd meet her in your backyard."

"Well, she's spending a long weekend with me and Brooke."

"Oh," Josh said, clearly impressed.

"She's a great cook, and I can use all the help I can get," Marilyn said practically.

"Hey, I'm a decent cook myself. Why didn't you tell me you needed a helping hand?"

Marilyn blinked, wondering if the man had completely forgotten their former encounters and their declarations to maintain a distant friendship. She glanced toward his left leg and grasped at any opportunity to change the subject. "Glad to see your cast is off. How does your leg feel?"

"Almost as good as new," he said lightly. "It still gives me some pain now and then, but that's expected. Is there something I can help you take outside?"

"Sure," Marilyn said, keeping her gaze firmly downcast. She turned to the refrigerator and began removing the appropriate hamburger trimmings.

"So how's everything with Gregory?" Joshua asked, his discreet voice implying nothing but genuine concern.

Marilyn stilled, gritted her teeth, and forced herself not to cry. "Fine, I guess. The same." If she were absolutely honest about her present feelings, she would have to admit that she dreaded Brooke's reaction to the canceled vacation. But none of that was Joshua Langham's concern. She felt him moving closer and wanted to scream as the ever-increasing knot in her midsection tightened all the more. She retrieved a tray laden with lettuce, tomatoes, onions, and pickles and placed them in Joshua's waiting hands.

"Have you received any more of those strange envelopes?" Marilyn asked, wondering how that question had sprang from her lips.

Joshua's hesitation prompted her into doing what she had purposed not to do. She glanced up into the velvety softness of his gentle eyes—eyes that were troubled.

"I continued to get the envelopes until about two weeks ago, then they suddenly stopped. I'm hoping it's over now. When the FBI used me as the key witness in Leopard's sentencing, they suggested I enter their witness protection program, but I declined. At the time, I didn't figure Clark would retaliate. I guess part of it was the familiarity factor. I had known him for so long. Anyway, up until a few months ago, I thought I had made the right decision. Now..."

"Exactly how did the FBI fit into all this?" Marilyn asked, her curiosity taking control.

He produced a wary smile. "I guess I just spilled part of the beans from my mysterious past, huh?"

"Yeah, I guess," Marilyn whispered. The two of them might as well have been sweethearts, muttering sweet nothings. Their conversation had gradually decreased in volume until the words seemed to caress the very air.

"So, am I a man of mystery to you?"

Marilyn's eyes widened. "What's that supposed to mean?"

"Just wondering if this panther on my shoulder and all that it implies somehow fascinates you."

"It wouldn't matter if it did," Marilyn snapped, irritated at herself for being so transparent with her thoughts, so easily snared into the web of his intrigue.

"Maybe not to you..."

"And what's *that* supposed to mean?" she queried.

She stiffly turned to grab the mustard, mayonnaise, and ketchup from the refrigerator then shut the door with a decided click.

"Never mind."

She narrowed her eyes, wondering if the man were trying to flirt with her. Had she or had she not been convincing in her declaration that she wasn't interested in another relationship? At one point, he had even warned her to stay away from him because of the dangers those envelopes implied. She supposed that since those envelopes had stopped, he was now more than willing to develop a closer friendship.

"I have this feeling that your intentions in bringing Tab back weren't exactly pure," Marilyn blurted as they simultaneously turned toward the back door.

Pausing, he slowly swiveled to face her, humor lighting his kind eyes. Gradually, he produced the grin that always crumbled every vestige of Marilyn's emotional barrier.

"Stop smiling like that," she snapped.

"Why?"

"Just because—"

"Because you like it more than you want to admit?"

Her mouth fell open in astonishment. Her mind whirled in irritation. Her face warmed. "How dare you! That's the most arrogant—"

"No, it's the truth!"

Marilyn gasped once more, wondering what his congregation would think of him at this moment.

"And since we're baring all here, I might as well confess that no, my intentions weren't pure when I brought your cat back. I smelled what you were cooking, and I was ravenous. I grabbed the first opportunity I could find to come and have a free meal! That just happened to be your cat up my tree."

"You're shameless!" Marilyn accused, ready to tell him to go back home.

"Yes..." He glanced at the tray of lettuce. "And lonely." Josh looked up at her, a candid, searching, longing question playing upon his features. A question so silent, so forceful that words would have lessened its potency.

A rush of warmth started at Marilyn's feet and surged to the roots of her hair, leaving her feeling as if she would melt. Just as the day she tried to remove the gelatin from his hair, she was once again in the grip of a force that wrapped its pleasurable arms around her to coax her closer to Joshua.

Lonely? He said he is lonely? I comprehend lonely. I've walked hand in hand with lonely. I know how it feels to have your soul ripped from your body and excommunicated to a cold, desolate land. And I survived. So can you. She didn't need the complications of another man...another minister in her life. She would rather take her chances with Mr. Lonely.

But have you prayed about this potential relationship? What's God's will in this? The disturbing thoughts echoed through her mind.

The back door swung open. "Hey, you two. We're ready to eat! I haven't had a hamburger in a year," Kim Lan called, stepping into the kitchen with Brooke on her hip. "Oops!" Her lips remained puckered, her expressive, almond-shaped eyes rounded. Her embarrassed expression said she clearly understood the intensity of the moment. She glanced from Marilyn to Josh and back to Marilyn. "Uh, we'll just wait outside."

"No, that's quite all right," Marilyn said, rushing past them and into the heat of the waiting evening.

Ten

"Whew! You and Mr. Wonderful have exhausted me." Kim collapsed next to Marilyn on the overstuffed, striped couch and propped her feet on the coffee table, next to Marilyn's.

"Why do you say that?" Marilyn asked through a stifled yawn. Brooke had gone to sleep the minute she hit the bed, and Marilyn would do the same. She hadn't had the chance to tell her daughter about Gregory's change in plans, so she decided to let Greg tell her. She was tired, really tired, of being responsible for his messes.

"I mean, there's enough electrical tension between you and Joshua to light up all of New York."

Marilyn looked at her friend's sandaled feet, whose toenails were meticulously painted the same shade of bronze as her fingernails. Wondering what it must be like to actually have the time to get a manicure *and* a pedicure, Marilyn darted a sideways glance at Kim. She thought about making light of her friend's remark but decided it was no use. They had been friends so long that any diversionary tactic would be wasted effort.

"I'm beginning to wish I had moved anywhere but on this street," Marilyn said wearily, covering her eyes.

"Brooke certainly loves him."

"So, since Brooke loves him, I'm supposed to just waltz down the aisle and live happily ever after?" Marilyn expressively waved her hand for added emphasis.

"Well, no," Kim said slowly, "but you might at least give the guy a chance, Marilyn. If you looked at me the way you looked at him, I'd probably never come back."

"That was the whole idea. I don't want him thinking he can just come over here any time he gets ready to romance me. I mean, good grief, it's already cozy enough with Brooke going over there two or three evenings a week."

"What are you afraid of?" Kim Lan asked turning toward Marilyn and scrutinizing her with that look she'd developed after one class of Psychology 101.

"Stop it!" Marilyn demanded, grabbing a blue-striped pillow and whacking her friend over the head.

"Stop what?"

"Stop looking at me like that! You're not here to psycho-analyze me. Just lay off! I won't deny that Joshua Langham is…is…is probably just the kind of man I'd…I'd…I could fall in love with," Marilyn grudgingly admitted.

"So the facts are out!"

"And I won't even deny that he does, sometimes, affect my pulse."

"As in every time you see him?"

Marilyn purposed to ignore Kim's pointed remarks. "But that doesn't mean I'm going to develop a relationship with him. Like I've already told you and him, you couldn't—"

"Pay me to get involved with another man," Kim Lan finished in sisterly satire. "And she's even prayed about this one!"

"Oh, give me a break, will you?"

"Okay, okay!" Kim Lan raised her hands in resignation. "You're a tough case, Marilyn Douglas, that's all I've got to say."

"You're a fine one to point fingers. Like you prayed about whether or not to snatch that opportunity to be a model."

Marilyn, feeling as if she probably shouldn't have opened that subject, nonetheless rolled her eyes in a reflection of Kim Lan's own mockery.

The supermodel grabbed the TV's remote control and clicked on the evening news.

"Ohhhh, now we're stooping to our own attempts at diverting the conversation."

The oriental beauty clicked off the television and abruptly turned to face Marilyn. "Have you ever truly sought God, Marilyn?"

She blinked in surprise. Marilyn had expected any question but this one from Kim Lan. She had been too ensconced in her own spiritual struggles to consider Kim Lan's experience with God. But here she sat, challenging Marilyn with a question she didn't want to answer.

"Well," she said lamely, "there was a time when—"

"How long has it been since you felt—really felt—as if you were intimate with God?—When He was as real to you as he was to the people in the Bible?"

"Ummm…"

Kim Lan crossed her arms, relaxed against the sofa, and stared at the blank television screen. "I've been doing a lot of thinking and reading lately. It seems that God has been drawing me closer to Him, but I'm not certain what to do about it."

"Do you still go to church?"

"Yes. I've been going to church with Ted, but it seems so—"

"Ted?"

"Ted Curry."

"Ted Curry?" Marilyn stared bug-eyed at her friend. "*The* Ted Curry, the heartthrob of America?"

"Oh...didn't I tell you we started seeing each other about a month ago?"

"No, you didn't, Honey!" Marilyn wondered why, given the circles in which Kim Lan ran, she was so surprised by this bit of news. Sometimes, it was hard to see her familiar friend as the supermodel she was.

"Well, we are," Kim Lan said practically, as if the whole relationship were with someone of no consequence. "And what about you?"

"What?" Marilyn squinted her eyes in confusion. Kim Lan had the annoying habit of throwing hairpin curves into most any conversation.

"What about you? Are you attending church?"

Marilyn swallowed. "Well...I've been going on some Sunday mornings...occasionally, to a large church not far from here. And I've been letting Brooke go with Mom and Dad to Joshua's church."

"That's nice."

"Nice? It's actually borderline miraculous. Four months ago, I wouldn't have even darkened the door of a church."

"So, you do feel like God is helping you with some healing?"

"Yes. I'm trying to do all I can to follow through on forgiving Greg, and I'm praying about trying to forgive him for abandoning Brooke. But there are still some mornings I wake up and there's this horrible flash of despising him. Then I remind myself that I'm not in that place anymore, and I pray for God's strength."

"There have been some swimsuit issues I've posed for that I'm beginning to wish I had never done."

Perplexed, Marilyn looked at her friend and realized this was yet another of Kim Lan's hairpin conversational curves. "Oh?"

"Yes." The lithe model stood and, straightening her silk pajamas, restlessly walked toward the front window where she peaked past the closed drapes to look at the front lawn.

"So, are you thinking of getting out of modeling or..." Marilyn groped for some lead on Kim Lan's thoughts.

"No," she said quickly, almost too quickly. "Oh, I don't even know why I brought all that up." With a teasing smile, she turned back to Marilyn. "I think Joshua is looking over here from his front window."

"Oh?" Marilyn did her best to sound disinterested.

"Yep. It looks like he's eating something out of a bowl and just standing there, watching. Want to peak?"

"No I don't," Marilyn said pointedly. She abruptly stood and stretched her tired muscles. "I think it's time to go to bed."

The phone rang, and Kim sprang toward it. "That's Sonsee."

"How do you know?"

"She called for you when Josh was here. It rang when I came in, so I answered it and told her to call back."

"Thanks for taking my messages," Marilyn said playfully.

"Hello," Kim Lan quipped into the receiver. "Hi! I thought it was you." Kim's eyes widened in pleasant surprise. "Oh, hi!" She covered the mouthpiece. "It's the whole gang," she said eagerly. "Do you have another phone?"

"In my bedroom."

"Go get it."

Smiling, Marilyn walked toward her room, anxious to hear from all her sisters. "The gang," as Kim Lan called them, hadn't had a conference call since the night after Marilyn had moved. Even though she had spoken with each of them individually during the last few weeks, she always enjoyed these phone calls when they all got together. After these group calls, she looked forward all the more to their biannual reunions.

She picked up the receiver of the traditional Victorian telephone that sat on her nightstand.

"Hey, guys," she called into the mouthpiece.

A chorus of hellos followed. Then Sonsee, Melissa, Sammie, Victoria, and Jac all jumped into the conversation at once with a round of questions.

"So, tell us more....He was over for hamburgers? When's the wedding? Kim says you two have it bad!"

Marilyn produced a stifled growl. "I'm going to kill you, Kim Lan!" she said through gritted teeth. "What did you tell Sonsee when she called, anyway?"

"Honey, I didn't tell her anything that wasn't the absolute truth," she said with a feigned, southern drawl.

"Please don't kill her," Sonsee said practically. "I don't have time for a funeral right now. My schedule is full. It takes *time* to save the lives of animals!"

Kim, Melissa, Sammie, Victoria, and Jac all responded with a chorus of laughter.

"Yes, have some respect for our schedules, would you?" Melissa parried. "I'm still in the middle of building my new medical office here!"

Marilyn rolled her eyes and settled onto the side of her bed. "I've told every one of you more than once—and I mean it, I'm not interested in another relationship!"

"You're starting to sound like a broken record," Sonsee teased.

"And I can tell you why," Kim Lan said playfully. "I've seen him with my own eyes!"

"Would you guys stop it?" Marilyn demanded in a mockingly huffy tone. "Whose side are you on anyway?"

"His, darlin'," Sammie said with her Texas drawl. "We want to see you happily married."

"Yeah, and miserable," Marilyn said in the voice of Scrooge himself.

The pregnant silence that ensued left Marilyn a bit uncomfortable. Of the seven of them, only Sammie and Victoria were married. For some reason, Marilyn found herself wondering if all were well in their paradises.

As Kim Lan was so apt to do, she booted the sisterly banter into a different direction and the conversational ball swiftly rolled along. Marilyn, sitting but a few feet from a front window, began to contemplate Kim Lan's claim that Joshua was standing at his window watching. At once she felt the urge to peak past the closed curtains to see him herself, but a sense of self-restraint suggested that would be nothing short of foolishness.

Why should I care if Josh is at his window? she told herself firmly.

Nonetheless, she silently stood, clicked off the lamp, adjusted the phone cord, and stepped toward her window. Despite her better judgment, Marilyn inched open the side of the curtains, peered across the street, and allowed her eyes to adjust to the evening shadows. Just as Kim Lan had said, Josh's dark silhouette graced the living room window. He appeared to be eating from a bowl. Marilyn figured it was ice cream. He seemed to have a propensity toward the stuff, given the mounds he consumed after the hamburgers.

As the sisters continued their amiable chatter, Marilyn wondered what the man was doing. Surely he wasn't watching her house. That would border on weird and obsessive. She reflected on the possibilities and shoved them from her mind. Joshua Langham was not weird and obsessive. He was too average to be weird, and too laid back to be obsessive. Marilyn glanced up the street to see the dark figure of what looked like an old man hobbling down the street, cane in hand. He stooped to scratch the ears of a large dog that looked like Blue. Marilyn wasn't certain, but she thought perhaps he even gave the animal a treat.

Within a minute, Joshua walked from the window and she noticed his front door opening. Then a faint whistle. Blue bounded away from the man on the street and rushed toward Joshua's front door. So that was it. Josh had been allowing Blue his final trip outdoors for the night. But who was the old man on the street? Marilyn glanced back to where he had been, and he appeared to have vanished. But he could very easily have faded into the shadows or gone into his own home. The neighborhood was full of retirees. Perhaps old Mr. Taylor three houses down was just out for a night stroll, which would be entirely strange.

With a nonchalant shrug, Marilyn turned from the window and once more focused her attention on the phone conversation. But what had been a chorus of chatter that had played in the background of her mind was silent. She had the strong feeling that someone had asked her a question she had missed. Then she noticed Kim Lan tiptoeing into her bedroom.

"What are you doing?" Marilyn hissed.

The remaining sisters howled with glee.

"We were talking and talking and talking and noticed you got quiet," Sonsee said.

"Yeah. So we asked you if the cat had gotten your tongue," Melissa said.

"And you didn't say a word," Jac and Sammie chimed in.

"So Kim said she'd just go see what you were up to," Victoria said. "When you still didn't respond, I told them you must be checking out Joshua, who was standing at his window watching you."

"He wasn't watching me!" Marilyn snapped, clicking on the lamp. "He was waiting on his dog to finish with his little trip outside." She pretended she was going to strangle Kim Lan.

"Help! Now she's trying to strangle me!"

"You guys are too much," Marilyn said through a fond chuckle. "Good grief, you'd think the bunch of you were sixteen instead of thirty-something."

"Hey! Stop it with that thirty-something, business," Kim Lan said in shock.

"Yeah! Everybody in America believes Kim is only twenty-four!" Sonsee defended.

"And holding," Kim Lan proclaimed.

The sisterly banter continued, and, as usual, Marilyn was uplifted by her friends' companionship. But despite the teasing, she figured they were praying for her. That perhaps their prayers, accompanied by the prayers of her parents, had been what had given her the strength to decide to forgive Gregory. Especially the prayers of Sonsee.

Dear Sonsee, ever the prayer warrior. What would I do without you? Or without any of my sisters, for that matter? she mused.

Like a decrepit old man, Clark McClure hobbled along the street in front of Panther's house. He didn't dare break out of his elderly gentleman gait, even with the darkness as his cover. No telling who might be watching, and Clark didn't want to leave a trace of his visit. When Panther had let the Saint Bernard outside to relieve himself, Leopard had called the friendly animal to him and extended the remains of some cheese crackers left in his pocket from a late evening snack. The dog had gleefully munched the crackers and begged for more. With a satisfied chuckle, Leopard planned to firm up the friendship with the dog. Once that little task was accomplished, the animal would gladly gobble down the deadly treat Clark planned to give him.

He paused in the shadows to examine Panther's small house. Absently, Clark reached through the hole in his right pocket and stroked the switchblade strapped to his thigh. Leopard had tarried fifteen years for this revenge. He would savor its every stage. Whether he actually killed Panther this week or not, this trip would be precious—a week of holding the ability to end Panther's life with the shift of his whim and the blade of a knife. Like a wildcat toying with a pathetically injured mouse, Leopard would extend his claws and mercilessly bat Josh about until he was frantic with panic. He gave a satisfied grunt that rumbled deeply in his throat as the taste of retaliation left him heady with power.

Eleven

~

The next morning, the doorbell rang before Marilyn, Brooke, and Kim Lan had finished breakfast.

"Saved by the bell," Kim said, laying the half-eaten croissant back onto her plate. "I have eaten more since I got here than I usually eat in a week. I have got to stop. My trainer is going to kill me."

With a chortle, Marilyn moved toward the front door and caught a glimpse of a red Cadillac in the driveway. "It's your Daddy, Brooke!" she called over her shoulder. Despite the bitter disappointments Gregory had dealt her, Marilyn had never once criticized him to her daughter. Something within her soul insisted that would only make the situation harder on Brooke. Instead, Marilyn had tried to make each of his visits seem like something special.

"Daddy! Daddy!" Brooke squealed, rushing past Marilyn as she opened the door. "Daddy! Is today the day we go on our vacation?"

"I haven't told her," Marilyn mouthed. "You can." She produced the most challenging look she could muster and dared Greg to back out of this one.

With the resigned wilt of exhaustion, Gregory dropped to his knees, gathered Brooke into his arms, and began the difficult task. Marilyn walked to the kitchen to prepare Brooke a bag of snacks and some baby wipes for "just in case" spills.

By the time Marilyn arrived back to the front door, Gregory was winding up his thorough explanation.

"That's okay, Daddy," Brooke said, wisely nodding her head. "I was worried about Joss anyway."

"Joss?" Gregory looked up at Marilyn.

"He's a friend in the neighborhood," she said swiftly.

"Yes," Brooke said. "I was afraid he would cry if I was gone so long."

"Well," Gregory said, fondly tousling her hair, "that just works out great for everyone then, doesn't it? I wouldn't want to make your little friend cry."

"Joss isn't little," Brooke said sagely.

"Oh?"

Marilyn gritted her teeth.

"No," Kim said from close behind. "He lives across the street and is all grown up. He had hamburgers with us last night," she continued while nibbling the very croissant she had rejected minutes before.

"Hello, Kim Lan," Gregory said evenly. The dislike evident in his words blatantly plastered itself across his face.

"Hello," Kim replied with a plastic smile. She had made the mistake of telling Gregory exactly what she thought of him for leaving his family. Since then neither had any spare love for the other.

If Marilyn had ever been blessed with a biological sister, she would have never lived the part more accurately than Kim Lan. Not only was the lanky model loyal through all, but she was too frank for words at times. Once more, Marilyn wanted to stifle Kim Lan's words. She was not interested in a relationship with Joshua Langham, and she didn't want Kim implying that she was—not even to Gregory. Not that Marilyn cared one flip about what Gregory thought at this stage, but the fewer people who were making romantic assumptions, the better she liked it.

"Joshua is all grown up? I see," Gregory said smoothly, glancing at Marilyn as if he understood all too well.

"There's Joss now!" Brooke said, bolting out the door toward the road.

"Brooke! Brooke!" Marilyn called hurrying past Greg and toward her daughter. "Brooke Lan Thatcher! You stop right now, and don't you go across that road unless—"

Joshua stepped from his yard, trotted across the street, and walked onto Marilyn's lawn.

"Hey, Ladybug," he said fondly, scooping the smiling child into his arms.

"Joss!" Brooke said, her face beaming. "Guess what?"

"What?" He tickled her tummy.

Through a gleeful giggle, Brooke said, "You don't have to cry now. I'm coming back tonight!"

"What?" Josh directed an inquiring gaze toward Marilyn, but his attention was swiftly snared by Gregory who neared the trio.

Quickly, Marilyn drew a hard and fast analogy between the man holding Brooke and the man who had once been her husband. The stark reality of Gregory's haughty, materialistic demeanor compared to Josh's humble, down-to-earth manner left Marilyn reeling in astonishment. Greg had always seemed the aloof, privileged sort. That was part of what had attracted her to him in the first place. But with Greg standing beside Josh, who wore the usual gym shorts and T-shirt, her ex-husband seemed like a piece of marred quartz crystal next to a brilliant diamond. Greg was by far more handsome in the traditional sense, by far more meticulously dressed, but Joshua Langham's glowing character boldly outshone her former mate.

Was this the man I lay awake and sobbed over for almost a solid year? Marilyn lambasted herself for ever being attracted to him in the first place. *I should have seen from the start that the man was shallow and selfish. If I'd only married someone like Joshua—*

She stopped those thoughts in midstream.

I shouldn't be having such thoughts. I couldn't care less about Joshua Langham and whether or not his character glows or wanes. He is in no way going to be a part of my life.

Haltingly, she introduced the two men who suspiciously eyed each other.

"Well, I guess we need to be going," Greg said with even civility as he reached for his daughter. "We'll be back tonight as planned, Marilyn."

"Yes, that's fine," Marilyn said, relieved that the awkward moment was dissolving. She handed Greg the small canvas bag that held Brooke's supplies

As he took it, Greg peered into her eyes as if he were partly surprised and partly...jealous. Marilyn wanted to burst into riotous laughter. Was the man who discarded her actually jealous that another man might be interested in her? Dumfounded, she watched as Greg loaded Brooke into the luxury automobile and sped away.

"I don't think he liked me," Joshua said simply.

Blinking, Marilyn turned her attention toward him. She had been so flabbergasted by the implications of Greg's absurd reaction that she had completely forgotten about Josh. A chuckle burst from her lips, and a few more followed.

"I don't think he did, either."

"Well, I'm glad you're getting a laugh out of it," Josh said, his eyes dancing merrily.

Marilyn's chortles subsided as a companionable silence settled between them.

"I enjoyed last night." The expectant tilt of his lips seemed to suggest he awaited her response like a beau starved for any encouragement from his belle of choice.

"Thanks." Marilyn suddenly felt more than guilty for the cold treatment she had dealt him once they had actually started eating. She wanted to apologize; she really did. But wouldn't apologizing only hint that Josh might have a place in her life? Nervously, she toyed with the button on the silky indigo shirt Kim Lan had given her.

"I'm sorry if I came across as pushy last night," he said at last. "I didn't mean to barge in and then..." He hesitated, then didn't continue.

Marilyn prayed that the earth would simply open and swallow her. Falling to the center of the earth would be much easier than dealing with the contrite honesty in Joshua Langham's eyes. *Why, God, why?* she wailed within. *Why did You allow me to move across the street from this man? I am not interested in another relationship!*

But that same haunting thought that had tormented her after her first meeting with Joshua began a disturbing chant within: *It's the calling. It's the calling. It's the calling...to be a pastor's wife.*

"Oh...that's—that's okay about last night. I'm s-sorry too," Marilyn stuttered, backing away from Joshua as if he were a poisonous viper. "I—I—uh—I guess I need to get back to my c-company now." She turned and hastened toward the porch, all the while feeling his gaze upon her. Without a backward glance, Marilyn stumbled up the stairs, rushed into the house, slammed the door, and collapsed against it.

A mischievous smile covering her face, Kim Lan turned from her post by the front door, where she had obviously been spying. "Oooo, Honey," she said in a feigned southern accent, "y'all got it bad for each other!"

"Oh, go eat the rest of the croissants," Marilyn snapped.

Sunday morning, Joshua preached as he had never preached in his whole life. His sermon was on seeking God with your whole being, and it was more for him than for anyone. Just before the closing prayer, he paused and looked over the congregation of folks who had become dear to him in the past few months. He felt such a kindred spirit with each of them, such an awesome awareness that they loved him and were willing to overlook any blunders of their new pastor.

Already the congregation of roughly seventy was growing under Joshua's ministry. Even a few hard cases in the community, people everyone else had given up on, had accepted Christ as their Savior due to Joshua's unconditional love and soft words. Joshua spotted an old man, wearing shaded glasses, sitting on the back pew and wondered if this was yet another person who had been around town his whole life but was just now entering the house of God. As the elderly gentleman stroked his scraggly gray beard, Joshua made a mental note to make sure he got the man's address and phone number.

Joshua asked the congregation to stand and called on Marilyn's father to lead in closing prayer. But Joshua's mind wasn't on the prayer. His thoughts rested on his own struggles with the demons of his past. Despite all his efforts within the church, despite all the congregation's work, despite all the blessings of God, Joshua still felt inadequate and burdened with his wrong choices.

And for some reason, meeting Marilyn had only heightened his sense of loss. He desperately wanted a wife and family. If he had stayed on the straight and narrow, he might well be going home to a house cluttered with the wonderful evidence of children. A house that smelled of pot roast. A house where he playfully grumbled because his closet was stuffed with dresses. Instead, he would enter an empty, spotless house where a bologna sandwich awaited him. As Mr. Douglas' prayer came to a close, Josh gripped the pulpit and begged God to somehow deliver him from all these tormenting emotions.

The sounds of shuffling papers and an adjourning congregation alerted Joshua to the fact that the prayer had ended. He should have been standing at the back door by now, greeting church members. Leaving his Bible and notes on the pulpit, he rushed toward his usual post, but a small familiar hand found his. "Joss! Joss! Look! I brought my new baby today! And guess what..."

Smiling in delight, Joshua scooped Brooke into his welcoming arms.

"What?" he asked, momentarily postponing his trip to the back.

"Guess what I named him?"

"Umm..." Joshua closed his eyes and pretended to concentrate. "Rumpelstiltskin," he said playfully.

"No, you silly! I named him Joss!" Brooke said, her brown eyes glowing with something close to hero worship.

A father's love stirred within Joshua. And if Marilyn agreed, he would have married her at that moment, not because he was in love with her, but because he was in love with Brooke. The child desperately needed an at-home daddy. And Josh...well Josh desperately needed a family. But he shouldn't marry Marilyn for any other reasons than his love for her—and he wasn't in love with her. Attracted, yes, but the love part had yet to take root. That took time, and time was not something Marilyn was willing to give him.

Yesterday when she had virtually run from him, Joshua had initially laughed. After all, he clearly understood the fire of attraction he saw in her eyes. If that attraction was strong enough to make her run, he had mused, perhaps he just needed to change the direction of her running. But after his first reaction, Marilyn's running had cloaked Joshua with a spirit of hopelessness. If she were that intent on escaping him, the whole situation might indeed be impossible.

Gently he kissed Brooke's cheek and walked to the back of the sanctuary. Even though he had missed shaking the hands of several regulars, he was able to intersect the old gentleman before he exited.

"Hello," Joshua said as he extended his hand. "I'm Pastor Joshua Langham. Glad to have you today."

"Hello, sonny. Enjoyed your sermon." The old man, who smelled of a dumpster, extended grubby fingers that protruded from tattered, open-fingered gloves.

"Thanks. It's great to have you here." Joshua wondered why the old man would be wearing gloves, given the Arkansas summer heat, but he soon dismissed the thought. Just like everyone, the old man needed unconditional love, no questions asked. Joshua would extend that love and hopefully win him to the Lord.

"Great to be here. Name's Magruder, John Magruder." The old gentleman leaned heavily on his ancient gnarled cane and lightly touched Brooke's arm. "You've got a mighty cute daughter there."

"Oh, he's not my daddy," Brooke said in her usual, open manner. "He's just my neighbor. And…and my best friend." She emphasized her claim by hugging Joshua's neck.

Josh beamed despite himself.

"Brooke! There you are!" Natalie Douglas, a graying, blue-eyed version of Marilyn, rushed forward. "I'm so sorry," she apologized, retrieving Brooke from Joshua's arms.

"Oh, it's quite all right," Joshua said with an assuring smile. "She wasn't in any way bothering me."

"I'd say." Fred Douglas, tall and lean, stood just behind his wife. His keen, brown eyes evaluated the situation in a way that left Joshua a bit uncomfortable.

"This is my grandpa," Brooke said to the elderly gentleman who took in the whole scene. "He peels oranges *the best.*"

"Does he?" The old man tousled Brooke's hair.

"Do you have plans for lunch, Mr. Magruder?" Joshua asked as Natalie and Jacob swept Brooke away with them.

"No, can't say that I do."

"I would love for you to join me. I was planning a fine, home-cooked meal at the local cafe."

"Sounds too good to pass up," Magruder said.

Joshua shook a few more hands, extended a few more greetings, accepted a few more compliments for his "outstanding sermon." He turned back to the old man.

"Do you want to follow me in your car or..."

"Don't own a car myself. I could use a lift, if that's okay with you."

"Great. I should be out shortly. I drive the green Ford truck parked on the east side of the parking lot. You can't miss it."

Leopard shuffled out the door and graciously accepted the kind remarks from the various church members. The whole setup made him sick. These church members were so obviously in love with their pastor that they were blissfully blind to any faults he might have. Well, that little misconception will be corrected.

Clark was raised in a small church, so he understood the power of one or two disgruntled members. He would make sure that more than one or two members were disillusioned with their "perfect" pastor. That is, if he was able to stop himself from exacting his ultimate revenge before he could ruin Panther's reputation. Through the hole cut in his pocket, Clark again fingered the switchblade. Only time would tell what his final decision would be. Presently he needed to continue his act and make sure no one suspected he was a muscular, virile male with a gnawing need for vengeance.

Sweating beneath the Arkansas sun, Clark sidled up to the forest-green pickup and waited. The ninety-two degree heat seemed incidental compared to the red-hot rage boiling from the pit of his soul. He had been waiting fifteen years for this moment. A few minutes in the broiling sun wouldn't matter in the least.

Twelve

Settling on one of the twin beds in Brooke's room, Marilyn sipped a cup of raspberry mocha coffee and watched as Kim Lan laid the final toiletry items into her soft leather suitcase. The supermodel wore the disguise for travel that Marilyn had come to expect. After early church, Kim Lan washed off all makeup and twisted her waist-length hair into a matronly bun. She changed into worn-out jeans and a tattered, tie-dyed T-shirt. Add to that the floppy denim hat and dark glasses she would don before leaving, and Kim Lan was seldom recognized when out in public.

The friends had attended the early service so Kim could pack and leave in time to catch her early afternoon flight back to New York. As usual, Brooke had attended church with her grandparents. Today they were going to a family reunion picnic immediately after church, which Marilyn had opted out of. The last family reunion she attended had been with Greg, and she did not want to answer the prying questions of her great aunts, in-law uncles, and fourth cousins twice removed. But Marilyn's mother, the proud grandparent that she was, wanted to show off her adorable granddaughter, and Marilyn had acquiesced.

"Well," Kim Lan said crisply, "I guess that's that!" She zipped the suitcase, plopped it onto the floor, and extended the handle in order to roll it behind her.

"So, have you decided what you're going to do about the shoot your agent called about yesterday?" Marilyn asked, savoring the aroma of the gourmet coffee Kim Lan had brought.

The tall model examined her perfectly manicured nails as if she were thinking of chewing them all off. "I guess I'm still praying about that one. It's still a month off, and I've got a week to give my answer," she said nervously. "We're talkin' buckets full of money on this one."

"Yeah, but..." Marilyn stopped herself. Who was she to be the moral thermometer for anyone? Marilyn had hated her ex-husband for longer than she wanted to admit, and the Bible specifically stated that was on par with murder. Even though Marilyn had repented and begun the forgiveness journey, she still felt inadequate to guide anyone.

"But what?" Kim Lan asked.

"Well, I was just thinking about what you said Friday night—that there were some swimsuit issues you had posed for you were starting to wish you hadn't done."

"Yes, I remember," Kim Lan said wearily. "But..." With a sigh, she shrugged and nervously toyed with her keys. "I guess when put face to face with a deal of this magnitude, it's kind of hard to turn down."

"But if it's something God doesn't approve of—"

"Oh, get real," Kim Lan snapped, gripping the brim of the floppy denim hat all the tighter. "Are you going to tell me you swim in your long johns?"

"Somehow wearing a modest, one-piece swimsuit for a family swim session seems a little different than this deal," Marilyn said, wishing the whole time she could stop her mouth from its determined blathering. How had she gotten herself into this one?

"So you don't think I should do it. Is that it?" Kim Lan challenged, her cheeks slightly flushed.

"I think that's pretty obvious. But," Marilyn took a cleansing breath, "you've got to decide. It's between you and God. I can't be the one to say."

Kim Lan once more eyed her fingernails.

"I'm sorry I started preaching," Marilyn said, producing an apologetic grin. "I guess I'm falling into my pastor's wife mode without even realizing it."

"It's okay." Sighing, Kim Lan sat down beside Marilyn, her shoulders hunched. The epitome of what many women dream of being but would never accomplish, Kim Lan was young, gorgeous, slender, wealthy, and admired across America. But during this visit, her dark, almond-shaped eyes had seemed haunted with a struggle of the soul.

"I started seeking God about six months ago," Kim Lan said reflectively. "I mean really seeking God. Not just showing up at church and enjoying my reputation as the 'Christian model.'" She drew imaginary quotation marks in the air. "I guess compared to most of the people in my circles, I'm a goody-two shoes." She turned toward Marilyn. "I figured seeking God would mean that He would..." She shrugged. "...That He would bless me."

All this talk suddenly made Marilyn highly nervous. Sure, she had the "right answers" to Kim Lan's modeling questions, but should she offer answers since she hadn't been seriously seeking God as she once had? Even though she certainly had begun the journey to spiritual recovery, there were still miles to go. She looked back over her life, over her teen years when she too, had been a goody-two-shoes. She thought about her college days and all the fun she had shared with her sisters. She mused over her decision to marry Gregory. Marilyn had felt led by God to be a pastor's wife, and Gregory had said he thought he should become a pastor. He was tall, dark, handsome, and she was in love. Their relationship seemed perfect. She recalled with vivid, painful clarity that she had just assumed God was smiling on her desire to marry Greg. So when he proposed, she had gladly accepted. The whole thing had seemed so right.

Then there were those years as a pastor's wife. Marilyn had naturally fallen into that role. She seldom missed a service—only when she was sick. She offered sound, biblical advice to anyone who asked. She unconditionally supported Gregory's ministry, and she had even grown spiritually. Her devotional time that had sometimes seemed boring during her teen years had turned into a daily encounter with God that she loathed to ever end. During those years as a pastor's wife, she had truly sought God as Kim Lan was mentioning. But Gregory's disavowal had left her an empty shell of her former self—mentally, emotionally, and spiritually. An empty shell capable of producing only darts of anger specifically fired at God and Greg.

Disturbed, Marilyn stared into the fragrant coffee and tried to concentrate on her friend's words.

"Anyway, what I've found is that God has blessed me for seeking Him, but I'm starting to notice this cycle of sorts," she said, jangling her keys. "He blesses me awhile then starts carving on me. I keep thinking of the potter-clay analogy. You know, that passage in Isaiah where he talks about God being the potter who formed us and is molding us."

Marilyn nodded, feeling that perhaps God was molding her as well.

"And I wonder if that's what's going on with this latest modeling offer. I feel such a battle within over whether or not to pose for this shooting."

"Well, if you suspect it isn't God's will, you know what to do," Marilyn said, amazed at how sure she sounded. Hadn't she been going through some of the same sorts of battles to which Kim Lan was admitting? A battle of her will against God's?

"But then I think of how many people I could help with that kind of money. And isn't that in the Bible, too? That we're to give to the needy?" Restlessly, Kim Lan stood. "Here I am talking about all this, and I'm going to miss my plane if I don't get with it."

Relieved to move on to another subject, Marilyn stood and deposited her coffee cup on Brooke's dresser. The two sisters exchanged a brief and poignant hug. "It's been great to have you here," Marilyn said, her eyes a bit misty. "I'm going to miss you."

"Oh, me too!" Kim Lan said sadly. "I can't wait until our sister reunion, when the whole gang gets together."

"It's just in three months," Marilyn said, following Kim as she began rolling her suitcase through the small house and to the front door. "I was thinking after New York, maybe we could do the next one here since Eureka Springs is such a tourist town."

"Sounds great to me!" Kim exclaimed. As she walked onto the front porch, she pushed her cheap, black sunglasses up the bridge of her nose and pulled the hat snugly in place. "Let's see…that will be next summer. By then we'll probably all be meeting at the house across the street." With a teasing lift to her mouth, she pointed to Josh's home.

"Oh would you pulleeezzze stop it!" Marilyn said, placing the back of her hand against her forehead as if she were about to swoon.

"Okay, okay, I give up!" Kim Lan said, raising a hand in resignation.

"You're kidding!" Marilyn gaped. "You *never* give up so easily."

"You're right," Kim Lan said in an impish whisper, her nose wrinkled in mischief.

Marilyn rolled her eyes and waved her final goodbyes to one of her dearest friends. As Kim Lan steered the rented Toyota up the street, Marilyn wondered what her final decision would be on posing for the swimsuit issue. Kim's modeling career had afforded her every luxury of the modern world, and Marilyn knew she had made some wise investments that left her wealthy. However, Kim Lan still struggled with saying no to big money because of the lessons learned from her impoverished childhood. Raised the poor daughter of a Vietnamese refugee and a disabled Vietnam veteran, Kim had often expressed her dreaded fear of being poor again. However, that background had also left the supermodel with a special place in her life for the needy. Marilyn had no idea how much money Kim regularly gave to organizations such as Christian Blind Mission International, but it was probably a large chunk.

With a reflective sigh, Marilyn walked into her small cottage and locked the front door, as if she were trying to block out any more thoughts of Kim Lan's troubling modeling decisions. For Kim Lan's struggles relentlessly pointed to areas of Marilyn's own life where she was not in full obedience to God. Pressing her lips together, she walked toward the tiny bathroom just outside her bedroom.

She noticed the nondescript, white envelope lying on the side of the bathroom sink and figured Kim must have accidentally left it. But on closer examination, Marilyn read her own name inscribed in the model's ornate handwriting. Marilyn slowly picked up the overstuffed envelope, already suspecting what it must hold. Several times during her stay, Kim

Lan had offered to give Marilyn "a few dollars to help make ends meet," but Marilyn had steadily refused. Her eyes stinging, her fingers trembling, Marilyn tore a jagged opening in the envelope. Much to her shock, several hundred dollar bills fluttered from the envelope to decorate the sink and floor. The tears that had once stung her eyes now spilled onto her cheeks. Quickly, Marilyn retrieved the money and began nervously counting them. Kim Lan had left exactly fifty 100-dollar bills. Five thousand dollars.

Swallowing against a sob, Marilyn spotted a note inside the envelope. Her fingers shaking uncontrollably, she opened the brief message.

> Dear Sis,
>
> You are probably the most stubborn woman I have ever met, unless you count me. I knew before I arrived that you would never take this money from me and that you certainly wouldn't cash a check. But during my prayer time, I felt so strongly that God was asking me to give you $5,000. I can earn far more than this in one shoot, so don't start feeling guilty about the amount. I want you to take the money and place it where you most need it. I know it's tough being a single mom and trying to make ends meet, so don't start trying to put on a brave face. Anyway, we sisters do have one request—that you please buy a computer. We miss you on the internet. (Besides, I think Brooke will enjoy it!)
>
> Hugs and Kisses,
>
> Kim

Marilyn sat on the side of the bathtub and sobbed.

Kim Lan guided the Toyota along Eureka Springs' winding, tree-lined lanes until she reached Spring Street. With the smells of new leather surrounding her, she wished for her jet-black Jaguar. Her forever worrying agent, Charlie Howell, continually nagged her about hiring a bodyguard and being a bit more careful when she drove herself, but Kim enjoyed her independence...and enjoyed the Jag. Furthermore, the idea of having a large brute continuously traipsing around after her left the super model less than thrilled. Her Park Avenue penthouse was located only twenty minutes from the organization for whom Charlie worked, the famous Forman Model Agency on Greene Street. So far, Kim Lan had enjoyed the agency's standard policy to hire a Lincoln Town Car and driver for her outings in the New York City area. But when she left New York, she disguised herself as she had today and either drove her Jag, chartered a plane, or flew first class.

As she headed south on Spring Street, she checked her watch, only to see the cheap timepiece had stopped. She pressed her lips in exasperation and eyed the traffic. Given the town's tourist nature, the main street was decidedly busy. "Not as bad as New York," Kim Lan muttered, eyeing her carry-on bag and contemplating digging out her diamond-studded Rolex. "But bad enough to make me late if I don't get out of here." She had spent entirely too much time talking to Marilyn. But talking to her sagacious friend proved hard not to do.

With a fond grin, she wondered if Marilyn had discovered the money by now. Kim knew that when she got home her answering machine would probably be blinking with a message from Marilyn.

She nervously checked her dead watch again, then glanced at the line of cars in front of her that had stopped for someone turning. As she halted, her attention was snared by a green Ford truck pulling into a mom-and-pop café. The truck looked vaguely familiar, and Kim Lan understood why when Joshua Langham got out of the driver's side. He wore a traditional black suit and a red tie—definitely looking the part of the caring pastor. Rushing to the passenger side, he assisted an elderly gentleman from the truck. The ancient, graying man with scraggly beard and shaded glasses looked as if he had seen many days better than the present. Without a doubt she was witnessing a Good Samaritan act in the making.

Thoughtfully nibbling on the end of her thumbnail, Kim Lan compared Joshua Langham to her actor boyfriend, Ted Curry. He was recently voted the most handsome man in America; Josh was simply average. Ted earned mountains of money; as a pastor, Joshua probably earned a pittance. Ted had loads of charm; Joshua had more, for his charm was genuine—always genuine. Ted turned his charm on and off as the situation required. Furthermore, Ted Curry seemed much less serious about any devotion to Christ, evidenced by his pressuring Kim Lan to become more intimate physically. Joshua Langham seemed the consummate gentleman, the ultimately dedicated Christian, a man of honor, who would never, absolutely never, be part of tempting another to sin.

"Come on! Live a little, Kim Lan," Ted often said. "Everybody sleeps around in this business. God understands that! We'll just ask forgiveness tomorrow. Besides, you're the only lady I've ever been with who hasn't been more than ready. What's the matter, Babe? Don't you think I'm sexy?" He usually tried to nuzzle her neck at that point or pressure her into heavy petting. However, Kim Lan was firm in her decision. Once Ted realized just how firm, he had started backing off a bit…just a bit. But Kim well understood that with only one encouraging nod from her, Ted would spring into action.

Part of what gave Kim Lan the strength to resist was that she had learned her lessons the hard way. Early in her skyrocketing modeling career, she had made the mistake of having an affair with an American superstar. When her mother found out about the affair, the news almost destroyed her. As much as Kim Lan would hate to sadden her mother again, presently she was more concerned with grieving the Lord.

She watched Joshua open the restaurant door for the old man and usher him inside. With a resigned sigh, she recognized that Joshua Langham was, by far, a better man than Ted Curry.

"Marilyn Douglas, you're crazy," she muttered. Realizing she was still nibbling her thumbnail, Kim Lan impatiently jerked her hand away from her mouth and looked at her marred nail. Not much damage had been done. She could repair it before tomorrow's shampoo advertisement shoot.

An impatient horn sounded from behind. Startled, Kim Lan noticed the cars in front of her had long since moved ahead. Immediately, she pressed the gas pedal and sped toward her celebrity life, toward Ted Curry's waiting arms, toward a tough modeling decision—a choice of the soul.

Thirteen

Marilyn stepped into her favorite eating establishment and felt as if she had leaped back in time. The Ozark Village Restaurant featured a collection of antiques, farm equipment, old signs, and bottles as a perfect backdrop for the traditional, southern buffet. The scrumptious smells of the country food always reminded her of the April 15 Income Tax Customer Appreciation Day, when the owner fed the whole town of Eureka Springs for free. Living in a small town certainly had its drawbacks, but then there were such delightful benefits as well.

Customarily, Marilyn looked toward her usual spot near the row of front windows. She blinked in surprise. Joshua Langham sat near her favorite booth with an elderly man sitting across from him. Stifling a groan, Marilyn fervently searched for the waitress who usually seated her. She was nowhere in sight.

Maybe if I just duck my head and walk toward the back, Joshua won't see me, she hoped. Marilyn would be forced to walk by him because the restaurant offered only a buffet. Perhaps she could wait until he left, then go to the assortment of food. Silently, she hurled invectives at herself for not eating the leftover tuna salad from last night. *What possessed me to want to dine here today?* she thought disgustedly. But this was her favorite eating place, and she was lonely.

As she ducked her head and prepared to dart toward the back, her spirit ached. The house had seemed so empty after Kim Lan left. Brooke wasn't even there to ease the pain of the silence, so she had decided eating out alone was better than eating alone at home.

"Marilyn?"

The considerate note in Josh's gentle voice seemed to dance up and down her spine. Marilyn stilled. Her plan to race to the back had miserably failed. In a split second, Marilyn rehearsed her options. She could ignore him, but since she had stopped when she heard his voice, he would know she was ignoring him. She could coldly glare at him in an attempt to stop any invitations to join him, but that would be rude. She could politely wish him a good day and continue her journey to the back, not giving him time to request her company. The final choice seemed the only option.

Conjuring a polite smile, she turned to him. "Oh, hello, Josh," she said nonchalantly. No one would ever guess the sight of his captivating smile left her anything but uninterested. "Great to see you," she said, then swiveled to pursue her grand escape. Desperate, she considered slipping out the back exit without eating. McDonald's was nearby. She could always grab something to eat there. As if she were in a nightmare, Marilyn pondered the insane possibility that Joshua might appear there, too.

"One?" a middle-aged brunette waitress asked, her old-fashioned prairie skirt swishing around her ankles as she came to a halt beside Marilyn.

"Yes, just one, Carla. At the back, please."

"That's the smoking section."

"Doesn't matter, just get me a seat in the back."

"Would you care to join us?" Josh asked from close by.

Marilyn stifled a moan. *Now what?* She looked into Joshua's limpid gray eyes and desperately wanted to answer with a firm no. She had no business enjoying a meal with a man who threatened—yes, threatened—her heart. Joshua Langham was exactly the kind of man she could fall in love with. If she had never married Gregory, if he had never betrayed her, Marilyn most likely would have welcomed a relationship with someone like Josh. But she forced herself to remember the excruciating pain Greg had dealt her, to remember tht she could not afford to do anything but keep her distance from Josh.

As the silence stretched between them like a gaping, emotional canyon, Josh produced a coaxing smile that bordered on the pathetic.

"Please?" he whispered.

Her pulse jumped, and Marilyn looked down at her tightly clasped hands. Either the man was exceptional at acting plaintive or he was as lonely as she was.

At last, she answered.

"Of course."

Joshua beamed. "Great."

Within seconds Carla Evans, smiling as if she were Cupid, told Marilyn she would return to take her beverage order. Marilyn wondered how long it would take before her mother discovered she had eaten out with Joshua. The waitress was a friend of Natalie's, and Marilyn envisioned Carla immediately rushing to the back to call Natalie with the hot news.

"Marilyn, this is my new friend, John Magruder," Joshua said as Marilyn joined them. "Mr. Magruder visited us in church this morning."

"Hello," Marilyn said, nodding politely. As she sat next to Joshua, she noted dessert dishes with the remains of peach cobbler and assumed the two had already finished their meal.

The unkempt elderly gentleman returned her greeting, and Marilyn received the strangest sensation he was examining her like a cobra who sizes up a helpless field mouse. A chill slithered down her spine, and she quickly looked toward the buffet as the man's aroma, something akin to a stale dumpster, sent a sickening spin through her midsection.

"Would this happen to be the mother of that fine young lady you were holding this morning?" Mr. Magruder asked.

"Yes, as a matter of fact, she is," Josh said, directing a smile to Marilyn. "He met Brooke."

"Oh, you met my daughter?" Marilyn questioned as that creepy feeling from earlier seemed to dissipate. Perhaps his recognizing a family resemblance with Brooke was the reason for his scrutiny of her. Nonetheless, the man looked as if he came straight off the streets of alcoholic row, and Marilyn wasn't sure she trusted him.

"Yes, I met her. The little tyke reminds me of my Kelly when she was 'bout that age."

"So...tell me about your family," Joshua suggested in a voice that said he cared.

Marilyn momentarily forgot her concerns over the scraggly old man. Neglecting thoughts of the aromatic buffet, she focused on Joshua as he truly listened to the man's story of losing his family by his own foolish choices. Joshua Langham possessed an unmatched gift of tenderness. Mix that with his all-masculine demeanor, and Marilyn wondered how many women the man had snared without even realizing it. Perhaps her reaction to Joshua was not so abnormal. There must have been scores of women who would have married him.

Joshua glanced toward her. Startled, Marilyn held his gaze for only a few seconds. Seconds that felt like an eternity. Seconds that told her he understood the effect he had on her. His Friday-night declaration that she liked his smile more than she wanted to admit seemed to resonate between them like a taunting chant.

Abruptly Marilyn broke his gaze, forcing herself to stare at the wooden table. But the worn grain blurred. Did she affect Joshua as much as he affected her? Or was she nothing but another plaything on a long list of his flirtations? Without half an effort, Josh had Kim eating out of his hand an hour after their acquaintance. Marilyn thought of the sinister past that his panther tattoo suggested. If his past were indeed dark, then it must have involved women as well.

But he's a pastor now, for pete's sake, she thought. Immediately, she gave herself a thorough, inward shake. *Well, so what! So was Greg!*

Marilyn had to get out. Being so close to Joshua had completely erased her appetite. She must have been nuts to have agreed to sit with him, let alone *by* him.

"If the two of you don't mind," Mr. Magruder said, dotting the corners of his mustached mouth with his paper napkin. "I believe I will excuse myself. I always try to take a long nap on Sunday afternoons, and—"

"I'll be glad to drive you home," Joshua offered swiftly.

"No, no, that's perfectly fine." He held up a grimy hand, partially covered by a tattered glove. "I can see myself home." The old man scooted to the end of the booth as if he had enjoyed enough of their company.

"Services tonight are at six. If you need a ride to church—"

"Okay," he called over his shoulder as he hobbled past the tables, now deserted in the aftermath of the lunch rush.

With genuine concern etched on his face, Joshua watched the old man struggle with opening the door before exiting.

"I'm guessing he's just a vagrant passing through, but I can't get that verse out of my head, 'Whatever you did for one of the least of these brothers of mine, you did for me,'" Joshua said, a note of sorrow in his voice. "There's so much more for him if he'd only turn his life over to God."

As much as Marilyn would like to empathize with the old man, the methods of her prompt and sure escape posed themselves as her most important task of the moment. An awkward silence settled around them, and Marilyn feigned concentration on the worn table. Soon she felt Josh watching her. Her peripheral vision confirmed it. He was too close. Entirely too close. Marilyn needed to scoot his way only half an inch and the two would be rubbing shoulders. She should move to the other side of the booth. Now.

"And what would you like to drink today, Marilyn?" Carla asked, giving Marilyn the impression that the waitress had repeated her query more than once. She looked up into merry blue eyes that were far too inquisitive for comfort.

This was her chance! Her chance to decline an order, make her excuses, and leave. But somehow she couldn't. As she had ridden the emotional pendulum from the moment she met Joshua, so she rode it now. The man who, three minutes before, she had assumed to be a former ladies' man, Marilyn now hated to treat rudely. As Kim Lan had mentioned, she had been close to uncivil Friday night. Saturday, she ran from him. In return, he had virtually begged her to have lunch with him.

"I think I'll just have a glass of tea, Carla," she heard herself saying.

"Great. Help yourself to the buffet."

"Thanks."

Carla, smiling with a hint of conspiracy, picked up the old man's remaining dishes.

"Thanks for clearing that spot," Marilyn said, amazed at how natural she sounded. "I think I'll move over there once I get my food. Gives me more elbow room." No one would have ever imagined her main motive was to put as much room as possible between her and the man sitting entirely too close. But after she had helped herself to the buffet and settled into her new place, she wondered if the move across the table was so wise. Now she was forced to look directly into Joshua's face. And the unadulterated admiration spilling from his eyes left Marilyn all the more shaken. She forced herself to focus on the meatloaf and mashed potatoes on her plate and prayed she would be able to choke it down.

"So, how did Brooke enjoy her outing yesterday?" Josh asked softly.

His ordinary words seemed to caress Marilyn's mind. *Stop it!* she wanted to snap, just as she had when he'd smiled at her in the kitchen. But she didn't. Instead, she simply answered, "I think she had a good time." As she nervously tormented a paper napkin she continued, "Brooke was tired when she got home. I was afraid she would be disappointed that Gregory changed their plans at the last minute, but as things turned out..."

"I remember she was afraid if she was gone all week I would cry."

Marilyn produced a slight chuckle. "Isn't it funny how children assign their own emotions to everyone else? Since she sometimes cries when I leave her, she thinks we would cry if she were gone a few days."

"Maybe I would have," Joshua said, a wistful note to his voice. "She's been quite an addition to my life."

The admission caught Marilyn off guard, and she once more gazed into eyes that openly admired her. As always, the effect was mesmerizing. Her pulse began its slow, telltale tattoo. Her palms moistened. She longed, despite her common sense, to feel Joshua's lips against hers.

"Thanks for letting Brooke come over," he said solemnly. "It's been quite a summer for me."

Carla arrived with the glass of iced tea, and Marilyn scrutinized the tiny ice cubes floating in amber liquid. "Well, I guess my motives aren't exactly pure." She produced a tight smile. "I..." She cleared her throat. "It's been hard for Brooke, not having an at-home dad." She shrugged. "My father has done a wonderful job of stepping into that role as much as he can, but he has such a time with his arthritis. And, well, Brooke needed someone who was able to play chase and toss her into the air—a father figure, I guess." Marilyn nervously toyed with the button on another of Kim Lan's extra silk blouses. She swallowed against the lump in her throat as she thought of the fact that her darling daughter no longer had a father at home. The fact that Josh, as if by God's own miraculous design, had stepped into that role. The fact that he had obviously fallen in love with her daughter and might easily fall in love with her. They could be one, big happy family. Brooke would, once again, have an at-home daddy.

Marilyn reached for her tea glass and took an enormous gulp. The cold liquid chilled her throat and seemed to turn to ice in the pit of her stomach.

"I'm honored that you trust me," Joshua said, yet a worried frown furrowed his brows. "But we haven't known each other long, and in a way, it worries me that you trusted me so readily. In today's world—"

"You're the first person—you're the *only* person—I've allowed her to do this with," she said, with an edge to her voice.

"I'm sorry. I didn't mean to question your judgment. It's just that—"

"Well, according to my mother, I could trust you with—with Brooke's life. It's not like I haven't asked a few questions here and there," she blurted.

"Okay, okay, okay!" He held up both hands. "I said I was sorry."

She hesitated to speak her thoughts, but something inside propelled her headlong into the conversation. "Despite—um—despite whatever happened in the past, I can tell you're trustworthy now. It doesn't take a brain surgeon to figure out you're a man of honor."

There. The truth was out between them, and it seemed to gloriously frolic around the table and right into Joshua's eyes. Once more, he beamed. Ironically, her own words contradicted her musings about Joshua's past. Despite his past, he would never harm her daughter. He might fascinate every female from a supermodel to a little old lady, but the Joshua Langham she knew would never deliberately mistreat a living soul.

"So, if you can trust me with your daughter, why can't you trust me with yourself?" He uttered the question so softly that it was almost indiscernible.

Marilyn's head snapped up in shock. "What?" she gasped. When he opened his mouth to repeat the words, she held up her hand. "No...n-no, that's okay. I heard you the first time." She reached for her tea and swallowed another mouthful. At last, Marilyn said what she should have said long ago: "I need to go now." Her legs trembling, she scooted across the booth's wooden seat and stood.

"Marilyn, please," Joshua said, laying a hand on hers.

Her fingers seemed to explode with tingles. She jerked from his warm touch as if it were the devouring tongues of an unquenchable fire.

"Marilyn..." He glanced across the deserted restaurant as if he didn't want to be overheard. "You can't deny that we share an incredible attraction," he whispered. "Let's face it, this is no ordinary—"

"And what is your experience with ordinary attraction?" she returned in a soft yet intense voice.

"What's that supposed to mean?"

"It's supposed to mean...it's supposed to mean..." She looked into his eyes, full of challenge and vulnerability mixed in a way that wrenched her heart. "It's supposed to mean that I figure you were a ladies' man in your former life when...when you got that panther tattoo because...because...you're just too—too appealing for your own good. And I figure you probably attracted a whole line of women."

He remained silent. Stricken and silent.

"Tell me it isn't true," Marilyn whispered, wondering why it even mattered. This was the Josh of here and now. Marilyn understood that the right thing to do was accept him as he was, a man whose past was forgiven, not drag up dark deeds that were over. But she was a human being, and something in her needed the answer. Perhaps she wanted to think that she was the only female who had swooned with his charisma. If only...if only she could learn that a hundred women before her hadn't felt the same way she felt.

"Nothing I have done in my past in any way changes this...this thing we have between us."

"So I was right," she muttered.

"God help me, Marilyn," he lamented. Placing elbows on the table he cradled his head in his hands and tightly curled taut fingers into his hair as if he were ready to rend it by the roots. "I wish I could tell you differently. Oh, how I wish I could tell you no. But it was a time in my life when I was running from God and from everything that was right. You have no idea how often I've lambasted myself—how often I still condemn myself over my own stupidity."

Marilyn spontaneously reached to touch his shoulder but stopped midway. The irony of this whole wretched conversation was that, whether Josh had slept with a thousand women or none, that in no way changed reality. She would not pursue a relationship with him. Why had she even asked him about the past?

Silently, she turned and walked out of the restaurant, her legs trembling as if she had run thirty miles. She didn't notice until she unlocked the door of her Chevrolet that Joshua watched her from his spot near the front window. She paused, took two steps toward the restaurant, and stopped. She could not allow herself the luxury of getting too close to him again. She had been wounded by a man more than she ever wanted to be wounded again. Another relationship would only make her vulnerable once more. That was not something she was willing to do right now. Not for God. Not for anybody.

Within seconds she started her car and turned the air conditioner to its maximum setting to blast away the summer heat. Just as she was backing out from her parking space, Marilyn remembered she hadn't even thought of paying for her untouched lunch. She debated about whether or not to rush back in, pay her ticket, and quickly leave. After moments of deliberation, Marilyn decided to just call Carla and tell her she would settle the debt tomorrow.

As soon as that minor detail was resolved, Marilyn observed a troubled Josh exiting the restaurant, striding past his Ford truck, and straight toward her car. Apparently, he was not through with their conversation.

But I am. Hands violently shaking, she moved the console gear shift into the drive position and sped away. In her rearview mirror, she caught a final glimpse of Joshua watching her.

Deep in her soul, the rumbles of thunder predicted an approaching storm. Joshua Langham, with all his charm, did not seem the sort of man who appreciated a woman walking out on a conversation, let alone driving off and leaving him standing in the parking lot. Gripping the steering wheel, Marilyn dreaded going home because Joshua lived right across the street. If he had followed her outside to finish their conversation, he very likely would walk from his house to hers to speak his mind. As she drove the car through the curving, tree-lined lanes, Marilyn contemplated taking a long, leisurely trip to nowhere. She could very easily head north, pull off at a roadside park, and dawdle away her afternoon. Hopefully, by then, Joshua would truly accept the futility of pursuing her and forget the whole conversation.

Marilyn checked her trusted Timex. Five after two. Her parents might be returning Brooke within the next half hour. If her father had his way, attendance at the family reunion picnic would be short lived. But, on the other hand, her mother might talk him into staying all day. There was no way of second guessing those two. Marilyn needed to be home in case they arrived early with Brooke.

She turned toward her neighborhood and guiltily glanced in her mirror. Joshua was following her.

Fourteen

Leopard slammed the door of his economy motel room and stalked into the small bathroom. Hurling insults at Joshua Langham, he stopped in front of the mirror and gazed at his own reflection. Since he had taken such special pains with the beard and wig to ensure any youthful skin would be covered, he looked something akin to a werewolf. The long, shaggy wig and lengthy beard obscured any trace of his thirty-something complexion. The glasses, tinted gray, also veiled the sharpness of his keen amber-colored eyes—eyes Panther might well remember.

Abruptly, Clark removed the glasses and began peeling the beard from his irritated skin. At last his face was free of the annoying adhesive, and he reached underneath the wig to unfastened the elastic bands that held it snugly in place. Clark shed the smelly clothes he had deposited in the dumpster during the night for that "well-worn" odor. Before getting into the shower, he reached down to his lean thigh and unbuckled the strap holding the switchblade firmly in place. Then, impulsively scratching his irritated face, Clark stepped into the shower and turned on the spray as hot as he could tolerate. He hated that horrible scent and wondered how he had managed to eat with that smell surrounding him.

But Clark would do anything—anything—to ensure the completion of his vengeance. He had made contact with more than positive results. After washing the layer of lather from his face, he smiled with satisfaction. Nothing about Joshua Langham's circumstances surprised Leopard in the least. The man had always been able to smooth talk his way in and out of a snake pit. He was nothing more than a lying con artist. He had probably already lied to that blonde who had joined them at lunch. No telling what lines he was feeding her. But none of that would matter in a few short weeks. By then, all Joshua Langham's underhanded fallacies would cease.

His skin protesting against the hot water, Leopard finished washing, turned off the water, and reached for the towel. Part one of his well-laid plan had been orchestrated with full success. Now on to part two.

Joshua hadn't planned to grow so aggravated at Marilyn, but the closer he got to their neighborhood, the more annoyed he became. Her avoidance tactics bordered on rude. He had spent many hours entertaining this woman's child, and what had his efforts gotten him? A cold shoulder and judgment. Josh wasn't exactly thrilled about his past, but at the same time he could do nothing to change it.

Why in the name of common sense is Marilyn acting like I'm some kind of lesser man because of my previous choices? I've asked for and received God's forgiveness. I've remained celibate for fifteen years. I've clung to the power of the Holy Spirit to live a righteous life above reproach. Who is she to cast stones? Josh's mind wouldn't stop churning. And the more he fumed, the angrier he became.

He pulled his trusty pickup into the driveway, moved the gear shift to park, and glanced up at his rearview mirror.

Marilyn, head bent, shoulders hunched, rushed from her car toward her front door. A voice within Joshua suggested he quietly go into his home and give Marilyn some space. But the longer he watched her trying to avoid him, the more he wanted to confront her. Not only had she walked away from their conversation in the restaurant, but she had also coldly driven from the parking lot, leaving him standing there like an idiot. He had even taken the time to pay for her meal—and what kind of thanks did he get?

Gritting his teeth, Joshua opened the truck door, got out, and stormed toward Marilyn's house. She stood on her porch now and seemed to be wrestling with the ancient door lock. Several times, she cast anxious glances over her shoulder. Just as Josh spanned her four porch steps, the door swung inward. Marilyn rushed into the cottage, closing the door behind her. Josh grabbed the knob, flung open the door, and followed her in.

"What are you doing?" she snapped as he closed the door with a determined thud.

He whirled to face her. "I've come to get a few things straight with you!"

Marilyn blanched.

And Josh, for the first time since he left the restaurant, hesitated in his wrath. He didn't grow angry very often, not this angry, anyway. But once he did, he was usually furious. His mother had even told him his eyes looked as if they were filled with flames when he was irate. Curling his fists, he stalked toward the picture window and tried his best to gain a firm control of the rage that pummeled his soul. All Marilyn had done was treat him the way he had treated himself—with disgust and rejection. She treated him like an outcast. Her turning away from him had done nothing but dig the wound in his soul a little deeper and enforce everything he felt about himself.

Once again a soft voice in the recesses of his spirit suggested he should go home and address these issues after he calmed down. Instead, he turned to face Marilyn again. "I didn't appreciate your walking out on me," he said in a deceptively soft voice.

She stood across the living room, clutching her purse, looking much like a frightened dove preparing to take wing.

"You saw me coming toward you in the parking lot, and you still drove off. That was rude, Marilyn."

"I'm sorry. It's just that—"

"You have no right—no right whatsoever to pass judgment on me for my past." He took a few steps toward her.

"I..." She stumbled backward.

"I took a vow of celibacy when I accepted Christ fifteen years ago, and I am truly ashamed of everything I have done—including breaking the law."

"You're a criminal?"

Joshua wanted to rip out his own tongue. Bit by bit, he was telling Marilyn the story of his brush with the law and his near imprisonment. He should have just gone home as that still, small voice had suggested—accept the obvious, leave Marilyn alone, and enjoy his relationship with Brooke. Why continue to knock on Marilyn's door when she was yelling, "Go away"? He didn't want to discuss the details of his involvement with Leopard or his past relationships.

Why am I even at her house in the first place, Josh wondered abruptly. *What am I going to prove? Nothing. A big, fat nothing.*

Clenching his teeth, Joshua purposefully strode toward the front door. He would do what he should have done in the first place—go home and regain his composure. Later, he would reopen this conversation and proceed with caution. But as he gripped the doorknob, a hand on his arm stopped him.

Marilyn couldn't explain the insistent urge that had overtaken her. Only one demand raged through her brain—the demand to discover exactly why Josh had tangled with the law and exactly what that panther on his shoulder meant. From the moment she'd seen the panther two months ago, she had pondered its implications. Those thoughts had escalated into a full-blown hurricane of curiosity. She had to hear the story, or she would explode.

Joshua stilled. Shoulders slumped in defeat, he kept his back to her.

She breathed deeply, hoping to invoke an equilibrium upon her thoughts. "I'm—I'm sorry about leaving you at the restaurant like that. I should have...should have never asked you about your past and about any...um...other old relationships you had. It's really none of my business. It's just that..." *Why am I babbling about Joshua's former relationships when I want to know the details about the panther story?*

"That what?" Josh slowly turned to face her. The rage in his eyes vanished and was replaced with a dull, broken ache that seemed to spill from his soul.

Marilyn became increasingly aware that she was holding his arm. Abruptly she released her grip.

Joshua searched her face as if he were looking for any sign of encouragement. When his hungry gaze settled on her lips, Marilyn desperately tried to school her features into an expression of bland disinterest, but she feared all she accomplished was desperation. This was crazy. This was beyond crazy. How had her curiosity about his past transported her to this island of magnetism?

"Marilyn?" he asked, his voice noticeably husky.

"Josh, don't—don't do this. I didn't intend..." She held up her hands as if to fend him off. Instead, he managed to step into the circle of her arms and cradle her to him.

"Ah, Marilyn," he breathed against her neck.

Marilyn closed her eyes as all good judgment fled. She shouldn't enjoy this moment. She really shouldn't. But the feel of his strong arms around her, the faint smell of his aftershave, the warmth of his embrace all created a cloud of pleasure that settled around her and dashed aside every reason why this shouldn't be. She thought he was going to kiss her, and even though she shouldn't let him, she didn't have the strength of mind to stop him. As their tender embrace lengthened, Marilyn sensed an iron will of restraint operating within Joshua. A restraint that kindled the fires of respect in Marilyn. The respect rapidly grew in its potency and beckoned Marilyn to a closer relationship with him.

Gently, silently, strongly, Joshua pulled away. "I'm sorry," he muttered, reclaiming his post by the picture window. "I shouldn't have. I won't ever do that again until...unless..."

The unfinished thought hung between them, and Marilyn struggled for his meaning until her distraught mind settled on one concept. Was he saying he wouldn't approach her again unless they got married? There it was again. The "m" word! The word she *did not* want to hear or contemplate! Her momentarily defunct fear revived with full vigor.

"I am not going to marry you!" she blurted before she comprehended that her mouth was bent on expressing her horrified thoughts.

Josh gradually turned to face her, a strangely curious expression cloaking his every feature. "Who said anything about marriage?" he asked in surprise.

"I...um...I..." Her face heating past the comfort zone, she cleared her throat.

The incredulous chuckle he produced led Marilyn to firmly believe she had beyond a doubt misunderstood his meaning.

"Oh, I get it," he said, and amused gleam in his eyes. "You thought I was going to say, 'I won't ever do that again unless we get married'!"

Her face heated all the more. For once in her life, Marilyn was irrefutably without words, without a coherent thought, without one scrap of dignity left intact.

And Joshua Langham...Josh was loving it. He crossed his arms and smiled like a large feline who had just outwitted the neighborhood bulldog.

Where once respect had glowed for Joshua, now ire sprouted. "Well, exactly what were you going to say?" she snapped.

"I was going to say that..." He paused for another well-placed chuckle. "I was going to say that I won't ever do that again unless you change your mind about us. I felt as if I were perhaps pushing myself on you, and I certainly didn't want you to feel as if I were...were...assuming I could just take privileges. I was trying to be a gentleman."

"And what about now?" Stiffly she clenched her fist. "Would you say your...your laughing at me is the behavior of a gentleman?" She waved her arm for emphasis.

He pressed his lips together as if he were covering a smile, but another chortle burst forth despite his gallant attempts.

"Oh...just—just—just go home!" Marilyn bolted into the tiny kitchen and stood gripping the counter, waiting for the sound of the front door to open and close. But no sound came. As the kitchen clock ticked off the seconds, Marilyn sensed Joshua was not going to leave. At last his footsteps neared then stopped behind her.

Without warning, her eyes stung, her lips trembled, her legs began to shake. The more her humiliation and despair revealed itself, the more incensed she became.

"Marilyn."

The contrite note in his voice only increased her tears. "I said go home," she said, clinging to her fury.

"I'm sorry."

"Just go home," she ground out, choking on a sob. She should be apologizing instead of continuing in her rudeness. Nonetheless, she cleaved to the anger because the anger was better than the overwhelming fear that washed over her soul like stale, bitter water. Despite all her vehement mental opposition against a relationship with Joshua, the two of them were gradually growing in their acquaintance, so much that Joshua had actually taken her in his arms and she had enjoyed it. This triggered her dread of another romantic relationship, especially with another minister.

Joshua didn't say a word, but she felt his resistance to her request that he leave.

Marilyn tried to suppress another sob, but to no avail. The sob pushed itself from her and was quickly followed by a few companions. The feelings slamming her soul spanned far beyond her initial humiliation. She desperately wanted to curl up under the covers and never show her face to Joshua again. Now the sobs were reproducing at an incredible rate, and with each sob the desire to melt from existence increased all the more.

"Ah, Marilyn," Joshua said as he placed a comforting hand on her shoulder. "I'm so sorry. I shouldn't have laughed at you."

Covering her face, Marilyn did what her head told her not to do. She turned toward this kind, considerate man and allowed him to once more wrap his arms around her. As he gently patted her back, Joshua rested his head on top of hers. At long last, the tears spawned by humiliation and apprehension abated, and Marilyn found her voice.

"I am so scared," she rasped.

"I know...I know." He stroked her hair, and in that moment Marilyn sensed that he comprehended everything she was feeling. No other explanation was needed. "I should have never laughed at you," he repeated.

"It's okay," she said weakly, enjoying his warmth. She couldn't ever remember feeling so cherished, not even in the first year of her marriage. Gregory had always seemed more interested in being the dictator of their home and making sure his desires were met than contemplating any of her needs. A voice inside Marilyn whispered that she should break away from Joshua's embrace, but another need overrode that advice.

What had started as a moment of comfort soon began to stir Marilyn's senses. The chemistry between them was like a stick of dynamite with a very, very short fuse. Presently, Marilyn was feeling anything but comfort. Joshua's heart, rapidly thudding against her cheek, attested that he, too, was far from tranquil. Nonetheless, Marilyn again perceived that Josh's iron will of restraint was strongly intact. Awkwardly, she pulled her face away from his starched white shirt, now damp from her tears.

"Your shirt's wet," she said pragmatically.

As if he didn't hear her, Joshua placed his hands on either side of her face and stroked her cheeks with his thumbs. Only one choice posed itself—for Marilyn to look upward, through Joshua's eyes, into his soul. There she seemed engulfed in a melancholic, misty cloud of remorse.

"I am so sorry about my past choices. I have regretted my former relationships ever since I found the Lord, but I must tell you that I have never regretted my choices more than today. I was young and stupid and thought I had the world by the tail. The Ten Commandments to me were just a long list of rules my parents stuffed down my throat, and I had no idea—absolutely no idea—that they were actually a plan from a loving God to keep me from doing things that would harm me. I thought 'thou shalt not commit adultery' was just something to keep me from having fun. I had no idea I was taking a sledgehammer and putting a dent in my soul every time I..." Abruptly, he turned from her, stepped toward the kitchen sink, and forlornly stared out the window.

The torment in his demeanor left Marilyn breathless. His earlier, vehement words seemed to echo off the walls: *You have no right—no right whatsoever to pass judgment on me for my past.* Yet Joshua appeared to be doing to himself what he had demanded she not do. She opened her mouth to tell him that accepting Christ as your Savior meant He wiped away the past and all things became new. A Christian no longer had to live in the past. Again, she had all the right answers. She had given them to so many people when she was a pastor's wife. But Josh possessed a firm "head knowledge" of all this and more. Likewise, Marilyn mentally grasped much of what the Bible said about trusting—radically trusting—God's guidance. But sometimes in her own life there existed a gap between what she knew to be truth and what she embraced as truth. Could it be that until the heart embraced truth, its impact was significantly abated? She blinked with the power of her thoughts and chose to definitely not speak her pat answers to Joshua's problems.

"Clark McClure and I were best friends in high school and college," Joshua began in a hollow voice.

Suddenly feeling as if she were in a conversation with Kim Lan, Marilyn squinted, trying to understand Joshua's turn in the conversation.

"Clark was often on the edge of the law, and quite frankly, I usually didn't participate in any of his shady deals. I was more interested in breaking the laws of God than the laws of society." Pausing, he turned to face her, wearily crossing his arms, and leaning against the counter. "I think Clark even dealt in drugs some. We shared an apartment, and there were some odd characters who often showed up from nowhere, talked briefly with Clark, and left. I never wanted to be part of the drug scene." He rubbed his face like a man truly vexed. "I just extended my stupidity in other directions." Pausing, Joshua studied the aging, dull kitchen tile. "When Clark brought home the stuff he had printed off his brother's computer, I didn't understand until after we read it the seriousness of the files he had somehow managed to hack his way into."

Marilyn's mind spun as if she had been caught in the winds of a late-afternoon Arkansas storm. Clark? The edge of the law? Drugs? Computer hacking?

The firm knock on the front door barely penetrated her whirling thoughts as she stared at Joshua with round-eyed interest. Finally, she must be hearing the true story. Of all times for someone to be at the door!

Ignore them. They'll go away. The urgent thought seemed rational. Then she remembered Brooke and her parents.

Marilyn glanced at her watch to discover yet another hour had lapsed. It was just after three.

The knock sounded once more, this time louder.

"Are you going to get that?" Josh asked.

"Yes, of course." Marilyn turned for the doorway then stopped dead in her tracks. If this was indeed her parents, what would they think if they saw Joshua in her house? "I think this is Mom and Dad," she said meaningfully, hoping Joshua would take the hint and stay in the kitchen. "They're supposed to bring Brooke by some time this afternoon. They've been at a family reunion."

"Great," he said, falling in beside her.

"No," she urgently whispered, as if her parents could hear. "You stay in the kitchen. I don't want them to suspect—"

"Oh, I see." Joshua's brows rose with understanding as an impish light twinkled in his eyes. "You're ashamed of me."

"No," she hissed. "I don't want them to get any ideas about..."

"And what about me? Do you want me to have ideas?"

The knock now sounded at the back door. "Marilyn?" her father called.

"Oh, great! Now they're at the back."

"So what am I supposed to do now? Want me to crawl into the refrigerator?"

Darting Josh a tempestuous look, Marilyn resigned herself to the inevitable and opened the back door.

Fifteen

◦

Her cheerful mother, stoic father, and a cranky little girl clambered across the threshold. "We tried you at the front door, but couldn't get you to answer," Natalie said.

"Sorry," Marilyn muttered, bending to pick up a groggy Brooke. "We were talking."

"Oh," her parents said in unison, staring at Joshua.

"Hi," he said with a casual smile.

"Hi," the Douglases responded.

"Joss." Brooke leaned toward Joshua, extending her arms with the open trust of a child.

"She almost went to sleep on the way home," Natalie said. "She played hard today."

"So did we," Fred said, a downward turn to his mouth.

"Oh, you," Natalie playfully patted his arm. "He never wants to stay long at these reunions."

"It's because they wear me out. I'm ready for a nap." He stifled a yawn and languidly rubbed his wrinkled face, tanned from the hours in the sun as a postman and gardener. "Let's go."

"Okay, go on to the car," Natalie said. "I'll be there in a minute. There's something I need to ask Marilyn."

Rolling his eyes, Fred ambled toward the door. "How many times have I heard *that* one?" he muttered as he walked outside.

"Have you been crying, dear? Is everything all right?" Natalie whispered as soon as the door closed.

Marilyn didn't want to discuss her reasons for crying in front of Josh. "We can talk later," she said under her breath, casting a furtive glance toward Joshua. But he was gone. Marilyn peered past the kitchen doorway to see him walking toward the worn rocking chair in the living room, Brooke's head resting on his shoulder.

She looked back into her mother's concerned face. Still, she didn't feel comfortable discussing the whole ordeal. She glanced at her hands, tightly balled into fists.

Marilyn and her mother had always been closer than most mothers and daughters. As Marilyn stepped into adulthood, the two of them had been more like sisters. But for some reason, Marilyn had felt constrained about sharing this dilemma about Joshua. Perhaps because Natalie, ever the matchmaker, seemed more a champion of Joshua's views than Marilyn's.

"I hope Pastor Josh hasn't upset you," Natalie began.

Marilyn bit her lips and hedged for time.

"He's a terribly nice man, but..." Natalie continued.

"We did have words, but everything is fine," Marilyn interrupted.

"Well, dear," Natalie said as she laid a gentle hand on her daughter's shoulder, "lovers' quarrels happen to the best of us."

"Mother!" Marilyn hissed defensively. "We are not in love! Why is everyone from Kim Lan to Sonsee to you to Carla at the cafe convinced that we've got something going?"

Natalie blinked, her eyes taking on the injured look of a wounded doe. "I'm sorry, dear. I didn't mean...I just assumed... the way the sparks fly when...and Brooke talks about him nonstop. Your father and I just assumed..."

Marilyn's mind filled with frustration. She was forced to acknowledge that everything her mom said was absolutely true. And only a zombie would miss the sparks flying when she and Josh were together.

"I'm sorry," Marilyn said. "I didn't mean to blast at you." Crossing her arms, she struggled to keep the sharp note from her voice. "It's just that I'm not ready for a relationship, Mom. I'm really not." This day would undoubtedly go down as one of the most exasperating of her entire life. "I can't help it if Joshua is attractive or Brooke thinks he's grand." She raised her hands in a plaintive plea. "I'm just not ready."

"I understand," Natalie said, her eyes taking on the practical spark Marilyn had seen many times. "And I promise not to bring it up again. No more questions or comments from me."

"Thanks!" Marilyn said with a relieved sigh. One of the reasons mother and daughter could maintain a friendship was that Natalie had never tried to control Marilyn once she had grown up. Natalie had been a godly influence. She had led her daughter, and she had inspired Marilyn to emulate her. But she had never tried to force Marilyn's hand on any issue. Natalie Douglas respected her daughter enough to give her the space she needed.

Natalie turned toward the door.

"Oh, and Mother?"

"Yes?" she answered as she swiveled to face Marilyn, a thinly veiled nuance of concern clouding her expression.

"I accidentally ran into Josh today at the Ozark Village Restaurant. We shared lunch, and if Carla calls with the 'hot news,' please explain to her that Joshua Langham and I are *not* dating."

"Don't worry. I will."

"I just don't want the whole town—"

"Of course not, dear! I'll take care of it." Natalie reached to embrace her only child then backed away to peer deeply into her eyes. "I am praying for you every day. For you and little Brooke."

"I know," Marilyn whispered.

Natalie's eyes filled with tears. The soft lines around her mouth crinkled as she fought the emotions. "I just want the best for the two of you. That's why I worry about you all alone now."

"It's okay." Marilyn gently stroked her mother's face. "But we're okay. Honest."

"Yes. But when Greg did what he did, Fred and I grieved so much for you." Natalie covered Marilyn's hand and squeezed it. "I've been strong for you, Marilyn. And I haven't mentioned it, but I've often wanted to—to just somehow retaliate against Greg myself. A few times during the divorce, I thought your father was going to do just that." Natalie shook her head. "But we had to come to terms with it and forgive him."

Marilyn sighed as she once again contemplated the ripple effects of that seven-letter-word "divorce." The pain of death. The death of a family. Gregory's decision had harmed more people than he, in his selfishness, could ever comprehend.

"And I guess that when I saw you and Josh together in the hospital that day after the tornado and saw how the sparks were flying, then when Brooke started talking about him all the time, I just assumed... All I want is for you to be happy again, Marilyn."

Marilyn bit her lips as new tears stung her eyes. The incredible love her parents had always shown her was not something she ever took for granted. "Thanks, Mom. I understand. I'd feel the same way if it were Brooke. But I'm just not ready." Marilyn absently gazed out the window to see a bank of clouds gathering above. "I wonder if I'll ever be ready."

The comforting silence that ensued left Marilyn free to ponder her own fears. Fears that seemed to tower higher than the Ozarks surrounding Eureka Springs. The back door clicked as the sound of distant thunder filled the kitchen. Marilyn turned to see that she was alone. Her spirit softened with the memory of the love and gentle understanding that had shone from her mother's eyes. But Marilyn also remembered those troubled clouds that had darkened Natalie's demeanor just as the gathering clouds now darkened the sky. Natalie was clearly worried about her daughter, and Marilyn pondered the means to ease her anxiety.

With a sigh, she trudged toward the living room to find Joshua gently rocking Brooke. The child's head rested on his chest, and Josh had propped his cheek against her blonde tresses. The tune of the soft lullaby he hummed wrapped around Marilyn's mind to produce an inconsolable ache. For several silent seconds, she stood watching the scene, torn between the conflicting desires to either snatch Brooke from Josh's arms or embrace the moment as a treasured memory.

Another rumble of thunder and a rustle of the trees. The pre-storm winds might as well have been blowing through her soul.

Whipping around, Marilyn rushed back into the kitchen. Deftly, she grabbed a big-handled basket sitting beside the back door then stepped outside and gently snapped the door shut. Before the storm began, she wanted to pick the numerous ripe tomatoes she had noticed that morning and check to make sure the vines were firmly attached to their individual trellises—anything to get away from that scene in her living room.

Joshua glanced over his shoulder to watch Marilyn stalk back into the kitchen. He had heard her approach and he discerned she was watching. He hoped she would join him. Instead, she had distanced herself from him again. She seemed to be forever doing exactly that. The back door opened then clicked as she shut it.

With a resigned sigh, Josh gently kissed Brooke's forehead. He drank in the child's angelic demeanor and a protective surge flooded him. In that instant, Joshua Langham experienced a father's love, an enlightenment that he would stop at nothing to defend Brooke. He bestowed another kiss on her cherub cheek and once more wondered if Gregory Thatcher had been insane when he walked away from such a lovely lady and enchanting child.

Maybe one day Gregory's loss will be my gain, he thought joyfully. But as soon as the familiar thought entered his mind, he squelched it. There was no need to get his hopes up. Carefully, he stood and cradled Brooke close to his chest. Even though Josh felt that he may have won new ground in his almost nonexistent relationship with Marilyn, they were still miles from a commitment—a commitment that might never be. Joshua tiptoed down the hallway until he arrived at an ajar door that opened into a room decorated with dolls. He stepped into the room and tenderly deposited Brooke on the white, wrought iron day-bed.

A rumble of thunder sounded overhead, and the trees began their telltale shifting. Concerned, Josh hurried from the room. He hadn't heard Marilyn come back into the house. Memories of that rare tornado that could have killed them all swirled through Joshua's mind. Despite the claims that it was the tornado of the century for Eureka Springs, he hadn't been the same since that stormy night. Every time a new storm approached, he cringed.

Joshua stepped into the kitchen and pulled aside the cheerful curtain decorated with blue geese. Marilyn hovered over the row of tomato plants, swiftly gathering the red fruit and depositing them into her oversized basket. Josh cast another cautious glance toward the ominous gray clouds. His jaw tightened.

Marilyn glanced skyward, looked back at the garden, then hurriedly progressed to the next plant as if she were determined to gather the remaining tomatoes before the storm broke. Drumming his fingers against the countertop, Joshua continued to watch her. At last she trotted toward the house. Satisfied, Josh turned from the window and headed for the front door. He did not want to be in her home when she returned because he had probably already pushed the boundaries. If Marilyn had wanted to further converse with him, she would have joined him when he was rocking Brooke. The last thing he needed to do was overstay his welcome. As he heard the back door open, he opened the front door, stepped onto the porch, and silently shut the door behind him. The first fat rain drops splashed against the porch steps, and Joshua dashed across the yard toward his bachelor home.

Clark McClure settled onto the back church pew while the pianist began the evening service's prelude with a round of "Amazing Grace." As the service at last got underway, the whole ordeal nauseated Clark. Joshua sat in the typical pastor's spot behind the podium and said the usual amens. The music director opened with a few choruses—choruses that Clark remembered from childhood. In disdain he glanced around the dated sanctuary, decorated in golds and greens, and wondered if anything in churches across America had changed since he was a kid. He might as well have been in the sanctuary he and Josh had been forced to attend during high school. Josh's father had been the pastor, and Leopard's father had been a deacon. Leopard and Panther had been in charge of general anarchy. Whatever possessed Josh to become a minister was beyond Clark's sphere of understanding.

As the service wore on, Leopard anticipated the long-awaited event. The event he had counted on. The event that would give him the chance to snoop—the tedious pastoral prayer that marked the opening of most sermons.

Tonight's service offered no exception. Once Josh began the prayer, Leopard slipped from the back pew and hobbled toward the foyer. Knowing Joshua would soon be busy with his sermon, Leopard gambled that he wouldn't be interrupted. A quick inspection this morning had revealed that the pastor's office resided across from the restrooms at the end of the hallway. Noiselessly, he closed the sanctuary door and, relying on his cane, feigned a limp as he walked toward the restrooms—and the pastor's office.

Clark cast a furtive glance over his shoulder and steeled himself against briskly striding toward the office. As the sound of Joshua's prayer dimmed in the distance, Clark firmly reminded himself that he must continue his act. No one appeared to be watching, but he refused to open himself to suspicion that he was anything more than an old man in need of a bath and a dose of "divine love."

He paused at the door marked "Pastor's Office" only long enough to glance up the hallway and make certain no one was watching. Deftly, he pulled a tattered handkerchief from his pocket, wrapped it around the doorknob, and tested to see if the door was locked. As he had hoped, the knob turned freely, the door swung inward. And Clark slithered through the opening like a serpent straight from the pit of Hades. Silently he closed the door behind him, lowered the blinds, and removed the penlight from his coat pocket. Only traces of evening light filtered through the closed blinds, and the penlight's tiny beam proved as handy as he had anticipated. He didn't want to turn on the overhead light in case someone passing might notice it seeping under the doorway and become suspicious.

Leopard flicked the narrow beam across the cluttered office. On the east wall, an overburdened bookcase appeared to house an abundance of reference books. The ancient desk held a comfortable collection of worn books, Bibles, opened mail, and computer software. Joshua Langham, despite his claims to religion, had changed precious little. He was still just as much a clutterbug as he was a ladies' man.

Skillfully Leopard began his work. Careful to use the bedraggled handkerchief to cover every handle on which he tugged, Clark opened each drawer of the ancient desk. As quickly as possible, he rifled through the various assortment of papers. His only valuable find—two keys on a nondescript key ring. The keys rested in the lap drawer beside the paper clips. A note scrawled on a piece of attached cardboard said, "house." With a pleased smirk, Clark dropped the keys into his worn jacket's pocket. He certainly had not been looking for keys to Joshua's house, but finding them so readily available would keep him from having to break a window later in the week.

Next, the file cabinet. One by one he inspected the files, but the overflowing drawers proved void of the desired object. Desperately, he placed the penlight between his teeth and dug to the bottom of the jumbled papers in the cabinet's last drawer. Nothing.

Irritated, he closed the drawer and pointed the light toward the bookshelves that lined the east wall. Upon his initial glance minutes before, the shelves appeared to harbor only reference works. But another perusal alerted Clark to a collection of books that strongly resembled the record books.

Leopard grinned in triumph. He rushed toward the books, reached for the largest one, then halted. Leaving fingerprints was not an option. Cautiously he placed the handkerchief along the spine, pulled out the book, deposited it on the shelf's ledge, and allowed it to plop open. Just as he had hoped, the names and addresses of church members lay before him.

With a satisfied chuckle, Leopard replaced the book, turned off the penlight, and stepped toward the lone window. He reopened the blinds and, still using the handkerchief, turned the window's simple lock. Adroitly, he tugged upward on the window to ensure its ready opening. Assured of the window's cooperation, he lowered it and silently turned toward the door. He had been gone from the sanctuary long enough.

Slowly, Leopard opened the office door a hair's width and scanned the hallway. No one. As soundlessly as he had entered, Leopard stepped from the office, closed the door, and turned toward the nearby water fountain. Only when he reached to turn on the water did he perceive that his hands were slightly trembling.

"Are you okay?" a concerned voice asked from behind.

Leopard hid the compulsive jump and turned to face the fresh-faced usher who had seated him that morning. "Yes, sonny, I'm fine. Just fine."

"Are you sure? I saw you leave and I was afraid you were having problems. I checked the restroom, and..."

"I guess I was caught in the act." Clark feebly rubbed his face. "I was feeling a bit faint and laid down in one of the Sunday school rooms." Clark pointed at a nearby room.

"Do you need me to call a doctor?"

"Oh no...no. I'll be okay. It's just one of those things. I'm not as young as I used to be," Clark said, cleverly inserting a particularly pathetic note into his elderly voice. "I believe I will head on back home, though. Please give my regards to the kind pastor. Tell him I'll try to make it next week."

"Do you need a ride?"

"No. No, that's quite all right. I can manage." Clark sluggishly limped up the hallway, into the foyer, and out the front door.

Sixteen

◡

Kim Lan walked across the threshold of her plush New York penthouse. The austere black-and-white decor that usually appealed to her penchant for understated elegance seemed sterile in comparison to Marilyn's homey cottage. The silence Kim often embraced likewise had lost its appeal in the light of Brooke's spontaneous laughter. As she locked the door behind her, her feet protested anew, and she slipped off the cheap loafers.

Her first-class flight had been uneventful. As usual, her disguise of no makeup, the matronly bun, hat, and sunglasses had worked, and she reveled in being able to maintain her freedom. Nonetheless, the stress of flying left her ready for bed. She rolled her suitcase into the apartment's only bedroom—a suite as large as the living room. Unceremoniously, she dumped the suitcase on an oriental settee and unzipped it. In seconds she had retrieved the toiletry items she needed and started toward the bathroom. A glance at the answering machine on her black lacquer nightstand caused her to detour.

Kim Lan pushed the answering machine's message button, then tugged on the nearby drape cord. The polished cotton drapes, the color of wine, swished open to reveal an expansive picture window that covered most of the wall. In the distance lay New York City's scenic skyline, ablaze with lights. Kim Lan listened to the messages as they played one by one.

Her agent, Charlie Howell, was nervous. He was always nervous. He wanted to be sure she made her six A.M. shoot for that shampoo advertisement. She checked the crystal-ensconced Bulova on her nightstand and decided that if she didn't get to bed soon she would get precious little sleep.

Her boyfriend, Ted Curry, asked to come over once she got home. He claimed to miss her terribly. Immediately, Kim Lan thought of Joshua Langham and the differences between him and Ted. As Ted's silky voice continued, Joshua's qualities blurred in the face of the movie star's blatant allure. Gradually she began to ache for the feel of Ted's arms around her. The necessity of her early bedtime prevented her from inviting him over tonight, but she would certainly return his call.

Marilyn's message was third. The tearful note in her appreciative voice left Kim Lan's eyes misty. The five grand was nothing but pocket change for her, but it meant the world to Marilyn.

Turning from the window, she listened to the fourth message. Sonsee, her voice urgent, wanted to talk to Kim Lan *now.*

She padded toward the restroom only to stop in her tracks when the fifth and final caller spoke. "Kim Lan, this is Gregory Thatcher. Call me when it's convenient for you." She heard his phone number but didn't comprehend it. What could Gregory Thatcher want with her? A combination of interest and dread tumbled through her mind. She and Gregory weren't exactly members of the mutual admiration society, and Kim Lan wasn't enamored with the idea of holding any sort of conversation with the man. Nonetheless, the fact that he called her left her curious about his intent.

Presently, Kim focused on getting ready for bed. She would return the calls later. Within fifteen minutes, she crawled between the satin sheets, the color of cream, and reached for the cordless phone. From memory, she punched in Sonsee's number and waited.

After the first ring, Sonsee picked up the receiver. "Hello Kim," she said with assurance.

"How did you know it was me?" Kim Lan asked, drowsily staring up through the netting which covered the ebony poster bed. "Oh, I forgot. You've got that obnoxious caller ID thingy."

"You should get one sometime."

"Maybe you should just get a life," Kim teased.

"Believe me, I've *got* a life."

The two friends chuckled in unison.

"So what's up?" Kim asked as she snuggled deeper into the blankets that smelled of melon linen spray.

"Melissa called about two hours ago. She had been on the phone with Marilyn and was worried."

"Oh?"

"Marilyn snapped at her and told her to mind her own business and hung up on her."

"You mean *our* Marilyn? Ms. Congeniality?"

"Yes. Melissa called me in tears, so I called Marilyn. She said she didn't want to talk about it and didn't exactly sound like she had graduated from Miss Berrymore's charm school, either. In all honesty, I've never felt such walls between me and Marilyn. I thought maybe since you were there this weekend... Melissa is really upset."

"Hmm." Kim Lan paused to ponder this new turn of events. Of all the times in the last ten years when one or more of the seven friends had shared a few harsh words and eventually made up, Marilyn had always chosen to rise above the conflict and remain Christlike throughout. She had never snapped at any of her sisters. Oh, there had been those odd moments when she was grouchy, but as far as a full-blown conflict, Marilyn had not been a participant and had never taken sides.

"What happened?" Kim Lan asked at last. "Did Melissa make the grave mistake of bringing up Joshua Langham?"

"Yes. How'd you guess?"

"How did I guess?" Kim Lan rolled her eyes. "Listen, honey chil'," she said with a feigned, southern accent, "you know I've just spent the weekend with those two and they've got it bad. But Marilyn is fighting it like you wouldn't believe."

"What's the deal? Is she crazy?"

"Yep." Kim Lan crinkled the satin sheet between her forefinger and thumb and chortled. "That's the only explanation I can come up with. The man is the personification of wonderful. He's not exactly the most handsome guy I've ever met, but he's got enough charm for all of New York. Brooke loves him, and he's for real."

"So, what's Marilyn's problem?"

Kim Lan sighed. "I guess she's been burned once, by another minister, and, well, you figure it out."

"Gregory 'The Jerk' Thatcher ought to be hanged at sunrise."

"I agree. Want to meet me at the corral and see that he's taken care of?"

"You're too funny," Sonsee said, chuckling.

"I actually saw Greg this weekend."

"And..."

"He's the same as always. I think he still wants to hang *me* at sunrise."

"Just because you had the guts to tell him what he was doing was wrong?"

"He *knows* he was wrong, and I think he regrets leaving Marilyn."

"Oh?"

"You should have seen him when he realized Marilyn and Josh might have a thing going. He turned about three shades of green—as in the color of raging jealousy."

"That's ridiculous. He's the one—"

"Right. But the whole thing has been ridiculous from the start. Believe it or not, I had a message from him when I got home."

"So have you called him back?"

"Not yet. I'll probably wait until tomorrow. I don't want to talk to him, and I'm not sure I can restrict my commentary to his chosen subject."

"I'm there," Sonsee said with resignation. "And just about the time I decide to drive to Little Rock and let him have it, God gets me by the lapel and gives me a good shake. I'm trying to forgive the man, but sometimes I have a serious relapse, especially when I start thinking about Brooke."

"I know how you feel. I think Marilyn's doing better than even I am in that department."

"So what do you think about her? I want to call Melissa back."

"Tell Melissa not to take it personally. I just think Marilyn's stressed out to the breaking point. She told me her mother and father have hinted that they'd like to see her and Josh together. Joshua, I think, has probably made a pass or two himself. I caught them in the kitchen—"

"Details! Details!"

Kim Lan held up her hand. "I wish I *had* the details."

"Do you think he kissed her?"

"Are you kidding, Honey? Marilyn would probably call the police. I'm telling you, Sonsee, she's got a bad case of 'touch me nots' where he's concerned."

"Well, I've been praying for her."

"Keep it up. I think this whole thing with a single, attractive minister living across the street from Marilyn seems a little bit too 'convenient.' I'm not certain that God isn't at work here."

"So do you think Marilyn's fighting God's will on this?"

A tendril of tension slithered through Kim Lan as she recalled her own struggles with whether or not to pose for the upcoming swimsuit issue. Why was she even commenting on Marilyn's battle, when she had a royal conflict of her own underway. "I don't think I should say, but it just seems suspicious to me. After all, she did at one time firmly believe the Lord had called her to be a pastor's wife."

"Hmm. You've added a new dimension to the whole picture. I think anyone struggling with God is going to be miserable."

Kim's own misery seemed to well up with her friend's words.

"Thanks," Sonsee said. "This call has helped tremendously. I'm going to give Melissa a ring and hopefully help make her feel better."

"I'd bet my last box of eclairs that Marilyn calls Melissa no later than tomorrow night to apologize."

"I hope. I hate it when any of the sisters are crossing swords."

"Me, too. But, hey, our friendships are stronger than any conflict. They'll work it out. I have the utmost faith in both of them."

"Thanks, Kim Lan. And keep me updated on what happens with Gregory."

"Oh, I will. I'll call you right after I call him."

Kim hung up the phone and thoughtfully chewed her lip. Should she call Gregory tonight or wait until tomorrow, as she had told Sonsee? She glanced at the nearby clock and decided to wait until tomorrow. She didn't need any dark circles under her eyes in the morning. A before-bed chat with Gregory would undoubtedly leave her in the throws of insomnia. Tomorrow. She would call him tomorrow.

Languidly, she dialed another number from memory—Ted's number. She would arrange for him to meet her after the shampoo shoot.

❧

Clark McClure stood outside the office window he had unlocked only hours before. Glancing over his shoulder, he peered through the inky, moonless night to make certain no one watched. The small church sat on the edge of town on Highway 62, and this particular window faced a wooded pasture that spanned the base of an Ozark mountain. Midnight's damp smells, chirping crickets, and the shriek of an occasional screech owl all swirled together as the perfect atmosphere for such a devious deed. In one fell swoop, Leopard raised the aluminum window, lifted himself into the office, and deftly lowered the glass pane. Briefly pulling the blinds away from the window, he cast a last glance across the empty pasture to reconfirm a lack of witnesses. Fortunately, the dense cloud cover blocked the moon and stars' golden glows. Perhaps fate was smiling on him.

As usual, he had driven within walking distance of his destination, parked the rental car, and trudged the remaining span. He had toyed with the idea of just driving into the church parking lot, but dashed it aside. Even in his old man disguise, Leopard was taking no chances at being caught or traced to this location at this hour. Wasting little time, he double-checked to make certain the blinds were snugly closed, clicked on his penlight, and walked toward the bookcase. Tonight, he had chosen to wear worn jeans and a long-sleeved shirt. The stinking "old man" clothes had seemed too bulky for crawling through windows. Furthermore, Clark was tired of the odor. Instead of the bedraggled cotton gloves, Clark had chosen a pair of thin, leather gloves that snugly fit his hands and would prevent any fingerprints. Like an accomplished jewel thief, he retrieved the record book from the shelf and paused.

All evening he had deliberated whether to copy the addresses at the church or use the hotel's office room. Neither option seemed flawless. The longer he stayed at the church, the greater the risk of being caught. But using the hotel copy machine increased his risk of someone in this small town growing suspicious of his copying from a church record book. Furthermore, making copies at the hotel's office room also meant removing the book from the premises. At last, Clark decided to use the copy machine he had spied in the adjoining workroom.

Silently he moved toward the door that opened into the next room. Within seconds, he turned the knob, slipped into the cluttered quarters, and flicked the penlight's narrow beam across the room. The aging copy machine sat on a decrepit wooden table. On the opposite wall, a longer table held various office paraphernalia, including paper. With the musty smells of office supplies engulfing him, Leopard switched on the machine, checked the paper drawer, and began his task.

Within half an hour, he had finished the job. Every name and address in that church record book now belonged to him. He could contact each of them, provide the degrading information about their pastor, and destroy the Panther's reputation before he destroyed the man. Sneering, Leopard grabbed a fist full of paper from the table behind him and settled the sheets in the deplenished tray. He wanted to leave everything exactly as he found it.

Joshua steered his trusty truck into the dark churchyard. After two hours of insomnia, he had decided to get up, don his "pastoral" gym shorts and T-shirt, and pay a visit to his computer. Before he came to Eureka Springs, he hadn't been able to afford a computer for his personal use, but the church had dutifully insisted upon buying a new one for his office. Joshua hadn't even attempted a token protest. Instead, he had smiled like a kid on Christmas morning and readily accepted their offer before they changed their minds. Still in the throes of learning about his new office companion, the sleepless Joshua decided to pay yet another midnight visit to better acquaint himself. This was the third such visit in recent weeks. He was learning that anything was better than lying in bed thinking of Marilyn, thinking of the futility of his growing feelings for her, and thinking of the torment of living across the street from her, being eternally kept at arm's length. How would his congregation picture him, if they discovered his thoughts were turning more and more toward his attractive neighbor?

With a dry chuckle, Joshua stepped from the truck. He figured most of the congregation would be glad if he and

Marilyn became an item, especially Marilyn's folks. Several times in recent weeks, numerous members had teasingly hinted about their need of a pastor's wife. Once or twice a single niece or third cousin twice removed had arrived as a "special guest we would like you to meet." Josh had taken it all in stride until he met Marilyn.

Shoving images of her from his mind, Josh unlocked the church's main entrance and stepped into the foyer. With the familiar smells of church hymnals and fresh flowers enveloping him, Josh paused to relock the door. No sense in taking any chances. Forcing himself to focus on the task at hand, he meandered up the church hall, opened his office door, and clicked on the light.

∞

Leopard reached down to gather the photocopies as the office door opened and closed. Next the light clicked on. Leopard stilled. His mind reeled. His gut clenched. Swiftly he moved into action. He removed the penlight from between his teeth and switched it off. Swiveling, he crouched and noiselessly slithered under the worktable that bore the extra copy paper and other supplies.

Who could be at the church at such a late hour? Was it Joshua or another intruder? Leopard peered from his hiding spot and noticed he had failed to turn off the copy machine. Biting back a groan, he deposited the record book and copies on the indoor/outdoor carpet. Instinctively, he touched his thigh to feel the imprint of the switchblade beneath his jeans.

The person in the other room took several steps and stopped. The chair behind the desk squeaked and the sound of the computer booting up soon followed.

Joshua. The person has to be Joshua. Leopard shifted from a squat to resting on his knees. Although his position still cramped him, he managed to reach through the hole in his right pocket and gently extract the switchblade from its leather holder. He pushed the appropriate button, and the blade sprang to life with a faint swish of metal against metal.

He could kill Joshua now, and no one would suspect him. This was the perfect setup; the best opportunity for the consummate revenge. Why wait?

The door to the supply room eased open with a faint sigh. Joshua, glancing around the room as if he sensed a presence, stepped toward the running copy machine. Curiously he looked across the shadowed room then shrugged. "Kids," he muttered to no one then turned off the machine.

Leopard's leg muscles twitched with the adrenaline flowing from his dark soul. He should complete his revenge now... now...now. The word echoed through his mind like a primeval chant.

As Panther turned toward his office, Leopard crept from his hiding place. In two short lunges, he could be close enough to slit Reverend Langham's throat from behind before the man comprehended what struck him.

But is that what you want? a sinister voice whispered from the dank caverns in his mind. *Even if he sees your face before he dies, you are an old man to him, not Leopard. He will most likely never understand who killed him. And you will not have the pleasure of destroying everything he's built.*

A simple death would not appease Leopard's perverted need for the consummate revenge pounding through his veins.

Josh stepped into the office and closed the door behind him. The perfect moment had ended. Leopard's leg muscles stopped their twitching, his pulse decreased, and his breathing evened to a normal rate. Silently he hunched back under the table and tarried. He reminded himself that Panther's house keys remained in the hotel room. On any given night, he could waltz through the door of Joshua's cottage and end his life. He had waited fifteen long years to complete his revenge. He would savor the process to the fullest.

Seventeen

The next afternoon, Marilyn sat in the living room, wearily rocking Brooke. The last twelve hours had been nothing short of miserable. Brooke started vomiting at one in the morning and had continued off and on until an hour ago. This morning the pediatrician had said Brooke probably ate something at the family reunion that gave her food poisoning. The good doctor prescribed the appropriate medication, which had reduced Brooke's misery and stopped the vomiting by noon. Although Marilyn had been able to grab a shower and a change of clothing that morning, she hadn't bothered with hair or makeup. She didn't care what she looked like or even who she saw. She only wanted some sleep.

With a pathetic whimper, Brooke stirred and Marilyn lovingly stroked her back. "It's okay, Honey. Mom's right here."

"I want Daddy," Brooke whined.

"Ssshhh," Marilyn soothed, the very thought of Greg leaving her all the more weary.

During the wee hours of the morning, between Brooke's bouts in the bathroom, Marilyn had lain awake and pleaded with God to somehow complete her forgiveness of the man she had once completely trusted. Although the forgiveness journey had started the day she opened the family albums, she still struggled with seasons of wanting to do something markedly nasty to Gregory.

190

But last night, with the Arkansas stars softly twinkling against the velvet sky, Marilyn had seen a new glimpse of the real Greg. A man who had destroyed, not only her life, but his own life, too. She wondered, even now in the light of day, how long he would live before seeing he had made a horrible mistake. Before seeing that his sin had damaged his own child. Before seeing that a man couldn't just walk away from his family without his conscience one day catching up with him. These new thoughts had ushered in an astounding pity for Gregory Thatcher. Truly he had blindly discarded treasures from God.

"I want Joss..." Brooke said drowsily.

Marilyn tried not to let her mind roam in *that* direction. The idea of Joshua Langham coming into her home brought feelings of unwelcomed warmth. But she needed help from somebody—even if it was Joshua. Her sleep deprivation had finally affected her logic. Marilyn feared that if she didn't get rest soon she might well do something incorrectly, such as giving Brooke the wrong medicine or the wrong dosage. She gazed toward Joshua's quaint cottage, much like her own, and pondered the option of calling him. His truck sat in the driveway so he was home, but he might well be busy with church-related work. As much as she wanted to avoid Joshua, any help at this moment was welcome.

On the other hand, her mom had offered to come over that morning when Marilyn had phoned with the news of Brooke's illness. At the time, Marilyn had been handling the situation and sensed that Brooke wanted and needed her own mother. Fortunately, Marilyn's boss, Ginger Lovelady, was also a mother and insisted Marilyn stay with the ailing Brooke. Now that Brooke seemed to be calming down, Marilyn's stamina was spent. She hated to call her mother because she felt she depended on her mom too much as things stood. At last she decided she had no other choice.

The phone rang. Clutching Brooke, Marilyn staggered toward the cordless receiver, retrieved it, and plopped onto the striped sofa. Most likely, this would be her mother. With resignation, Marilyn pressed the answer button and resolved to go ahead and ask her to come over.

The voice that greeted her was not that of her mother. A concerned, masculine voice caressed her exhausted mind. "Marilyn, is everything okay?" Josh asked. "I noticed you didn't go to work this morning, and I was afraid maybe you were sick or something. I didn't call earlier because I didn't want to seem like a nosy neighbor, but I finally decided to see if you needed help."

Marilyn, fatigued beyond words, blinked against stinging eyes. The kind note in Josh's voice was exactly what she didn't need at the moment. That sort of sympathetic concern could very well drive her off the cliff of emotional stability.

"Marilyn? Is everything okay?"

"Brooke has been vomiting. I was up with her all night, and I haven't slept."

"I'll be right over." The line went dead.

Marilyn rested her head against the back of the couch, relieved. She should probably be aggravated over Josh's assumption that he had the right to just pop over whenever he chose. He had come and gone all weekend as if it were the natural thing to do. However, Marilyn dismissed any notion that suggested Josh wasn't welcome. She desperately needed help.

· Josh tapped lightly on the front door.

"It's open," Marilyn called seconds before Josh stepped into the room.

Brooke raised her head and extended her arms.

"Hi, Ladybug." He tenderly lifted her into his embrace. "What's the matter?"

"I throwed up," Brooke said against his neck.

"Go on, Marilyn," Josh whispered, waving toward the hallway. "You look beat. Get some sleep. I'll take it from here."

"Don't you have church stuff to do?"

"Mondays are my days off."

How well Marilyn remembered Mondays in the parsonage. Monday had been the down day, the day of repose and rejuvenation. Joshua appeared rested, relaxed, and ready to help. Marilyn decided to forget all the reasons why she shouldn't allow this alluring gentleman to further entrench himself into her home life. Groggily, she stood and walked toward her bedroom, only stopping long enough to give him instructions for Brooke's prescriptions.

"Don't let me sleep too long," she called over her shoulder as she trudged toward her room.

"I won't," he said, settling into the rocking chair.

Marilyn collapsed onto her unmade brass bed and kicked her loafers off the edge. As she wrapped herself in the comforter, a cloak of anxiety enfolded her mind. Melissa. Of all the seven sisters, *Melissa Moore* was undoubtedly the one most like an interrogator—albeit a caring one. Kim Lan was a tease. Sonsee was pleasantly nosy in an amiable sort of way. Sammie Jones masked her inquisitive nature with southern charm that normally got her questions answered anyway. Victoria Roberts usually figured if somebody wanted to tell her something she would. Otherwise, Victoria left the subject alone. And Jac, pragmatic private detective that she was, saw precious little worth in investigating her friend's personal lives when she needed to be focusing on her current case. However, when the group was together, all the sisters usually joined in the banter and laughter if one of them started the questions.

Marilyn had dealt with almost all the sisterly inquiries she could handle. She had spent a tiring weekend fending off Kim Lan's teasing, an afternoon dealing with a combination of her mother and Carla's insinuations, and parrying Joshua's overtures. When Melissa began her questions, Marilyn had broken with the pressure of yet another person trying to push her toward Joshua Langham. She had snapped at one of her dearest friends, then hung up on her. As sleep nibbled the corners of her mind, a wave of shame washed over her. When she awoke, she would call Melissa and beg her forgiveness. The woman didn't deserve the treatment Marilyn had dealt her. *Dear God,* she prayed as the haze of sleep descended upon her, *please forgive me, and help Melissa forgive me.*

Kim Lan stared at her reflection in the lighted mirror. The heavy application of makeup hid the dark circles under her almond shaped eyes. The shampoo advertisement had taken longer than she thought. And now she sat in the cluttered studio dressing room, her head pounding, wondering why she was even here. The glamour lifestyle certainly held its share of grinding work.

Everyone applauded her advertisement performance, including the aging president of the shampoo company, who had offered Kim Lan a ride in his limousine and a night on the town. He'd said that the advertisement would undoubtedly sell at least a million bottles of his product. Kim had assured him she wouldn't have agreed to the shooting if she didn't believe his shampoo superior to many on the market. Then she kindly turned down his offer of a night or two in his company. Even if Ted Curry weren't in her life, the "shampoo king" had a wife and two teenage daughters at home. Kim Lan was not in the business of breaking up families. Period.

With a sigh, she rubbed her aching feet, removed the bathrobe she had used in the shoot, and donned the casual suit she had worn that morning. Fortunately, she had tomorrow off.

A knock at the door preceded Kim Lan's exit by only seconds. Her agent stood on the other side, holding a dozen roses, grinning from ear to ear.

"Hi, Charlie," she said through a stifled yawn.

"You were great, Baby, just great!" Charlie was a short, red-headed "fireball of an agent," who looked like an aging Mickey Rooney. He extended the flowers to Kim Lan, and she buried her nose in the fragrant softness.

"Thanks. You spoil me."

"Honey, as much dough as you rake in for me, I can't spoil you enough. Thought any more about that swimsuit issue? They're still waiting for your final confirmation."

Kim Lan turned for her leather handbag and wrinkled her brow as a tense lump developed in the pit of her stomach. "I still haven't decided."

"How can you not decide?" Charlie insisted, following her into a hallway, covered with a rich burgundy carpet.

Kim Lan began the short trek to the front door of the studio and wished Charlie would just stop it with the swimsuit issue questions. Couldn't the man see she needed time on this one?

"They're offering more money than you've ever made on a shoot yet. You could swear off work for a year."

"Yes, and so could you," she said with a bit more venom than intended. A quick glance toward Charlie's aggravated demeanor said he felt the venom full force. "I'm sorry." She placed a hand on his shoulder. "You're in this business to make money. Your concern is understandable. I know I've delayed my decision, and it's down to the wire. But there's more going on with me right now than just the money."

"Well, whoever he is, you'd better tell him to lighten up." The gleam in his sharp green eyes said Charlie figured Ted was behind her hesitation. Kim Lan bit back a grin. Ted thought Kim exposing most of her lithe body to the world was nothing but a bonus for him. He gloated in dating the most glamorous woman in New York.

"The way things stand, Kim Lan," Charlie continued, "if you hedge too much, they'll ask someone else to be the lead model. Competition is tough. There are women lined up at Forman's who'd give their eyeteeth to have this opportunity."

"I know, Charlie, I know," she said, allowing the doorman to open the glass doors for her exit. She scanned the portico and spotted the ebony Town Car and driver waiting nearby.

Charlie rolled his eyes. "They're counting on the tentative agreement we reached months ago. They fully expect you to—"

"I can't help what they fully expect," Kim Lan said abruptly. At once she sympathized with Marilyn. This must be exactly what her dear friend was feeling—being pushed from all sides to develop a relationship with Joshua. And Kim Lan had participated in a great deal of teasing over the past weekend. She saw for the first time that she owed Marilyn a grave apology. No wonder she'd snapped at Melissa.

"I see, so we're playing hard to get," he said, narrowing his eyes. "They've already offered you top dollar, Kim Lan, I can't see that they will increase—"

"I'm not stalling for more money," she said firmly. "And I'm sorry for being so snappy, but I just don't want to discuss this any further today."

She glanced to her left and watched as the black car approached and stopped. Despite the fact that Charlie's flushed cheeks and compressed lips suggested he thought he was losing the battle over the swimsuit issue, his words seemed to seduce Kim Lan like the mesmerizing eyes of a deadly viper. *They're offering more money than you've ever made on a shoot yet. You could swear off work for a year....If you hedge too much, they'll ask someone else to be the lead model. Competition is tough. There are women lined up in every agency who'd give their eyeteeth to have this opportunity.*

Kim stepped toward the car. "Don't worry, Charlie," she called, not certain what prompted her consoling remarks. "I'll give you my decision soon."

The doorman tumbled all over himself to make certain Kim Lan was comfortably seated. The soft leather seat ensconced her, and she relished the feelings of luxury. It was nice, but nothing quite beat her Jag. She would have preferred to drive it around town, but the traffic was beyond hideous and finding a parking place was a nightmare.

As the driver pulled into the Manhattan traffic, she breathed a prayer of relief that they were avoiding rush hour.

Relaxing, Kim Lan closed her eyes and inhaled the smell of supple leather. Immediately she recalled a saxophonist's rendition of "Have Thine Own Way, Lord" that had filled the senses of her soul that morning while she dressed. At five in the morning the tune had soothed her and helped her set her focus on the Lord. But in the wake of Charlie's blatant pushes toward that swimsuit issue and her own wavering, the very song that had soothed her earlier now rubbed against the grain of her humanness.

Abruptly she turned her mind to the upcoming encounter with Ted Curry. He had agreed to meet her at the apartment lobby at three. She glanced at her Rolex, which proclaimed she was already thirty minutes late.

Within half an hour she entered the exclusive apartment building on Park Avenue. The foyer looked more like that of a luxury hotel than a place of permanent residence. The marble floors, elegant front desk, and strategically placed pillars reflected the elegance of Kim Lan's penthouse. With the brass and glass furnishings, gourmet restaurant, indoor pool, exquisite art, exercise room, maid service, room service, and huge hostess suites available for entertaining, the rich and famous residents usually didn't mind the exorbitant cost.

"Miss Lowery," the doorman said, nodding with respect as she passed him, "Mr. Curry awaits you."

Kim Lan glanced across the foyer to see Ted—tanned, handsome, self-assured—slumped into one of the overstuffed, leather settees, watching her from across the room. With the sensual smile ever in place, he twirled a pair of silver-framed sunglasses by the ear piece.

As usual, Kim Lan's pulse jumped. Whatever "it" was, the man had it. All of America agreed. For the most part, so did Kim Lan. Fleeting thoughts of Joshua Langham's genuine nature drowned in the face of Ted's blatant good looks. The two of them did make a grand couple. Wherever they went, heads turned in appreciation. With a flirting grin, she wiggled her fingers at him. He had called again that morning before she had left for the advertisement shoot. But the fire in Ted's eyes suggested they hadn't spoken in weeks. In seconds he was at her side, his arm possessively around her waist.

"Hey, Babe!" he said softly. "Missed you."

"Missed you, too," she said, immersed in the effects of shocking blue eyes contrasted with a dark complexion. As a young girl, she dreamed of one day having a husband who looked much like Ted. If Kim Lan were honest with herself, she would have to admit she had never grown past feeling as if she were that impoverished, dowdy child of mixed heritage. Could all this fame, wealth, and even Ted Curry truly be hers?

The two of them turned toward the elevators, surrounded by marble.

"Excuse me, Miss Lowery!" the receptionist called from behind the front desk.

"Yes, Millie?" Kim Lan moved from the warmth of Ted's hold and gracefully walked toward the desk.

"You have a message from…from a…" She studied her notepad. "From a Gregory Thatcher. He said he had tried to call you several times at your apartment and wasn't having luck touching base. He wanted me to ask you to call at your convenience."

Kim Lan frowned. *At my convenience?* The man proved just as persistent as he always had been and clearly disregarded her convenience. "Okay, thanks." She turned around and bumped into Ted. "Oops, sorry," she said as he steadied her. "I didn't know you'd followed me."

"I guess it's a good thing I did," he said, a teasing nuance to his troubled words. "Is there something you should tell me? Who's this Greg guy?"

A deeper look into Ted's eyes revealed a dark cloud of apprehension that the teasing glimmer couldn't quite mask.

Could it be that Ted Curry, American heartthrob, was actually a bit unsure of himself?

"He's just my friend Marilyn's ex-husband. She's the one I was visiting this weekend." Grabbing his hand, Kim rushed toward the opening elevator. "He left a message on my machine last night, and I didn't call him. I planned to call him tonight. He's probably left a couple of more messages on my machine today. The man never gives up."

"What could he want?" Ted asked, as the elevator rose to the top floor.

Kim Lan smiled. "I have no idea. But he's married again and can't stand me, if that makes you feel any better." She raised her eyebrows. "I briefly saw him this weekend at Marilyn's."

The dark clouds in Ted's demeanor dissipated, and he gently toyed with her waist-length hair. "I can't imagine a man not being able to stand you."

She peered at Ted and wondered exactly how deep his feelings ran for her. The two of them had only been an item about a month, and she had wondered from the start how long it would last. Due to the fact that any woman in New York or Los Angeles would throw herself into the man's arms, Kim had been skeptical that he could actually fall in love with her. But today, standing in this elevator, she began to suspect that perhaps Ted Curry was smitten a little more than the tabloids wanted to admit. They hadn't been seeing each other long enough to be fully in love, but...

A giddy feeling fluttered through her as she fancied the possibilities of marrying Ted. It would be a fairy tale come true.

But is this God's will for you? The thought came to her unbidden.

He says he's a Christian, she argued.

Shallow at best.

He's a knockout, she parried.

He's egocentric.

He thinks I'm great, she thought defensively.

But he loves himself more.

Only yesterday, she had decided Marilyn was crazy for giving Joshua the cold shoulder. Yet in the face of Ted's good looks, Joshua's attributes seemed to blur.

Could there be a "Joshua" for me?

She dismissed her disturbing thoughts. "Joshuas" didn't run in the circles she now frequented. And who else had looks like Ted Curry?

Kim opened the door of her penthouse to the sound of the telephone ringing. "I'd bet my last box of eclairs that's Gregory now."

"Want me to get it?"

"Sure." Kim Lan kicked off her Italian sandals and left them askew on the white carpet. She padded into the ornate kitchen that was more a showplace than a room of culinary endeavor. As she opened the refrigerator and retrieved a couple of colas, she suspected Ted would prefer something a little stronger, but she never touched the stuff.

He appeared in the doorway, his hand over the mouthpiece of the cordless phone. "One Gregory Thatcher, as you suspected."

"You didn't interrogate him or anything, did you?" she asked in jest.

"He'd better be your friend's ex-husband. And he'd better not like you," he playfully growled against her ear.

Kim handed Ted his cola and swallowed a giggle.

"Hello," she said.

"Kim Lan, Gregory here."

"Hi, Gregory," she said in guarded tones.

"I don't think there's any reason for either of us to waste time on pleasantries, so I'm just going to get to the reason I called."

"Please do," she said stiffly, following Ted into her expansive living room.

Ted's eyes widened inquisitively as he settled onto the black leather sofa and pulled Kim Lan down next to him.

"What's going on with Marilyn and that man across the street?" Gregory demanded.

"Why?" Kim Lan asked, stalling for time. What business was it of Gregory's who Marilyn chose as friends?

"Because Brooke is my daughter, and I have a right to find out if she's going to have a stepfather."

"You should have thought about that before you left them."

Aggravated, Kim Lan rose, walked toward the oversized picture window, and squinted against the early evening sun blazing upon the congested traffic.

"At this point, I think you've pretty much given up all rights to the choice of whether or not Brooke has a stepfather." Kim Lan did little to hide her irritation. "You certainly gave Marilyn little choice in Brooke's having a stepmother."

"Listen, I didn't call to get a condescending lecture on my choices, especially not from a woman who's involved with the likes of Ted Curry."

"You've looked at one too many tabloids," Kim Lan said with calm assurance. "I'm a woman of strong biblical standards. Ted and I aren't married, so we aren't—"

"Forget that," he snapped. "I didn't call for the lowdown on your love life or the lack thereof. I called to—"

"What's the matter, Gregory?" she asked pointedly. "Are you having second thoughts now?"

With a decided click, he ended the call. Kim Lan, smiling in satisfaction, placed the receiver back into its cradle.

Eighteen

◡

"Marilyn...Marilyn..."

The annoying voice seemed to come from a distant land.

"Marilyn, it's time to wake up."

The voice is masculine. Definitely masculine. And considerate.

"Marilyn, your parents are here with supper."

Greg? No...not Greg. He's gone. He isn't that tender, either.

"Hey, Goldilocks, wake up!"

The firm shake jolted Marilyn into the realm of reality.

Joshua's indulgent smile immediately greeted her. "Are you going to sleep your life away?"

"What time is it?"

"Six."

"Six?" Marilyn sat straight up. "Where's Brooke? How is Brooke? I can't believe I slept so long."

"Brooke's fine. She dozed off and on all afternoon, but she's in the kitchen now with your mother, chattering like a magpie."

"How do they do it?" Marilyn asked through a yawn.

"Who? What?"

"Kids. How do they swing from being sick as a dog to full-blown energy in a matter of hours?"

"Beats me," he said, shrugging. "You're the parent, here, not me."

Marilyn rubbed her eyes and stood. Certainly, she felt less than fresh, but she wasn't the zombie she had been when she first went to sleep.

"I'm going to reclaim my post in the kitchen," Josh said. "Your mother has me setting the table and your father putting ice in the glasses. She's quite a slave driver when it comes to pulling a meal together."

"Are you staying for dinner?"

"Of course." He raised his brows. "I've earned a free meal, wouldn't you say?"

"You're shameless," she said through a drowsy chuckle.

"It's the only way to be when you're a bachelor and hungry," he said as he walked toward the door.

Despite every ounce of better judgment, Marilyn liked Joshua Langham immensely. He was just the kind of man she would have married, if only...

Marilyn Douglas Thatcher, you are not going to get married again. Ever. Stop it! Stop it! Stop it!

A look in her dresser mirror dashed aside all thoughts of Joshua and instigated a muffled groan. She looked awful: haggard, unkempt, with dark circles under her eyes.

Upon the heels of her verbal distress, Joshua appeared in the doorway and gave her a questioning glance. Immediately the source of her discontent registered on his countenance.

"You look just fine to me," he said.

Before Marilyn understood his intent, Joshua stepped back into the room, bestowed a spontaneous kiss on her forehead, and hurried out the door.

Breathless, speechless, thoughtless, Marilyn stared at the empty doorway. A slow cascade of tingles began a delicious trail from her forehead, across her cheeks, down her spine.

Her face heated. Her palms moistened. Her mind spun as if she were on a roller coaster. Marilyn collapsed onto the bed.

Joshua stood at the kitchen table, positioning the last plate in its place. Broodingly, he stared toward the tiny dining-room window surrounded by cheerful, sunflower curtains that turned the ordinary room into a realm improved by a woman's touch. The curtains blurred in a spiral of yellow, blue, and taupe, and the merry sunflowers were lost on Josh.

Why in the name of common sense did I kiss Marilyn? What possessed me?

Perhaps it was the endearing moment of watching her awaken. Or the teasing manner in which she told him he was shameless. Or her doe-brown eyes, bemused from sleep.

Whatever had prompted the violation of Marilyn's invisible boundaries, Joshua had gone too far. He should have never, *never* kissed Marilyn. Yesterday, he had taken her into his arms. Today, he had kissed her. All weekend, Joshua had been over for one reason or another. Given her honest admission of being afraid of a relationship, Joshua had most likely pushed her past the point of no return.

Within seconds, his suspicions were confirmed beyond doubt. Marilyn entered the dining room and shot him an indignant glare. Mrs. Douglas walked in at that moment, the proud bearer of a scrumptious-looking casserole. Marilyn's father, on her heels, carried a salad and a basket of rolls. Joshua assumed that only their presence stopped Marilyn from telling him he could kindly take himself *and* his empty stomach home.

The tension that settled around dinner heightened with each second that ticked by. Nothing seemed to assuage the constricted atmosphere. Not Brooke's simple laugh as she enjoyed the chicken soup Grandma had made especially for her. Not Mrs. Douglas' attempts at cheer. Not Mr. Douglas' questions about Joshua's new computer. Not Marilyn's feigned politeness.

"Would you care for some more cheesecake, Pastor?" Mrs. Douglas asked, a questioning gleam in her eyes that went far beyond her inquiry about dessert. All during the meal, she had watched her daughter and the attractive pastor with a combination of concern and curiosity.

"No thank you," Joshua said, shooting Marilyn a wary glance. "I think I've probably outstayed my welcome. I need to head on home, anyway. I've got things to do."

"Don't go, Joss," Brooke whined, her limpid brown eyes the replicas of her mother's. "I want to play some more."

"Josh has been here all afternoon. You've worn him out, I'm sure," Marilyn said without emotion.

Fred Douglas turned keen eyes toward his daughter then darted a glance at Joshua as well. His brows raised a questioning fraction, as if to ask Joshua exactly what was wrong with his usually cheerful daughter. Joshua produced an almost nonexistent shrug and stood.

"I'll see you out. We can use the back door," Marilyn said ominously, as if she were going to her own assassination—or his.

Joshua, who had severely castigated himself for his rash action, recognized that Marilyn was preparing her own verbal confrontation. As he followed her out and shut the door behind them, a root of ire sprouted within. He had spent the whole afternoon helping Marilyn with Brooke, and she was apparently beyond angry over one tiny slip on his part.

She turned to face him, her flashing eyes, reddened cheeks, and flared nostrils clearly expressing her rage. "Don't you ever kiss me again!" she said through gritted teeth.

"At least give me a chance to apologize before you explode all over me, Marilyn," Joshua said defensively. "I'm sorry. I shouldn't have. I didn't plan to. It just happened. It wasn't my intent to—"

"I'll tell you what your intents are," she said, pointing a finger at his nose. "You started out this weekend by inviting yourself over for dinner Friday night. Then you tried to make a pass at me in the kitchen. Then Saturday—"

"What about Saturday? What did I do wrong then?"

"I'm not sure, but you were around, that's for sure. And yesterday, before I knew it, you were hugging me. And today you *kissed* me!" her voice broke on a high note.

"And you didn't like it?"

"That's beside the point."

"The point is, you liked it too much." He stepped toward her. "That's what's got you all in a huff! You want me around to help out with Brooke because she loves me, but you say you don't want me so much as touching you, even though your heart says the opposite." Joshua took another step forward.

She stumbled backward. "Don't you come near me!"

"Why not?" Some perverse voice within prompted him to step even closer.

She moved back.

He continued to walk forward until she bumped into the house.

Heaven help him, she was beautiful. Not in the way Kim Lan Lowery was, but in a fresh, wholesome, natural way. Marilyn's beauty was exactly the kind Joshua would like to look at the rest of his life. He envisioned them working together, serving the Lord as one, drawing closer as the years progressed. Yes, he could love Marilyn Douglas Thatcher. If he were given a few months to enrich their acquaintance, he could love her with his whole heart.

If only she would let him.

The fury that had once sparked from her eyes slowly dissipated as Joshua did little to hide his blatant adoration. New emotions seemed to flow from her soul—admiration, respect, longing.

"Leave me alone, Joshua," she said weakly. "I can't...I won't...I'm not ready."

"And how much have you prayed about this?" He asked, gently stroking her cheek. "About us?"

"I..."

"Have you prayed about it at all, Marilyn?"

"I..." She licked her lips, and Joshua longed to taste their sweetness.

"Well, I'll tell you I *have* prayed about us. I've prayed a lot lately."

As she continued to helplessly stare into his eyes, the only sounds were a dove gently cooing and the crickets forever chirping. Fiercely, Joshua's pulse hammered.

"I think you're the answer to my prayers. I also think you're fighting God on this one, Marilyn."

"Go home and leave me alone," she said, a weak spark of anger back in her eyes.

"I'll go," Josh said evenly, "but there's one thing I'm going to leave you to think about."

She pressed her lips together in stubborn assent to his request. "What?"

"I'm going to kiss you. And I'm going to kiss you right."

The obstinance cloaking her features slowly melted into expectant despair.

Joshua began lowering his head to hers.

She looked at his mouth.

"Push me away, Marilyn," he muttered.

She didn't move.

He paused mere centimeters from her lips, so close their breath mingled as one.

"You can stop me now. Stop me."

As much as Josh wanted to feel her in his arms, he would give her time to step away. He would control himself. He would rely on God for the strength that had sustained him these past fifteen years. He hadn't kissed but one other woman in over a decade. He would not blow his vow of self-control. Nonetheless, he desperately hoped Marilyn would not reject him. How many nights had he dreamed of sharing their first kiss?

As the breathless seconds ticked on, Joshua sensed that she, too, had contemplated this moment, regardless of her continued verbal denial. The realization came only seconds before she tilted her chin upward and closed the distance between them with surprising force.

Joshua had expected fireworks, but he had never anticipated the way Marilyn clung to him, the longing with which she responded, the embrace of two people destined to be together. As the kiss lengthened, alarm bells began to sound within his mind. He was enjoying this far too much. He needed to back away.

Breaking the kiss took every ounce of willpower he could muster, but Joshua distanced himself from Marilyn. Awkwardly, he slackened their embrace and put several inches between them. Her uneven breathing and her hazy eyes attested that Marilyn was just as affected as he. Joshua backed away even more.

No more kissing. Enough for now. Maybe enough until we—if we—get married.

Joshua didn't want to do anything to weaken his resolve to remain celibate until marriage. As a man of God, he would take no risks.

"Now," he said softly, "I will only come back if you ask."

Trying to regain her equilibrium, Marilyn helplessly stared up into Joshua's eyes. *Wow!* How had her fury over a simple peck on the forehead led into an earth-moving kiss? A kiss she had done nothing to stop. A kiss she had flagrantly met halfway. A kiss impossible to forget.

In seconds, she relived every encounter she'd had with Joshua since the day she met him. She had suspected they would eventually wind up like this. That was a large part of the reason she had run from him once she discovered he was a pastor.

The back doorknob rattled several times. A lengthy pause. Marilyn purposefully distanced herself from Josh as the door gradually opened. Natalie Douglas, discreetly peering out, extended the phone to Marilyn.

"It's Gregory." Natalie appraised the two with a discerning glimmer in her eyes.

Her face heating, Marilyn took the phone. Obviously her mother perceived exactly what had happened. Marilyn touched her lips and wondered if they were red. What a time to get a call from Greg. What could he want?

"I forgot to tell you," Joshua said, as Natalie retreated into the house. "He called earlier."

"Why didn't you just let the machine get it?" Marilyn snapped.

"I didn't want the ringing to wake you up," he snapped back.

The last thing she needed was Greg to start assuming... but why let his assumptions concern her?

"Hello," she said warily.

"Marilyn, what's going on?" Greg demanded.

"What are you talking about?" she countered, already on the defensive.

"I'm talking about you and that man across the street."

"What business is that of yours?" she asked, her voice rising.

"Listen, I called and he answered earlier today. What was he doing there?"

"Brooke has been sick. He offered to come over to help. That was it!" She raised her hand for added emphasis.

"What's wrong with Brooke?"

"She had a virus. She was throwing up."

"Did she ask for me?"

"She *always* asks for you, Greg. She has asked for you since the day you left!"

"How is she now?"

"As good as new."

"You'd better hope that Joshua Langham doesn't do anything to hurt her," he threatened.

Marilyn gasped in fury. "You've got a lot of gall to say that when your wife has already spanked Brooke when she didn't deserve it."

"How did you find out about that?"

"Brooke told me. Have you forgotten? Four-year-olds tell all."

"I told Sheila never to spank her again," Gregory said, a hint of exasperation in his voice. "Even if Brooke deserves it, Sheila is to divert all disciplinary decisions to me."

"And I'm supposed to believe everything from now on is going to be just hunky dory?" The last thing she ever wanted to do when she gave birth to Brooke was ship her off one weekend a month so another woman could mother her—or simply tolerate her, as the case might be. This setup was in no way what Marilyn would call "having the good life."

"Stop trying to change the subject, Marilyn!"

"Listen—"

"Don't think I don't see what's going on. I've already talked with Kim Lan about your neighbor," Greg said as if he understood more than he was saying.

"You called Kim about Joshua?!" Marilyn's rising wrath tied her midsection into an aching knot and sent a burst of trembling from head to toe.

"I have a right to know if my daughter is going to have a stepfather," he said indignantly.

"No you don't," Marilyn snarled. "How dare you! You— of all people!" A soft voice in the deepest recesses of her soul began whispering peace to Marilyn. A peace that gracefully blew a cool, calming mist upon the fires of her furor. Immediately, she recalled her prayer from last night during all the crisis with Brooke. A prayer in which she'd beseeched God to continue helping her forgive Gregory for leaving her a single parent. A prayer that had somehow enabled her to see him in a new light. And that light revealed just what a miserable, wretched soul he was. In those wee morning hours, shrouded in moments of insight, Marilyn had pitied this man because he had discarded the greatest honor in the world—comforting his own child during an illness. And now this same man was on the phone, demanding an explanation about her relationship with Joshua. She now suspected that his questions about Joshua must be the result of suppressed guilt. New pity engulfed Marilyn. Gregory Thatcher had dug a hole for himself, a hole that might one day swallow him up.

"Marilyn?" he barked. "Are you still there?"

"Yes, I'm here, Gregory," she said with a calm resignation that astounded her.

Silence.

"You made your choices," she said simply. Her trembling gradually decreasing, she marveled that a man who once believed he was called of God, a man who had stood before a whole congregation every Sunday morning, could be reduced to such a life. "Go to your wife. She needs you," Marilyn said like an assertive older sister before disconnecting the call.

"I'm impressed," Joshua said softly.

Joshua! She'd forgotten he was even here. She gazed at him in wide-eyed scrutiny.

"The fruit of the spirit is self-control. Whew! You aced that one, lady!" Joshua congratulated as he crossed his arms.

"Yes—after I thought about crawling through the phone and strangling him." Covering her eyes, Marilyn massaged her temples.

"I feel sorry for him," Joshua said.

Marilyn's head snapped up. Astounded, she saw on Josh's every feature the same insight God had recently bestowed upon her. "Me, too," she said with wonder. "I never thought I'd ever hear myself say that, but I *do* feel sorry for him."

"Maybe his loss will one day be my gain, huh?"

As he reached to stroke her cheek, his words echoed between them.

Nineteen

〜

Marilyn stepped away from Joshua and his pleasurable caress. They did not need to repeat that kiss from earlier, despite Marilyn's traitorous yearnings.

Choosing to study the toes of her worn loafers, Marilyn wondered how she had landed in this situation. She slowly began reflecting over the last couple of months. From the start, she had been wary of developing a relationship with Joshua. Her driving force in that fleeing had been fear. Fear of her own desire to be a loving wife—a desire that didn't go away just because her husband had abandoned his family and his ministry. Fear of trusting a man ever again. Fear of being devastated once more. An annoying Bible verse began a slow tattoo in the back of her mind: *For God has not given us a spirit of fear, but of power and of love and of a sound mind.*

Marilyn remembered Kim Lan's occasional remarks about whether or not she'd prayed about a relationship with Joshua. She also recalled her own determination to avoid the potential relationship, regardless of God's will. For the first time, she began to see that she might very well be running from God. The Lord had called her to ministry. Many people even said He had *gifted* her to be a pastor's wife. Could it be that God was reaffirming that call?

The old panic gripped her in its leprous talons, despite that echoing Bible verse about God giving her "a spirit of power, love, and a sound mind." At this moment, Marilyn felt anything but powerful. She didn't even want to talk about love, especially if it included Joshua Langham. And who could have a sound mind after the stress of *her* day?

"Will you pray about our seeing each other?" Joshua asked softly.

Marilyn nervously toyed with the hem of her oversized T-shirt and tried to avoid eye contact.

"Marilyn?" He gently lifted her chin, and she had little choice but to stare into the velvety gray softness of his eyes. "I'm not trying to pressure you. I'm not asking you to agree to anything—just to pray about it. I believe that God is a God of second chances. Maybe...maybe He's trying to give us both a second chance."

Unable to ignore the regretful note in his voice, Marilyn recalled the day before when Joshua had admitted his former life...the moments when he seemed to be berating himself for his past sins...the feel of his hands on her face as he said he regretted his past now more than ever. Marilyn wanted to tell Joshua that God had forgiven and forgotten his sins and obviously imparted to him the restraint of a moral man possessing high integrity. But somehow the words wouldn't come out. All she could say was, "Okay, I'll pray." Compulsively Marilyn swallowed, wondering if she was making the right decision.

Joshua's eyes danced as if he were a kid on Christmas morning. "Thanks," he said, stroking her cheek. Without another word, he turned and walked around her house toward his own home.

Squinting, Marilyn wondered how the man had managed to get her to agree to pray about seeing him when she had walked outside with the opposite intent. She sighed, sensing even before prayer what God's will was on this issue. From the first time she had met Joshua she perceived that perhaps her moving in across the street from an attractive, single pastor was no coincidence.

Her mind flashed forward into the potential future. She saw herself dressed in a tea-length, cream-colored gown standing near an altar. Joshua, handsome in his black tuxedo, stood next to her. Brooke was close by, a basket of rose petals in hand. The chapel was filled with friends and family. Her parents. Joshua's parents. Her six sisters.

Then she remembered another scene. A balcony at the Crescent Hotel in Eureka Springs. Sunrise. Only Gregory, Marilyn, the minister, and their parents. Gregory Thatcher promising to love, honor, and cherish her. His eyes sincere. His smile that of a man hopelessly smitten.

Her mind switched back to the first scene with Joshua in the candlelit chapel, promising to love, honor, and cherish her. His eyes sincere. His smile that of a man hopelessly smitten.

Marilyn trembled. Her head seemed to roar with an ocean of terror sweeping over her. Her hands grew clammy.

No! An urgent voice yelled from her soul. *No! No! No!*

The phone she was still holding rang, and Marilyn jumped at the sound of its intrusion. Warily, she looked at the cordless receiver, hoping Gregory wasn't on the other end. The second ring seemed to ominously announce another verbal encounter with her ex-husband. Gritting her teeth, Marilyn pushed the answer button and produced a suspicious, "Hello."

"Marilyn? It's me, Melissa," her friend said cautiously.

Immediately, Marilyn remembered her vow to call Melissa and apologize for treating her so rudely the night before.

"Oh, Melissa, I'm so sorry for last night," she blurted before Melissa could say another word. "I was *awful*. I was going to call you tonight. If you were here, I'd get down and kiss your feet and beg your forgiveness. You have no idea what kind of pressure I've been under lately. And then last night Brooke spent most of the night throwing up." Marilyn's voice broke, despite her valiant attempt to maintain composure.

"Oh, Marilyn," Melissa said, her own voice a bit wobbly. "I called to apologize to *you*. I'm just the mouth of the south. I should have never asked you all those pointed questions about...about...I'm not even going to mention his name."

"Please don't," Marilyn said with a humorless chuckle. "It seems like everybody and their brother—including a waitress at a cafe—is trying to push me toward him, and..."

"I understand. Don't say another word. It's just that we've all—all your sisters—have been so burdened for you and I guess we were all just *too thrilled* to hear that an attractive, single male was actually living across the street. Naturally, we assumed—I assumed..."

Marilyn sighed, feeling all the more guilty for her rude actions. "Well, if it's any consolation, and if you can keep a secret, I *did* tell Joshua I'd pray about seeing him."

For once in her life, Melissa Moore was silent. At last she said, "You know I can't keep secrets." The sound of a smile laced her voice. "Why did you have to tell me? Now I'm morally obligated to call everyone—Sonsee, Kim, Sammie, Victoria, and Jac.

"If you do, I will be forced to sew your lips together!" Marilyn threatened.

Melissa howled with laughter.

"I'm not kidding, Melissa! Kim harassed me all weekend. I've about had all I can stand for awhile. The only reason I told you was because I felt sorry...Hey! Wait a minute!" she teased. "Was this just another one of your interrogator tactics to get me to feeling sorry for you and then tell all?"

"Yes!" Melissa said with a new squeal of laughter. "And it worked!"

Marilyn rolled her eyes. "I think you missed your calling. Forget being a doctor. You should have been a member of the KGB, specializing in bright lights and brainwashing."

"I promise. I won't tell a living soul your secret. Scout's honor."

"Why do I think your fingers are crossed?"

"Because they are!"

Thus the sisterly banter continued until Brooke found her way out to her mom, wrapped her arms around Marilyn's leg, and begged to be picked up. Marilyn, noticing the pallor of Brooke's cheeks, recognized that her pint-sized daughter's recuperative energy had vanished. She picked up Brooke, stepped back into the house, and ended the phone call with Melissa. Marilyn's mom and dad, busy in the kitchen, insisted on finishing the cleanup while she tucked Brooke into bed for an early night. The digital clock on Brooke's dresser proclaimed what the evening shadows had already suggested: Eight o'clock was swiftly approaching.

"Mommy, read me a book," Brooke said groggily.

"Okay, Sugar." Marilyn snuggled next to her daughter and retrieved a book from the pile on the floor they'd left the night before. Before Marilyn had read halfway through *The Cat in the Hat,* sleep claimed Brooke.

Closing the book, Marilyn gazed in adoration at Brooke's angelic face. Of all the regrets she had from her marriage, she never regretted giving birth to Brooke. Ironically, the very situation that had brought the most pain into her life had also delivered the most joy. Although her marriage had not been paradise, God had miraculously given her a cherub of her very own. A little girl who bore only trace resemblance to Gregory.

With a sigh, she wondered if Greg would be as attentive once Sheila gave birth. The thought of his pulling away from Brooke brought Marilyn both pain and relief. Pain because Brooke needed her father. Relief because Marilyn wouldn't have to deal with him as much. A constricting vine of guilt entwined her soul.

That thought is nothing short of selfish, she scolded.

Of course she wanted what was best for her child. Since having two at-home parents had been denied Brooke, Marilyn would help her daughter enjoy the times she spent with Greg, regardless of how difficult he could be or how awkward the whole setup.

But Marilyn would soon discover that her encounters with him would go from awkward to volatile.

Twenty

Three nights later, Leopard knelt in the shadows beside the shrubbery. He pushed the light on his digital wrist-watch and noted the time: 9:59. He watched. He waited. He anticipated Joshua's letting that oversized mutt out any minute, just as he had the last three nights. Clark patted the pocket of his dark cotton shirt to once again assure himself he had the keys from Joshua's desk. He also double-checked the switchblade strapped to his thigh. Opening a sealed sandwich bag filled with poisoned hamburger meat, Clark prepared for his dark deed.

First he would kill the Saint Bernard. Then he would visit Panther.

This afternoon, he had prepared the last envelope to mail to Joshua's congregation then packed his bags. In the morning, Clark would board his flight to Los Angeles via Dallas. In Texas, he planned to mail the letters that would begin the destruction of Panther's reputation.

Joshua's front door opened to emit a homey glow that dispelled some of the inky darkness. "Go on, Boy," Joshua said kindly. The cheerful dog ran into the yard, tongue lolling, then turned straight to the bushes where Leopard knelt. The last two nights, Leopard had waited in the bushes for the animal and given him a special treat. Tonight, the treat would be deadly.

"Hey, you stupid mutt," Leopard said pleasantly, "want a bite?" He dumped the hamburger meat on the ground and watched with satisfaction as the dumb animal virtually inhaled the tainted meat. Wagging his tail, the saggy-eyed dog even sniffed Leopard's hands for more.

"No more," Clark said with satisfaction, ignoring the plaintive whine for his attention. The man at the feed store had said that the lime-green gopher poison, nothing more than feed grain coated in strychnine, worked quickly and thoroughly. The fool had thought Clark wanted the stuff for gophers.

"I hate dogs," he said without feeling. "I've always been more of a cat man, myself."

The large canine at last padded away in search of adventure.

Leopard pulled a piece of the nicotine gum from his left pants pocket and began chomping it with vigor. When he had time on his hands, he missed the brown cigars that had once been his constant companion. But any sacrifice was worth the reward of seeing Panther destroyed.

Joshua showered and donned his usual pajama shorts. He ambled into the living room and plopped into his favorite recliner. He'd catch the late news, beckon Blue back into the house, and call it a night. With his legs side by side on the recliner's foot rest, he noticed that the left leg had made substantial progress in regaining its original muscle tone since the cast had come off.

The last few days had been more than hectic for the minister of a growing church, and exhaustion draped around his shoulders like a burden he couldn't shake. As the weatherman droned on about the August heat wave, Joshua propped his head against the back of the recliner. The weather forecast became a foggy backdrop for his mind's drowsy wanderings. He hadn't seen or heard from Marilyn in three days. While Joshua hoped her prayerful consideration would result in positive news, he was finally at rest about the whole situation.

The Lord understood Joshua was long past ready to become a married man. Nonetheless, Josh wanted God's will more than he wanted to get married. He had broken off a relationship four years before...the only relationship he had developed since he had found the Lord. Jennifer Black had seemed exactly right for him. Their names even sounded good together, Jennifer and Joshua. Everyone—his parents, her parents, their friends—all thought they should get married. But the further they progressed in their relationship, the more troubled Joshua became. At last the two had mutually agreed to break up. The classy brunette wept grievously, despite their reciprocal assent to end the acquaintance. In the privacy of his apartment, Joshua had shed a few tears himself. But the longer time rocked on, the more Joshua perceived that Jennifer had not been the woman for him. He had heard through the grapevine that she'd married a year ago. Joshua was truly happy for her.

But here he sat, still a bachelor, still praying for God's will in his matrimonial prospects. Closing his eyes, Josh relaxed against the chair. His limbs felt as if they were weighted with bricks. His mind roamed to the moments he had been forced to admit his dark past to Marilyn. How he wished he could have told her he had saved himself for his wife—for *her*. Marilyn deserved a man who...

His thoughts trailed from his falling away from God's commands to the situation with the FBI that had almost landed him in prison. As he began the mental accusations, which had been his bane the last several years, a disturbing thought broke in on Joshua's mind.

I have forgiven you. As far as I am concerned, you never committed those sins.

Joshua sat straight up as a rush of tingles swelled upon his spine. His eyes stung. His mind whirled with the rare experience of his soul hearing God's voice.

"Oh, Father," Joshua breathed, "how do I get over these regrets? Here I am, encouraging other people to let go of their pasts, and I can't seem to stop accusing myself. I knew I was breaking hearts, Lord, but I didn't realize I was breaking my own heart—and Yours—as well. What was I thinking? And it was only Your grace that kept me out of prison." The problem was, Joshua understood all the verses, all the theology, behind forgiveness, but when it came to himself, it just didn't seem to penetrate his soul. A whirlwind of frustration assaulted him. *How many times have I prayed the same prayer? How many times have I begged God to release me from the guilt? How many times have I hit a brick wall?*

Fresh defeat settled upon him once more. Punching the remote control with more force than necessary, Joshua clicked off the television, then trudged up the hallway and into his spartan room. He switched on the bedside lamp, jerked back the comforter, and plopped into bed. Mercilessly, Joshua whacked the pillows together and propped himself against them. He grabbed his Bible from the nightstand and flipped to Psalm 51, highlighted in red. He had memorized it, but seeing it in print always gave him more comfort. Verses 1-3, 10, 13, and 17 especially lifted his spirit:

Have mercy on me, O God, according to your
unfailing love; according to your great compassion
blot out my transgressions. Wash away all my iniquity
and cleanse me from my sin. For I know my transgressions, and my sin is always before me....Create in
me a pure heart, O God, and renew a steadfast spirit
within me....Then I will teach transgressors your
ways, and sinners will turn back to you....The sacri-
fices of God are a broken spirit; a broken and contrite heart, O God, you will not despise.

These verses always brought encouragement. David, an
adulterer and murderer, had bemoaned his sin just as Joshua
bemoaned his dark choices. He remembered telling Marilyn
only three days ago that God was a God of second chances.
David's life proved that.

*Why can't I embrace God's second chance and shake this
spirit of bondage that torments me?*

As he continued to meditate on the Word, a new awareness sprang upon him. Somewhere between God's forgiveness and deliverance from the past, he was trapped. Trapped
in the corridors of his mind. Somehow, he must find the key
that would unlock the door of this endless, accusatory maze
that forever tortured him.

But how? He knew all the right answers. There must be
a place beyond a head knowledge of answers, a sphere of
heavenly peace. He longed for God to take him to that
serenity.

When he had collapsed into the recliner, Joshua hadn't
thought he could grow any more weary. Until now. Presently,
he felt as if he could sleep twenty-four hours. Josh reached to
turn off the lamp, only to remember he had left Blue outside.

With an exasperated huff, Joshua swung his feet to the
floor and lumbered down the short hallway to the kitchen

door. He unlocked and opened the wooden door and pushed against the old-fashioned screen door. As he scanned the yard, the tepid humidity of an Arkansas night bathed his chest and arms, and the smell of the freshly mowed lawn teased his nostrils.

"Blue!" Josh called, careful not to raise his voice above neighborly etiquette. He gave a brief whistle. "Blue!" Narrowing his eyes, Joshua squinted and strained to see into the dark yard. He flipped off the kitchen light, allowed his eyes to adjust to the darkness, and walked onto the back steps. "Blue!" He descended the steps and peered across the yard. Still no sign of the dog that had become something akin to a child to him. When Josh was home, the two were inseparable. But apparently, Blue had decided to go on an exploration this evening.

He stepped back into the house, locked the back door, and went to the front door, just in case Blue might be out there. Once more, the dog did not respond.

Debating his choices, Joshua decided to do what he had done on the occasional nights when Blue decided to roam. He padded back into his bedroom and raised the window by his bed about three inches. As in the past, Blue would undoubtedly be whining outside the window within the hour.

Leopard pushed the light button on his digital watch and checked the time once more. Almost an hour had lapsed since Joshua released the Saint Bernard into the yard. Once the dog had eaten the tainted meat, he dashed across the street, and Clark hadn't seen him since. Perhaps he was already experiencing the convulsions strychnine always produced. Whatever the case, the mutt was out of the way. The goal had been accomplished.

Relaxing for the first time since nightfall, Clark scooted from the cover of the bushes to lean against a massive oak only a few feet away. Still in the shadows, he waited. The next two hours ticked by like two centuries. In those hours, Leopard relived the horrors of prison. The survival of the fittest. The slavery of the weak. Clark, having always been wiry but strong, had decided early in his sentence that his only defense was building his body through weight lifting. That pursuit, he was sure, had saved his life and his sanity.

Panther should have gone to prison.

Panther should have gone to prison.

Panther should have gone to prison.

The troubling words turned into a chant that fueled the fires of fury forever burning in his gut. Fires that seemed spawned from the belly of evil. With his rage at its hottest, Clark checked his watch once more to see that one o'clock had at last arrived. Joshua should finally be in the throes of a sound sleep.

Standing, Leopard brushed the loose grass from his worn trousers. In irritation, he scratched at the aggravating beard and stealthily plodded toward the back door. Once there, he glanced over his shoulder, more from habit than a genuine concern that he would be detected. Clark, leashing his churning wrath, tugged gently on the ancient screen door, which opened with only the vaguest squeak. His hands shaking from a combination of hostility and nerves, he double-checked the switchblade. Next, he inserted his gloved fingers into his shirt pocket and pulled out the keys. Holding his breath, hot with vengeance, he prepared to insert the key into the lock. Just as Adam and Eve had opened a gateway to sin, so Leopard would open the door to his own revenge, allowing the requital to spew in whatever direction it so chose. Tonight. Tonight was his. His to do with as he pleased.

As the memories of prison continued to feed his spirit's voracious blaze, Clark inserted the key into the lock, eased open the door, and silently stepped into the kitchen. He reached through the hole in his pocket, removed the switchblade from the leather strap, and pressed the switch on its side. The deadly instrument sprang to life with the faint swish of razor-sharp metal.

Marilyn almost never suffered from insomnia. Being a single mother, employed full time usually kept her ready for sleep at any given moment. Why she should have insomniac tendencies tonight was beyond comprehension. As usual, she had been exhausted when she plopped into bed. So exhausted, she had forgone the Bible reading and prayer that had begun to typify her nightly ritual.

Her moments of sifting through the pictures in the photo box weeks ago had begun the slow and painful journey of setting aside her animosity and once more fully embracing her Lord and Savior. Kim Lan's comments on seeking God earlier that week had only intensified Marilyn's own awareness that she desperately needed the Lord in her life on an intimate level. Furthermore, agreeing to pray about Joshua's request led Marilyn toward a doorway. On the other side of that doorway was a new depth of relinquishing her "rights" to God. Still, Marilyn stood at the door, afraid to open it and afraid not to. All these musings continued to toss her about on a tempestuous sea of aching dilemma.

For what seemed like the thousandth time, she checked the digital clock on her nightstand to see one o'clock blaring back at her in annoying red. Her head aching with her valiant attempts to sleep, limbs heavy with fatigue, Marilyn sat up and adjusted the oversized nightshirt that had entwined itself around her legs. She grabbed her house robe from the end of the bed, stood, and traipsed toward the kitchen. Perhaps a tall glass of milk and a slice of her mother's homemade banana nut bread would help coax her to sleep.

"Thank You, Lord, that tomorrow's Friday," she muttered as she retrieved the milk from the refrigerator. This had been a long week, and she wasn't certain she had ever completely made up for the loss of Sunday night's sleep. Then there was the issue of praying about Joshua.

She deposited her milk on the counter, opened the aluminum foil surrounding the banana nut bread, and sliced a thick piece.

Thoughts of Joshua bombarded her. She had purposefully avoided contact with him since Monday, not even allowing Brooke to skip across the street as usually. Marilyn needed time for reflection. Tonight her mind seemed full of nothing but reflections concerning Josh—his average looks and winning personality and...*wow...what a great kisser!*

She felt as if the Lord were finally bringing her to a crossroads: She could be obedient and trust God in His leading about developing a relationship with Joshua or she could continue in her disobedience and run from the man every time she saw him. God seemed to be impressing upon her with renewed intensity that Gregory's disavowal had not relinquished the Lord's call upon her life. The call to be a pastor's wife. Marilyn gulped the milk, desperate for any diversion. But the diversion was short lived.

Her companionable conversation with Josh Monday night had done nothing but intensify the longing that had begun to take root in the garden of her soul. She wanted to have a *good* marriage—a marriage where submission to her husband wasn't a chore because he led the way in Christlike humility, submitting to the needs of his wife and family, willing to do anything, including washing their feet as Christ had washed his disciples' feet. Did such a man exist? Was that man Joshua? Would he take the biblical lead in creating a marriage where mutual submission, love, and respect went hand in hand?

Gregory had been more interested in making sure Marilyn submitted to him than trying to sacrifice himself for her. Somehow the man managed to methodically ignore what it meant to be Christ to his family, and he had solely focused on his wife's role. The result was no relationship—only a dictatorship where Gregory ruled and Marilyn slowly but surely built a wall around herself. Before Gregory's affair, there came a point where Marilyn never again wanted to have sex with him. When they were intimate, she felt more like a prostitute than a wife.

Marilyn sighed and took another bite of the moist bread. She had been wrong to not stand up to Gregory and request a more balanced view during the first year of their marriage. Because of this, their unbiblical relational pattern, if you could even call it a relationship, had become more and more entrenched until change had seemed impossible. So Marilyn had put on a smiley face and lived a lie, pretending all was well when it wasn't—until she could not pretend any longer.

Looking back, she recalled many times when the Lord seemed to be prompting her to calmly confront Greg, but she had always taken the coward's road and continued to smile and act her part. One thing she was slowly learning:

Radical obedience to God took courage. A courage God would have supplied in her marriage if only she had asked. But she hadn't asked. Instead, she had smiled. Smiled and pretended.

Then Gregory had had the affair. When Marilyn found out, she had been numb for a week. Yet she had honestly and practically sat down with Greg and, for the first time in their marriage, told him exactly how she felt. Then she admitted she had been as wrong as he was.

"If you'll forgive me, I'll forgive you," she said that late Friday evening, sitting across the dining room table from him. "And we can start from here. I think it would be a good idea to go for some marriage counseling. We can go to the counselor of your choice." Ironically, Marilyn had felt such peace, such conviction that her words were right. It was such a blessing to finally accept God's gift of courage and obey Him.

But Gregory, choosing to ignore the Word of God and cling to his erroneous beliefs, looked at her, told her she was an awful, rebellious wife, and that he wanted out of the marriage. Period. For a week Marilyn had begged him to stay. She had begged him the whole time he was moving out. Once he filed for divorce, she had quit begging.

"Poor Sheila," Marilyn muttered with great conviction. Undoubtedly, the vivacious brunette, eleven years Gregory's junior, thought she had landed a model husband when she tore Greg from his family.

Dear God, help her, Marilyn prayed earnestly. She stopped chewing, almost unable to believe what she had done. She had just prayed for the woman who had helped break up her marriage. The pity that had sprang to life the day she saw Sheila in Gregory's Cadillac once more manifested itself.

"Lord, give her wisdom in dealing with the man, especially now that another little one is on the way," Marilyn muttered as a lily of love sprouted from her pity. Astounded, she truly understood for the first time in her life the power of praying for an enemy. Slowly she took another sip of milk. As a new peace gradually engulfed her, she vowed to pray for Sheila and Greg every day. Yes, she would sincerely pray for the man who had destroyed their home. She would pray for him and ask the Lord to replace any remaining bitterness with the kind of love He would have for her ex-husband.

But, alas, images of Joshua filled her mind once more. On the heels of thoughts of Gregory, she mentally compared the two men and again recognized that Joshua Langham would understand what it meant to be Christ to his wife— to treasure her, to cherish her, to be willing to be crucified for her.

So what are you afraid of? The thought came unbidden into her mind. Marilyn blinked. If she released her fear, what would be her protection? She had clothed herself in a thick veil of foreboding paranoia that wouldn't allow her to trust another soul, especially if that soul happened to be masculine. If she released her apprehension, her protection would vanish.

Trust the Lord. Simply trust the Lord. He knows what's best for you. He wanted to give you the courage to confront Gregory early in your marriage, but you were afraid. Don't let fear rob you again. Reach out and take the courage God is willingly extending to you. These thoughts sent her into another tailspin, and she gulped the remainder of the milk. "Now," she said firmly, "you are going to bed. And you are going to sleep. As far as you are concerned, a decision about Joshua Langham can wait until tomorrow."

But as she passed the kitchen door, a loud bumping noise froze her in her tracks. She turned off the kitchen light and waited as her teeth clenched in dread. The bumping occurred again. This time it sounded as if someone were actually beating against the petite frame house. Marilyn swallowed hard against the nausea creeping up her throat. *Was someone trying to break in? Should she call the police...or Joshua?*

Marilyn always admired brave women like her sister Jac Lightfoot. Jac would never consider calling the police or even a man. She would rely on her martial arts skills and her own strength of character. But not Marilyn. She might be a wonder mom, but she was *not* Wonder Woman.

The knocking stopped. Trembling violently, Marilyn turned on the porch light, pulled back the kitchen curtain a fraction of an inch, and strained to see the source of the noise. Any moment, she expected to spy a dark figure looming toward the house, intent on breaking and entering. But she saw nothing.

The jarring noise came again. Stifling a scream, Marilyn dropped the curtain and jerked away from the window.

Twenty-One

Penlight in hand, Leopard crept across the kitchen floor, careful not to make a sound. Gradually, he maneuvered the distance to the hallway like a slithering, silent serpent, determined to accomplish his deadly deed.

Panther should have gone to prison.
Panther should have gone to prison.
Panther should have gone to prison.

The vengeful chant pulled images to the forefront of his mind. An image of Joshua Langham ratting to the FBI. An image of himself having no option but to plead guilty to gathering and delivering defense information to aid a foreign government. Espionage, they called it. Punishable by death or by imprisonment for years—or—for life.

All these past incidents surrounded Leopard like a swarm of fierce hornets bent on inflicting a tortuous death. At the end of the hallway, Leopard clicked off his penlight and paused between two doors, slightly ajar. He gently pushed against the door to the left to see what appeared to be an empty guest room. With a satisfied smile, he nudged the right door until it opened completely. Switchblade in hand, he approached the still figure slumbering in the bed. The blinds to the right of the bed were raised, the window opened a few inches. Spears of moonlight spilled across Joshua's relaxed face, creating a collection of shadows and highlights.

Leopard's leg muscles twitched as he stilled himself against springing on the bed and mercilessly ending Panther's life. Grinding his teeth, he decided to just go ahead and kill him. He was here. The chance was perfect. Sticking to the plan to first destroy Panther's reputation paled in comparison with his insatiable need to see his ex-friend dead. He could deny that gnawing need no longer.

The symptomatic trembling that had earlier evidenced his fury ceased. In its place a cold determination now reigned. His hand steady, his muscles poised for brutal action, Leopard stepped within inches of the bed, extended the switchblade to within centimeters of Panther's rib cage, and paused for a final perusal of the man who betrayed him. Could it be that after fifteen years in prison he was at last getting his revenge? The reality seemed as sweet as honey to his soul.

The phone rang.

Shocked, Leopard stared at the cordless phone on the nightstand as if he had never seen a phone in his life. At the second ring Joshua stirred in his sleep. Leopard, reacting from instinct rather than logic, took several steps backward and crouched behind the open closet door. As the phone produced its third ring, Clark's logic set in. He could go ahead and kill Joshua before he completely awoke. A phone's ringing shouldn't stop him from his mission. He prepared to stand just as Josh fumbled with the phone and produced a dazed, "Hello."

"Marilyn?" he said more distinctively. A pause. "Okay, I'll be right over."

Leopard, still clutching the switchblade, breathed in shallow, silent spurts as Joshua turned on the bedside lamp and fumbled in the closet. Clark could shove the door closed on Panther, trap him in the closet, and...

No. Up until a few moments ago, he had pledged to savor this experience as long as possible. Part of that savoring included devastating Joshua emotionally before he destroyed him physically. What was better? A quick murder now or a slow, pleasurable process through which Joshua would be pushed to the brink of insanity before he died?

Leopard relaxed his grip on the switchblade. He would wait just as he had planned from the start. With Joshua stumbling from the room, Leopard reached into his back pocket and pulled out a sealed white envelope—packed with the message identical to the one Josh's whole congregation would receive in a matter of days. Sounds of the front door opening and closing left Clark free to stand. He stepped from behind the closet door, dropped the envelope on the dresser, and exited the house.

Marilyn hung up the phone and rushed to Brooke's room to make certain her daughter was safe. As she suspected, Brooke lay in her twin-sized bed sleeping peacefully. Although the knocking had once again ceased, Marilyn compulsively checked to make sure the two wood-framed windows in Brooke's room were locked. She rushed up the hallway toward the living room to await Joshua.

The light tap on the front door was nothing short of a message of hope. Without pause, Marilyn stepped toward the front door. "Josh?" she asked, her hand on the dead bolt.

"Yes. It's me."

Relieved, she unlocked the door and flung it open. Joshua stood on the threshold wearing an ebony shirt wrong side out, gray jogging shorts, and tennis shoes with no socks. He clutched a baseball bat and gave Marilyn a blurry-eyed, yet protective stare.

"Where's the noise?" he asked, sweeping past her.

"At the back. Near the kitchen door." Marilyn barely took the time to relock the door before rushing after him to the dark kitchen.

Joshua pushed aside the kitchen curtain to peer into the backyard, illuminated by the porch light. Still shaking with fear, Marilyn stood in the kitchen doorway and deliberated about leaving Joshua to the task. But she couldn't. She would never forgive herself if he were seriously injured while she was cowering in the living room.

"I don't see anything. When was the last time you heard the noise?" he whispered.

"When I called you."

"Okay." He raised the bat and approached the back door. "I'm going to open the door. Get ready."

"What exactly do you want me to do?"

"Just stay where you are for now. If anything happens…call the police."

"Okay."

Slowly, Joshua turned the dead bolt lock. It clicked with the sound of metal against metal. The aging knob produced a faint squeak. Next, the door swung inward only an inch and a yellow glow pierced the room's shadows.

Marilyn, ready to dash toward the phone, gripped her fingers until they ached.

Joshua carefully opened the door a bit wider. He pushed against the screen door and placed one foot outside.

"Joshua…"

He turned to face her, brows lifted.

"Be careful."

A slight smile. He nodded and stepped outside. Immediately, he snapped the door shut behind him, and a low muffled moan filtered through the heavy wooden door. Certain someone had assaulted him, Marilyn rushed forward and tried to open the door.

Joshua's pale face greeted her. "Don't come out here," he demanded.

"What is it?"

"It's Blue. He's dead."

Two hours later Joshua pulled the Ford truck back into his driveway. Listlessly he got out and walked across the street to lightly tap on Marilyn's front door. She'd told him she would wait up for him, but Josh didn't want to awaken her if she had gone back to bed.

Coffee mug in hand, she immediately opened the door. Josh noted she had changed from the house robe into a pair of faded cut-offs and an oversized T-shirt. Regardless, Marilyn was still a sight to behold for his gritty eyes. Joshua had about decided the woman would look good in a feed sack.

"So what did Dr. Lovelady say?" she asked as he stepped into the living room.

"Somebody poisoned Blue. Dr. Lovelady did a quick autopsy and said his stomach was full of raw hamburger meat, mixed with gopher bait. The stuff is lime-green. She said when she sees a stomach with contents of that color, it's gopher bait, no questions asked. According to her, gopher poisoning is nothing more than feed grain coated in strychnine." Joshua rubbed his eyes and collapsed on the striped sofa. "Dr. Lovelady said it causes horrid convulsions."

"That must have been the noise I heard."

"Poor boy, he was knocking against your house because he was in the final stages of death." Joshua propped his elbows on his knees and covered his weary face with his hands.

"I'm so sorry," Marilyn said, settling on the couch beside him.

"It's okay." Joshua controlled his emotions. "I just left Blue with her. She said she'd take care of the body. I didn't want to look at his face another second." He sighed. "It's probably ridiculous for a grown man to get so attached to a dog, but..."

Marilyn touched his arm. "I'd probably howl for a week if my cat died. We do get attached to animals. We just do. They become a part of the family."

"I just can't imagine who'd poison him." Joshua held her gaze as those empty envelopes he had dismissed seemed to float between them—but that was ridiculous. There was no way those envelopes from Leopard could be connected with Blue's death.

"Well, I hate to tell you this, but if Blue was getting into somebody's yard and causing havoc or anything of that nature, there are some people around here who are mean enough and value their backyard chicken coops enough—"

"Yes, but I thought I was so careful to keep him close." Joshua leaned back in the couch and pinched his bottom lip. "I *did* leave him out longer than necessary last night. I was thinking, and the time got away from me. By the time I got around to calling Blue back in, he was long gone. He's pulled that stunt a few times before. Usually, he'll sit outside my window and whine when he's ready to come in. So I left my bedroom window up, hoping I'd hear him if he came back home."

A companionable silence settled between them and Joshua watched the hand on the brass wall clock tick off the seconds. His heavy emotions urged him to find a moment of release.

"Thanks for coming over," Marilyn said softly. "I'm not terribly brave when it comes to noises."

"I'm glad you're not. I'd rather you be safe than sorry." He smiled slightly, taking in the weary paleness of a pretty lady. "I told you to call me when you decided about seeing me," he teased in a tired voice. "But I didn't expect a call in the middle of the night."

"Well, you know me, once I make a decision, I'm quick to action." Marilyn stood and walked toward the front window, as if to purposefully put distance between them.

"Meaning?" Joshua asked, his pulse jumping with the implications of her flippant answer.

She cleared her throat. "I think it's a little ridiculous to deny that we have this strong attraction for each other, but..."

"But?"

"There's more to this whole situation than just how we feel."

"Such as?"

"Do you, as a minister, want to be involved with a divorced woman? Let's face the facts."

"I have no problem with it in your case. I believe the Bible clearly offers you freedom to pursue another relationship—and even remarry—in your circumstances. From what I understand, you tried to get Greg to stay, and he still chose to continue in his adultery. It's not like the two of you just couldn't get along and divorced. In that case, I'd have to tell you to try to reconcile with your husband, and if he refused, to remain single. But this business of adultery, and then his marrying the other woman, Marilyn—"

"And if he hadn't married her, I *still,* even now, would be willing to reconcile for Brooke's sake," Marilyn said softly, her eyes a bit misty. "But that's no longer an option. I tried to get him to go to counseling. I admitted that I had been wrong in some areas. And I *was* wrong in some stuff, but he was too! I desperately didn't want our family to be destroyed. It's like...like an emotional abortion." She raised her hand in defeat. "Maybe if I had been a better wife?"

"You can't blame yourself for his sin," Joshua said softly.

Again Josh was struck by the magnitude of what Greg had thrown away. He ached for this lovely lady and her delightful daughter.

Standing, Joshua approached Marilyn, desperately wanting to pull her into his arms and soothe away her pain. But he hesitated. He didn't want to do anything that might make Marilyn feel as if he were pushing her.

"Gregory made a choice against God's will. You may very well have both been wrong in some areas of your marriage, but that did not, and does not, justify adultery."

"But if I drove him to it—"

"Marilyn, I'm sorry, but I have a hard time believing that a woman who is willing to forgive adultery and reconcile with a man who has deserted her *drove* him to an affair. Listen..." Joshua stepped forward, gently taking her hand in his. "He made a choice. It was a choice instigated by Satan, not by God. You cannot take the blame for his sin," he repeated.

"You sound like Kim Lan." Marilyn moved away from his touch, confirming Joshua's decision to use constraint.

"If so, Kim Lan is right."

Marilyn sipped her coffee and thoughtfully stared into the cup. "Can you believe that Greg used to make disparaging remarks about Kim's lack of spirituality?"

"Perhaps he saw himself in her."

"What do you mean?" she asked, peering into his eyes.

Josh shrugged. "Well, I think Kim Lan...maybe...let's just say I think Kim is a baby Christian."

"Yes, but she's seeking God more than she ever has."

"I sensed that from some of the things she said. I think it's great. We need more people in prominent positions like hers who will stand up for Christ," Joshua said earnestly. "But Gregory seems like the type..."

"Yes," Marilyn said flatly, "I'm beginning to wonder why I didn't see that before I married him. Looking back, I think I just went along with the flow more than seeking God over whether or not to marry him. Maybe what my mother called "cold feet" was really the Lord warning me about marrying Gregory? We were in love, and he was supposedly called to be a pastor, and I was *definitely* called to be a pastor's wife." Marilyn sighed. "I guess I just figured in my humanity that the whole thing seemed logical and the best opportunity for blissful matrimony."

"I'm beginning to think that just because something is a good opportunity doesn't mean it's a *God* opportunity. For instance, just before taking this church I was offered a staff position at a megachurch in Houston. I was tempted, but I couldn't get peace about it. I had to choose between the smaller church here and that prestigious position in Houston. The pay was better, the house was better, and they were even going to give me a car. But I just couldn't get comfortable with it. Apparently God had someone else for that position. It's sometimes tough to say no to a good opportunity.

I imagine marrying Greg at the time seemed like the best thing to do.

"Anyway, when I took the church here," Josh continued, "I knew I was doing the right thing. Now I'm so glad I did...for a variety of reasons." His admiring smile left the meaning clear.

A new bout of uncertainty overwhelmed Marilyn. Despite all the ground she was covering spiritually, despite her thoughts on getting better aquainted with Josh, a tiny, fear-full voice from within suggested she run from Josh's admiration.

"I guess Kim needs to hear that bit about the good opportunity versus God opportunity business." Marilyn voiced the first thought that flashed through her mind—anything to change Josh's focus.

"Oh?"

"There are some tough choices she's going to have to make soon," Marilyn said as she debated whether or not to share Kim Lan's struggle. Her tongue was loosed, and she continued, "She's been offered a pile of money to pose for another swimsuit issue. She's trying to decide whether or not to take the job. I just wish she didn't have to debate the decision. This choice is a little clearer than deciding which church to take. But at least she's to a point where she is feeling convicted about such shoots."

Joshua nodded his head in understanding.

"I just think that—" Marilyn took a sip of coffee, "that as women of God we shouldn't purposefully invite men to..." She shrugged, wondering what had possessed her to ramble on about the subject. "It's one thing to wear a modest swimsuit for the purpose of swimming, and it's another thing altogether to..." Marilyn bit her lip and produced an embarrassed smile.

Eyes dancing with laughter, Joshua silently appraised her.

"What's so funny?" she demanded.

"Just you. You sound like you're giving a presentation to the teenage girls at church titled, 'What It Means to Dress as a Godly Woman.'"

Groaning, Marilyn covered her eyes. "You're right. Why is it I slip into that mode so easily?"

A thoughtful silence settled between them, and the tension that had been tightly coiled within Marilyn since Josh returned from the vet's seemed to be slowly unraveling. This was the first time she had truly relaxed with him. She had been so busy trying to dodge him that she hadn't let herself have much of a normal conversation with him. But she was immensely enjoying herself now, whether she should be or not. Once more that persistent, fearful voice tried to warn her. This time Marilyn swept it aside.

"Anyway, back to your question…" Josh crossed his arms. "I don't see a problem with anyone opposing our seeing each other. If I did, I wouldn't be here."

A lone owl's faint call echoed from afar. Marilyn tugged aside the curtain and peered into the darkness, wondering if the owl was lonely.

"Well, I've been thinking…" She paused as the owl's barely discernable hoot reached her ears again. He did sound lonely. So lonely. Marilyn's heart twisted. She and the owl had much in common.

"I guess we should see each other," she said practically, once and for all making her decision.

"Ooo…" Josh winced. "Do you have to sound so happy about it?"

Swiveling to face him, her lips twitched against a smile. "But I'm *not* agreeing to marry you," she said, shaking her finger at him.

"Yeah, I've heard that rumor," he said through a chuckle. "Seems you've said the same thing before."

She rolled her eyes. "Did you have to bring that up?"

Sobering, he stroked her cheek, and Marilyn steeled herself against the power of their attraction. This time she couldn't quiet the resurrection of that fearful voice.

Dear God, she pleaded, *please tell me I haven't lost my mind.* But there was the owl's call, reminding...the loneliness...that haunting loneliness.

"Seriously, Marilyn, I don't think we need to rush into anything. All I ask is that you stop running from me." He paused for a grin. "Give us a chance to try to get better acquainted."

"Good. That's exactly the way I feel. I just...I..." She swallowed hard and lowered her gaze.

"You're still scared?"

"A little—no...*to death*." When she looked back at him, his understanding eyes touched her spirit. With an effort she restrained herself from falling into his arms.

"I understand. I'd probably feel the same way."

She nodded.

"Well," Marilyn said practically, "I guess now is as good a time as any to warn you to be prepared for general mayhem and interrogation from my friends once they find out about us."

"You mean there's more besides Kim Lan?"

"Oh, yes. There are seven of us who are especially close. We all went to the University of Texas at the same time, met there, and formed a close bond. We call ourselves the seven sisters. We have a sister reunion once every six months. It's all great fun."

"Sounds like it."

"But they *really do* act like my sisters most of the time."
She rolled her eyes.

"And that's bad?"

"Well," she shrugged, "they've teased me mercilessly since
they found out you were across the street."

"So, you've been talking about me?" Joshua produced a
delightful grin.

Marilyn narrowed her eyes. "Whether I wanted to or not.
Once Kim Lan found out about you..."

Joshua closed the distance between them and gently
tugged Marilyn into the circle of his arms.

Careful not to spill her coffee, Marilyn rested her head
against his chest and savored the feel of his heart's strong,
steady beats. That quiet voice of fear had no chance of survival in the face of Josh's warm embrace.

"I think your friends and I will get along just fine," he
said with a smile in his voice. "But I think we'll get along
better."

⌒

Kim Lan awoke for her usual five-in-the-morning
workout. Her mind spinning with a weighty decision, she
needed to talk to a friend. If it weren't four o'clock in
Arkansas, she would have called Marilyn. Instead, she impatiently arose, donned her exercise gear, left her penthouse,
and took the elevator down to the workout room that featured state-of-the-art machines. The equipment's bright silver
hue contrasted with the royal blue carpet to create the same
aesthetic appeal of every room in this luxury apartment
building. As usual, no one else was there this early. Kim Lan
liked working out alone. It gave her time to think.

She mounted the stationary bicycle and began the warm up. The decision over the swimsuit issue wouldn't stop plaguing her. She had only two days left to decide. Charlie had called yesterday evening to say the magazine had upped their offer. Apparently her hedging had instigated their action. The offer of more money only heightened Kim Lan's deliberation. After all, the money was the reason she would be doing the shoot. And it was a bundle. More than her parents ever dreamed of making. Although Kim Lan had built them a comfortable home in Boston, this money would mean she could do even more for them—and others. *And yourself,* a voice whispered from the back of her mind.

Sighing, she admitted the truth. She would enjoy the extra money. Kim Lan always enjoyed the extra money. She relished the "rich and famous" lifestyle and never—absolutely never—wanted to go back to the poverty-stricken existence of her youth. She had been too poor and too plain to be counted as one of the popular, pretty girls in school. Only in her college years had she blossomed into the exotic beauty that now mesmerized America.

Ferociously, she tackled the machines, as if a hard workout could somehow exorcise the battle raging within. Regardless of her insatiable need for more money, she suspected that the Lord would not be pleased were she to pose for this swimsuit issue. Only six nights ago, she had told Marilyn she had begun to wish she had never posed for similar shoots. Kim Lan had begun a journey of seeking God and that journey was methodically revealing areas of her inward being that had not been in line with the Word of God. For years, she had believed that if men lusted after her, it was their problem. But was it? Especially if she understood that her immodest dress would invite lust?

*But you can't think in those terms when making profes-
sional decisions,* she told herself. *You'll never see the men
who look at your photos. If they do lust, it will be after the
image in the photo, not after the real me. The whole thing is
a mirage. It's just a game they're all playing. What's the harm
in playing along? Besides, the swimsuit issue is always the
hottest. And they want to do a pullout centerfold of me. This
would really strengthen my career.* She stopped for a
moment and switched machines. Her thoughts continued to
boil. *This isn't a religious decision. This is a career decision.
God understands I need to make a living. Besides, who would
turn down such an offer? Just like Charlie said, there are
women lined up in every modeling agency in New York
who'd say yes in an instant. No one—not even my pastor,
will think a thing of this shoot. And it will mean more
money...more money...more money...*

An hour later, Kim Lan deposited the twenty-pound
weights back onto their shelf. Sweat dripping into her eyes,
she grabbed a towel from the stainless steel rack, blotted
her face, and draped the towel around her neck. Charlie was
pushing her toward the shoot. Ted was pushing her toward
the shoot. And her own need for money seemed to be siding
with them. Perhaps God indeed would understand. After all,
He was a God of mercy and love, wasn't He? Surely, He
could look past any discrepancy in this pose, if there even
was a discrepancy. Plus, this would be the last one. The
absolute last one.

As she slowly walked back to the elevators and ultimately
stepped into her penthouse, she made her final decision. A
decision that left her at long last free of this tormenting deliberation. She would do the swimsuit issue. Kim Lan walked
into her bedroom, picked up the phone, called Charlie
before she changed her mind.

Twenty-Two

‿

The next morning, Joshua rolled over in bed and tried to block out the morning sun by tightly squeezing his lids together. At last he opened one eye to read the alarm clock: 8:36. With a sigh, he rolled out of bed. He felt as tired as he had been the night before when he went to bed. Fully expecting the sound of Blue's welcoming "wuff," Josh looked toward the hallway to see nothing.

Then he remembered. His best friend was dead. Blinking against his stinging eyes, Joshua rubbed his face and stood in front of his dresser. The haggard fellow who looked back at him in no way resembled the man Marilyn Thatcher had just agreed to see. Despite his sore soul's longings for Blue, Josh smiled. It was a tired smile, but it also was a smile of expectancy.

He scrubbed his fingers through his short, springy hair, glad it was deciding to fall into place this morning. Just as he turned for the closet, Josh noticed the unmarked white envelope lying on his dresser. Trying to remember what the envelope contained, he picked it up. Strange. He couldn't remember leaving it there. He checked to find the seal unbroken.

"Must be something from the office," he muttered. He tugged against the seal, deftly removed the folded white paper, and opened it. The words assaulted his mind and left

248

his mouth dry, his mind spinning. He stared at a copy of an old newspaper article titled, "The One Who Got Away." Josh remembered the exposition well. Dated fifteen years ago, the commentary suggested that he should have been indicted along with Clark. When the whole ordeal occurred, the media played havoc with the story. Two twenty-year-old men involved in an attempt at espionage. One of them trapped by the military police while the other one confessed to the FBI. One man called "Panther," the other called "Leopard." The opportunities for sensationalism were too great for the California papers not to stretch the story to the maximum. The writer of this article most certainly did some stretching.

How did the article arrive on my dresser? His mind immediately flashed to Blue's death. *Had the person who strategically placed this envelope on my dresser also killed Blue? It makes sense: Kill the dog so I won't hear an intruder. But when had the person entered? Better yet, who was it?* Only one name blazed through Joshua's mind: *Leopard.*

Once more, those empty envelopes invaded Joshua's thoughts. When they had stopped arriving, he had assumed Leopard had decided to stop playing his sick game. With disgust, he thought about his musings from the night before, about his desires to once and for all put the torment of the past behind him. Now it seemed his past was rising up like a monster to devour him alive. Since he had decided not to go to the police when the envelopes had started showing up, he had burned or discarded them and sighed with relief when they stopped. But now, he wished he had saved them.

Josh sat on the edge of his bed as a contrasting notion invaded his mind. So, what if he still had the envelopes? There was no evidence that the person who mailed the envelopes also deposited this editorial on his dresser. Swallowing against a tight throat, Joshua wondered if there was any indication of breaking and entering into his home. If Leopard had left fingerprints or *anything*, perhaps he could be implicated. Josh jumped up and, like a crazed man, went from window to window searching for any sign of an intruder. His frantic search at last led him back to his bedroom where he stopped in front of the window he had inched up the night before.

Could Leopard have slipped through this window and left the envelope when I left for my middle-of-the-night trip to Marilyn's and the vet's? Josh's skin crawled. And he decided, at last, that he must call the police. With a sinking heart, he realized he also needed to distance himself from Marilyn. He didn't want to take the chance of her being harmed because she happened to be with him.

⌒

By ten o'clock Marilyn pushed back her chair in the veterinarian's office and yawned for what felt like the millionth time.

"That's what you get for those late night dates," Dr. Lovelady said, stifling her own yawn as she walked toward the coffeepot.

"If you can call a dead dog a date," Marilyn said languidly.

Brushing back a lock of reddish hair touched with gray, the tall doctor refilled Marilyn's coffee cup. "I made it double strength this morning," she said through a smirk.

"Tastes like it," Marilyn said dryly.

"Hey, that's what you get for being late!"

"Sorry." Marilyn sipped the strong, bitter liquid. "It won't happen again. I've learned my lesson." She raised her right hand. "I, Marilyn Douglas Thatcher, do solemnly promise to be early from this day forth so I can make every pot of coffee."

"It can't be *that* bad," the middle-aged vet said.

"Well, it is keeping me awake. I guess that's all that counts."

Dr. Lovelady chuckled, leaned against the nearby file cabinet, and adjusted her white lab coat. "I remember thinking some time or other before I decided to become a vet that this would be an easier profession than, say, a medical doctor because I wouldn't have my sleep disturbed." She produced a caustic snort. "What a hoot!"

"I'm sorry about last night..." Marilyn began.

Ginger raised her hand. "Don't be. It wasn't the first time I've had a middle-of-the-night call, and it certainly won't be the last. That's what I'm here for."

"I just wish we could find out who poisoned him." Marilyn glimpsed a spider web near the leg of her wooden desk and bent to sweep it away.

"The person was probably some old, cranky neighbor who didn't like Blue around his backyard chicken coop," Dr. Lovelady said. "I've seen stuff like that happen too many times."

"That's exactly what I told Josh."

The doctor's next patient, a Siamese with an attitude, entered escorting its well-trained owner, and Marilyn was plopped back into the throes of managing the files, the phones, and her own thoughts. Something ominous seemed to be nagging at the back of her mind. Joshua had received some strange envelopes that connected him to a character named "Leopard," who had done something seriously illegal. Marilyn still didn't have all the details on the story, and she was beginning to despair of ever learning them. Once those envelopes stopped arriving, Josh relaxed about the possibilities of his past resurrecting to harm him. But could his dog's poisoning be in any way connected to his dark past? The easiest explanation seemed to be the neighbor/chicken coop scenario. But was that the accurate explanation?

"Marilyn?"

She looked up from shuffling papers at an apologetic Joshua who was standing on the other side of the typical waist-high wall that separated her desk from the waiting room.

"Yes?" she answered, wondering if her thoughts had conjured him up. He certainly was a welcome sight to her droopy eyes.

"Would it be possible for you to take a short break? There's something we need to discuss."

"Umm..." Marilyn eyed the waiting room, currently void of patients. She looked at the appointment book that listed no further commitments until one o'clock. Then she checked her watch to discover one more hour had ticked by.

"Let me check with Dr. Lovelady. I think she's about through with the Siamese. If so, she probably won't mind if I take an early lunch."

"Great."

Within five minutes, Marilyn had removed her lab coat and allowed Joshua to open the clinic's heavy wooden door for her. He placed a hand on her back with a familiarity that left Marilyn a bit wobbly in the knees.

"Let's just go to McDonald's," he said, his face grim.

"You're such a romantic," she teased. But a forbidding sense of trouble nibbled at her mind.

"Yep," he said flatly, looking around the parking lot as if he were afraid someone were watching. "You go ahead and take your car." He pointed toward the cobalt-blue Chevrolet parked beneath a tree. "I'll follow you in my truck. I'll explain when we get to McDonald's."

"Okay." She was tempted to question him on the spot but refrained. Something had Josh in a grimmer mood than she had ever seen him. Marilyn got into her two-year-old car and turned the air conditioner on high to ease the August heat. Fortunately, the money Kim Lan had given her had let her pay on the balance of her vehicle after she set aside just enough for the new computer. All she needed now was someone to help her with the purchase because she felt somewhat inadequate in that area. Perhaps she could ask Joshua's advice today. But given his present mood and the looming conversation, she wondered if that was such a good idea.

She drove the short distance to McDonald's. In silence, Joshua opened her car door for her. In silence, the two of them entered the cool restaurant. The smells of hamburgers and fresh french fries did precious little to ease the tension. Something was wrong. Really wrong.

"Want to order?" Josh asked.

"No. That's okay. Let's talk first."

"Okay." He scanned the restaurant and pointed toward an isolated booth in a far corner. "Is that fine?"

"Yes." In seconds, Marilyn settled across from him.

"This is going to seem strange to you after I literally chased you and got down on my knees to plead that you'd agree to pray about seeing me." He stared at her with enough torment in his eyes to fill an ocean, his meaning more than clear.

"This has to be the shortest courtship on record," Marilyn said quietly.

He grabbed a fist full of his short, springy hair as if to rend it by the roots. "I think Clark McClure is the one who poisoned Blue."

"You mean that Leopard person who sent you those empty envelopes?"

"Yes, the very same."

Marilyn recalled Joshua's edict the day she visited him in the hospital after seeing that envelope from Leopard: *Stay away from me. Just go home and pretend I don't exist.*

"How can you be sure it's him?"

"I can't, but someone left a copy of an old article about me on my dresser last night. The article is one of the few ones where the writer suggested I should have gone to prison when Clark did. I can't think of anyone else who would have an article of that nature."

A chill scurried down her spine. "Have you called the police?"

"Yes."

"And?"

"An officer came over, heard my story, and told me there's not enough evidence. He did find some traces of hamburger meat with bits of lime-green stuff in it near the bushes. He also found the print of what looks like the heel of a canvas shoe. But there's nothing that points to any individual. He even dusted my window for fingerprints."

"And..."

"He couldn't get any. He said it's not like what you see on the movies where they always get prints."

"So, somebody broke into your house and left an article on your dresser without so much as a trace?" she asked in disbelief.

"You got it. I was certain he must have entered through my bedroom window because I had left it partially open when I went to bed, hoping Blue would wake me up." He sighed and rubbed his eyes, heavy with fatigue. "Listening to that policeman, you'd think Leopard had a key or something. But that's ridiculous!"

Biting her lips, Marilyn looked at the tabletop, the color of one of Brooke's wheat-toned crayons. "What about the key under the rock by your front door?"

"I checked that. It's still there. And I have a hard time believing that someone who'd be devious enough to come into my house in the middle of the night would be conscientious enough to use the key then put it back."

Marilyn nodded in agreement. "And do you have any extra keys anywhere else?"

"No." Silently he toyed with a package of ketchup left by the last diners. "Wait a minute!" His head snapped up. "I did leave a couple of extra house keys in my desk drawer at the church office. I had them made the day I locked myself out of the house. I'm not the best person about keeping up with keys." He produced a pathetic smile. "I guess I'm a bit disorganized at times."

"That's okay," Marilyn said. "Don't feel like the Lone Ranger. I'm the worst closet slob you've ever seen. None of my closets are organized for long, and there are a few of 'em that are dangerous to even open."

"Oh?"

"Yes. Avalanche city!"

They joined in a mutual chuckle that lasted only seconds before they both sobered to contemplate the seriousness of Joshua's present situation.

"So what are you going to do?" Marilyn asked softly.

"Right now, there's not anything I can do—other than keep my distance from you and Brooke," he said with a disappointed wilt to his words. "I think it would probably be a good idea to encourage Brooke to stay on your side of the road for awhile. I'd hate to be out playing with her if Leopard decided to drive by and shoot at me. And I'd hate to be taking you out to dinner, start the truck, and have it explode."

"Surely you don't think he'd—"

"Nothing would surprise me at this point. The FBI offered the witness protection program after I turned him in, but I didn't figure I'd need it. Besides, who wants to change identities with all that entails? At the time, all that seemed like it should be for people who witness against the mafia or something, not against a twenty-year-old former friend." He placed his forehead against the heels of his hands.

Renewed curiosity raged through Marilyn. "Um...Josh..."

"Hmm?" He looked up at her.

"You never *did* finish telling me that story. Would you mind?"

He looked at the table. "I can't remember where I left off, so much has happened."

"I think you had just told me that Clark brought a computer printout to your apartment."

"That's right." He sighed. "I guess I sorta left you hanging, huh?"

She nodded.

"Well, to make a long story short, those files were military secrets. They pinpointed the names and locations of American spies in the Middle East."

"Oh, no."

"At first, Clark and I were just intrigued. I was too ignorant to see where Clark was going with the whole business. The next day he suggested we should sell the secrets to the Middle East. He said he figured they would give us at least a million bucks for the info." Josh continued to play with the ketchup packet. "At first, I did entertain the idea that Clark and I could sell the printout, leave the country, and live the good life in Switzerland for a long time. Then my usually defunct conscience set in. I couldn't get past something I had learned growing up: 'Thou shalt not steal.' Never mind that I was blowing any chance of keeping most of the other Ten Commandments, but for some reason that one just started annoying me."

"Undoubtedly God."

"Undoubtedly. Anyway, I knew Clark shouldn't have stolen those files and that selling them was just as wrong, so I told him I couldn't comply." He tossed the ketchup packet aside. "I'd love to tell you it was only the 'thou shalt not steal' part that prompted my decision, but I can't. I was also scared stiff to think we might get caught. But Clark told me if I didn't go along he'd turn me over to the police and tell them I was the one who printed the file." Joshua peered out the window, into the busy parking lot.

"So, you…" Marilyn prompted, sitting on the edge of her seat.

"So, I didn't feel like I had a choice. Clark said he was able to get in touch with someone who put him in touch with some representatives from Iraq. We were scheduled to meet them together one Friday afternoon in an alley near our apartment. They were going to hand us a briefcase full of money, and we were going to hand over the printout. I was working in a surfing supply store at the time. Clark was at the apartment. He called me right before he left, making sure I was going to be there. I told him I was," Josh swallowed hard, "but I was scared. Really, really scared. And…" Narrowing his eyes, he looked directly at Marilyn. "And I didn't show up. I decided to go to the FBI instead. I told them everything. Then Clark's contacts turned out to be the military police—they had set him up."

Marilyn whistled.

"It's called espionage, and it got him a solid prison sentence. It's been fifteen years, and he's undoubtedly out now, probably for good behavior."

"And he's got revenge on the brain, you think?"

"What do you think?"

"I think we'd better do some serious praying." Even though building a relationship with Joshua still ignited a flame of fear, Marilyn was, without a doubt, disappointed that they had to put a halt to their courtship.

Joshua was by no means perfect. He had a past—a dark past. But so did she. Both of them had made mistakes and paid the consequences. However, as Joshua had told her, God was a God of second chances. This week, in all her praying, she had come to the conclusion that if the Lord could take murderers like Moses, David, and Paul and turn them into biblical greats, then perhaps He could take the rags of her life and create a beauty that never would have existed without the agony of loss. Sighing, she hoped Joshua could one day say the same of this mysterious situation.

"I will pray for you, Joshua. I'll pray every day."

"Thanks," he said, standing up.

Hesitating, Marilyn looked up. "There's one other thing I think I should say, Josh."

"Oh?" He sat back down and nervously glanced around the restaurant.

"Yes. I already apologized to you about...about bringing up your past the other day at the restaurant. But I—I just wanted to tell you that—that..." She cleared her throat and began worrying the packet of ketchup Joshua had tossed aside. "I in no way hold any of your past against you. I don't feel anything about it, except a great deal of respect that after—after you...hmm...experienced...well, that you have stayed true to your vow of celibacy for fifteen years. I guess the other day I was just more curious for some perverse reason that seems to have faded away. I—"

He covered her hand. "Maybe you were just being human," he said with a sad smile.

"Well, I guess that's true. But—but what I'm trying to say is there's no reason to keep beating yourself up over it all." Marilyn cleared her throat again and continued to address the ketchup. "God has forgiven you, and somehow this week I seem to have come to grips with some stuff, too, and one Bible verse keeps coming to me." She held up one of her hands and smiled. "It's in Philippians, and you probably already know it."

"Go ahead and say it anyway," he requested softly.

"Forgetting what is behind and straining toward what is ahead, I press on toward the goal to win the prize for which God has called me heavenward in Christ Jesus."

He smiled, and all traces of the former wariness momentarily vanished. "I needed to hear that right now."

"Good."

"Do you have any suggestions about how to—how to make that work? My problem is that I have memorized all the right verses. I understand all the appropriate concepts. I can even counsel people and recommend books for them to read that are supposed to help them with the same problems I'm having." He waved his hand in exasperation. "But I just seem stuck. It's like in this one area of my life I'm caught somewhere between knowing the truth and allowing the truth to set me free."

Marilyn stared at him like a startled doe, her mind devoid of any suggestions. According to her mother, this man had a Master of Divinity degree in biblical studies. She couldn't tell him anything he didn't already know. At last she asked, "I guess you've prayed about it?"

"Yes," he said, a defeated shadow in his eyes.

"Well, I guess it's just a matter of truly accepting the fact that Christ has forgiven you for those sins. It seems to me that as long as you hang on to the right to lambaste yourself you haven't truly embraced the Lord's forgiveness," Marilyn offered. "I guess you could picture yourself bundling all those sins up in a bag and nailing the bag to Jesus' cross, then just leaving them there. As long as you hold on to the right to beat yourself up, then you're saying that Christ's crucifixion just wasn't enough."

"Wow! That's good stuff," Josh said, a glimmer of respect in his eyes.

"Yes, and I have no idea where it came from."

"Maybe from the Lord," Joshua said simply. "I've read stuff like that in the past, but somehow—hearing it from you now...and that business about nailing the bundle to the cross..." He shook his head and smiled. "I think I've got some bundling and nailing to do."

Marilyn sighed. "I probably do, too."

Eventually, Joshua stood. "As much as I hate to put an end to this, O Wise One, I feel like we need to be seen together as little as possible." Once more he glanced around the restaurant that was whirring with the lunch crowd. "I can't shake the feeling that I'm being watched every second of every day now."

Worriedly Marilyn rose to her feet. "Like I said, I'll be praying for you."

Taking Marilyn by surprise, Joshua bent and gently brushed his lips against her forehead. "Thanks. And you take care of the Ladybug." His words held a tone of finality that left Marilyn chilled.

"I will," she said,

"Go get in line and get yourself some lunch. I'm going to head out." Without another word, he trudged out the door, shoulders hunched, head lowered.

Marilyn steeled herself against chasing him, against telling him that she already cared for him so deeply that it scared her, against begging him to be extremely careful. She lightly touched her forehead and wondered if she would ever again feel his kiss, experience his embrace. "Oh, Lord," she whispered, covering her lips with shaking fingers, "protect him."

Twenty-Three

⌒

Monday evening after work, Marilyn stopped by her mother's to pick up Brooke. She pulled into the driveway of the rock house where she was raised and put her trusty Chevrolet into park. The day had been beyond hectic, and her neck and shoulders ached. Her job as office manager included being a general "go-fer" and veterinary assistant. One particular German shepherd, whom a muzzle highly offended, had been quite a handful.

Sighing, Marilyn got out of the car and trudged across the grass that showed signs of the late summer heat. The cicadas shrieked in the evening warmth. It seemed to Marilyn that the hotter the weather, the louder the insects. They were exceptionally loud today.

Sweeping aside the beads of perspiration that dotted her forehead, she walked up the porch steps and thought about the one person she had tried to avoid thinking of all day— Joshua. She hadn't seen him, except for yesterday morning and evening when she'd attended church with her parents. He had seemed distant, distracted, and determined to keep plenty of space between them. His obviously frigid demeanor had left her a bit perturbed. Even though she understood his reasons, she nonetheless expected the man to at least sneak her a private smile. But she didn't even get a crumb of recognition. He had briefly hugged Brooke, both Sunday morning and Sunday night. However, Marilyn had managed to distract the child, and mother and daughter had moved along with the flow of church members bustling out the door.

For a woman who had literally run from Joshua, she certainly had changed her outlook. Or perhaps God had changed it. Marilyn produced a dry chuckle and gently tapped on her mother's front door before entering. The cool air immediately chilled the film of perspiration along her forehead.

"Hello, dear," Natalie said from across the cozy room. Her eyes rimmed in red, she bent before the floral couch and silently finished buckling Brooke's sandals.

"Mom!" Brooke yelled as she smiled with glee.

"Hi, darling, I missed you," Marilyn said, extending her arms. Brooke flung herself into her mother's embrace.

"Grandma's cryin'." Pulling away, the little girl nodded her head sagely.

"Brooke, sweetie, would you sit right here and watch a new video Grandma was saving for you for Christmas? I sneaked it out today for a special treat." Natalie gave a telltale sniffle as she inserted the video into the VCR and turned on the television.

"Yes!" Brooke cried, clapping her hands with glee.

"Good. There's something your mom and I need to talk about. We'll be in the kitchen if you need us."

"Okay," Brooke said, already focused on the television.

Marilyn, frowning with concern, followed her mother to the recently remodeled kitchen where she was presented with the newspaper article entitled, "The One Who Got Away." The article Joshua had described to her at McDonald's. The exposition featured a photo of Joshua dashing from an indistinguishable brick building, head bent, as if he were warding off reporters.

"Where did you get this?" Marilyn croaked, her pulse throbbing.

"It came in the mail today," Natalie said in a wobbly voice. "Everybody in the church got one. The phone's been ringing off the hook."

Torn with anguish, Marilyn blinked against her own tears. "I've heard the story behind this," she said, skimming the condemning words. "This piece isn't factual."

"I figured it wasn't," Natalie said, blowing her nose on a paper towel. "But there are a couple of people in our church who are always bent on believing the worst. Mrs. Simms is saying we should call a church meeting and demand Pastor Langham's resignation."

"But...but....they can't do that!" Marilyn sputtered, suddenly wanting to defend Joshua from the ills of such an undertaking. "Josh was a key informer on this case. Besides, this happened fifteen years ago. He's lived a life above reproach for all those years. And...and isn't this business of finding Christ all about forgiveness and starting life anew—or isn't it?"

"Yes, but you know how the Gilberts are. They were instrumental in removing our last pastor because they didn't like him."

"I'll go and talk to them if I have to. I'll tell them...I'll tell them..."

"They've always thought the world of you. I don't think they ever got over your break up with John before college. They sure wanted you to be their daughter-in-law."

"I'll tell them I'm thinking about marrying Joshua," Marilyn blurted. "And if they hurt him, they'll be hurting me...and...and...little Brooke. This is going to devastate Josh."

Marilyn stopped short as she noticed Natalie's raised brows and teary, inquisitive eyes round with speculation. As if her own words had just sunk into her mind, Marilyn stared back at her mother, her eyes just as round. "I told Joshua on Monday night that I'd pray about seeing him. So I prayed about it and decided that was what the Lord wanted."

"Has he already proposed?"

"N-no... we haven't known each other long enough. We aren't even in love yet. It's just that..." Marilyn dashed away her own tears. "Oh, Mother, I just have this feeling about him. That's a big part of the reason I ran from him in the first place."

"I had the same feeling about him from early on. I guess that's why I assumed you two would get along." Natalie tore off a paper towel and handed it to Marilyn.

"Oh, Mother, you and your paper towels. As much as you cry, you'd think you'd keep a box of tissue in every room of the house."

"I did have a box in here. Last Friday, Brooke pulled them all out one by one and laid the cat on top of them while I was in the laundry room."

The two shared a short burst of laughter.

"Well! So you and Josh are going to see each other," Natalie said. "But honestly, I'd never guess the two of you were an item, not with the way he treated you Sunday. I was rather disappointed, myself."

Marilyn rubbed her temples. "I can't tell you why, but we were only an official item about nine hours. Right now, we're keeping our distance for a very practical reason."

"Does it have anything to do with the article we received."

"Yes."

"Someone is trying to ruin Joshua."

Silently Marilyn held her mother's discerning gaze.

"Is it the man he turned into the FBI?" Natalie queried.

Marilyn still remained silent. She had promised Joshua not to leak a word to anyone.

"Is Josh in danger?"

Covering her trembling lips with the tips of her fingers, Marilyn glanced at the nearby oven, which was producing the wonderful aroma of chocolate cake.

"And that's the reason you two broke it off so quickly? Because he's worried about you and Brooke?"

"Mother, how do you always figure out everything?"

"The same way you figure out when Brooke's been naughty and doesn't want to tell you. It's a mother thing." She fiddled with the ceramic spoon holder atop the ebony oven. After a weighty silence she continued, "Well, your father's talking to Mrs. Simms and the Gilberts right now. As a respected member of the church board, if he can't get them to back down, no one can."

$$\backsim$$

Three weeks later, Kim Lan stood in a luxurious Hawaiian condominium. Her eyes full of tears, she stared at herself in the full-length mirror. Clad in a tiger-stripe bikini that left almost nothing to the imagination, she had just finished the final pose on the private beach a few feet away from the condominium.

According to Charlie, who had dropped by after meeting with other clients, this shoot was her best work. But inside, Kim Lan felt like an Old Testament maiden who had sold herself to the worshippers of Baal. The photographers' words still rang in her mind to produce a nauseating punctuation to the fact that she had blatantly disobeyed God:

*Great job, Kim Lan. Keep it up, Baby! Hold that sexy look.
You're going to have all the men in America at your feet. Yes!
Yes! Yes! Now, turn your hips a little to the left and drape
yourself over that rock like you're about to melt all over it.
That's it. That's it, Baby. This is the reason they say you're the
best...*

With disgust, she tore the swimsuit from her body, strode
toward the brass-and-glass decorated bathroom, turned the
water on as hot as she could stand it, and stepped beneath
the spray. She tried to wash away the horrible guilt that had
descended upon her. A guilt that left her feeling like Eve in
the Garden of Eden with her mouth full of delicious fruit,
conviction spilling from her lips. "Oh, God, forgive me. I am
so sorry," Kim prayed. She coughed against the drops of hot
water that sprayed into her mouth.

But what about next time? a haunting voice asked. *You
can say you're sorry for this time, but have you committed to
never doing this again?*

Kim gritted her teeth, wondering, indeed, what she would
do about the next time. After her early morning workout
several weeks ago, she had mentally declared this would be
the last shoot of this sort. Now that declaration seemed lame.
The photographer was already saying he wanted her next
year, and even on a similar shoot in a few months. Saying
no would certainly cut into her earning potential.

An intense battle flared up within Kim Lan, and her own
words to Marilyn mocked her: *What I've found out is that
God has blessed me for seeking Him, but I'm starting to notice
this cycle of sorts. I keep thinking of the potter–clay analogy
from Isaiah. And well, I wonder if that's what's going on with
this latest modeling offer. I feel such a battle within over
whether or not to pose for this shoot.*

The battle wasn't over.

Ferociously, Kim Lan lathered with the scented soap whose name bore her signature. Quickly she rinsed and turned off the water. Fervently, she rubbed herself dry, all the while feeling as if her chest would explode with the conviction of a Holy God. She had disobeyed Him. A remedy for her rebellion meant more than a swift "I'm sorry" with plans to repeat the sin. God was requiring her full repentance, her turning away from a life of tantalizing men to lust.

She donned her silk pajamas and plopped onto the king-sized bed, face down, her waist-length hair wrapped in a towel atop her head.

I wonder what Charlie and The Forman Agency would think if I stopped doing this type of modeling? What would the other models think? What would my fans think? What would God think? These questions swirled through her mind like an accusing mantra, bent on rending her soul.

Think about it, a rational voice insisted. *You have done nothing to break the Ten Commandments.* Mentally, she ticked all ten off in her mind and affirmed she hadn't consciously broken even one of them.

However, I'm certainly enabling a nation full of men to break one. Millions of men will dream of being with me. Some will probably fantasize committing adultery with me.

Kim Lan sat straight up. The shower had done nothing to wash away the feeling that she was in a cesspool. And a final question lambasted her thoughts.

Am I a woman of God or not?

She thought of Marilyn, of her obvious disapproval of the swimsuit shoot. Kim Lan had conveniently avoided the subject since that weekend when Charlie had called, and Marilyn hadn't brought it up either. Marilyn, despite her anguish in losing Greg, had always struck a chord of admiration among all the sisters. She seemed to have something special going on with God. Marilyn Thatcher, struggles and all, was indeed a woman of God.

But are you? Exactly how serious are you about the Lord?

The bedside phone rang. She looked at the cream-colored receiver as if it were a foreign object. Without thinking, she answered.

"Kim Lan!" Charlie said boisterously. "Since I still have some business to take care of here, I thought I'd join the celebration. I'm about to leave for the restaurant. Want me to have my driver pick you up? We can go together."

She hesitated. She'd forgotten the final dinner with the photographer, the magazine publisher, and the rest of the models. According to the publisher, this swimsuit issue was undoubtedly the hottest, and Kim Lan was without exception the most enticing of them all. As with the president of the shampoo company, Kim Lan suspected the magazine publisher would ignore the fact he was married for a few nights if she would. *But I won't,* she affirmed to herself.

"Hey! Are you there?" Charlie asked.

"Yes." Her internal turmoil had swept aside all thoughts of the celebration dinner. Kim Lan glanced toward her open suitcase sitting beside the mirrored closet doors. What she really wanted to do was pack her bags, forget tomorrow's chartered flight, and go back home tonight. She possessed no desire whatsoever to celebrate her disobedience to God.

"So what do you think?" Charlie asked.

Are you a woman of God or not?

She chewed on her perfectly polished thumbnail then blurted the answer that ended her mental anguish. "Yes, I am."

"Great, I'll be there in—"

"No. I mean—I mean—" She glanced toward the tiger-striped bikini near the full-length mirror framed in cherry wood. A new undulation of holy conviction splashed against her. "I mean I *am* a woman of God."

"What?"

"Charlie," she blurted with determination, "I should have never done this shoot. This sort of thing is only one step removed from pornography."

"Are you getting religious on me, Kim Lan?"

"No, I'm not getting religious on you, Charlie! I'm making a few decisions that I think will please God. I am a Christian, and I have no business—*no business*—doing the kind of poses I just completed." She took a decisive breath and plunged forward. "And I've decided I won't do another shoot like the one I did today. Don't even call me when they offer. The answer is no. N–O–" she spelled.

"But—but—but—" Charlie sputtered. "These are your biggest money-makers."

"I can't help it. I refuse to entice a nation full of men to lust after me ever again. If a women's magazine calls and wants me to pose in the latest *decent* swimwear for the sake of showing and selling the *swimwear* then I'll consider it. But this business of putting on a micro-bikini and melting all over boulders and lying in the surf for a men's magazine is over."

"Do you understand how this is going to affect your career?"

"I don't care how this is going to affect my career. I've finally come to the point that I'd rather please God!"

"Ah, Kim Lan, you're just having a mood," he soothed in a patronizing voice. "Maybe tomorrow you'll feel differently."

"No," she said in exasperation. "This has nothing to do with a mood. It has to do with obeying God." Kim Lan stood, feeling as if a giant weight were falling from her shoulders. "Furthermore, I don't want to even see this issue when it comes out. There's nothing I can legally do at this point to stop them from printing the photos. I've signed the contract. I fully understand all that, but I regret it!"

"Have you lost your mind?" Charlie yelled.

"No, I haven't lost my mind," she ground out. "I'm finding my right mind. I'm through with selling myself like this. It's wrong. It's unbiblical. And...and it makes me feel dirty."

Silence.

"Furthermore, I'm calling to see if I can arrange a flight back home tonight. I need to go home." Kim Lan's voice broke as an incredible peace filled her soul and ended the friction of her spiritual turmoil.

"Okay, okay," Charlie said as if he didn't want to further agitate her. "But what do I tell the people expecting to see you tonight?"

"Tell them...tell them the truth, Charlie."

He sighed.

"I'll talk to you later," she said in tired triumph. "I've got some packing to do."

Kim Lan hung up the phone, walked to the string bikini, picked it up, and dropped the thing in the nearest trash can.

Twenty-Four

~

"Hi," Joshua said, his eyes heavy with fatigue.

"Hi," Marilyn answered, shocked by Joshua's presence on her porch.

"Aren't you going to ask me in?"

"Okay." She opened the door wider and stepped aside as he entered. Other than an occasional neighborly glimpse of him, Marilyn hadn't seen Joshua since the weekend she visited her mother's church. After his cold, distant treatment she had decided to continue attending the larger church in town while allowing Brooke to go with her parents. During the last few weeks, Marilyn had managed to distract her daughter enough in the evenings to keep her mind off of visiting Josh...for the most part. Although the child occasionally asked for him, Marilyn simply told her, "Josh is busy right now," and left it at that.

Josh walked into her living room and plopped onto the striped couch as if he were dragging a bucketful of bricks securely attached to his neck.

The phone rang, and Marilyn looked toward it, feeling as if something ominous was underway. Even though she hadn't seen Josh in person, he had called her once two weeks ago and awkwardly requested prayer for a special board meeting. Joshua had, of course, discovered that the whole church received copies of the incriminating editorial.

272

Although some members had been disgruntled over the editorial, the church board had arranged an immediate open meeting that resulted in their unanimous, continued support of their young pastor. Marilyn had praised the Lord with her parents and continued to bombard heaven with prayers for Joshua's safety.

The phone continued its ringing, and Marilyn thought about unplugging it. She didn't want to hear another stressful report concerning the man she had grown to care for so very deeply.

"Are you going to get that?" Josh asked, an aura of defeat cloaking his demeanor. "It's probably somebody with the news."

"The news?"

"Yes. Leopard sent another article."

Marilyn groaned and reached for the phone.

"Marilyn, it's me," Natalie said, her voice trembling.

"Joshua's already here," Marilyn said simply. "He says there's been another article."

"Yes. And this one's as bad as the other one—maybe worse. It would appear our pastor has been a ladies' man. Is that true?"

"It's true," Marilyn rasped, her mind racing with the implications of her mother's words. What kind of news release was this one?

"But that was fifteen years ago," Marilyn continued.

"That's obvious by the photo in the article. But I think this is just too much for Mrs. Simms and the Gilberts, and a few others who wanted to kick him out with the last article. This time I think they have a significant number of folks behind them."

Marilyn looked toward Joshua and silently held his troubled gaze.

"I won't keep you," Natalie continued. "And it's none of my business, but that man is going to need you right now."

"Yes, I know," Marilyn whispered. Never breaking eye contact with Josh, she bid her mom adieu and hung up.

"Your mother?" Joshua asked.

"Yes."

Silently Josh retrieved a sheet of folded paper from his shirt pocket and extended it toward Marilyn.

Fingers trembling, she took it, opened it, and began to read the incriminating article. "Joshua Langham (above) struts his stuff with model Marty Norton as his partner in crime faces time in prison..." Appalled, Marilyn skimmed the rest of the article that detailed Joshua's scandalous interacting with the opposite sex, leaving no doubt of his infamy. Briefly she scrutinized the photo of a younger Joshua clutching a gorgeous woman, obviously in full swing to a popular dance tune.

"I had a brief affair with her," he said flatly. "Anyway, she was a model who never made it all that big. That picture was taken before I turned in Clark, but they didn't print it until after our story hit the media. The photographer originally took the shot because of Marty, not me."

Stunned, Marilyn handed the copy of the article back to him.

Grimly, Josh snatched the piece of paper from her, angrily wadded it, and hurled it across the room.

"Have you called the police?" Marilyn asked, settling beside him on the couch.

"Yes."

"And?"

"There's nothing they can do. The first article was postmarked in Dallas. This one was postmarked in Oregon. According to the police, there's no way to prove these even came from Leopard. And even if they did prove he mailed them, nothing about the mailing is illegal. It is not illegal to send empty envelopes to people. It is not illegal to mail copied newspaper articles to anyone."

"But poisoning a person's dog is a misdemeanor."

"But how do we prove he did it?" Joshua asked, raising both hands in exasperation. "I was so relieved after that last church board meeting when everyone seemed so...so accepting. I knew there were a few who wanted to toss me out on my ear, but the vast majority supported me. I thought maybe the whole thing would blow over. But it's not blowing over." Leaning forward, Joshua propped his elbows on his knees, placed his head in his hands, and curled his fingers into his hair. "It's getting worse." He paused. "I've called a church meeting for tonight."

"Tonight?"

"Yes. At eight. I'm going to stand before all of them and explain the best that I can about everything that happened. Will you come?" He asked, not moving a muscle.

"Okay," Marilyn whispered without reserve.

"Where's the Ladybug?"

"Gregory has had her all week. He's supposed to bring her back tomorrow." Marilyn, sweeping a strand of annoying hair from her eyes, ached for her daughter. All week she had wondered whether Sheila was treating Brooke with love or mere tolerance.

"What's going on with him?" Josh asked flatly.

"Nothing really."

"He isn't bothering you anymore...about us?"

"No." Marilyn stared out the front window at a lone cardinal that had landed on her porch rail. "How do you think Clark got the addresses of the whole church?"

"I'm not certain, but—"

"Do you keep a church roll in your office?"

"Yes."

"Do you think he—"

"I've thought of everything. But I've about decided he must have somehow copied the roll book." Leaning back, Joshua stared at the ceiling. "Remember the extra house keys I told you about in my desk at church?"

"Yes."

"Gone."

"So, he must have somehow gotten into your office and taken the keys. Do you think he just–just– Do you have a copy machine in your office at church?" Marilyn asked, shifting to fully face him.

"Yes. And there was a night when I went to the office at midnight to work on my new computer—not long before Blue was poisoned—and the copy machine had been left on." Straightening, he looked her square in the eyes with much the same expression as a hunted animal. "I assumed it must have been kids."

"But..."

"Now, I'm wondering."

Marilyn shook her head in wonder. "What do you think he'll do next?"

"I think he's going to try to kill me," Josh said without blinking.

She bit her bottom lip. "How can you be so certain?"

"Because I understand him. He wouldn't be wasting his time on me unless he has other plans." Joshua stood and walked across the room. His back to her, he continued, "I'm beginning to think I was crazy not to enter that witness protection program. Naive and crazy."

"Well," Marilyn said as she walked to his side, "you didn't. And there's no way to change the past. But we can pray for the future and for your safety." Intuitively she placed her hand in Joshua's to encourage him, only to notice his fingers were chilled. Marilyn wrapped her other hand around the outside of his hand. "Your hands are cold."

"I'm chilled to the bone."

"Why don't we go to the church together and pray at the altar before everyone gets there."

He produced a tired smile. "You're a great lady." Gently, Josh bestowed a kiss on her forehead.

"And you—" Marilyn took a quivering breath. "You're a great man."

At 7:30 Leopard cruised the Arkansas curves that eventually led him to Emporia Street—Joshua's neighborhood. This trip he had chosen to drive from California instead of fly. The last two days had been long, but the handgun he carried was well worth the drive. The thirty-eight revolver he bought on the street would have been detected by airport security. Tonight, after he killed Joshua, Clark would toss the gun into a local restaurant dumpster, drive to the airport in Bentonville, leave the stolen Buick in the parking lot, and board a plane back home.

At last, his revenge would be complete. The fact that he had finally come this far made Leopard giddy.

He barely braked as he rolled parallel to Joshua's house and scrutinized the small home. Joshua's truck claimed the driveway. Within an hour, Leopard would leave the sedan at a nearby park, walk back to Emporia Street, hide in the bushes, and watch. When the perfect moment came, he would end Panther's life.

Clark figured by now, Joshua's church members were so riled they were ready to ask for their pastor's resignation. Leopard understood all too well the mentality of a small country church. His own parents had attended such a church when he was a child. He remembered the cyclical feuds in which the members participated. He even recalled his folks criticizing the pastor a few times themselves. In short, Clark had been around the church scene long enough to witness a whole congregation turn into of a den of vipers with little warning.

As he pressed the accelerator, Clark glanced in his rearview mirror to see Panther meeting that blonde from the restaurant in his front yard. Leopard slowed the vehicle and peered into the rear-view mirror as the two got into Joshua's truck. With a twist of his lips, Leopard made a snap decision. He would follow them. Wickedly chuckling, he muttered, "Kiss your stinkin' life goodbye, you traitor."

Marilyn quietly followed Joshua into the church where she grew up. Without a word, he switched on the lights as he went. The gold-and-green color scheme produced a gentle softening to the atmosphere. The classic stained-glass windows beckoned Marilyn into the sanctuary and carried her back to her childhood.

At last, Joshua turned to her and helplessly stared into her eyes as if he were looking for any sign of strength in her. Marilyn understood the way he felt all too well. She clearly recognized the emotions spilling from his eyes. She had felt exactly the way he looked the day she arrived on her parents' doorstep with a broken life and a two-year-old who

wailed for her daddy every night. Now it was Marilyn's turn
to be strong.

"Let's pray," she said, taking his hand in hers.

Silently the two of them walked toward the ancient altar
and knelt side by side. They propped elbows on the dull surface, worn by many a soul who had sought God there.
Groping for direction, Marilyn pondered whether she should
pray first, wait for Josh to pray, or just breathe her heavenward pleas in silence. However, Joshua gave a telltale sniff,
and Marilyn dashed a glance his way. His elbows were
braced on the altar, his hands covered his face, and his
shoulders shook.

Marilyn bit her lips to stay her own tears and decided to
go ahead and pray. "Oh, Father God," she said, her voice
quivering, "we pray that You will calm those who will be
here tonight who might plan to come against Josh. Lord, he
is Your man. Thank You so much for his life and for—for all
he's meant to me, to me and to Brooke." Marilyn sniffed as
a tear trickled down the side of her nose. "And, Lord, while
I'm on the subject, I pray that You will guide Josh and me
in our relationship. Forgive me for being so hardheaded,
Father. Forgive me for anything I might have said that was
harmful to Josh." Pausing, Marilyn gulped, not certain she
understood why her prayer had taken the turn it did.

Immediately, she felt a strong arm around her shoulders.
"Father," Joshua breathed, "thank You for Marilyn. Thank
You for the light she and little Brooke have brought into my
life. Oh, Lord, please...please spare me. Don't let me be
killed now—not now, when...when I've met the woman of
my dreams." He stifled a broken sob.

"Father God," Marilyn continued, the tears now plopping
from her cheeks onto the altar, "speak peace to us. Give
Josh the courage to face those who are about to arrive. Don't

let the powers of darkness overtake his ministry. Keep him in Your hands."

The following silence was broken only by their diminishing sniffles. Joshua looked under the altar and produced a box of tissue. Gratefully, Marilyn grabbed a handful.

"Thanks," Josh whispered, tucking one of Marilyn's hands into the palm of his.

Marilyn nodded and, powerless to do much else, gazed into his eyes. What she saw there warmed her damp cheeks. Adoration. Respect. And...love. Yes, the beginnings of mature love.

The church door opened and closed, then footsteps sounded from the foyer. Marilyn followed Josh in scrambling to her feet and turning to face the first arriving church members. Within fifteen minutes, people lined the pews and Joshua stood behind a podium he had placed in front of the altar. He retrieved a microphone from the platform and nervously cleared his throat. After leading a brief prayer, Josh darted a nervous glance to Marilyn and began.

Clark, leaning on the cane, hobbled into the church foyer, his mind raging with what could possibly be going on at Panther's church this evening. Perhaps...did he dare hope that he could somehow be witness to the church excommunicating their pastor? The possibility left him reeling with delight. He debated whether to limp into the sanctuary, but decided instead to stay outside the door and eavesdrop. If this happened to be a sickening church service, then he would go back to Joshua's house and wait until he returned. However, a joyful voice inside him suggested that Panther's church service days were over—with this congregation anyway.

After finding a chair by the door, Leopard sat down. He inserted his hand into the right pocket of his baggy pants and groped through the hole until he caressed the thirty-eight strapped to his leg. His fingers stroked the handgun as a vile craving rushed upon his depraved soul spotted with evil. Deep in his heart of darkness, a lean feline's voracious roar erupted and echoed off the corridors of his twisted mind. Panting with expectation, he gradually narrowed his eyes and strained to catch every word that began to trickle from the sanctuary.

"I'm glad you're all here. I understand there has been another newspaper article that has been mailed to everyone in the church," Joshua said, darting another glance toward Marilyn.

Trying to encourage him, she smiled. However, she progressively tensed with each passing second. Josh cleared his throat, and no one said a word. The silence reminded Marilyn of a cemetery at midnight. Desperately, she wanted to turn around from her spot in the second pew and view the expressions of everyone present.

"I have at one time or another alluded to my dark past, but I have never gone into details. Even during the meeting a few weeks ago after that first article was mailed, I skimmed over a lot." He smiled sadly. "I've never lied once about my past, but there's quite a bit I'm ashamed of and much I haven't mentioned." From that point, Josh simply shared his

story, leaving no stones unturned. He even stated that he
believed his old friend was trying to ruin him.

Marilyn, eyes filled with unshed tears, felt as if a rosebud
were gradually opening up within her. A rosebud of love.
The same love she had seen in Joshua's eyes minutes before
when they knelt at the altar. Joshua Langham may have
made some wrong choices in his life, but no one could
reproach him now. Obviously he was a man who knew God
and desperately wanted to follow His path.

"I can't finish this story," Josh continued, nervously slipping his hand into the pocket of his pleated slacks, "without
telling all of you that I have spent many years beating myself
up for my sinful past. I have regretted every choice I ever
made that was contrary to the Word of God, I—"

"Then why'd you do it all?" a gravely, masculine voice
challenged.

Marilyn reflexively turned around to see Mr. Gilbert,
tanned and rugged, rising to his feet. Now in his sixties, Marilyn couldn't remember Isaac Gilbert ever doing much more
than grumbling. No matter what happened at church, he
usually believed himself obligated to supply the complaints.
Trying to gauge the reaction of the rest of the congregation,
Marilyn scanned their faces. Some were aghast at Gilbert's
outburst; others looked as if they wanted an answer to his
question, especially the sour, aging Mrs. Simms.

Marilyn glance toward Joshua, whose face slowly drained
of color.

"I think we need a pastor who is squeaky clean. Not one
who's dragging his sins and a long line of felonies around
with him," Gilbert said.

"Amen," someone mumbled from the back pew.

"Mr. Gilbert," Joshua began, his voice less than certain,
"I'm not dragging my past with me." He looked directly at

Marilyn, and his eyes took on a spark of new courage. "I've bundled those sins up and nailed them to the cross. As far as God is concerned, I've never committed one sin. And..."

Marilyn gave an encouraging smile.

"As far as *I* am concerned, my sins are covered by the blood of Jesus."

"But what kind of an example are you to our children and grandchildren?" Mrs. Simms barked, sanctimoniously patting the back of her gray hair.

"I'll tell you the kind of example he's setting," a soft voice insisted from the other side of the sanctuary.

Deciding that being discreet simply was not the current protocol, Marilyn turned the other direction to look toward the speaker. Mrs. Holmes. Dear Mrs. Holmes. She never said much, but her God-centered life and loving spirit usually spoke for her.

"Pastor Josh has been a great source of hope for me. I have a son 'bout the same age as our pastor. But...but...he's not..." Tears brimming her eyes, she shook her head.

Marilyn's own eyes were stinging again. She sniffed. Why did she always feel the need to cry when anyone else started?

"Anyway," Mrs. Holmes said, toying with a button on her faded blouse, "he's an alcoholic. There for awhile I was so...so discouraged. I didn't even feel as if the Lord was hearing my prayers about my boy. Then pastor Josh came. And even though he never did detail—until lately—all his past, he told me and my husband to never give up because there was a time when he—*even he*—lived a life of sin. And I don't guess I've ever told you, Pastor, but your example has meant the world to me." Gripping the pew in front of her, she humbly reclaimed her seat.

284 Debra White Smith

The congregation produced a ripple of "amens" that gradually expunged the hopelessness from Joshua's demeanor.

"I'd just like to say," Fred Douglas began, coming to his feet, "that as the senior member of the church board, I don't see how these articles in any way affect our church or our present choice in pastor. As far as I am concerned, he has *clearly* answered any questions we might have. I don't see that there's a problem."

"That's because your daughter's going to marry him," Leona Gilbert mumbled just loud enough for everyone to hear.

Marilyn felt as if tongues of fire flickered along her cheeks. Stone silence followed. Joshua ducked his head, and Marilyn thought she detected the slightest smile curving the corners of his mouth. *How can he be laughing? Has the man become delirious under pressure?* she wondered.

Someone sat next to Marilyn. She looked to see her own mother with a determined glint in her blue eyes. Natalie leaned toward Marilyn and began to whisper.

"There's been a rumor."

So I gathered.

"I think it probably wouldn't hurt at this point for you to validate our pastor and also clarify your relationship with him."

"But that's nobody's business," Marilyn hissed.

"Not under normal circumstances. But these are not normal circumstances. There's a church full of people that would like to hear that Joshua Langham is as much a gentleman as he now claims to be."

Gritting her teeth, Marilyn stared in consternation at her mother. "The last thing I expected to do was give a speech."

"Well, sometimes we've got to do what we don't want to do." Natalie Douglas seemed to dare her daughter to look

away. "Last month you said you'd go to the Gilberts and
Mrs. Simms and tell them you and Joshua were praying
about getting married..." her voice trailed off meaningfully.

"Mother!" Marilyn whispered. "You can't be suggesting—"

"It might mean the difference between Joshua's staying
and leaving," Natalie said with conviction.

Trapped by her mom's candid scrutiny, Marilyn deliberated her options. At this point, she debated if she even had
any options.

Twenty-Five

The cool September darkness draped around Leopard like a comfortable cloak. As stealthy as a deceptive feline, he crept from the shadows of the bushes in Joshua's yard to the back door. He had listened long enough to the church meeting. His plan had unfolded as beautifully as he presumed. Clark's lips turned up at the corners as he relished the death of Joshua Langham's reputation. With gloved hands, he deftly inserted the key into the lock, turned it, and the door opened with the faintest of squeaks. The kitchen smells of a recently cooked meal enveloped Clark. He shut the door, padded across the kitchen tile, and stepped into the living room. Eyes narrowed, he appraised the choices of chairs and decided on the recliner in the corner. Joshua most likely would be well into the living room before he spotted Leopard. That was exactly what Clark wanted. Then it would be too late.

Scratching at the irritating beard, he settled into the recliner, laid the thirty-eight on the chair's armrest, and waited. The old urge for his thin brown cigars manifested itself, and Panther grinned wickedly. Once his mission was complete, he would be free to smoke a whole pack of cigars, if he so chose. But for now, he continued to abstain. He didn't want to alert Joshua with the distinct odor of tobacco. He wanted no evidence to point back to him. No traces at all.

Joshua, distracted by the covert conversation between Marilyn and her mother, found it difficult to follow the general line of muttering that had claimed the congregation. Presently, an indescribable veil of peace descended upon his soul—enough peace that he could even find Leona Gilbert's comment about his marrying Marilyn somewhat amusing. Seeing Marilyn's face grow scarlet had even added to his inward laughter. Perhaps the stress of this whole mess had made him demented. Whatever the case, his earlier despair had turned to serenity with a touch of humor.

Lord, he prayed inwardly, *if these people ask for my resignation, I will freely give it. I will hold no malice. You have taken care of me since the day I accepted You as my Savior. You will continue to take care of me. My life and my ministry are in Your hands.*

The tranquility intensified. His soul soaked up the spirit of contentment. He rested in Christ. Despite the outcome of tonight's meeting, he would survive. His ministry would survive. Even if the people here rejected him, there were other congregations and other places to serve.

A movement from the second pew snatched Joshua's attention. Marilyn, her face pale, stood. Startled, Joshua prepared to acknowledge her right to speak, but Marilyn didn't give him the chance. With a determined set to her lips, she quietly entered the aisle to walk to his side.

The congregation hushed. All attention focused on Marilyn.

She held Joshua's gaze for a brief, yet potent second then reached for the microphone he held. Blinking in surprise, Joshua relinquished it and took a deep breath.

"Most of you watched me grow up," Marilyn began, her voice noticeably shaky. "I was raised in this church." She paused long enough to glance over the congregation with a challenging gleam in her eyes. "Whether you would admit it or not, most of you have heard the details of my divorce." She took a quivering breath and rapidly blinked.

Joshua noticed a rush of tears in her eyes, then they abated. Admiring her self-control, he grasped her words like a man who has been thrown a lifeline.

"I tried with every scrap of my being to get my former husband to stay in our marriage, but he chose the other woman," she stated practically. "Most of you know I've been back in Eureka Springs for over two years now. But only this summer did I finally receive the healing from God that allowed me to darken a church door without feelings of..." She gulped and gripped the mike with both hands. "Without dark feelings.

"Well, in June I accepted a full-time position with Dr. Lovelady and was able to rent my own place. As things turned out, I moved across the street from your pastor."

With great fondness, Joshua recalled the moment he had met Marilyn. She had been wearing a pair of blue jean cut-offs, an oversized T-shirt, and a blatant case of indignation due to the shape of her garden. Yet to Joshua's eyes, she had looked nothing short of a dream come true. The all-American woman. And as he had thought on that momentous day, so Joshua repeated his sentiments, *God bless America.*

With a hard swallow, Marilyn continued. "Well, apparently some of you have now heard a rumor that Josh and I are—are involved in a relationship. And I must tell you that in all my acquaintance with Joshua Langham, he has never, *absolutely never,* been anything more than a perfect gentleman. Personally, I can't help what his past is, and neither

can he, but I can testify to you that his present is very much
in line with the Word of God. I firmly believe he is indeed
a man of his word and a man of God." She intently peered
at Joshua, her brown eyes a reflection of varying emotions,
a combination of "I can't believe I'm standing up here saying
all this," and "I'll do everything in my power to validate your
honor," and "I'm scared stiff," and…"I love you."

Yes, Joshua saw traces of new love stirring within Marilyn's soul. Despite all her vows of not being interested in a
relationship, he had somehow won her heart. *Thank You,
Lord!* his heart exclaimed.

Still she stared at him, and the congregation seemed to be
holding its breath for her next words. "And…we aren't
rushing into anything," she said slowly, "but Josh and I are
praying about maybe one day getting married."

A fountain of glee sprang up within Joshua, and he felt
as if he would explode with unbelievable joy.

"We are?" he blurted.

The congregation burst into a round of boisterous laughter.
Laughter that chased away the negative atmosphere that initially seemed to rob Josh of his very breath. Laughter that
found its way onto Marilyn's own face. Joshua joined in, and
he placed his arm around Marilyn's waist, bestowed a light
kiss on her forehead, and grinned like a man who had just
discovered the world's greatest treasure.

"Excuse me," Mr. Gilbert barked as he once more stood.
"None of this, no matter how cute it is, changes the situation."

"Amen," Mrs. Simms declared.

"That's the truth," Mrs. Gilbert said, vigorously nodding,
and a few heads on the back pews joined in the nodding.

Once more the crowd quieted. No one moved. Joshua
ached with the pending loss of members. Thankfully, he now
saw the majority of the church supported him. However, there
would always be those who refused to understand.

"I've been a member of this church for forty years," Isaac Gilbert continued, his treacherous eyes like the beady orbs of a venomous serpent. "And we ain't never had such a man as our pastor. All our pastors before now have been decently married with a clean background, not some—some playboy who should've been a jailbird."

The group produced a collective gasp, and Joshua gritted his teeth, trying hard not to respond in defensive anger.

"And here's the deal," Isaac said, tucking a thumb under the strap of his worn overalls. "I ain't gonna stay in a church with such a pastor. If this group wants to keep the likes of him, then I'm going to take my money and my time and go somewhere where the pastor is the decent sort." Chin at an arrogant angle, he clamped his lips together as if he dared anyone to refute his righteous claims.

"That's right," someone mumbled.

"Well," Joshua began, desperately praying for something to say, "Mr. Gilbert, I have appreciated your—your past support. You and your wife mean a lot to me."

"Hmm," Mrs. Gilbert muttered and produced a petty sniff.

"But isn't a story like mine the reason we're here? Didn't God send His Son to die for sinners, so that those who have grieved Him can come to know Him and serve Him? If we remove everyone with a past from the church and from ministry, in some places we won't have many people left."

"Amen," the congregation said in unity.

But a darker opinion erupted from the back pew. "That all sounds real pretty and flowery," Mr. Gilbert shouted, pointing his finger at Josh's nose. "But I don't trust you any farther than I can throw ya. You're still nothing but a—"

"I'm a sinner, saved by God's grace," Joshua said, amazed at the calmness that swept over him. "And once I devoted my all to Him, God unfolded an amazing life before me. Furthermore—"

"Mr. Gilbert." Marilyn grabbed the microphone, her voice not quite as patient as Joshua's. "God is a God of second chances. Just think about it. Good grief, Paul himself was a murderer!"

"That's right," several in the crowd affirmed.

"But the Lord got a grip on him and turned him into someone who has reached the world for the cause of Christ."

A red flush crept up Isaac Gilbert's face. Silently he glared at Marilyn, then shifted his attention once more to Joshua.

"Let's go, Leona," he ground out. Shoulders rigid, he stepped from the pew and stomped up the aisle. His wife, head held high, followed in his wake. Mrs. Simms and approximately twelve other members followed suit. The church door slammed twice, then silence claimed the sanctuary. A gracious, placid silence.

"We need to remember them in prayer," Joshua said simply, a mixture of concern and relief overtaking him.

"I think we need to remember *you* in prayer," the wiry Fred Douglas stated as he stood. "Let's gather around our pastor at the altar," he said with great compassion. The church members acquiesced to Fred's request and all began to stand and move forward.

Joshua took the mike from Marilyn, placed it on the front pew, grasped her hand in his, and knelt at the altar. The hands that touched his back seemed to impart the very touch of God upon his soul. And whatever happened, Josh knew his Lord was in control.

Marilyn, emotionally exhausted, pulled her Chevy into her driveway next to where she usually parked. The illumination of her headlights had revealed that the other car in the drive was a red Cadillac.

She smiled, wondering why Greg had returned Brooke early. They weren't due to arrive until in the morning. Anticipating the feel of her precious daughter in her arms, Marilyn put the car into park, turned off the ignition, scrambled from the driver's seat, and ran toward the luxury automobile. Fully expecting Greg and Brooke to be waiting in the car, she spontaneously opened the passenger door, intent on giving her daughter an affectionate welcome—but the car was empty.

Puzzled, Marilyn looked toward her front porch to see no one there, either. Her car's incessantly dinging bell reminded her she had not closed the door, retrieved her purse, or removed the keys from the ignition. Marilyn rushed back to the car, grabbed her purse and keys, slammed the door, and ran toward the house.

As soon as she inserted the key into the lock, the front door swung open.

Gregory stood on the other side, silently appraising her with melancholy eyes.

Marilyn raised questioning brows. "Where's Brooke?"

"She went to sleep on the way here. I tucked her into her bed."

Ignoring him, Marilyn dropped her purse and keys on the couch, rushed through the living room, down the hallway, and into her daughter's room. The light from the hallway cast a cozy gleam across the sight of the sleeping child. Brooke lay against her pillow, eyes closed, a stuffed bear firmly entrenched in the crook of her arm. Marilyn covered her lips with trembling fingers and knelt beside her daughter's bed.

"Mama missed you, Darling," she whispered, brushing aside a strand of white blonde hair from Brooke's cheek. Delicately, Marilyn touched her lips against Brooke's forehead and pulled away. She searched her daughter's relaxed demeanor for any signs of discontentment. Had Sheila been kind to Brooke? Only a conversation with Brooke would answer Marilyn's concern.

With a sigh, Marilyn stood and cast another loving look at her charming daughter. The week had been a long one. A sinister voice tempted her to begin a new round of resentful accusations toward Greg, but Marilyn stopped the thoughts even before they had a chance to take root and flourish.

You have forgiven Gregory. You have nailed your resentment to the cross. You must not pass a heritage of bitterness to your daughter, she reminded herself.

Wearily tucking a strand of hair behind her ear, Marilyn contemplated having to face Gregory in the living room. She certainly didn't want to interact in another heated discussion about Josh. Hopefully, Greg had quietly slipped out and begun the journey home. But once she entered the living room again, all her hopes died in the face of his presence.

"Is she still asleep?" Gregory asked, his arms folded as he stood near the wall on which hung an assortment of Brooke's photos.

"Yes." For lack of anything else to do, Marilyn picked up her keys and leather purse from the couch and deposited them in their usual spot on a table a few feet from the front door. "Why did you bring her home early?"

"She was crying for you." He swung around and focused his attention on the pictures.

Brooke's life of constantly missing one or the other of her parents brought fresh tears to Marilyn's eyes.

"How did you get in here, anyway?" she asked, desperately wishing he would move toward the door.

"I picked the back-door lock," he said without apology.

A twinge of irritation sprouted in Marilyn's chest, and she stiffened.

Briefly he glanced toward her. "I'm sorry if that offends you, but Brooke was asleep in the car, and I didn't know how long you'd be gone. Even though the nights are cooler than last week, there's still enough summer left to make the car stuffy."

"That's fine," she said begrudgingly, feeling as if it were anything but fine. While one side of Marilyn was glad Gregory had thought of Brooke's comfort, another side didn't like the idea of her ex-husband intruding into her house without invitation.

"Here's this month's check, before I forget it." He reached into the pocket of his pleated shorts and handed her the money.

"Thanks." Avoiding eye contact, Marilyn took the sealed white envelope and placed it into her handbag.

"I added a little extra again," he said softly.

Narrowing her eyes, Marilyn studied him, wondering exactly what his motives were. In the almost two-and-a-half years since their divorce, he had kept an impeccable record in child support payments. But only this summer had he started adding extra. "I appreciate it," she said, a note of doubt in her voice. "Every little bit helps, but—"

"How are you?" he asked, his green eyes suddenly taking on a glimmer of guilt.

"I—I'm—I'm fine," she stammered. Walking across the room, she stood behind the straight-backed rocking chair and gripped the top rung. The hair on the back of her neck prickled, and she wondered what Greg thought he was up to. He lacked the haughty "I'm better than you" expression that often characterized their brief encounters. The dark circles she had noticed under his eyes the last time she saw him seemed darker. His shoulders weren't quite as erect, and his eyes...the eyes that had once snared Marilyn, were boring into her.

The years they had spent together seemed to twine around them, weaving an ever-tighter web of tension.

For better. Yes, there had been laughter even though their marriage wasn't perfect. Especially the first Christmas with Brooke—

For worse. Greg's mother passed away the second year of their marriage from cancer. Marilyn had held Greg while he sobbed.

In sickness. Despite his bent to arrogance, one winter Greg had practically drowned Marilyn in chicken soup and Sprite when she had a nasty case of the flu.

In health. They had managed to sneak away to a log cabin in Branson one spring weekend. That was probably the weekend Brooke was conceived.

But all of that was over. Their marriage had died because Gregory had made his choice. A choice that left them both dealing with the difficult situation of shuffling Brooke back and forth like luggage. Even now, the thought that her daughter was forced to endure such upheaval left Marilyn trying to subdue the fury.

Abruptly, Greg turned back to the photos of Brooke. "I miss her when we're apart," he said in a tormented voice.

Marilyn gripped the chair tighter as her heart began to thump out hard, even beats.

"I see," she said in a barely audible voice.

Gradually, he turned to face her again, and the mask he once hid behind lay at his feet. Marilyn stared into the countenance of a person in mental, emotional, and spiritual torture. Few men could surpass Gregory Thatcher's classic good looks. Few men could surpass his presence behind the pulpit. Few men could surpass the charisma with which he had led his church. But none of that had been enough to keep him from making those detestable choices and falling into blatant sin. In the face of his disavowal, all his good qualities seemed like a package wrapped in gold but empty on the inside. Mentally, Marilyn once again compared Gregory to Joshua.

There is really no comparison, she decided. *Joshua... Joshua Langham is the real deal. Gregory Thatcher just thinks he is.*

"And I miss you," he said at last, his words a faint wisp of sound woven with the thick tension filling the room.

Marilyn swallowed hard against a lump forming in her throat. Gritting her teeth, she blinked against the threatening tears. Tears of frustration, of sorrow, of almost three years worth of agony. With more willpower than she thought possible, she abstained from crying.

"I made a terrible, *terrible* mistake," he said, wearily rubbing the base of his neck.

"I tried to tell you that, Gregory, the night you told me you were moving out, but you wouldn't listen." Marilyn raised her hands in exasperation.

"Can't you just give us another chance?" he asked, his lips trembling.

Marilyn felt as if all the air left her lungs. The room began to spin. Her temples hammered. Goosebumps prickled along her arms.

"What about Sheila?" she gasped. "Didn't you make a commitment to her? And...and what...what about the baby?"

"She miscarried," he said flatly. "The doctor doesn't think she will ever carry a child full term."

"So it will be just the two of you."

"Maybe. Maybe not," he said as if the words were wrenched from him. "She's gone into a terrible depression, and—"

"And locked you out?" Marilyn asked, trying to hide any traces of mockery.

Hopelessly Gregory stared at her.

The mockery vanished. To be replaced by pity. That night when Brooke was sick with that virus, Marilyn had suffered for the man who had trashed a treasure and didn't seem to realize it. Now she ached anew with the fact that Gregory indeed had comprehended his loss. He had thrown away a jewel without a backward glance.

Until now. Marilyn decided that nothing was more pitiful than the person who devalues the priceless, unless that person has been the arrogant, dictator sort. Seeing Gregory so broken and distraught seemed the ultimate cruelty.

But he brought the agony upon himself, she reminded herself.

"I'm not certain—if we'll stay together," he said, taking a step toward Marilyn. "And—and I just—just want my family back."

Marilyn put additional distance between them. "Gregory," she said with more grit than she felt. "You have made a commitment to Sheila, and you need to stick by that. This is not the senior prom, and you are not going steady. This is *marriage.* You can't just switch partners every time it suits you."

"Are you saying you won't—"

"I'm saying that—" Despite her better judgment, Marilyn actually momentarily considered the possibility of going back to him. For Brooke. For the sake of what was lost. But immediately, she dashed aside all such thoughts. "I'm saying that if you had never married Sheila, and even though I don't love you anymore, I would try to rebuild what we had for the sake of Brooke. For the sake of our family. But Gregory, you left me for Sheila, and you *married* her. Now, you want to leave Sheila for me! What's going to stop you from doing this again in a couple of years?"

"But—"

"And..." Marilyn trembled so violently she thought she would collapse, "I'm not going to do that to Sheila. I wouldn't put another human being through what I've suffered these last few years. It's almost worse than death. It *is* a death. It's the death of a family!" she said, her voice breaking on a high note. "I tried to tell you this almost three years ago, but you wouldn't listen. I begged you. I pleaded with you. I tried to tell you where we both were wrong and that changing marriage partners wouldn't fix the problem. All you've done is take your bunch of problems into the next marriage. But you wouldn't listen to me—"

"I'm listening now." Closing the distance between them, he gently gripped her arms.

With the smell of his cologne filling her senses, Marilyn pulled away and stumbled backward until she bumped into the wall. "Don't touch me," she said as a trickle of sweat drained down her tense spine. "You have no right. You threw that right away."

"Is your decision because of that jerk across the street?" he asked, his lips twisting bitterly.

"Joshua isn't a jerk," Marilyn said firmly. "And, no, even if Joshua weren't in my life, my answer would remain the same."

"Are you going to marry him?" Greg demanded, his nostrils flaring.

"I'm praying about it." Raising her chin, Marilyn pressed her lips together.

Greg produced a caustic laugh. "Don't tell me you think God will bless that!"

Marilyn gasped, wondering how Gregory Thatcher could think that God had appointed him as His spokesperson. "I'm not going to pretend for one second that marrying Joshua would have been God's Plan A for me and Brooke. I think you and I both understand what Plan A should have been." Her thoughts went back to the night before her wedding, to the overwhelming doubts she had dashed aside. She wondered, as she had a hundred times, if marrying Greg had been God's perfect will for her life.

"Well, I'm offering you Plan A again," he said sarcastically. "And you aren't taking, so I can only assume that Joshua Langham—"

"No! No! No!" She stomped her foot. "I have told you once, I will tell you again. My decision about your offer has nothing to do with Joshua. I told you earlier this summer that I didn't want to get involved with another man—and that includes you!"

"But you are considering Joshua?" An ugly, jealous spark flashed in his eyes. "Now you're contradicting yourself!"

"So I'm contradicting myself!" Marilyn raised her arms in exasperation. "You contradicted everything you told me the day we got married, Gregory!"

Eyes narrowed, he worked his jaw muscles and glared down at her. "I won't be making this offer ever again," he said as if he were issuing a threat. He raised his chin a fraction, and Marilyn recognized traces of the manipulator from her past.

She silently held his gaze, never wavering in her resolve.

"You witch," he snarled contemptuously.

Reflexively, Marilyn's hand jerked as the driving urge to slap him spawned her response. But she stopped before ever raising her hand. The instant surge of fury passed, to be replaced by renewed determination...determination and peace...peace and thanksgiving. As she coldly stared at him, her mind raced to the future, to the possibility that one day she might somehow wonder if she should have accepted Greg's offer. But in two tiny words, he had given her the answer. He had changed precious little. His commitment to her the second time would be no greater than the first. In turning him down, she was making the only choice for her and the best choice for Brooke. Thoughts of Greg possibly deserting Brooke a second time hardened Marilyn's resolution.

Turning on his heel, Greg stomped toward the front door.

"Oh, Gregory?"

He swiveled to face her.

"I'm praying for you." Marilyn whispered, looking down at her shaking hands, astounded that she had the strength to speak, let alone in civil tones. "For you and for Sheila."

His eyes widened in surprise.

"And I've been fairly blunt, but I want to tell you that I've forgiven you. I hold no animosity toward you whatsoever—not even for what was said tonight."

Face impassive, Greg looked at his sneakers.

"I—think that if—if you and Sheila would find a good marriage counselor, maybe—"

Without allowing her to finish, Greg stepped out of the house and closed the door behind him.

Marilyn walked toward the couch and collapsed.

"I'm impressed," a voice said from the dining room.

Startled, Marilyn jumped up and faced the intruder.

Twenty-Six

Leopard paced Joshua's living room as if it were his cage. Only minutes ago, he'd heard Joshua's truck pull into the driveway. Panting with anticipation, Leopard had sprung from his chair to peek past the closed drapes and scrutinize his prey. But the full moon's illumination revealed Joshua walking across the street instead of approaching his own front door. Then Leopard recalled seeing that blonde from the restaurant earlier today when he watched them in his rearview mirror. She had walked over to Panther's house from across the street. Panther never strayed far from a female acquaintance, and Leopard didn't believe for one second that being a minister in any way slowed down Josh's extracurricular activities.

Weighing his options, Clark continued to pace the living room. *Joshua might not come back until the morning. But if I wait for him, I might not make it to Bentonville in time to catch the morning flight home. And my next supervisory visit with my parole officer is in two days. I have to make that appointment. If I don't, they'll know I've violated my parole. And that would mean a return trip to the world of bars.*

Pushing the light button on his watch, Leopard noted the time: 9:53. He would give Joshua exactly fifteen minutes. If he didn't come home, then Clark would go after him.

"Hey, I'm sorry," Joshua said. Depositing the bottle of sparkling grape juice on a nearby table, he approached the pale-faced Marilyn. "I thought you heard me walking through the dining room."

"No, I didn't hear you," she said, her drawn brows and compressed lips proving her genuine irritation. "Joshua Langham, if you *ever* do something like that again, I'll—I'll—"

"You'll what?" He took her hands in his, and without reserve, bathed her in the most adoring gaze he could muster.

"I'll...I'll...stop that!" She broke away from him and walked across the room to stand in front of the wall graced with family photos.

"Hey," Josh coaxed as he followed her, placing gentle hands on her shoulder. "I'm sorry. Really. I—"

She sniffled. Her shoulders hunched, and a broken sob erupted from her.

"Marilyn?" Turning her to face him, he pulled her close. At once, he understood how frazzled the confrontation with Gregory had left her. But hearing the same confrontation had fueled Josh with enough hope to paint the skies with "I love you" banners to Marilyn. In the recesses of his mind, he had harbored the tiniest of fears that perhaps Marilyn wasn't over her former husband. But tonight she had told Greg she wouldn't take him back—no matter what!

"Oh, Josh," she said through the tears, "how did my life get to be such a mess?"

He bestowed a tender kiss on her forehead and reveled in the scent of her sporty perfume. "As an official part of your life, I'm highly offended," he teased through a smile.

"I didn't mean it that way," she said, a note of spunk coming through despite her tears.

"I understand." He said as he stroked her shoulder-length hair, enjoying the silkiness beneath his fingers. "But maybe the worst is over. I don't think he'll ever make another scene like that one."

"How much did you hear?"

"Everything, I think."

"Why are you even here?" Her tears diminishing, she pulled away from him. "And how did you get in?"

Joshua stepped toward the end table where the bottle of grape juice was sitting. He grabbed a few tissues from the nearby box, extended them toward her, and held up the bottle.

She dabbled at her cheeks. "That looks suspiciously like—"

"It's sparkling grape juice," he supplied. "I stopped by the store on the way home from church and bought it for us to celebrate our success. Have you ever had sparkling grape juice?"

"No." She produced some final sniffles.

"It's much like grape soda, only better. Anyway, when I got out of the truck, I started over here and noticed Greg's car in the drive. At first, I thought about going back home, but then I got worried. I thought you said he wasn't due to bring Brooke back until in the morning, and it seemed late for him to be here. I didn't like the idea of…" He shrugged. "So I decided to go around to the back door, and provide a backup—just in case."

"Don't tell me you picked the lock." Marilyn pressed the tissue against the corners of her eyes for the last time.

"No, actually the door was unlocked."

"Well, Gregory picked the lock and must have left it unlocked."

"Would you like me to install a dead bolt for you?"

"I would be *delighted* if you'd install one."

"And what about the front door?"

"It's covered."

"Great, then, consider me your local knight in shining armor. Your dead bolt wish is my command." Josh gallantly bowed.

"Oh, brother." Marilyn rolled her eyes and unceremoniously grabbed the grape juice from his grip. "How 'bout we get some plastic dinosaur cups and drink the juice."

"Dinosaur cups!" Josh exclaimed. "I was thinking in terms of fine crystal goblets."

"Yeah, right. Like I've ever owned anything like that. You need to call Kim Lan if you want that kind of treatment."

"No thanks. I'll stay with you," Josh said with a smile. He followed her into the kitchen and watched as she reached to the back of her cabinet to pull out two long-stemmed glasses, the color of sapphires.

"These are a good imitation of fine crystal," she said practically. "Maybe they will work better than the plastic dinosaur cups."

"Either is fine with me," Josh said, peeling away the gold foil that covered the bottle top. He unscrewed the cap and filled the glasses she held out. Setting the bottle on the kitchen counter, he took one of the glasses. "Here's celebrating a won battle at church! And…a won battle in your living room."

Obviously thinking Josh was through, she began sipping the juice.

He smiled as a designing suggestion roamed through his mind and left his mouth. "*And* celebrating the fact that you are praying about marrying me, even though I have never asked you."

Marilyn sputtered and choked.

◇~—

Leopard stopped pacing and pushed the light on his watch. Thirteen minutes had lapsed since his vow to wait fifteen minutes. "Close enough," he muttered. Obviously, Joshua was not coming home tonight. Grabbing his cane, Clark slipped out Joshua's back door and crept around the side of the house. The stars in the clear September sky seemed to watch him like a thousand golden feline eyes. The chirping crickets shrieked an unrelenting chant that propelled Clark forward. The night air, barely touched by the fingers of fall, filled his lungs and fueled his vengeance. He stroked the thirty-eight and anticipated its buck against the power of a departing bullet.

Finally the night of retribution had arrived.

Clark approached the house across the street and soundlessly ascended the concrete steps. He paused outside the front door, doubled his fist, and hesitated before knocking. Perhaps he should make certain Joshua had indeed gone into this house. To no avail, Clark strained to see through the blinds that covered the aging door's window. He stepped toward the large living room window to see if there might be an opening in the tightly closed drapes. Nothing.

Momentarily abandoning his old man gait, Clark propped his cane against the doorframe, rushed down the porch steps, slipped around the side of the house, and hovered within inches of the frame home. Silently he picked his way through the flower bed, pausing only when a spider web brushed his cheek and tangled itself in his bothersome beard. Dashing aside the annoying web, Clark paused beside the first window to which he came. Cautiously, he inched his face toward the window and peered through the half-opened blinds into a comfortably cluttered living room, aglow with lamplight. But no Panther.

With an impatient grunt, Clark ducked, then sneaked under that window to pause beside the next one. A pair of thin, flowered curtains graced that window, and Clark strained to see into what looked like a tiny dining nook. Another room, void of occupants. *Perhaps Panther isn't in this house,* he thought.

Leopard continued his exploration until he came to the last window on this side of the house. A window covered by a curtain that opened in two tiny spots to reveal a limited view of what appeared to be the kitchen. A kitchen where two people stood, drinking what looked like wine.

Clark grinned in satisfaction. His calculations had been correct. Joshua Langham, forever the ladies' man, was up to his usual tricks. The blonde appeared to be thoroughly duped.

Leopard frowned. He hadn't planned on killing anyone but Panther. However, if murdering Panther meant having to shoot his girlfriend as well, then so be it. Tomorrow, Clark had a plane to catch. The next day, he had a parole officer to meet. He couldn't let the inconvenience of another murder hinder his well-laid plans. At once, his mind flashed to that moment in church when Panther had picked up the blonde-haired child. He wondered if the little girl was in the house. *If I kill the mother, should I kill the child?*

He thought of his two nephews. He remembered his own childhood. He recalled the prison inmates who had harmed or killed children and how the other men—even himself—

had especially detested them. Despite his hardness, he cringed with the thought of aiming a gun at a child and pulling the trigger.

No. I won't kill the little girl. If she is in the house, I'll leave her sleeping. In the morning, she'll find the bodies of her mother and Joshua. That would most certainly be a shock, but she should thank me for sparing her life.

Feeling as if the floor had shifted, Marilyn coughed against the carbonated grape juice.

Joshua chuckled beneath his breath. "Are you going to be okay?"

"Yes." She gasped and produced a few final hacks. Awkwardly, she swirled her grape juice around in the glass and searched for words. "I'm sorry," she mumbled at last. "I didn't mean to be jumping to any conclusions, but I just thought—"

"Jumping to conclusions?" Joshua laughed outright, and Marilyn looked up to encounter a spark of mischief still alive in his eyes. "That wasn't the problem at all. I just felt a little let down because I never got the chance to propose."

"Oh." Marilyn gulped the bubbly juice and set the empty glass on the counter with a faint click.

"And I haven't even shopped for the ring, and...I was wondering...could you please tell me...do we have a date set yet?"

Trying to hide the fact that she was drowning in embarrassment, Marilyn narrowed her eyes and glared at him.

"Your face is red." He touched her cheek with the backs of his fingers.

"I guess you're satisfied then?"

He smiled lazily, set his glass on the counter, and pulled her close. Tenderly, Josh bestowed a light kiss on her tear-stained cheek. Marilyn swallowed against the tingles that showered her like a thousand falling stars.

"I guess it's time for me to go home," Joshua said against her ear. "I didn't intend to stay long—only long enough to thank you for tonight. It meant the world to me to have you stand up with me and...and...ah Marilyn," he whispered. "I've missed you so much these last weeks. Your being right across the street and not being able to see you because I was so afraid was so hard. And I probably have no business being over here tonight, but for once, I just couldn't stay away.

"All teasing aside, I'd give my right arm for you to agree to marry me. And I promise I'll always—always—treat you right."

Marilyn soaked up the essence of this man from whom she had initially run. This man whom she had grown to respect. This man whom she was beginning to love.

"I'm still a little scared," she said honestly. "But... but...like I said tonight, I am praying about it. I guess I just figured that you didn't enter relationships lightly and the fact that you even wanted me to agree to see you was proof within itself that you were already praying about...about..."

"Yes. You are absolutely right," Joshua said as he pulled away. "I am praying. I have been praying since the day Blue tore up your garden. I felt an immediate attraction to you, but I think we'd both agree that doesn't mean a relationship is in God's will."

"At this point, the thing I want most is His perfect will. I have made enough mistakes," Marilyn said quietly.

"I feel the exact same way." With a sad smile, Josh stroked the side of her face with his index finger. "Meanwhile, the fact still remains that I shouldn't be over here, not until this business with Leopard is over."

Marilyn tensed and tried to blot the dark images from her mind. "Have you tried calling him? That probably sounds crazy, but maybe if he learned you weren't cowering, he'd get over the thrill of whatever he's up to."

"I thought of that myself last week," Joshua said. "I called information, but his number is unlisted. I was able to get his father's number."

"And?"

"I called Mr. McClure, trying to get Clark's number. To make a long story short, he wouldn't give it to me and hung up on me."

"Do they blame you for Clark's trip to prison?"

"Undoubtedly."

A faint knock sounded at the front door. Marilyn looked toward the sound.

"Are you expecting anyone?" Josh asked.

"No." She nervously bit her lower lip. "I just hope that's not Gregory again."

"Want me to get the door?"

Marilyn contemplated Joshua's ready-to-help demeanor, wishing she could somehow allow him to weather her battles. But that was impossible. She shook her head. "No, but thanks for asking."

"Okay. I'll wait here," he said. "Every damsel in distress needs a good watchdog."

"Thanks," she said, walking from the kitchen.

In a matter of seconds, Marilyn turned on the porch light and discreetly peered past the blinds on the front door window. A familiar old man stood on the other side, leaning on his gnarled cane, patiently awaiting her answer. She paused, wondering why the man looked so familiar. At last she remembered that day at the cafe when she had joined Josh for lunch. She couldn't remember his name, but he had been with Josh that day. He had initially given Marilyn a few forbidding chills, and she hesitated about opening the door to him. But later Joshua had mentioned he thought the man was homeless. Apparently he was still in town and needed help. Forcing aside a new round of misgivings, she turned the dead bolt lock and opened the door.

Kim Lan touched the solid brass lamp on her oriental nightstand. A soft, golden glow draped across the elegant room. She glared at the Bulova beside her bed.

I've been in bed an hour and I'm still not asleep!

Viciously, she jabbed her pillow and plopped back on it to stare at the netting, the color of cream, which served as a canopy for the black lacquer bed.

Her recent modeling decision over the sexual poses now mocked her. Last night, Kim Lan had ridden the plane home like a warrior who had won a victory. With great relief, she had waltzed into her penthouse in the wee hours of the morning, collapsed on the bed, and slept like a woman with a free conscience.

But as the leisurely day wore on, she began to feel as if a myriad tiny doubts leapt from the walls, attached themselves to her body, and burdened her mind with all sorts of speculations. Furthermore, when Ted arrived hours ago to escort her to dinner, his reaction to her news only added to her qualms.

"Are you nuts?" he'd asked over the Caesar salad. "You make a bundle on those types of shoots."

Kim Lan had helplessly stared at the fine silver and crystal that typified most of her dates with Ted. "But I just didn't feel that, as a woman of God—"

"Really, Kim Lan, I think when you're talking about that kind of money, God understands."

She had silently appraised his convinced expression and wondered if perhaps she had been taken by a moment of overactive conscience in Hawaii.

Restlessly, she stirred in the bed, and a new thought seized her: *Call Marilyn.*

Kim Lan mentally calculated the time in Arkansas—just after ten. Should she call her friend so late? She might be asleep by now. Certainly Brooke would be in bed. Kim Lan didn't want to awaken either of them.

Call Marilyn.

Her heart yearned for an affirmative voice on her decision. Marilyn would zealously support her, and she could certainly use the verbal affirmation tonight. Yet the hour proved so late.

Once again, Kim Lan mused over the reason for her modeling decision. "Oh Father," she breathed, "did I do the right thing?" That one small prayer opened the floodgates of heaven. Just as in that Hawaiian condominium, Kim Lan experienced an overwhelming peace that transcended all the doubts. Despite what Charlie or Ted or anyone said, she had indeed made the right choice. The choice of a woman of God.

With a sigh, she decided to wait until in the morning to call Marilyn. Tomorrow was Saturday. They would have ample time to talk. And she had other things to tell Marilyn as well. She looked at the three-carat diamond gracing her ring finger and smiled as it sparkled with blue fire despite the limited light. At dinner, Ted had surprised her with a proposal. She certainly hadn't expected Ted to pop the question so early in their acquaintance. Taken aback, she had at first grappled for a response and even told him she wasn't certain their goals in life were the same. Kim Lan had asked him to please allow her a few weeks to consider his request. She had hated to sound like she thought herself spiritually superior to Ted, but more and more she longed for a man who would join her in seeking God, not just in making an obligatory appearance at church on Sunday. However, Ted, shocked by her hesitation, had at last extracted Kim Lan's true thoughts. With his intense blue eyes shining like limpid orbs of a man in love, he immediately vowed to be everything she desired. He even promised to never again mention their having sex before marriage.

At the evening's end, after Ted's ardent pledges, Kim Lan decided to go ahead and tentatively accept the ring if he would agree to postpone their formal announcement of the engagement. After all, Ted Curry was the most eligible bachelor in the United States. The closest thing to American royalty. Kim Lan saw no harm in seriously considering his offer. Even though she had never prayed about marrying him, she would begin doing so soon. Their relationship seemed to be falling together so smoothly, and perhaps her increasing loyalty to the Lord would continue to influence Ted toward a more devoted walk with God. After all, he had spoken of the Lord tonight in terms he had never used before.

Twenty-Seven

Joshua tiptoed into the small dining room, stopped, and listened to see if the guest was Gregory. He didn't trust that man for one second.

"Oh, hello, Mr...." Marilyn hesitated.

"Magruder. John Magruder."

Josh recognized the name and the faltering voice of the elderly gentleman whom he had dismissed as a vagabond who would not return.

"Yes, Mr. Magruder," Marilyn continued, "I'm sorry your name eluded me. Was there something…"

"Actually, yes. I was on the porch of the young pastor's home, awaiting his arrival. When he drove up, I noticed he came over here. I'm sorry if I am intruding, ma'am, but I desperately needed a place to sleep tonight. Is Pastor Langham here?"

"Yes, yes he is," Marilyn said, a sympathetic smile in her voice. "Won't you step in, and I'll get him. We were just in the kitchen."

Not waiting on Marilyn, Joshua walked into the living room as she shut the door and automatically locked it. Mr. Magruder hovered near the doorway, and Marilyn walked toward the dining room, only to look up and see Joshua. "Oh, there you are," she said. "Mr. Magruder wanted a word with you."

"Hello." Josh approached the old man and extended his hand. "Did I hear you say you needed a place to sleep tonight?"

The aging gentleman's brief smile was barely detectable beneath his scraggly beard and mustache. Instead of extending his hand to Joshua's, he dropped the cane, stood straight up, inserted his hand into his pocket, and pulled out what looked like a thirty-eight caliber revolver with a menacing silencer on its end.

Stunned, Joshua stilled, then adroitly stepped between Marilyn and the gun. "What do you want?" he demanded. "If it's money…" He reached toward his back pocket.

Mr. Magruder chuckled wickedly and shook his head. "Don't want your money," he snarled in a voice that began to sound less aged and more familiar. "I want your life." Magruder savagely tore at his beard to drop it to the floor. The mustache was next. He tossed aside the glasses and ripped off the gray wig.

His legs trembling, his gut quaking, his mind whirling in disbelief, Joshua speechlessly stared at the man only feet away—Leopard.

"You stinkin' idiot," Clark growled. "You don't deserve the quick death I'm going to give you." Leopard waved the gun toward the far wall. "I want both of you to stand over there."

"Go ahead and kill me if you have to," Joshua said. "But please don't kill Marilyn." Fleetingly, he thought of Brooke. *Does Leopard remember that Marilyn has a little girl? Will he kill Brooke too?*

As if Joshua's thoughts had conjured up the child, she whimpered from close behind. "Mommy…I waked up."

Instinctively, Joshua glanced over his shoulder to see Brooke, standing between the living room and dining room, rubbing her eyes, hair tousled, dressed in a rumpled red top and shorts. Immediately, Josh glanced back at Leopard, whose attention also momentarily rested with Brooke.

Jump him! The thought struck Josh one second before he flung his body full force upon Leopard. The surprised Clark grunted as he slammed against the door then toppled to the floor with Joshua landing on top.

As Joshua struggled to secure a grip on Clark's right wrist, the retreating sounds of Marilyn's footfalls and Brooke's confused cries preceded the back door slamming.

Face contorted, the furious foe squirmed beneath Joshua's weight. "I'm going to kill you…you…" he panted, adding a long list of gutter words to his declaration.

Joshua's panic escalated into desperation. Sweat beading on his forehead and spine, he at last clamped both hands over Clark's right wrist. An arrow of triumph pierced Joshua's terror. But like a rabid beast, Leopard sank his teeth into his enemy's hand while simultaneously socking Josh in the gut with his free hand. The air rushed from Joshua's lungs in the form of an erupting yell. The concurrent pain that shot from his bleeding hand made him release his grip, which once again granted Leopard the advantage.

⟨ ⟩

Marilyn, clutching Brooke close, rounded the house and gripped the car keys she had grabbed from the table near the door. Glancing over her shoulder, she looked toward the front window to see two writhing silhouettes standing in the living room locked in battle. Whimpering, Brooke clamped her arms around her mother's neck all the tighter. Marilyn produced her own tiny cry as one thought hurled its way past her terror: *Cell phone. Cell phone. Cell phone.*

A few weeks ago, her father had insisted Marilyn get the phone and keep it in her car. At first, Marilyn had resisted, seeing the communication device as nothing but a luxury she could hardly afford. But Fred Douglas, certain his daughter desperately needed the phone for safety purposes, insisted on footing the whole bill. As Marilyn clutched Brooke in one arm and clawed at the door handle, she thanked God her father had been so adamant about the phone.

Breathing a prayer for Joshua, she opened the car door, plopped a crying Brooke into the passenger seat, toppled onto the driver's seat, slammed the door, and inserted the key into the ignition. She picked up the phone and decided to make her call before starting the car. With hands shaking uncontrollably, she turned on the phone and began dialing 911. At last she pushed the send button and waited.

"Come on...come on..." she muttered, not wanting to drive off until she made certain help was on the way. The warring silhouettes in her living room continued their struggle, and Marilyn panted as if *she* were the one fighting.

Brooke's whimpering escalated to wails. "I'm scared! I want Daddy!"

"It's okay. It's okay, Honey," Marilyn crooned, her own voice catching on a sob. Marilyn patted her daughter's leg, and Brooke gripped her arm.

"That man that Joss jumped on is—is *mean,* Mommy! Is he h-hurting Joss? I want J-J-Joss!"

Just as the emergency operator spoke her greeting, one of the silhouettes collapsed as if he had been shot. Marilyn caught her breath, and her eyes filled with tears. The man left standing momentarily hesitated then darted toward the door.

Dear God, let Josh be okay, Marilyn pleaded as her front door opened. But Joshua wasn't the one who stepped onto the lighted porch. A gut-wrenching sob tore at her. *Is Joshua dead?* Marilyn's whole being spun with images of Joshua's cold, still form in a casket. *No!* she wanted to scream. *No! Oh, Lord, please...NO!*

"Hello...Hello..." the operator said urgently, "are you there?"

"I'm—I'm here," Marilyn cried, watching as Leopard descended the trio of porch steps and paused at the bottom to scan the yard. She debated whether to crank the car and try to speed away or just duck and hide. If she cranked the car, he would certainly discover her hiding spot. And what would stop him from shooting into the moving car? Deciding to hide, she flopped over the console. However, with Brooke's weeping growing louder by the second Marilyn wondered exactly what would prevent Leopard from finding them.

"There's been a shooting," Marilyn hissed into the phone. "Send police and ambulance."

Hating to traumatize the child any more, Marilyn saw no recourse but to clamp her free hand over Brooke's screaming mouth and hold her against the seat. She couldn't hear the operator any other way, and Marilyn certainly didn't want Brooke alerting Leopard to their location.

"Are you calling from a cell phone?" the operator rushed. "I'm not picking up an address for this number."

Brooke, squirming against Marilyn's firm hold, grew all the more frantic.

"Cell phone. I'm on my cell phone. In the car," Marilyn rushed as Brooke's tears dampened her hand. "I'm at 35 Emporia Street."

"Okay. I'm sending help now. Can you stay on the phone with me?"

"I—"

The driver's side door handle rattled. Gulping, Marilyn pressed the phone's power button and disconnected the call. As the door began to open, she released Brooke and shoved the phone under the passenger seat. The dome light blinked then came on. Brooke's screeching escalated. Feeling Leopard peering at her, Marilyn groped for the passenger door handle. If she could just open the door and shove Brooke out...

"You didn't think you could get away, did you?" Clark growled, pressing the end of the handgun against the back of Marilyn's head.

Marilyn stilled. The cold circle of steel seemed to eat into her skull. Her stomach threatened to empty itself. "Please... please..." she choked out as Brooke sobbed uncontrollably and dug her short fingernails into Marilyn's forearm. "Don't...don't kill me and my daughter."

❧

Kim Lan had just turned off the light and once more settled against the pillow when her phone rang. She groped through the darkness to once more touch the brass lamp. Squinting against the soft glow, she picked up the cordless phone, but her usual "hello" was cut short.

"Were you awake?" Sonsee asked.

"Yes, and it's a good thing. It's after eleven here," Kim Lan said through a weary yawn.

"I know. I went to bed early but I suddenly woke up about five minutes ago with this horrible feeling about Marilyn," she rushed. "I tried to call her, but no one answered the phone. The machine finally picked up. That doesn't seem right to me. She's almost always home by nine because of Brooke's bedtime. I've been praying for her like crazy. I'm pacing the floor. I'm scared, Kim. I feel like something awful is happening."

Kim Lan swallowed against a lump in her throat. "You're not going to believe this, but I had this urge to call Marilyn a few minutes ago myself, but I decided it was too late and I'd wait until in the morning."

"We have to pray for her," Sonsee urged.

"Okay. Okay. You keep praying. I'll try to call this time."

"Good. Call me back."

"Right. I will."

Without so much as a goodbye, Sonsee hung up.

Kim Lan dialed Marilyn's number and waited as the phone began its usual peel. By the fourth ring, her palms produced a film of nervous sweat. Marilyn's answering machine usually picked up in six or seven rings.

"Now," Leopard growled. "I want you to sit up nice and slow, and we're going back into the house."

"But—but what about Brooke?" Marilyn, gradually sitting up, coughed against a sob as those images of Josh in his casket grew more distinct by the second. "Please... please... just let Brooke stay in the car. She—she—"

"I'm afraid that's not possible. She has seen me."

The faint sound of a telephone's ring cut through the night. Marilyn looked toward her front door, still ajar. "That's my phone," she said, grasping for any diversion.

"So what! It's a telephone. They ring sometimes," Leopard barked. "Now get out!"

"Mommy, Mommy, Mommy! Don't go, Mommy!" Brooke clambered over the console and landed in her mother's lap, wedging Marilyn between the steering wheel and the seat.

"Get out!"

Marilyn, weak with trembling, sent one last desperate glance toward her house. On the other side of her closed drapes, a man's shadow moved sluggishly.

"Joshua!" Marilyn's shriek mingled with Brooke's dreadful wails.

Leopard, momentarily abandoning his deadly intent, jerked his head up and stared toward the house. A maniacal laugh exploded from him as he turned from the car and hurled himself toward the house. During all the time Leopard had harassed Joshua, during the last minutes when Marilyn had discovered the identity of John Magruder, she had lived in astonishment at Leopard's seemingly perfect plan for revenge. He had clearly envisioned every possibility of being identified and avoided any incriminating evidence. The whole thing had appeared flawless. Until now.

"You should have never left me here," Marilyn said through gritted teeth. She unceremoniously deposited Brooke in the passenger floor board. "Stay there and don't move," she admonished her trembling child.

With uncommon valor, Marilyn shut the door, cranked the engine, put the headlights on bright, and slammed the car into drive. She pressed the accelerator without reserve and directed the vehicle straight toward Leopard. He turned in wide-eyed shock and started to lift his handgun. With a decisive thud, the Chevrolet struck Clark, and Marilyn slammed on her brakes as he rolled across the hood to crash into the windshield and plummet to the ground. Violently shaking, Marilyn threw the vehicle into reverse and backed up, the wheels spinning with the force of her rapid acceleration. The headlights revealed a crumpled, motionless form.

At last, Kim Lan could breathe. Someone picked up Marilyn's phone, but only after the answering machine started the recorded message. A pain-filled, unrecognizable voice coughed a garbled message.

"This is Kim Lan!" she screamed over the machine's greeting. "Who is this?"

"C-call p-police," the man rasped before a toppling noise attested to the receiver's being dropped.

Apprehension engulfed her as the sound of an approaching siren filtered over the phone line. "Marilyn! Marilyn!" Kim Lan screamed into the receiver, her mind conjuring the worst. *"Mar-i-lyn!" Oh Lord...dear Father...Jesus...please don't let her be dead!* she pleaded. "Marilyn! Marilyn!" A lament erupted from Kim Lan as she scrambled from the bed and began pacing the room. *What about little Brooke? Oh, Lord, don't let Brooke be—*"Marilyn!"

The multiple sirens now blared so loudly they sounded as if they must be in Marilyn's yard.

"Marilyn!" Tears blurring her vision, Kim Lan swished aside the dinner gown she had draped across the oriental bench and collapsed onto its hard surface.

A barely perceptible moaning mingled with the rushing of feet. Then the distinctive notes of Marilyn's voice.

"Marilyn!" Kim Lan yelled again. "Marilyn!"

At last, someone picked up the receiver. "Hello," Marilyn said breathlessly.

"Marilyn? It's Kim Lan. What's going on?"

Holding Brooke close, Marilyn collapsed beside Joshua who now lay on the sofa. A dark-red stain of coagulating blood oozed from below his left shoulder and marred his shirt as he tottered on the brink of consciousness. Two paramedics with a gurney gently nudged her aside, and Marilyn bent to bestow an assuring kiss on Joshua's forehead. She wanted to tell him he was going to be fine but couldn't seem to get any words past the lump in her throat. *What if he isn't going to be fine?* she worried. Her eyes filled with unshed tears, and Brooke began another round of hysterical screams.

"Joss! Joss! Mommy, Joss is dead! He's dead, Mommy!"

"*Marilyn!* What's going on?" Kim Lan demanded again.

"J-Josh has been sh-shot!"

"Are you and Brooke okay?"

"Fine. We're—we're fine. Terrified, but fine. Can't talk any more. Pray!" Marilyn pushed the phone's off button and tossed it onto the striped couch now stained with blood. Then she gently pressed Brooke's head against her shoulder. "Shhh, Honey. Josh isn't dead. He just has a bad boo-boo."

The paramedics elevated the gurney that now held Joshua and began rolling him toward the front door. Marilyn hesitated on the door's threshold and struggled between two desires: to follow Joshua to the hospital or to stay home and calm her disturbed daughter. Being a mother won out. A tear trickling down her cheek, Marilyn watched the paramedics as they loaded Josh into the ambulance. Near Marilyn's car, another paramedic hovered over Leopard's unconscious form, as a second ambulance pulled up.

The flashing lights, the late hour, the smell of blood, the taste of terror all swirled together and Marilyn felt like an empty shell—devoid of spirit. One by one, the neighbors' lights came on, and people began to discreetly step onto their porches. A grim-faced police officer, in search of details, approached Marilyn. With a sigh, she prepared to endure a battery of fatiguing questions.

By ten the next morning, Marilyn felt as if she hadn't slept in a week. She walked into the ICU waiting room of Carroll County Regional Medical Center and hoped the staff would allow her to see Josh for a few minutes during visitation. His getting shot had certainly deepened Marilyn's realization of how much he meant to her. The thought that he could have been easily killed left Marilyn wanting to grab him and not let go.

Shortly after she entered the waiting room, a kindly, middle-aged man who strongly resembled Joshua stood and walked toward her. The plump lady by his side stood as well. "Are you by chance Marilyn Thatcher?" the man asked as he neared.

"Yes. Yes, I am," Marilyn acknowledged as she produced a tired smile.

"I'm Joshua Langham, Senior." He turned to the smiling woman at his elbow. "This is my wife, Theda."

"Oh...hello...so you did make it. My mom told me the two of you were contacted last night and that you were going to try to catch a flight here."

"Yes. We made it. The nurses let us in for five minutes with Josh about an hour ago," Theda said with a kind smile. The soft, approving light in her brown eyes left Marilyn feeling as if she were encompassed in the warmth of friendship.

"How is he?" Marilyn asked, groping for any new word of Joshua's progress.

"The surgeon removed the bullet, but they wouldn't have left him in ICU without reason," Theda stated quietly.

"He seems to be doing fine, though," Mr. Langham said, examining Marilyn as if he were trying to come to a verdict on her behalf. "There for awhile he was having trouble with his blood pressure"

"Yes, that's what the nurse told me when I called this morning," Marilyn said.

"But everything seems to be stabilizing now," Mrs. Langham finished.

"I'm assuming someone told Josh I've been calling?" Marilyn asked.

"Oh, yes," Theda said.

"Once he was conscious, the nurses informed him every time you called," Mr. Langham said with an assuring smile. "Josh told us to watch for you."

Marilyn squirmed inwardly, more than sure of the reasons for the aging couple's interest in her. Her cheeks warmed slightly, and she cast an embarrassed glance out the floor-to-ceiling windows that lined the east wall. She wondered what Joshua had told them. Certainly he couldn't have told them much. This morning, the nurse had informed Marilyn that he gained consciousness and began talking around 7:30. However, she couldn't imagine his having the strength to tell his parents about their relationship. Clearly, they must be in a state of raging curiosity.

"How about a cup of coffee or tea?" Mrs. Langham asked skillfully changing the subject and pointing toward the supply of complimentary refreshments.

Groping for any diversion, Marilyn gladly walked toward the coffeepot. "I could certainly use a pick-me-up. It's been a long night and morning." She reached for a styrofoam cup as Mrs. Langham removed the carafe and offered to fill her cup with the steaming liquid. Joshua Senior ambled toward the windows and peered out over rolling Arkansas hills.

Deftly, Marilyn added sugar and creamer to her coffee and searched for absolutely anything to say. Drawing a total blank, she sipped the rich, hot liquid instead.

Theda patted Marilyn's arm in seeming conspiracy. "I think you are an answer to my fifteen-year-long prayer."

Sputtering, Marilyn coughed against the coffee that was misdirected by her sudden intake of air.

"Is there a Marilyn Thatcher here?" a nurse curtly asked from the doorway.

Relieved, Marilyn raised her hand and hacked against the traces of coffee still lodged in her windpipe.

"Joshua Langham is asking for you in ICU."

Theda squeezed Marilyn's hand. "I'm sorry if I seemed... It's just that..." She sighed as her eyes, surrounded by soft wrinkles, filled with unshed tears. "It's been a terrible scare, and quite frankly, finding out about you and your sweet daughter has been the light in the whole ordeal. Joshua hasn't said a word before now, but..."

Marilyn, moved by Theda's honesty, decided right then and there she would always love Joshua's mother. "Probably because...well...because we've—we've been praying about our relationship. And there hasn't been that much to tell."

A thoughtful gleam appeared in Theda's eyes as she silently shook her head. "I understand, but I'm extremely thankful for you already." She shrugged. "I guess I shouldn't say more right now."

Marilyn glanced toward the nurse, who waited less than patiently. Tossing a pleasant goodbye to the Langhams, she set her coffee cup near the coffee pot and approached the doorway.

"Joshua Langham is asking to see you," she said succinctly, tucking a strand of dark hair under her nurse's cap. "We usually don't come after guests like this, but Mr. Langham won't stop asking for you, and he's starting to get agitated."

Striving to keep up with the fast-paced nurse, Marilyn followed her into the ICU ward. The smells of clean sheets and antiseptic enveloped her as she passed several small rooms, none of which proved to be Joshua's. At last the nurse stopped and ushered Marilyn into a room with a tag bearing Joshua's name attached to the door.

"Keep it to five minutes. We don't want to tire him," the nurse commanded as if she were an army sergeant.

Mutely nodding, Marilyn walked toward the bed where a pale Joshua lay, languidly observing her entry. "Hi," he said with a slight smile—a smile that was a mere shadow of the arresting variety to which he usually exposed her. The IV, bed rails, monitors, and blood pressure band attached to his arm only added to his pathetic appearance. How could this be the virile man with whom she had stood last night in front of his congregation?

Marilyn's lips trembled. Her eyes stung. Her legs shook. "Hi, yourself," she whispered as he reached for her hand.

"Hey, no crying allowed," he slurred.

"I—I'm n-not crying." Marilyn brushed aside a tear as it trickled from the corner of her cheek.

"Do I look that bad?"

"You look wonderful."

"So do you." His heavy eyes drooped. "Where's the Ladybug?"

"With my mom. I would have been here sooner, but she was so upset it was hard to pull away. Finally, I just had to come."

Marilyn recalled a similar conversation in June. Josh, in a hospital bed, asking about Brooke. Thoughts of Brooke reminded her of the picture her daughter drew for Josh. She pulled the piece of red construction paper from the side pocket of her leather purse.

"Brooke drew this for you," she said, unfolding the childish artwork. "This is supposed to be a picture of your house with you and her in the front yard."

He lifted a hand to touch the picture. "It's not complete. You're not there." His head tilted to the side, and Josh began to doze.

"I think you're right," she whispered. Looking over her shoulder, Marilyn expected the army sergeant nurse to come back at any moment. She bent to kiss Joshua on the forehead then turned to leave.

"Don't...don't go," he said softly tugging at her hand. "I...I w-wanted to ask you about—about Leopard."

"From all I can gather, he's here in the hospital under police guard. According to the officer, he's got broken ribs, a concussion, and facial contusions. He'll be going back to prison soon."

"I guess you're quite a h-heroine, huh?" He winced with pain.

"Anything for you," she said.

Joshua sank into the arms of sleep once more, and Marilyn inched away from the bed. The same nurse appeared in the doorway and ushered Marilyn from the room. "He's going to be fine," she said, her stern face softening a bit.

"Thank you," Marilyn said through a shaking smile, "I needed to hear that."

Twenty-Eight

Marilyn sat among the talking group of sisters who had converged upon the hospitality suite where Kim Lan had arranged for them to meet. The spacious room in her Park Avenue apartment building featured the latest in modern decor. The designer had taken special pains to create an ambiance of a classy penthouse in rich hues of burgundy, teal, and black with enough tropical plants to seemingly supply an island with foliage.

As usual, everyone dressed in casual attire, despite the elegance surrounding them, which only added to the reunion's family atmosphere. Kim Lan, relaxing in one of the plush chairs, repeatedly glanced toward the doorway, as if she were expecting someone. Marilyn wondered if Ted Curry were planning on making an appearance. Veterinarian Sonsee LeBlanc, her auburn hair pulled into a no-nonsense ponytail, chatted with the brunette Melissa Moore about her new general practitioner's office complex. Sammie Jones, the fiery red-headed reporter was the total opposite of the ladylike homemaker, Victoria Roberts, who was petite and peaceful. The two of them joined private detective Jac Lightfoot at the food table laden with gourmet delicacies.

The hum of companionable talking and brief bursts of laughter left Marilyn with the desire to always be with her sisters like this—not just twice a year.

Kim Lan rose from her seat and settled beside Marilyn on the leather sofa. "Did you get a chance to call and check on Brooke?"

"Yes," Marilyn said tensely. "Mom said she was excited to see Greg."

"When was the last time you saw him?" Kim Lan asked, eyeing the exquisite diamond, gracing her ring finger.

"The night he asked me back. I've arranged for him to pick up Brooke at Mom's and Dad's from now on, so I have managed to avoid him."

"So you don't know if he and Sheila—"

"Haven't heard a thing. I'm still praying for them."

"You're incredible." Kim Lan shook her head, a glowing light of admiration shining from her ebony eyes.

"No, *God* is incredible," Marilyn said with conviction. "Any right attitude I have is of Him, not me. Left to myself..." Marilyn shuddered as she recalled almost slapping Greg when he called her a witch.

Silently, Marilyn mused over her emotions about Brooke's time with Greg. Allowing her daughter to go with him troubled Marilyn more than ever. Repeatedly, Greg was exhibiting enough errors in sound judgment to leave Marilyn uneasy, at best. Once more, she reflected over the wretched situation of shuffling Brooke around that had become the fabric of her life. Marilyn darted a heavenward prayer that God would give her the strength to continue trusting Him in all things, including Brooke's welfare.

"Are you enjoying yourself?" she asked, smiling into Kim Lan's eyes.

"Of course! Don't I seem like it?"

"You just seem a little nervous about something." Marilyn shrugged. "You keep looking at the door like you're expecting someone. Are we going to get to meet Ted?"

"No. He's in California on a shoot," Kim said with an enigmatic smile.

"Your ring is lovely," Marilyn said. She had been wanting to have a moment alone with Kim Lan since her arrival, but no opportunity presented itself until now.

"Thanks." Kim extended the ring to watch it sparkle with blue fire.

Marilyn debated whether to voice all the concerns that had flooded her the day Kim announced the tentative engagement to the movie star.

"I think I want some of the grapes," Kim Lan said as if she were skillfully sidestepping any chance of Marilyn's input.

"I could use another soda," Marilyn said.

Standing, Kim reached for Marilyn's hand and pulled her to her feet. Jac, Victoria, and Sammie arrived, their plates laden with goodies, and shamelessly took the seats Marilyn and Kim had just vacated on the sofa. After a round of sisterly chiding, Marilyn and Kim ambled toward the food table, a masterpiece in choice finger-foods.

Kim Lan picked up a cluster of grapes and nibbled one of them. Thoughtfully, she retrieved an oversized saucer and added some crab salad to her choice of delicacies. Silently, Marilyn chose a few morsels to continue the snack feast that usually characterized the friends' second night together. Despite their interest in the food, Marilyn felt as if the subject of Kim Lan's engagement refused to be dismissed.

She schooled her features into a casual expression and decided to dare plunge forward with her remarks. "So, how are you feeling about your engagement?" Alert to Kim's reaction, she focused on pouring a soda into a short glass full of ice. When Marilyn glanced up, she thought she detected a tiny doubt sprinting across Kim's face.

"Are you still praying about it, or..."

"Yes," Kim Lan said with reservation.

Marilyn recalled their phone call the day after Joshua's tangle with Leopard. The two had discussed many things, including Kim's choice not to continue in the sexually suggestive poses. However, the model's decision to consider Ted Curry's proposal left Marilyn uncomfortable. In some ways, Kim Lan's potential engagement seemed an exact contradiction to her claim of seeking God anew. Marilyn had never met Ted; however, the tabloids often left his lifestyle open to many, many questions. Then, she remembered the times she had been standing in the grocery checkout and seen a false lead line about Kim Lan. Furthermore, she reflected over the newspaper article that had twisted the facts about Joshua's involvement in Leopard's crime. A tinge of guilt marred her mind. Perhaps she was judging Ted unfairly.

Nevertheless, she at last decided to speak her thoughts. "Kim Lan," she began hesitantly, "you don't have to marry him just because he asked. I know he's supposed to be the most eligible bachelor in America, but..."

The exquisite beauty stiffened.

"Look..." Marilyn placed a consoling hand on her friend's arm, "I'm not trying to interfere, but take it from somebody who made one mistake...if—if there's ever a point where you feel like you're doing the wrong thing, then don't go through with it."

Nervously flipping her glossy, waist-length hair over her shoulder, Kim Lan turned toward the food table. "Have you tried the crab salad?" she casually asked, and Marilyn decided to drop the subject. Kim obviously wasn't comfortable discussing her pending engagement with Ted. Recalling her own touchiness when she first met Josh, Marilyn understood all too well her friend's need for some space. With a sigh, she took Kim's suggestion and helped herself to a scoop of crab salad.

Within seconds, a movement at the door caught Marilyn's attention. A familiar man stepped across the threshold. Marilyn's eyes widened in astonishment. She darted a glance to Kim Lan who beamed.

"Surprise!"

"Joshua?" Marilyn whispered as he closed the door and bathed her in an adoring gaze. "How—"

"I'm sneaky, that's how," Kim Lan said impishly. "As much as the gang wants to meet my man, they *really* want to meet *your* man." Grinning, Kim Lan looked at Josh who presently nabbed the attention of all the sisters.

Traces of new love produced a flutter in Marilyn's midsection as she noticed the bouquet of red roses in Joshua's hands. Marilyn deposited her plate on the edge of the service table and immediately rushed toward him. His focus never wavering, Josh met Marilyn near one of the lofty, exotic plants, bestowed a gentle kiss on her cheek, and placed the roses in her hands. "These are for you," he said against her ear as the sisters whooped like college cheerleaders. "And..." He reached into the pocket of his pleated pants to pull out a black velvet ring box. "So is this—" Josh opened the hinged box to reveal a winking solitaire on a gold band—"if you'll marry me."

Marilyn, blinking against tears, laughed incredulously as she contemplated the recent months. Even though she and Josh had begun discussing their marriage, both had remained in the prayerful consideration mode. They had even attended a premarriage seminar two weeks before—a seminar that had only heightened Marilyn's feelings that Joshua and she had a future together. However, both had resolved not to rashly commit to an engagement until they were absolutely certain of God's will. And both had agreed a long engagement would be the most advantageous. Marilyn could not, she simply *would not,* hurry into marriage.

Nevertheless, the glowing love cloaking Joshua's features spoke of nothing but certainty. Certainty and hope. And Marilyn could not deny that she, too, in recent days had found that supernatural assurance—the God-inspired optimism that life with Josh represented the Lord's perfect will for her and Brooke. Her heart pounding furiously, Marilyn whispered a faint, trembling yes.

Joshua, incited by the laughing delight of the sisters, wrapped his arms around Marilyn and firmly pressed his lips against hers. Taken by surprise, Marilyn blinked then decided to give her friends something to remember. Unrestrained, she threw her arms around Joshua's neck and thoroughly kissed him back.

The man had respectively kept a gentlemanly distance since their decision to deepen their acquaintance. Other than an occasional hug or a gentle brush of the lips, Joshua had maintained a definite air of restraint in their physical contact and carefully avoided being alone with Marilyn. His approach left her with a growing monumental respect for him...respect mingled with a dose of resigned frustration.

His sudden intake of air attested to his own astonishment, and Marilyn reveled in this rare moment. With the sisters applauding in the background, the kiss finally came to an end and Marilyn could not suppress her joyous laughter.

"How long have you known you were coming?" she asked as her friends began surrounding them, intent on meeting Marilyn's man.

"Two months," he admitted, his eyes sparkling with adoration. "Kim Lan called one day...the rest is history."

"She's a schemer," Marilyn said, making eye contact with the oriental beauty who giggled with triumph.

The whole gang chattered as they introduced themselves to Joshua. Marilyn took in the whole scene. She couldn't imagine life without her sisters. All of them were important in her life. All of them had supported her during laughter, tears, and struggles. And all of them depended on each other as only friends could.

Author's Note

Dear Reader,

I hope you enjoyed *Second Chances*. My heart's desire in writing this novel centered around featuring divorce as it really is—a heart-wrenching agony that leaves despair in its wake. My own parents divorced, and I understand firsthand the pain involved. Malachi 2:16 tells us that "God hates divorce" because it causes such heartache and scarring to those involved. Furthermore, those who have been touched by divorce will attest to its devastation. Truly, divorce is nothing short of an emotional abortion.

However, I also believe God's grace extends to those who are divorced. He is willing and able to forgive. While it is in no way my desire to condone divorce, I feel very strongly that in cases such as Marilyn's, where adultery is involved, God is indeed a God of second chances.

If you have been involved in a divorce, I hope this book will bring you to a deeper healing than you have known before.

If you know someone or are related to someone who is divorced, may this book help you better understand their plight and also help you to forgive, just as Marilyn's mother and father had to forgive Gregory.

If you are thinking about getting a divorce, please reconsider. Even if there has been adultery, God is ready and waiting to heal the brokenhearted. And where two people are willing to try, the Lord can miraculously repair a marriage. I purposefully painted the picture of Gregory Thatcher to show that many times the one who files for divorce later regrets his or her decision and wants their family back. But many times, it is too late.

Even though there are *some* cases—very few cases—where divorce is the answer, most of the time the break up of a marriage turns serious problems into a horrific event that destroys lives and cripples people for generations. Divorce creates a bigger problem on top of a problem. If your marriage is in trouble, I encourage you and your spouse to pray together, read God's Word together, and, as a couple, seek out other Christians you trust and can be honest with. God will bless your efforts.

After seventeen years of marriage, my husband and I are deeply committed to the Lord and to each other. Even though we have a wonderful relationship, every marriage has its difficult moments. With prayer, understanding, compassion, forgiveness, and a willingness to serve, we have not only kept our marriage together, but it continues to grow stronger every year. We are now more in love than we've ever been and have more romance in our relationship than we've ever known.

I pray that your marriage will be the same.

In His Service,
Debra White Smith

Debra White Smith impacts and entertains readers with her life-changing books, including *Romancing Your Husband, Romancing Your Wife, 101 Ways to Romance Your Marriage,* and her popular fiction—The Austen series and the Sisters Suspense series. The founder of Real Life Ministries, Debra touches lives through the written and spoken word by presenting real truth for real life and ministering to people where they are. She speaks at events across the nation and sings with her husband and children. Debra holds an M.A. in English.

To write Debra or contact her for speaking engagements, check out her website:

www.debrawhitesmith.com

or send mail to

Real Life Ministries
Debra White Smith
P.O. Box 1482
Jacksonville, TX 75766